WHEN SHE
WAS BAD

www.**transworldbooks**.co.uk

Do you love Tammy Cohen's books? Try these:

THE MISTRESS'S REVENGE
Her sharp debut novel written as a journal addressed by a former mistress to the married lover who dumped her.

'Gasp in recognition at this cracking tale'
Grazia

THE WAR OF THE WIVES
A happily married woman whose husband dies unexpectedly is confronted at his funeral by a woman who claims that she was his wife.

'Moving, funny and completely absorbing'
Prima

SOMEONE ELSE'S WEDDING
The story of a wife and her grown-up family whose secrets come shimmering to the surface at a wedding: told in real-time over thirty-six hours.

'Utterly gripping'
Lisa Jewell

THE BROKEN
A couple are sucked into their best friends' bitter
divorce with devastating results for all.

'A work of near-genius'
Daily Mail

DYING FOR CHRISTMAS
A young woman is held captive over the
twelve days of Christmas.

'Packs a killer twist'
Prima

FIRST ONE MISSING
The parents of missing children club together for
support. But all is not as it seems.

'Head and shoulders above the rest'
Daily Mail

Tammy Cohen (who previously wrote under her formal name Tamar Cohen) has written several acclaimed novels about family fall-out: *The Mistress's Revenge*, *The War of the Wives* and *Someone Else's Wedding*. *The Broken* was her first pyschological thriller, followed by *Dying for Christmas* and *First One Missing*.

She is a member of the Killer Women crime-writing collective and lives in North London with her partner and three (nearly) grown children, plus one badly behaved dog. Chat with her on Twitter @MsTamarCohen or at www.tammycohen.co.uk

WHEN SHE WAS BAD

Tammy Cohen

BLACK SWAN

TRANSWORLD PUBLISHERS
61–63 Uxbridge Road, London W5 5SA
www.transworldbooks.co.uk

Transworld is part of the Penguin Random House group of companies
whose addresses can be found at global.penguinrandomhouse.com

Penguin
Random House
UK

First published in Great Britain in 2016 by Black Swan
an imprint of Transworld Publishers

A CIP catalogue record for this book
is available from the British Library.

ISBN
9781784160197

Typeset in 11/14pt Sabon by Falcon Oast Graphic Art Ltd.
Printed and bound by Clays Ltd, Bungay, Suffolk.

Penguin Random House is committed to a sustainable
future for our business, our readers and our planet. This book is made from
Forest Stewardship Council® certified paper.

MIX
Paper from
responsible sources
FSC® C018179

1 3 5 7 9 10 8 6 4 2

For Michael

1

Anne

Imagine we could see the damage inside ourselves. Imagine it showed through us like contraband on an airport scanner. What would it be like, to walk around the city with it all on view – all the hurts and the betrayals and the things that diminished us; all the crushed dreams and the broken hearts? What would it be like to see the people our lives have made us? The people we are, under our skin.

I thought about that when I saw you on the news just now. I recognized you right away. '*Such an ordinary person*,' those people said. '*I can't believe someone like that could do something so terrible.*'

When I got the text this afternoon from Barbara Campbell telling me to turn on the news, I couldn't work out what she meant at first. The news was full of the usual stuff – the Republican leadership contest, the price of fuel, Syria, Russia. Nothing that meant anything special to me. I wondered whether Barbara was going a little senile. She retired a while back, so it's possible. Then I remembered that, of course, living over in England she meant the *British* news. Well, that flummoxed me. In the end I had to call Shannon and she popped in on her way home from work. She fixed it up in five minutes flat, running a cable from my laptop to the main TV screen so I could watch the BBC live.

I waited for Shannon to leave before I put it on. Before heading out, she hugged me for a long time, as is her custom, and I was grateful all over again. So many daughters grow out of that kind of close contact as they get older, as I did when I learned to recognize my mom's distinctive scent as last night's sweated-out booze. Parents are always a disappointment to their children, that's part of our role. But Shannon has never held it against me.

From Barbara's text, I'd guessed the news wouldn't be good. But when I saw the photographs, when I heard what you'd done . . . I had to stop myself from pouring out a large glass of white and drinking it down in one as if it was a shot of something short and strong and slammed on a bar. Instead, I took a deep breath in and tried to count to seven before releasing it as, on-screen, a woman in a blue raincoat stood outside a courtroom and recited the stark facts of your case.

'First court appearance,' said the woman's thin-lipped mouth. 'Confirmed name and address.' And, 'Judge set a date for trial.' Then the scene changed to a wide, tree-lined London street where a different woman was adding a bouquet of flowers to an impressive pile outside a glossy black gate, in front of a smart-looking Georgian townhouse. 'Crime that shocked a city . . .' the voiceover said. 'The accused worked with the victim . . . particularly brutal nature of the killing.' Then the focus skipped again to a modern office building in the financial heart of London. A young man interviewed on the sidewalk outside the main entrance shook his head in disbelief. 'Such an ordinary person,' he repeated.

But I know. I know the truth. And ordinary doesn't come into it.

2

Paula

'I still can't believe it.'

Paula knew it wasn't helping Gill to keep saying the same thing over and over, but the phrase seemed to be stuck in her throat. Every time she opened her mouth, up it came again.

'I wouldn't take it, if I were you, Gill. Find a shit-hot lawyer. Sue the arse off them.'

Typical Ewan. Always thinking there was something that could be *done* about everything. But he was still young. Hadn't yet learned that sometimes things happen to you, and there's not a damn thing you can do about it.

'I already talked to an employment lawyer, and the head of HR was in the meeting,' said Gill, smiling bravely, although her large brown eyes seemed to swim beneath a glaze of unshed tears. 'Yes, I could try legal action but apparently the money they're offering me on top of my statutory notice period is more than I'd get if I won an unfair dismissal claim, so it's not worth it.'

'But it's so unfair,' said Chloe, who'd already gone through three tissues which were scrunched up on the table in front of her, next to a near-empty glass of wine.

'We're such a good team, all of us. Why would they want to go and break us up?'

It wasn't surprising Chloe was taking her boss's dismissal so hard. Ever since Gill had taken her on as a junior she'd had an almost Svengali-type influence over her.

'They say we've been underperforming, Chloe,' said Gill, a telltale wobble in her voice. 'And they need a scapegoat. Which is me.'

Paula didn't think that was entirely fair. Of course she was sorry Gill was going. They'd worked together for eight years. They were friends. But the truth was, as Executive Manager, Gill had been coasting during the last couple of years. And productivity and profitability had definitely suffered as a result. So for her to claim to be some kind of sacrificial lamb was a bit much.

Directly across the table from her, Amira, who'd already downed two gin and tonics in the time Paula had taken to sip a third of her bitter lemon, leaned forwards conspiratorially so that the ends of her thick black hair trailed in a little puddle of lager.

'I bet Mark Hamilton patted you on the shoulder straight after he sacked you and said "no hard feelings",' she said to Gill. 'Am I right?'

Gill visibly winced at the word 'sacked' and Paula's heart went out to her. Amira could be so insensitive sometimes.

'Yeah. I think he did say something like that,' mumbled Gill. 'But I was in shock, so half of the things he said went straight over my head.'

'How about if we all refused to go back to work,' said Chloe, her cheeks flushed with earnestness and Pinot

Grigio. 'They couldn't sack us all, could they?'

'They've probably sacked us all already. Just for being here and not heads down at our desks like good little workers,' said Amira.

Paula tensed. She supported Gill, of course, and she hadn't needed persuading to accompany her to the pub after she got the devastating news of her dismissal that morning. But she couldn't put her own job at risk. Not when she was the only one in the house earning any money. Sweat prickled on her spine and she surreptitiously reached her arm behind her to peel the material of her top away from her back. It was so hot in here. Or was it? Paula's hormones were so haywire she'd lost the knack of regulating her own temperature and could lurch from cold to scorching and down to freezing again in a matter of seconds. Sometimes she got so hot it was as if her own blood was boiling inside her veins.

'Sorry about the wait. The Small Child is on bar duty again. Must be an Inset day at school.' Charlie put down the drinks he'd been carrying and slid back into his seat. Then he reached across the table and wrapped his surprisingly delicate fingers around the top of Gill's hand.

'Don't let the bastards grind you down,' he said softly. 'There are plenty more companies out there who'll snap you up. We'll all give you a glowing reference.'

Gill nodded with that fixed half-smile people use when they're trying not to cry.

Sarah broke the silence following Charlie's comment, arriving at the table breathless, mobile phone in hand.

'Sorry. Sorry. Childcare emergency. All sorted now.'

Charlie cleared his jacket off Sarah's chair so she

14

could sit down. Paula used to envy those two their close-ness, always slipping away after work to go drinking, arriving at their desks the next morning with raging hangovers and vague memories of pubs visited, random strangers met, cocktails downed. But since Sarah had had the boys, such outings had become a thing of the past. Nothing was ever the same after having children, was it?

The ends of Sarah's red hair had formed damp ringlets. Must be raining outside. That figured. Paula looked around the table – Sarah, Charlie, Chloe, Ewan, Amira, Gill, her. Already she was mourning the solid unit they'd been. Gill might not have been the most dynamic boss, but they'd all rolled along quite happily together on the whole. No fallings out. Minimal office politics. A dream team, as Chloe said.

Amira's phone beeped loudly, a kind of squawking noise that made them all jump. She glanced at her screen.

'Holy shit,' she said. 'Just got a message from Juliana who works in HR. You'll never guess who's going to be our new boss.'

'Who?' came a chorus of voices. Paula glanced at Gill, whose smile had got tighter, as if someone was stretching it out.

'Rachel Masters.'

Oh. Well. Paula tried to avoid industry gossip, but she'd heard the name through the grapevine. Difficult. Demanding. Divisive. Those were the sorts of words that preceded Rachel Masters. Still, she got results, apparently – and that's what counted in the end.

'Hang on,' said Sarah. 'I'm sure I heard some rumour about her. Some kind of trouble in the office.'

Gill nodded. 'I heard that too.' Her voice sounded almost gleeful.

Paula fought off a fierce wave of heat that surged up from somewhere beneath her ribcage and burst into flames around her lungs, blazing up into her shoulders and throat. Anxiety was like a spiteful child pinching her insides. They'd been here in the pub for over two hours, ever since Gill had come back from a meeting with Mark Hamilton, white-faced and shaking and accompanied by a security guard who stood watch while she gathered up her things from her glass office, partitioned off from the main office floor. It had been nearly lunchtime, so they'd all gone with Gill to the pub to find out what was going on. But now Paula couldn't stop worrying about what Mark Hamilton, the company MD, would say when he came down to talk to them all, as he surely would, and found no one there. What if he brought *her* with him, Rachel Masters? Unease spread through her like the prick, prick, prick of a tattooist's needle. She was the deputy. She ought to be setting an example.

'Sorry, Gill,' she said, feeling around under her chair for her handbag. 'We ought to be getting back.'

'No. We ought to stay here. Show Hamilton that he can't just do exactly what he wants,' said Ewan, passion making him look younger than his twenty-eight years.

'Er, I think you'll find he can do exactly what he wants,' said Amira. 'Mark Hamilton Recruitment is his company. The clue's in the name.'

In the end it was Gill who decided things.

'I need to get going anyway. I'm going to give myself

the afternoon off and then I'll get on the phone, start ringing some contacts about a new job. I'm not worried. I've had so many approaches over the years.'

Paula had worked with Gill long enough to recognize her brand of quiet bravado. Poor Gill. Though she had a steely side that she kept carefully hidden, this must be a terrible blow to her self-esteem. Still, thank God she was going home so they could get back to the office. Paula sneaked a quick look at her watch, and her stomach gave a savage lurch.

'Come on,' she chivvied the others while trying to free her arm which had become trapped in the sleeve of her raincoat.

'Yes, you lot go back,' said Gill brightly. 'I'll call a taxi to come and pick me up, with all my stuff.' She gestured to the cardboard box containing notebooks, a spare pair of shoes, the framed photograph of Gill with her two young nephews. 'Just make sure you keep me updated on what's going on. I shall expect a blow-by-blow account from each of you. And pictorial evidence of the infamous Rachel Masters.'

By the time they arrived at reception, five floors down from their office, Paula was out of breath. She really ought to start going to the gym or something, she thought, try to get rid of the extra two stone that seemed to have attached itself to her in the last couple of years without her even noticing it, so that now, at fifty-five, she hardly recognized herself. In the lift, she kept her head down, for fear of seeing her own mother looking back at her from the mirrored walls.

Why had she worn that awful old top today? The shapeless blue T-shirt was made of the kind of thin cotton that clings damply to clammy skin. If she'd known she was going to meet a new boss, she'd have made more of an effort. And she certainly wouldn't have worn these black trousers. At least the waistband was covered by her top, so you couldn't tell it was elasticated.

Bustling through the door of the office, her coat already half shrugged off, Paula's nerves were on edge. Please don't let Rachel Masters have arrived already. But a quick glance towards what used to be Gill's office confirmed her worst fears. The door was shut. Someone was in there.

For five minutes, Paula sat at her desk not knowing what to do. Though the blinds were down there was a narrow gap between the slats, through which she caught a glimpse of a woman bent over the desk that until that morning had been strewn with Gill's personal effects. Her face was partially hidden by a curtain of glossy dark hair. She couldn't get a good look, but she could tell immediately that Rachel Masters was ten, maybe fifteen years younger than her. That meant Paula had all the advantages of experience. Rachel would be glad of a safe pair of hands.

Emboldened, Paula took another peek and felt herself relax. Rachel Masters looked so alone there in that office. She was probably feeling much more nervous than they were and desperate for someone to come and introduce themselves. And as her new deputy, it really ought to be Paula herself.

Taking a deep breath, she crossed the few feet of blue carpet to her new boss's office.

'Yes,' came the reply to her knock.

Paula stepped through the door.

'I just wanted to welcome you—'

'Is it normal for the entire staff to take a two-hour lunch break?'

Rachel didn't look up and Paula was conscious of her smile shrivelling on her lips.

'No. We were just—'

'Can you call everyone together, please? I'd like to have a few words.'

'Of course. Out on the main floor?'

Finally Rachel glanced up at Paula from eyes of palest blue offset by spiky black lashes. Paula felt her cheeks burning.

'Well, unless we sit on each other's laps, we're hardly about to squeeze seven people in here, are we?'

Rachel's mouth, a red lipsticked slash, flattened into a tight smile.

Paula was aware of the sweat prickling under her arms and made a note to herself to keep her hands clamped to her sides. She felt her cheeks burning.

'Will do. You'll find we're a pretty friendly bunch.'

Again the smile that failed to reach the eyes.

'I'm not here to make friends.'

3

Anne

I was shocked, the first time I saw her. That's how naïve I was. I thought that somehow, what had happened to her would be written on her skin. Despite all my training, all those lectures and clinic hours and nights spent poring over textbooks, I didn't think you could be unmarked by something like that.

When I think about the young woman I was then, the one who slipped in through the run-down back entrance of the teaching hospital that first morning to avoid the scrum of reporters outside the front, feeling shyly self-important as she flashed her credentials to the police guarding the lift access, she doesn't seem like me at all but someone else entirely. A woman of principle, ambitious enough to worry that her blonde hair would stop her being taken seriously and vain enough to keep it long anyway. A woman who didn't smile often but when she did, you knew she meant it.

Nowadays my smile is like a facial tic. I hardly even know I'm doing it.

Going up in the lift, I was apprehensive but excited. I had that fluttering thing going on where you're both proud – *I must be good at my job* – but at the same time

20

terrified – *what if they find out I'm no good at my job?* Like most women who reach a certain level of success, I worried about being unmasked as a fraud.

I didn't know why I'd been picked. My PhD on the long-term effects of acute trauma in minors had won me some small amount of localized acclaim, and the university press had turned it into a book that sold well for an academic tome. I was up and coming, but I was by no means an authority. All these years later, I feel even less so, despite all the letters after my name and the corner office with the nameplate on the door, and the shelves with the foreign editions of my books lined up like trophies. If you stripped them away one by one, these trappings and badges of knowledge, I wonder if there'd be anything left underneath.

The rumours going around the department at the time said that Professor Kowalsky and I were lovers and that's why he'd picked me as his assistant in one of the two assessments he'd been charged with carrying out. No such rumours attached themselves to his choice of Dan Oppenheimer to assist him in the other one. Though the same level as me, Dan was far more ambitious and contributed well-regarded papers to several international journals. That the rumours about me and Kowalsky probably originated from Dan himself did little to lessen their sting.

Professor Kowalsky was waiting in the lobby. I say 'lobby' as if it was some kind of grand affair, but nothing was grand back then. A few squares of carpet tile of some dingy hue, a central ceiling light. And Ed Kowalsky standing there with a clipboard in his hands and all his teeth on show. He was trying to look like it was all in a day's work, but his hands gave him away, fluttering up to run his fingers through his hair again and again. He was proud of that hair.

'Dr Cater,' he said. And then: 'Anne.' He held my hand between both of his like he was pressing a flower.

'Professor Kowalsky . . .'

'Ed. Please.'

'Ed. I just want to tell you how incredibly grateful I am for this opportunity. A case this high profile, you must have had so many people asking for a chance to work with you.'

'Oh my gosh, yes.'

That's how he spoke.

'But you know, Anne, you have the right research background and, more to the point, you have sound practical experience of dealing with post-traumatized young children. Of course there were people more highly qualified than you who would have bitten my hand off to get near this case, but I have to be sure this is about the child and what's best for the child, not about professional ego. I don't want to walk into a bookstore next year and see an exposé of this case written by someone whose agenda was based on something other than helping the patient.'

In other words, he'd chosen me because I wouldn't try to capitalize on his case. I was too junior to be a threat. In view of this it seemed to me that Kowalsky might have underestimated the scale of Dan Oppenheimer's ambition, but in truth I didn't mind. I was flattered by the recognition. And yes, excited at the chance of working with a child that damaged and of helping repair some of that damage.

The corridor of the Psychiatry Department of La Luz City University Medical Facility was a sterile affair. Since then it's been painted in a mellow magnolia and there's some framed artwork on the walls. We had a memo before the prints went up, checking whether we considered them suitably 'non-stimulating'. We all joked about that for a long time afterwards. 'Nice jacket,' we'd say, 'but are you sure it's non-stimulating enough?'

Sometimes when I think about how I'm still here all these years later, I can't breathe. I keep a paper bag in the top drawer of the desk to blow into when the panic rises.

Room 238 was the most child-friendly of all the consulting rooms. There were padded grey chairs and a low coffee table in lieu of a desk, and a filing cabinet in the corner stuffed with specially chosen toys. On the coffee table was a stack of children's books. The *Sesame Street* annual was on the top, looking slightly frayed around the edges of its cardboard cover. Along the back wall was a shelving unit with more books and, discreetly positioned at the far end, a tape recorder.

'As you know, our role here is to assess rather than to treat,' Ed Kowalsky said. He was standing by the window with its slatted blinds which divided the view of the concrete and glass courthouse across the street into neat grey horizontal lines. I could tell he was too nervous to sit down. His hands were again busy with his hair. Flutter, pat, comb. Flutter, pat, comb.

'With that in mind, I propose we don't take notes during the sessions themselves. Obviously we'll record them, and then after Laurie has left we'll discuss and make proper records.'

Laurie. The news reports had referred to her as 'The

23

Minor' or 'Child L'. Her brother, David, whose own psychiatric assessment was being carried out in tandem by Ed and Dan Oppenheimer, was Child D. Hearing Laurie's name gave me a jolt. That was probably the first time I'd really thought about her as a child, rather than a case study. The understanding that someone real had gone through what she went through and seen what she'd seen, caused a painful tightening in my chest. What would that do to a person?

Suddenly, I was terribly aware that I was way out of my depth.

There was a knock.

'Come in,' said Ed Kowalsky and I watched him unzip his smile.

First through the door was a stocky middle-aged woman with a wide moon-face and neat brown hair tucked behind her ears. She was wearing a loose-fitting cream top in the kind of linen fabric that creases easily, and a calf-length brown skirt that rubbed against her sheer flesh-coloured pantyhose, creating a static field around her legs. A large canvas bag was slung over one shoulder, while on the other arm a thin leather watch-strap cut into her wrist so that the pale flesh bulged over it on either side. On the end of that arm, her plump fingers were closed around the hand of a child.

'Hi, y'all. I'm Debra Albright from the Child Welfare Agency. And this here is Laurie.'

You'll think I'm just saying this with the benefit of hindsight, but I swear as the small figure followed the social worker into the room, the temperature dropped around ten degrees. Cold prickled at the back of my neck despite the balmy, early-fall day outside.

'Hi, Laurie.' Ed dropped into a squat, his knees creaking as he did so, and held out a hand.

The little girl gave a shy smile that was like a light going on under her skin. Without letting go of her social worker, she reached out and shook Professor Kowalsky's hand. He shot me a brief sideways glance, so fleeting I would have missed it if I'd blinked, but I knew exactly what it meant. Despite everything that had happened to her, all the horror she had witnessed, Laurie hadn't shied away from human contact.

It was a hopeful sign.

Given everything that came afterwards, I now realize just how alert we were for such signs, and how vulnerable that made us.

And how dangerous.

4

Amira

Paula seemed flustered when she came out. Amira instantly dropped her head and frowned intently at her computer screen, trying to look deep in concentration and not as if she'd just been staring through the glass walls of the executive manager's office, attempting to lipread the conversation.

'Hello, everyone, can I have your attention?'

Paula was standing awkwardly on the periphery of the open-plan office, trying to project her voice. She half raised her hand and then dropped it instantly, her cheeks flaring pink, but not before Amira had caught a glimpse of dark circles under the arms of her colleague's pale-blue T-shirt. Poor Paula had been having a hard time of it recently. Not that she'd ever admit it.

'Could you all gather round, please? Rachel would like to say a few words.'

'Yeah, like "here's your P45",' muttered Charlie under his breath.

Amira's heart jolted. Though they'd all been making gallows-humour jokes about losing their jobs on the way back from the pub, the truth was, Amira was scared stiff at the possibility of being made redundant.

Two hundred and twenty-five thousand pounds' worth of scared. That's how big the mortgage was that she'd basically forced Tom to take on so that they could finally move into their own flat. Without her salary, they could not afford to carry on living there. And the way things were going in the recruitment world, she was unlikely to waltz straight into another job. She and Tom had been getting on so badly recently, partly due to the financial strain under which the move had put them, plus the added pressure of dealing with her perennially unhappy mother who still couldn't understand why they hadn't wanted to carry on living with her. Losing her job, Amira felt, could tip them over the edge.

The door to what Amira still thought of as Gill's office swung open and Rachel Masters stepped out. You couldn't deny she was attractive, with sleek black hair that fell past her shoulders, cheekbones sharp as Toblerones, oyster-coloured silk shirt tucked into a slim skirt and gym-toned legs ending in nude heels so high you suddenly realized how tiny she must be without them. Her face had that healthy outdoors glow that good quality make-up gives you and she was wearing a very particular scent that Amira couldn't identify. Musky, smoky – almost overpowering. She must have given herself a spray before she came out, Amira decided. Bit of Dutch courage. Seemed to be working wonders on Ewan though. He was a tall guy anyway, but he visibly pulled himself up straighter as the new boss passed, his handsome boy/man face turning to follow her as if drawn by an invisible string. Plonker. But you couldn't hold it against him any more than you could resent a puppy for jumping up at you. Amira knew she had a reputation for being too plain-spoken, so she had a soft spot for Ewan and his total lack of guile.

'Glad you all decided to show up finally.'

Rachel's high, girlish voice, so at odds with her fearsome reputation, came as a shock. She gazed steadily around at each of them in turn, until they were all shuffling their feet or staring down at the carpet.

'I'm aware a lot of you will be feeling upset about Gill's leaving and concerned about your own futures here. I'm not going to sugar-coat things. The department is in a precarious state. It's not entirely Gill's fault. She did a commendable job here for several years, but the industry has changed beyond recognition and the department failed to change with it. My job is to turn us around so we become more effective and super-attractive to new clients. But I'm not going to lie, it's going to be painful, and there may well need to be some further staff restructuring. I've been brought in to make the hard decisions and that's what I intend to do. I hope you'll all give me your utmost cooperation. After all, we ultimately want the same thing – a successful, profitable department we can be proud of.'

Rachel flashed a smile that was gone almost as soon as it began, but still she remained in place, her eyes sweeping around. Amira attempted to hold the new manager's gaze when it alighted on her, digging her nails into her palm, but in the end she looked away feeling as if she'd conceded something.

'Right. I'll be calling each of you into my office individually over the next couple of days so I can find out a bit more about you and how you see your role in the organization. And then we'll take it from there.'

She half turned, but Chloe stepped forward, practically blocking her way. Amira groaned when she saw that the willowy office assistant actually had her hand in the air like a small child in the classroom.

'Rachel, hi. Just wanted first to say "welcome" and secondly to ask—'

'I'm not taking questions at this point.' Rachel's high-pitched voice was clipped as if someone had slammed a door on it. 'If there's anything you need to know, you can ask when you come in to see me.'

Chloe's English-rose cheeks flushed red as Rachel clickety-clacked briskly back to her office on her vertiginous heels, and Amira felt sorry for the girl. She could be a pain in the bum sometimes and was an arse-licker extraordinaire, but she was only twenty-four, and was being paid peanuts to come into work every day. And she'd be mortified to be snubbed like that in front of Ewan, whom she was constantly trying to impress. As far as Amira could tell, no one in Chloe's life had ever said no to her, and she thought for a horrible moment that the younger woman was about to cry.

'I was only going to ask her if we should be doing anything to prepare for our interview.'

'Ah bless, you were asking for homework.'

Charlie didn't mean to be unkind, it was just his manner, but Amira knew Chloe wouldn't get it. She'd once overheard her telling Paula she felt Charlie's attitude to women bordered on sexual harassment because of his liberal use of 'sweetie' and 'love' when addressing colleagues. Paula had had to point out that he used the same endearments to the male members of staff and she shouldn't read too much into it.

'I'm sure you don't need to prepare anything, Chloe,' Paula snapped.

Amira glanced over curiously. That wasn't like Paula. Normally her responses to everything were so infuriatingly measured it made you want to say something outrageous, just to provoke her into a reaction. On closer inspection, Paula was not looking her usual placid, contained self. Her faded brown bob was neat as ever, but her face looked washed out, the features smudged and undefined.

Idly, Amira's gaze slid across from Paula to the glass box which she must now force herself to think of as Rachel's office. With a start, her eyes locked with those of her new boss. The woman was leaning back in her desk chair staring straight out. Her face, clear of the practised smile she'd been wearing earlier, was set hard – and even from a few yards away, Amira could see how tightly she was clutching the pen whose end she was clicking in and out, in and out with an unnerving rhythmic intensity.

Amira found herself glancing away, feeling unaccountably guilty – why? Yet really, mightn't it all turn out for the best? It was a shame Gill had to go, but they'd all known it was on the cards. The department's poor performance had been highlighted in the company's annual review and it was only a matter of time before someone was called to account – and Gill was the obvious candidate. So the change around wasn't entirely unexpected. There and then, Amira decided to keep her head down and wait for things to settle.

But as she opened up a PDF file that pinged into her inbox from the still-sulking Chloe, Amira couldn't quite shake off the memory of those metallic blue eyes burning like acid into her own.

5
Sarah

She was going to be late again. She'd had to wait for two tubes to go from the platform at Finsbury Park before she was finally able to squeeze into a carriage, where she ended up pressed into the armpit of a sweating young man in a shiny suit wearing too much aftershave and not enough deodorant. And then once she'd changed to a different line at King's Cross, the train had sat in a tunnel just outside Liverpool Street for ages, with Sarah's stress levels rising by the second. They were so close to her destination she could have practically jumped out and on to the platform, but instead she'd had to stand gripping the rail and trying to remember what that stress management leaflet they'd all been sent had said about finding your happy place in your mind. Bed – that would be her happy place.

Now she was running awkwardly up the stairs of the tube station and wishing she hadn't worn the black skirt that had never really fitted her properly again after the second baby was born. The skirt hadn't been her first choice. In honour of the new boss, she'd put on her best trousers, but then Sam had decided that his little brother Joe needed a nappy change, only Joe had got bored halfway through and gone toddling off to find his mum who'd just sat down to gulp her tea. Without thinking, she'd picked him up and plonked him on her knee, realizing too late why Sam had thought, in his three-year-old wisdom, that his brother needed his nappy changed. Off had come the trousers. She'd had to pull the skirt out from the wash-basket. 'These trousers say Dry Clean Only,' Oliver had called, squatting on his haunches by the washing machine, and if Sarah hadn't been in such a rush she'd have laughed out loud. Two babies in three years and he still thought she owned anything, *anything*, that had to be taken to the dry cleaner.

On the streets of the City, she bowed her head against the persistent drizzle that seemed to have arrived out of the blue while she was underground. The shower at home had done the very same thing that morning, spurting arcs of water horizontally across the bathroom with no forewarning at all. The rain, she knew, would make her red hair frizz. Despite the arsenal of anti-frizz products that crowded their cramped bathroom shelves to Oliver's endless frustration, Sarah's hair only had to get a snifter of atmospheric moisture and up it sprang around her head like something you'd use to scour a pan.

She had an unwelcome flashback to Rachel Masters's cool silk shirt and uncreased skirt. Pulling her phone out of her bag she glanced at the time. 9.10. Gill had always been very understanding about the occasional late start. She knew Sarah would more than make up for it by taking work home or staying late on Wednesdays when Oliver's mum took the boys. Though she didn't have children herself, she'd never made Sarah feel bad about it. Sarah remembered how nervous she'd been when she'd had to break it to Gill that she was pregnant again just months after returning to work from a year's maternity leave with Sam, and how relieved when, after a deep sigh, her boss had simply said: 'Congratulations.'

Sarah tried to remember whether Rachel had children or not, raking back through the bits and pieces of gossip that had floated across to them over the last twenty-four hours from acquaintances at other companies their new boss had worked for during her rapid rise through the ranks. She thought not. But that needn't necessarily make any difference. Her sister worked in sales and had once had a boss with four children who was so desperate to prove that being a mother hadn't softened her up that she was far harder on the parents among her staff than anyone else, refusing to make even the slightest of concessions. So you could never tell.

Sarah pushed through the glass doors into the reception area with its plastic pot plants on top of a narrow laminated desk, behind which sat the receptionist with the hair extensions; Sarah could never remember her name. The woman's electric-blue-painted nails were so long that it took her for ever to tap numbers in on her phone pad using just the tips of her fingers.

'Morning,' said Sarah, hurrying past while looping the cord of her plastic ID card around her neck. She had that unpleasant out-of-breath feeling, as if her lungs were being gently raked with an ice-scraper.

The receptionist glanced up but didn't respond.

On the fifth floor, Sarah scurried out of the lift and in

through the double doors that led to her open-plan office. As her desk was on the far side, she'd have to cross in front of Rachel Masters's glass cubicle. She glanced over and saw the black head bent over the desk. If she just took off her jacket at the door and carried it in her left hand, out of Rachel's line of sight, she might look like she was just sauntering back from the loo instead of arriving fifteen minutes late.

Safely seated at her desk, Sarah finally risked looking across. Rachel was still engrossed in whatever she was working on and didn't appear to have noticed. Sarah inhaled deeply, feeling the knot of anxiety that had been lodged inside her gradually unravel. Only then did she become aware of the strange atmosphere in the office.

'What's going on?' she hissed at Charlie.

He gave her a funny little sideways look, swivelling his head towards her while the rest of him remained firmly in work pose.

'We've been regulated,' he whispered. 'By the new Führer. Apparently we're wasting too much time on coffee and chitty-chatty. Once we're in the office we're expected to be in work mode straight away. Like that.'

He snapped his fingers in front of his face.

'What did she actually . . .'

Sarah's voice tailed off as the door to Rachel's office was flung open and her new boss strode out, pausing by Paula's desk to confer. Sarah's heart stopped as suddenly both women swung around to look her way.

'Sarah, could you come into my office, please.'

'You're in trou-ble, you're in trou-ble,' sang Charlie softly.

Sarah tried to smile but her mouth was dry as she

made her way across the office, aware that everyone else was tracking her movements. Rachel had said she would be calling them each in individually – she was probably the first. If only she'd had a chance to think about it, and put her thoughts in order. She'd meant to sit down last night and write out a bullet-point list of her achievements in her role, and how she thought productivity could improve – the sort of thing new bosses want to hear. But then Sam had had a tantrum about having his hair washed, and it had taken ages to calm him down, and after that he'd insisted on reading two story books instead of the usual one, and by the time she'd got downstairs she hadn't had the energy to do anything except pour herself a glass of wine and watch the telly.

Outside Rachel's door, she hesitated, unsure whether to knock. Unnecessary, she decided, seeing as Rachel had only that minute called her in.

'Hello,' she said, in a jolly voice she instantly regretted. She pulled back the spare chair facing Rachel, ready to sit down.

'Don't worry about a chair, you won't be here long enough to need it,' said Rachel Masters. Her face was hidden behind her hair, her eyes trained on the folder on her desk. The moment stretched out in agonizing silence until, finally, she looked up.

'Are you often late, Sarah?'

The jolt of those blue eyes. Like falling on ice. *Slam.*

'No. It was just the trains today were—'

'Only I've been informed that punctuality has been an issue with you in the past.'

Sarah felt her eyes instantly burn with hot tears.

36

Someone had gone behind her back and complained about her. Someone out there in the office. One of the people she called friends.

'Who told you?' she asked.

'It's not important. The important thing is that you are aware that no matter what arrangement you had with Gill, that's not how I run things. I expect all members of staff, regardless of circumstances, to be in work at 9 a.m. and to remain at work until 5.30 p.m. at the very earliest. And if for any reason you arrive later than 9 a.m., I expect you to come straight to see me to explain. Are we clear?'

Sarah nodded, not trusting herself to speak.

Back at her desk, she turned on her computer and logged in without looking at anyone else. She could feel them all sneaking glances over at her, but she kept her gaze fixed to her screen.

Already there was the hot, gut-churning burn of injustice, the sharp needle of clever words she didn't say, winning arguments she didn't use. Who did Rachel Masters think she was anyway? Sarah was thirty-seven years old, yet Rachel had talked to her like a naughty child. After half an hour or so of account checking on-screen, she finally got up the nerve to take her phone out of her bag. Holding it on her lap, she texted her husband.

Was late and got telling off from new bitch boss. Feel like crying.

As soon as she pressed send she felt substantially better. She imagined laughing with Oliver about it this evening over a large glass of wine. Rachel Masters might have a more high-powered job than her but she didn't have what Sarah had – a family, a husband, people who depended on her and upon whom she depended in turn.

Even so, when she made her way to the toilet an hour later – fear of being judged a time-waster finally losing out to post-natal bladder – she couldn't help but cast a suspicious gaze around at her colleagues. They'd always got on so well in the past. There had been the occasional niggle – someone's M&S smoothie going missing from the fridge, that time Amira hadn't handed on a message and Sarah had lost a key client – but on the whole it had been an easy-going team. But now as she threaded her way through her workmates' desks, still studiedly avoiding their eyes, a question ran through Sarah's mind on a continuous loop.

Was it you?

6

Anne

There's a steady stream of students who make the trip to
the fourth floor, along the corridor past the framed
photographs of the faculty, to knock on my door. When
this happens, I try to look nurturing, and call, 'Come
in,' in as welcoming a voice as I can muster. I have a
reputation, you see, as someone who is as much
concerned with the emotional well-being of the students
who pass through here as with their intellectual stimulation. They come to me with questions about assignment
deadlines or reading lists or resource materials, but what
they really want to talk about is whether psychiatry is
the right thing for them, or how to combat the home-
sickness that has taken over their minds until they can't
think about anything except how their mother looked
when she said goodbye, or the bar where their old friends
will be gathering without them on Friday night, or how
they've fallen behind because a careless boyfriend or
girlfriend has shattered their heart into little pieces that
they cannot for the life of them put back together
again.

And I listen, and commiserate, and tell them they're
not alone – and bring up examples of past students

who've stood in the same spot and wept similar tears and gone on to achieve great things – and they leave here feeling a little bit more robust. Some of them even email me later, to tell me I made a difference, that seeing me was a personal turning point in their university experience. I reply that I was just in the right place at the right time – that it was nothing. But I know that not everyone could do what I do. And no one seems to notice that it doesn't come naturally. No one seems to see that I wear my concern like a lab coat that I have shrugged on over my real clothes.

I like my students, and I feel for them, just realizing for the first time that they're not at the centre of the world, their solipsism dissolving in the face of their own anonymity here. It's just that empathy wasn't one of the life skills my mother passed on to me. A bottle of vodka a day tends to make a person self-absorbed.

I'm popular here, but I know many of the younger faculty must wish I'd retire. They're hungry for my job because they see it as a stepping stone to something else, a necessary middle stage in their career development. And here I sit like a boulder blocking the stream of their lives. But I give them no reason to push me out. I'm old, but we live in an era where age is legally protected even while secretly derided and resented. I still publish the odd paper, still give lectures, even if sometimes the back row complain they can't hear me. I won't go because I have nothing to go to. Now that Shannon has left home and Johnny and I are long since divorced, this is all I have.

But the young woman who was introduced by Professor Ed Kowalsky to Child L in that airless room all those years ago was a different person altogether. Not so cynical, and quietly trying my best.

'I'm so glad to meet you, Laurie.' Bending down so I was on her eye level. Trying not to think about what those eyes had seen.

So what was it like, that first session? What you really want to know is, how damaged was she?

The truth is, she presented as a normal four-year-old girl. By turns talkative, then clamming up, shy, then suddenly bursting with life.

We agreed we wouldn't ask her any leading questions that first session, just observe and be guided by her, but in the end she brought it up herself. Ed had asked her what games she most liked to play and she smiled and brought her hands up next to her mouth, her little fists clenched with excitement.

'Oooh, hide and seek.' She did a little skip.

'And where's your favourite place to hide?'

'In the kitchen, under the table, or in the bedroom closet. Mustn't hide in the basement. Mustn't hide there.' Laurie shook her head forcefully from side to side.

Ed didn't look at me, but I could feel it, the tension that entered the room like a cold draught. Debra the social worker wrapped her plump arms around herself.

'Why not the basement, Laurie? What's in there?'

I could sense the effort it was costing Ed to keep his voice steady and measured.

Laurie, who'd been standing facing him, suddenly turned away – and it was a shock to find her eyes fixed on mine.

'It,' she said. 'It is in there.'

After that she didn't want to talk much.

'She's tired,' Debra said, hoisting her canvas bag back on to her broad shoulder.

I'm embarrassed to admit that after the child left the room, I was light-headed with relief.

7

Paula

The figures were moving across the page like tiny black ants. Paula rubbed her eyes. This always happened when she was tired. Last night was the third in a row where she'd hardly slept. Her sleep had been erratic for months thanks to hideous hot flushes which woke her up in the early hours soaked with sweat – but since Rachel Masters had arrived, her insomnia had got worse. She'd go to bed early then spend hours lying awake fretting about work. The flushes, when they came, were savage – a rush of intense heat that sent her heart rate soaring. She'd fling back the duvet and lie on the sheet feeling like something melting in the sun. Through the paper-thin wall, she could hear the motorcycle-engine sound of Ian's snoring and she'd wonder again how it was possible to have separated from a man yet still have her sleep destroyed by him night after night.

At her desk, she tried once again to focus on the printout. It was an invoice that a catering client was disputing. The company had supplied seventeen agency staff to work at a series of functions the catering client was laying on. However, the client said that three of those temporary workers had been sent home early as they hadn't been up to the job. It happened sometimes. The staff they recruited were generally kids trying to earn money for gap years and university courses. Their hearts weren't in it.

On her desk, her mobile vibrated and a text message flashed up.

Out of bread and OJ. Had to go shop. U owe me £3.50.

She glanced at the time on her computer screen. 12.50. At least Cam would see daylight today. That was an improvement on yesterday. She remembered how naïve she'd once been, assuming her days of having to worry about her son would be over once he went off to uni. No one had ever warned her that he'd come back after he graduated. Still, at least he'd had some experience of being independent, unlike Amy, who'd messed up her A levels and anyway baulked at the £9,000 a year tuition fees. 'I'd much rather go straight into a career,' she'd said. Paula could tell her daughter had been envisaging something glamorous – advertising or PR maybe. Instead, she now worked six nights a week in the local pub.

'Paula, have you got a second?'

Her stomach contracted sharply. This happened every time Rachel spoke to her: it was her body's reflex reaction. She followed her new boss into her office, aware all of a sudden of the dowdiness of her long, oatmeal-coloured tunic. It felt like a mail sack in comparison to Rachel's body-hugging navy and orange dress that zipped all the way up the back from hem to neck, emphasizing her neat bottom and tiny waist.

'Sit.'

As if she was a dog. But of course she sat in the chair opposite as indicated by Rachel's faint inclination of the head. *Woof, woof.*

'I've been going through the records and frankly I can't imagine how Gill stayed in her job this long. The place is a total shambles. New client mailings that have never been followed up on, workers kept on the books despite repeated abuses of the rules. How on earth did you let things get into this state, Paula?'

Her? The unfairness of the charge took her breath away. All she'd done was sit at her desk and do what Gill asked her, and act as a first port of call so Gill wouldn't be bothered with all the hundreds of questions and niggling complaints that came up every single day . . . and now she was to be held responsible?

'I wasn't in charge.' As soon as she'd said it, she felt guilty. Gill was her friend. She ought to be defending her, rather than letting Rachel Masters slag her off behind her back. The woman had been here two and a bit days, and she already thought she could judge someone who'd done the job for eight years?

'Did you at least try to get changes introduced? Or are you the kind of deputy who just goes along with what the boss says, regardless?'

A lump was forming in Paula's throat. Yet she was fifty-five years old. She had been working in recruitment when Rachel Masters was still at school. How many times had Gill told her over the years how lucky she was to have such a capable right-hand woman? She ought to be able to just calmly explain that they'd all done their best in some very trying circumstances, particularly these last months. But at the same time, if Gill was going to be made a scapegoat, the last thing Paula wanted was to be lumped in with her.

'I didn't always agree with Gill. In fact, a few times I did try to get her to institute some changes, but . . . well . . . ultimately she had the final word.'

It was kind of true. Over the years Paula had come up with some suggestions for how to improve the running of the department, and Gill hadn't always taken them on board.

'I'll look forward to hearing some of those ideas in due course,' said Rachel. 'I'd also like you to be thinking about a list – in confidence, of course – of which members of staff you consider to be working efficiently and which are dead wood.'

'Dead wood?'

'That's right. I'm sure you have a few candidates in mind. Now, can you please send in Ewan Johnson to see me.'

Paula stood up, her unsaid words sitting like small stones on her tongue. She should stand up for Gill, she should refuse to inform on members of her team. Rachel needed to know that her divide and rule style of management would not work here.

'I'll go and get him.'

8

Ewan

Ewan swallowed hard. It wasn't like him to be nervous, but then again he couldn't remember the last time he'd had a reaction to a woman like the one he'd had to Rachel Masters. For the last three days his eyes had followed her around the office like an unwanted dog. It wasn't that she was particularly beautiful. She was attractive, but no more so than loads of other women he knew. But it was as though she'd entered his head by a secret door and now he couldn't work out how to get her out again.

'You all right?' he asked, sitting down with his legs slightly spread and forcing himself to hold her gaze.

'I'm fine, thank you, Ewan.'

Was she smiling? It was hard to say with her.

'So, tell me a bit about yourself.'

He normally loved talking about himself. If he was ever on *Mastermind* he would be his own specialist subject, that's what his flatmates said. Yet now he couldn't think of a single thing to say.

'Well, I . . . I'm from Coventry originally – or as we locals like to say ,"fookin' Cov".' He glanced at her to see how his joke had gone down, but her face was a polite mask, giving nothing away. 'I was accepted by Manchester Uni but ended up staying in Cov. I'd had enough of classrooms by then, wanted to see a bit of life.' It seemed important for her to know that he'd had choices. He'd chosen to stay at home rather than go to uni.

'Got my first job in sales – a call centre, actually. Within six months I was top of the leader board for closing cold-call sales. My boss said I could have gone all the way, but I'm more of a people person. I wanted a job with more one-to-one contact.'

The phrase had come out perfectly innocently. He hadn't meant anything by it, but now he could feel himself blushing. Underneath the table he stretched out his left leg in a movement that had become so automatic he no longer knew if it was caused by stiffness or habit.

Rachel was leaning back in her chair, making notes in a black moleskin notebook that he knew for a fact hadn't come from the stationery cupboard. She'd put on a pair of stern, black-framed glasses which made her pale-blue eyes look huge. He wondered how old she was. He'd always preferred older women. They didn't play so many games. He'd never been much good at reading between the lines.

'You've been IT Consultant for just under a year. Are you satisfied with that role?'

Ewan kept his smile glued on and his eyes on hers, even though under the desk he was digging the pointy end of his pen lid deep into his thigh.

'Er, obviously I've already got my sights set on the Senior Consultant title, but I know I shouldn't try to run before I can walk.'

A look passed over Rachel's face that might have been

disappointment. Instantly he regretted his ambiguous, clichéd answer.

'Where do you see yourself in five years?'

That was more like it.

'Basically where you're sitting now.'

She raised her eyebrow.

'In that case, you'll probably have some idea how the department runs?'

He nodded, unsure where this was going.

'So you'll be able to tell me exactly where the weak links are?'

She meant people. Well, everyone knew who those were. Paula was a nice old thing, but she was stuck in the last century when it came to work practices, refusing to try anything new, basically sitting there waiting to retire. And much as he'd always got on with Sarah, she was a waste of space as far as work went – always late and spending half her time on the phone to childminders and babysitting in-laws. But these two women were his friends. Workmates, anyway. He couldn't dob them in like that. Could he?

'I'm sure there are things we could all do better.' He knew it was a cop-out. And Rachel Masters knew it too. She took off her glasses and sat back in her chair.

'That's doubtless true, but it's not what I asked you. Very well, Ewan, that's all for now. If anything does come to mind, my door is always open.'

He got up to go, feeling deflated, as if someone had taken a pin and let all the air out of him.

'Oh, and Ewan, if you're serious about sitting where I am, you might want to bear in mind that work is not a popularity contest.'

9

Anne

Child L had been placed with foster parents out in the suburbs. Professor Kowalsky arranged for our second assessment to take place at the foster-family home where we'd have a chance to observe Laurie interacting with other people as well as to talk privately to her foster mother about any concerns she might have.

Ed had offered to drive us both there. He was supposed to pick me up from home, but he called and said he was running late and asked me to meet him at the hospital where Child D was being cared for, and where he and Dan Oppenheimer and other assorted professionals had been carrying out a range of assessments, though in view of the high level of trauma the boy had experienced their remit was necessarily different from our own.

Ed had told me to wait for him in the lobby, but curiosity got the better of me. I'd accepted I'd probably never get to meet Laurie's young brother David. Ed Kowalsky was unwavering in his determination to keep the two assessments separate so that neither Dan nor I risked being swayed by each other's opinions. But what harm could there be in just seeing him? I told myself it was a chance to gain a richer understanding of Laurie, by seeing what she had seen. But really, I was curious, just like everyone else. I wanted to see what the things he'd gone through could do to a child, the subtle imprint they would leave on his skin.

By this stage, weeks after the Egans had been arrested, interest in the case had died down. The TV crews that had been camped outside the hospital had packed up and gone home. So, armed with my university medical school pass, I was able to slip past the reception and get up to the third floor without any trouble. There my luck ran out. The door to the corridor where I knew David was staying required a code to open. But as I was about to turn around, I saw through the panel of safety glass a door opening further down the corridor.

As I watched, a young woman came out, holding the hand of a small child who was walking with an unsteady, lurching gait. The two of them stood waiting in the corridor facing away from me. I stepped back smartly just as the tall, stooping figure of Dan Oppenheimer emerged from the room, followed by Professor Kowalsky. As the three adults conferred, with Oppenheimer noting something down on a clipboard, the little boy turned and, for a split second, we looked at each other. I felt suddenly short of breath as I stared into those eyes that had seen so much horror. I know it sounds fanciful, but it seemed as if a look of recognition passed between us. Then, just as quickly, he was gone – whisked off down the corridor by the young woman. I myself darted back down the stairs, my nerves still jangling from the encounter.

In the passenger seat of Ed's station wagon, I tried to put the unsettling glimpse of Child D out of my head.

The car had two booster seats in the back and the cloth upholstery was covered in white dog hairs.

'Excuse the mess. Families – you know what it's like,' Ed said.

No, I didn't know what it was like.

The journey took about twenty-five minutes and I remember feeling ill at ease. It felt too intimate to be sitting up front alongside this man I barely knew with his toothy smile, surrounded by the evidence of a normal, healthy, happy family life. As we passed other cars, I imagined how we'd look – an ordinary couple out for a drive in their family motor. Perhaps off to a parents' meeting at the kids' school, or grabbing a quick lunch, enjoying rare time off together. Ed was only fifteen or so years older than me – a perfectly respectable age gap. The thought of being mistaken for his wife made me feel sticky with discomfort, and I angled my face away from him, nervously twirling a tendril of hair that had turned damp and frizzy with the heat.

The house where the foster family lived was situated in a cul-de-sac of detached homes maybe thirty or forty years old. The neighbourhood was pleasant, but not ostentatious. Some of the lawns were overgrown, others had brown patches where garden furniture had been recently moved. The cars in the driveways were solid without being flash. As we approached the front door, we could hear a dog barking insistently in one of the neighbouring backyards.

'Hello, hello, hello!'

Jana Green was not what I had been expecting. I'd imagined a buxom, matronly figure with warm folds a troubled child could tuck herself inside of, and an apron tied around a soft, yielding middle. But Jana was all angles and straight lines. Her long toffee-coloured hair was tied in a loose braid that hung down her back, revealing cheekbones that jutted from her face, sharp as flint. She was wearing a white tank-top and denim cut-off shorts that showed slim legs with surprisingly long shinbones. She exuded that kind of calm which is an energy in itself, like a force field around her.

'Lisa, that's my eldest, has taken the little ones off for an ice, to give us a bit of time to chat. They won't be long. I hope that's good with you guys?'

'Oh gosh. Excellent plan, Mrs Green.'

'Please. Call me Jana.'

'Jana.'

Ed Kowalsky rolled the word around in his mouth like a tasty snack and I could see he too was having to recalibrate his mental image of Laurie's home life in the light of this new, unexpected reality. In the light of Jana and her cut-offs.

We sat around a table in the dining part of the kitchen.

'You don't mind, do you?' Jana asked us. 'I hate to be formal.'

Ed produced a tape recorder from the briefcase he'd brought in, saying, 'Just pretend it's not there, Jana. It's simply for our own reference, that's all. So how would you say it's going so far with Laurie? I know it's early days.'

Jana picked up her coffee mug and started tapping one of her long thin fingers against the handle. Tap, tap, tap.

'She's great. Amazing, when you consider . . . I mean,

53

obviously there have been moments. Well, she's only four and a half years old. How could there not be?'

'Moments?' I asked the question more to hear my own voice than because it needed to be asked. Jana was clearly going to tell us anyway.

'She gets angry sometimes. The odd tantrum that maybe you'd expect her to have grown out of by now. But then given the circumstances . . .'

'Quite,' said Ed. 'And has she talked about home at all? About her parents? About her brother?'

'She's asked where they are. But she doesn't really seem that interested in finding out. It's almost like it's something that flits across her mind every now and then. Do you know what I mean? Oh, let me show you something.'

Jana put the mug down and dashed out of the room in a blur of tanned limbs. Without her, the atmosphere seemed flat. Ed and I exchanged strained smiles and immediately looked away again.

'Here it is.' She was carrying a sheet of A3 paper which she laid carefully down on the table between us. It was a child's painting, all primary colours. There was a red square house with a triangle roof and three lollipop people, two big, one small. There was a black fence to the side and a long sausage dog next to it.

'She said that was her with her mom and dad,' said Jana, pointing at the trio of people with their stick bodies and round, smiling heads.

'Interesting. So she didn't draw her brother at all,' said Ed.

'Oh, but she did.' Jana moved her finger across the paper to the shape I'd assumed was a dog.

'He's lying down,' she explained.

'Ah,' said Ed in a small voice.

'So that,' I pointed to the black railings, 'isn't a fence.'

'No,' Jana agreed. 'That's a cage.'

10

Amira

'Working lunch? What does that even mean?'

Amira couldn't stop thinking about it. And every time she thought about it, her nerve-endings started tingling uncomfortably like the beginnings of pins and needles all over her chest and arms.

'It'll be fine.' Tom didn't even look up from his laptop. 'She just wants to get you all into a more informal setting. It always happens that way. New boss. Feels she has to lay down the law in the office. Now she wants to show you all a more relaxed side. Bit of team bonding. It's straight out of *The New Boss Handbook*.'

Without moving from where she was lying prone on the sofa, Amira reached out her hand and picked up her empty glass from the coffee table.

'See this?' Still Tom didn't look up. 'Oi! See this?'

He glanced over and then immediately looked back down again.

'I'd rather bond with this glass than Rachel Masters,' Amira told him. 'She gives me the heebie-jeebies. I'm dreading our cosy one-to-one first thing tomorrow.'

'Yeah, well, you've just got to suck it up. Look on the bright side. With the size of our mortgage we're only going to have to be working for the next hundred years or so.'

Tom sounded bitter, and the tingling turned into an insistent jabbing. She knew he hated his auditing job. But he'd made the decision on his own to give up on the music stuff. She hadn't pushed him. It wasn't fair to make her feel guilty. Anyway, the band had always been a pipe dream. This was London, where it cost you fifty quid just to breathe the air. You couldn't live on creative juices alone. And her mother would literally have driven her bonkers if they'd stayed there any longer, always making a big deal about being so easy-going, so different from her own strict Indian parents, yet the master of the pained expression, or the big sigh accompanied by the dreaded phrase 'your father always dreamed you'd . . .' followed by whatever was the exact opposite of what Amira had just announced she would do.

Every day Amira still missed her gentle-giant dad, even though it would be eight years next month since he'd died. But she remembered him as a kind man with a big laugh that shot out of him like a volley of cannon-fire when he watched a silly TV programme or joked with one of his many relations back in Ireland, not the reproachful figure hunched over with disappointment that her mother tried to project. Families were so weird, weren't they? If they hadn't been related, Amira couldn't think of two people with less in common than her mother and her.

Amira's unease was still with her when she got up to go to work the next morning, along with the heavy throb of a hangover. She blamed those huge wine glasses they'd received as a moving-in present. Three of those and you'd drunk a bottle without even realizing it.

She hesitated over what to wear, spending so long in front of the mirror trying on and discarding clothes that she was late leaving and had to do run-walking all the way to the station, cursing the heels she'd foolishly decided on at the last minute.

This wasn't at all the way she'd seen her working life. She'd always presumed she'd do something worthwhile. Something that made a difference – charity work or advocacy or something – but instead she'd fallen into recruitment, thinking it was just a stopgap while she made up her mind what she really wanted to do. Six months had turned into a year and then another, and now five years had gone by and here she was pinioned in place under the weight of their monstrous mortgage.

Walking through the double doors into the office, Amira was struck all over again by the strange new atmosphere. In the Gill days, people would have been hovering by each other's desks, cradling cups of coffee and chatting before getting down to the business of the day. But now everyone was at their stations, computers on, eyes down. The daring few who risked walking past the new boss's office to the kitchen did so with heads bowed. Where they used to take it in turn to do a coffee round (well, some had more turns than others, it had to be said), now they made quick, solitary forays to the kettle, making single cups that took just minutes to prepare and could be carried surreptitiously through the office without drawing too much attention.

Waiting to be called into Rachel's office for her one-to-one, Amira texted Tom. *Shitting self. Guillotine poised above head.* Only as she clicked send did she notice her phone had auto-corrected 'guillotine' to 'guilt'. Great. So now Tom would start reading all sorts of weird meanings into a text that was supposed to be light-hearted. She toyed with the idea of texting him again to correct it, but decided against it. Let him wonder.

'Amira?'

Paula had materialized by her desk, noiselessly like a ghost.

'Rachel will see you now.'

Amira smiled, but Paula wasn't really looking at her directly, rather at a point slightly to her left. She seemed tired, Amira couldn't help noticing. Her pale eyes were made paler still by the smudged purple shadows underneath. It must be stressful, living in that little terraced house with an estranged husband and adult kids who, as far as Amira could see, did bugger all to help. If only Paula would stand up for herself a bit. She should have chucked Ian out when they split up, broke or not. He'd have had to stand on his own two feet then, give up that vinyl business that was never going to make him any money and go out and get a proper job.

Making her way across the office, Amira couldn't help feeling that everyone was clocking her uncharacteristically high heels and judging her for trying too hard.

Rachel Masters was in efficiency mode, lining up the edges of the stack of papers in front of her that turned out to be copies of Amira's annual reviews, plus various progress reports and even her original CV, sent in when she applied for the job.

She said some complimentary things about Amira's work appraisals and the positive comments that had been made by her supervisors. Then she laid down the heavy engraved silver pen she had been turning between her elegant fingers and said, 'Can I talk to you in complete confidence, Amira?'

Amira blinked. 'Of course.' She tried to make her voice sound steady, but some obstacle seemed to have lodged itself in her windpipe.

Rachel shot a glance through the closed glass door to the main office, to where the rest of the staff were working, and then she leaned in across the desk.

'This department has been underperforming for years. I've been brought in to weed out anyone who is just coasting, and reward those making a proper contribution. Now I know this is delicate as you've all been working together as a team, but I want to give you the heads-up that there will be a vacancy coming up at deputy level, and I'd like you to apply for it.'

'Wow, thank you. I don't know . . . Wow, so you'll be creating another deputy position?'

Amira couldn't remember the last time she'd used the word 'wow', and now she'd just said it twice in one sentence.

Rachel held Amira's gaze. Once, Amira's parents' house had subsided and steel rods had had to be drilled into the rock below to underpin it. That's just how Rachel's eyes felt now. Like steel rods boring into her own.

'No. There's just the one deputy position.'

'But Paula is . . . Oh.'

The realization rendered her wordless. Still Rachel's eyes didn't leave hers, cut glass pinioning her to the chair.

'So now you can appreciate the need for discretion. I

want people I can rely on, Amira. I'm not saying it's a foregone conclusion you'll get the job, but from what I can see, you'd make an excellent deputy. I hope you'll at least think about it.'

Hurrying back through the office, Amira made sure to avoid eye contact with any of her workmates. Safely installed behind her own desk, she was surprised by a wave of resentment that came seemingly from nowhere. How dare Rachel Masters put her in this position? They'd all worked alongside each other for years without problem and now in she came, trying to stir up trouble between them. But soon her anger turned on herself. Why hadn't she said something? Why hadn't she stuck up for Paula, told Rachel where to stick her promotion? Where was her moral compass?

Her phone vibrated with a text from Tom.

How's the guilt?

For a wild moment, she felt he must have sensed her monumental spinelessness from wherever he was, until she remembered about the auto-correct mistake in her earlier message.

From the corner of her eye, she saw Paula get up from her desk. Amira immediately switched her attention to her computer screen, pretending to be engrossed in the response of a tech client to the latest batch of cvs she'd sent him. Her desk was on the main route out to reception and the toilets so she wasn't concerned when Paula headed straight for her. However, her heart sank when her colleague stopped by her chair.

'How'd it go in there?' Paula asked with a smile so tight it was like a fold in paper. Amira saw how it strained at the sides of her face.

'Oh, you know,' she replied. 'Bit scary.'

Paula's face relaxed.

'You too? Yes, she is a bit intimidating. Maybe she'll let her guard down when we all go out to lunch.'

As she moved off, Amira battled an urge to go after her, to explain herself. It wasn't her fault. She hadn't encouraged Rachel or said anything to indicate she'd apply for the job. And obviously she wouldn't even countenance it. Not for a minute. Yet still, as Paula exited through the double doors to the lobby, Amira felt as if she'd betrayed her. Guilt sat in her stomach hard as a stone.

11

Charlie

'I don't do food in a box.'

'Sh! You're just going to have to swallow your principles and slum it for once.'

'I don't get it. What's so wrong with a plate?'

Charlie hated the restaurant chain with its Scandanavian-style blond wood tables and bright ethnic prints and the supposedly healthy menu where everything was sprinkled with pomegranate seeds and alfalfa and called Superfood this or Superfood that and then wrapped up in a doughy carbohydrate-sodden wrap.

He and Sarah were the last staff members queuing to order their food. The others were sitting around a large table by the window which was already strewn with cardboard boxes and plastic smoothie cups. Rachel Masters sat at one end picking at something green and leafy with a stubby wooden fork. To her left, Chloe was leaning forward and saying something with that red rash flaring up like the Olympic flame on her chest as it always did when she was nervous. Charlie felt sorry for the girl. She could be a bit silly sometimes and inclined to be self-absorbed, but it was hard to hold your own in an office of much older people. On Rachel's other side, Ewan was grasping a bulging wrap in both hands while gazing over its top at their new boss with an expectant smile poised on his lips, just waiting to pounce on a flippant remark or an encouraging look. Oh dear. Poor Ewan.

'Someone needs to pop Ewan back in his crate with a blanket over the top,' he whispered to Sarah as they made their way over to the table. 'Calm him down.'

'I thought he and Chloe had a thing?'

'Euw. Child-snatcher.'

'Perhaps you could tell us all the joke. We could do with a laugh.' Rachel's glossy lips were parted in a smile, but her eyes were cold. Charlie's own lips suddenly felt sun-shrivelled dry. He'd worked in recruitment for years. He was an experienced, conscientious member of the team. Gill had privately told him he was the backbone of the department, so why did he feel as if he was back in the primary-school playground suddenly, loitering by the girls' area, just praying to be left alone?

'Oh, we were just laughing about the food,' Sarah said. Charlie was shocked to see that her hand, clutching its little box of salad, was actually trembling.

'Yes,' he broke in quickly, wanting to rescue her. 'I mean, has anyone in the entire history of Death Row ever asked for a last meal of alfalfa sprouts or quinoa?'

He and Sarah both did those false laughs people do on TV – that come from the throat and not the belly.

'I thought it would be nice for us all to have a clearing-the-air session, away from the formality of the office,' said Rachel, addressing the whole table.

If Chloe's head nodded much more fervently it would surely detach itself from her body.

'I'm very aware that things have been difficult, the last few days. Transitions are always tricky. But I want to urge you to come to me with any questions or problems or complaints. Far better to have them out in the open where they can be addressed instead of whispering in corners, which only creates a bad atmosphere.'

Was she looking at him? There'd been a moment when he'd felt rather than seen her eyes on him, like fingernails digging in his flesh. Charlie shifted uneasily and plunged his wooden fork into his food. The organic, free-range, probably ashtanga-yoga-practising chicken tasted like something that had been spat out and then reconstituted, its texture unpleasantly claggy.

'I thought it would be good today to go round the table and for each of you to say one thing you think could improve the performance of this department.'

What was this, circle time?

He and Sarah shared a brief look. One of her eyebrows was infinitesimally raised. When was the last time she had plucked them, anyway? Charlie missed the days of Sarah BC (before children) when the two of them used to go out after work and sit in gay pubs eyeing up men and singing medleys of West End musicals. She was already with Oliver then, but they'd quite happily kept separate friends. Not that Charlie had anything against Oliver, just that Sarah was more fun when she wasn't with him. Now when he thought back to those days, she with her fiery red curls and ready gap-toothed smile and weakness for sweet, liqueur-based cocktails that they'd stock up on in two-for-one happy hours, it was like a different life, like a holiday that, once home, you struggled to believe had ever happened. In the last four years, Sarah had acquired two children, at least ten extra kilos and a permanent frown-line down the bridge of her nose. They rarely went out anywhere any more, and when they did she'd spend most of her time fielding phone calls from Oliver asking the whereabouts of favourite toys or why Sam was refusing to eat whatever mush she'd left for dinner, or why Joe wouldn't stop crying. More often than not they'd both go home more stressed rather than less.

'Sarah. I can see you're dying to share something with the rest of us. Let's have your thoughts.'

From the corner of his eye, Charlie watched Sarah's hands. She was literally wringing them together in her lap. He couldn't remember ever actually seeing someone do that before. Squeezing, then turning, squeezing, then turning.

'Me? Ha! Typical – it would have to be me!'

Sarah tended to do this when she was nervous – speak a stream of nonsense just to say something.

'OK. So what single thing could improve the department . . .'

She did that a lot as well. Repeated the question to buy time. *Come on*, he urged her silently. *Have faith in yourself.*

'Well, I think the temporary follow-up system could be made a little more efficient than it is now. That's the system for doing the after-debrief with clients for one-off functions and events, getting feedback, making sure things went smoothly. We've been doing it for about eighteen months but it's still a touch hit and miss.'

Rachel was still smiling at her, a smile as hard and bright as an overhead striplight.

'Thank you, Sarah. That's a great start. So you've been running this system for eighteen months. Who was responsible for it in the first place?'

Sarah gazed blankly at Rachel as if she was suddenly speaking in tongues.

'Come on. Someone must have come up with the system in the first place. It's only eighteen months old. Who was it?'

A faint sheen had appeared on Sarah's upper lip.

'I don't . . . I can't remember.'

'Someone must remember.'

Rachel cast her eyes around the table, her smile unwavering. Ewan shrugged theatrically, Amira looked up to the ceiling as if trying to dredge her memory. Only Chloe, who was too junior to be involved, was unbothered. The silence stretched over the table, tight as cling film. Finally Paula spoke.

'I think it was me, actually.' Her voice came out in a squeak like someone unused to speaking.

'Great. So you'll be able to say whether you think Sarah is right.'

'I didn't mean . . .' Sarah burst in, unable to stop herself, but then seemed not to have the faintest idea what she hadn't meant.

'I agree that the system might benefit from some . . . updating,' Paula began, 'but I certainly don't think it's responsible for the department underperforming. If anything, I think the problem lies with the staff structure. It's too apple-shaped, too wide around the middle.

Things are getting clogged up in the centre because no one is really sure who is handling what. There ought to be a more streamlined chain of command.'

Too wide around the middle? So basically she was saying there were too many people on the same mid-managerial level, which in effect, meant Sarah, Amira, Ewan and Charlie himself. For a few seconds, Charlie tried to think of an alternative meaning for what Paula had said, but judging by the expression on Amira and Sarah's faces, there wasn't one. Ewan was determinedly tucking into his wrap. Maybe he hadn't followed Paula's remark to its final logical conclusion, or maybe he thought he was safe somehow. Had Rachel said something to him? He certainly did seem to be cosying up to her. Anyway, Ewan had his own separate sphere of responsibility – recruiting IT personnel – so maybe he thought he wouldn't be affected.

Paula, whose face had worn a rosily defiant expression while defending her post-event follow-up system, was now looking ashen, as if she'd just realized the implications of what she'd said. Charlie was starting to feel an unfamiliar burning in the pit of his stomach. Was Paula really suggesting Rachel get rid of one of them? Just what was she playing at? It now seemed ironic that just yesterday he'd stood in front of Rachel Masters and been outraged on Paula's behalf when Rachel had brazenly asked if he was interested in Paula's job. Well, of course he'd been outraged. It was so underhand. Nonetheless, he'd agreed not to mention it to anyone and he'd been true to his word, though more out of respect for Paula herself than any loyalty to the new boss.

'I really wouldn't feel comfortable discussing any change of role when there's already someone doing that job,' he'd told Rachel. 'Particularly when it's someone I've worked very closely with for a number of years.'

If he'd expected her to be embarrassed, he was disappointed.

'Very creditable, I'm sure, Charlie. However, I should make it clear I'm anticipating a degree of staff realigning. Certain positions will inevitably become vacant in the reshuffle.'

Afterwards he wished he'd called her bluff, been more combative. Paula had been at the agency for ever. She predated the carpet in reception, and that was saying something. Rachel couldn't just get rid of her like that. There were strict protocols to be adhered to, verbal and written warnings, disciplinary hearings. And it wasn't even as if Paula was bad at her job – she just lacked a little spark. She was maybe a bit inclined to coast along doing everything the way it had always been done because what's not broken didn't need fixing. But though she might not be the most dynamic deputy in the world, she was reliable and experienced and she and Gill together had always been supportive to him.

Now, after what Paula had just said, or implied, about there being too many middle managers, he wondered if perhaps she could have found out that he'd been sounded out about her job and this was payback. But she wasn't like that, surely? Paula had never been the vindictive sort.

Charlie looked over at Amira who was in turn exchanging wide-eyed glances with Sarah. The tension at the table was like an uninvited guest who'd arrived without warning and was refusing to leave.

At the far end Rachel Masters speared a whole cherry tomato. Reddish juice trickled from her mouth, and she licked it with the pink tip of her tongue.

12

Anne

Some days I look around at my life, my nice office, my secure job that gives me respect and status, my smart daughter, my lovely house, my interesting eclectic group of friends, and think I wouldn't be here without my mother. Other days I look at it all and know I'd be somewhere better. My mother got me here. And she keeps me here.

'Work hard,' she told me, and then, 'Work even harder. You're attractive now, but looks fade. No one will give you anything for free.'

So I inherited from her the drive and determination to make it this far. And I also inherited from her the self-doubt that ensured I went no further, and the conviction that the cure for it lay in the bottom of a glass. The only difference between us is that she gave in to that conviction whereas I battle it, day after day, year after year.

But during those days when Child L's story continued to dominate the headlines, I was still in denial. Addiction was a failure of will, not of genetics, I'd think as I carefully sipped on the single glass of wine I allowed myself each day. Working on the Child L case was my chance to move irrevocably beyond my mother's reach, or rather the reach of her legacy to me. It would be a gate into the rose garden she'd never been able to access, an escape route away from her perpetual and paralysing disappointment. Whenever Dan Oppenheimer and his cronies would whisper about me in the canteen when I passed – those old rumours about exactly why Ed Kowalsky had picked me for the case, reasons that had more to do with my long blonde hair than my professional qualifications – I'd remind myself of where I was headed and the small-town narrowness I was going to leave behind.

Ed Kowalsky and I had a very specific remit. We were to assess Laurie over a period of weeks or months to ascertain the degree of psychological damage she had suffered; based on that, we would then make recommendations for her long-term future. Putting it bluntly, Laurie was four and a half years old. If we judged her to be deeply, even irrevocably, damaged by what she'd seen and experienced in the House of Horror (as the papers had predictably dubbed her family home), we would recommend her to a specialist children's psychiatric facility and she would be made a permanent ward of the state. However, if we felt the effects of such emotional trauma as she'd sustained would fade in due course, we would recommend her to be adopted. In this respect our assessment differed markedly from that of Laurie's younger brother, which Kowalsky was also overseeing with the assistance of Dan Oppenheimer. In Child D's case, it was assumed the psychological and physical scars would render adoption an impossibility, so the assessment was to determine his long-term treatment. Laurie, however, had a chance.

Things were very different back then. We didn't know all the things we do now about the long-term effects of early childhood trauma and the different ways it can come out in adolescence or adulthood. This was before all the controversy over False Memory Syndrome where adults, often undergoing psychological treatment, claimed to have recovered memories of infant abuse. We genuinely believed that as long as the damage was not too extreme, if a child was young enough, and placed in a stable, loving environment, he or she would form a new set of memories, and leave the past behind. In those days we thought the best chance of a new life was to sever all links with what had gone before and start afresh. If Laurie was approved for adoption, we'd already talked about placing her somewhere overseas where no one would know her story, and where the chances of her coming across the details in later life would be minimal. These were pre-internet days when it was still possible to lose oneself and stay lost. Or to lose someone else.

So there was a lot riding on us, and we wore our responsibilities particularly heavily on our third meeting with Laurie. This time Jana brought her into the medical school together with her own young son, Barney, a year Laurie's junior. Her older daughter, Lisa, was in class. For the first quarter of an hour we exchanged chit-chat while watching the children play. I was particularly keen to observe the interaction between the two. After all, Laurie had been brought up essentially as an only child. She wasn't used to sharing. To that end I brought out a simple but brightly coloured building-block game.

'Here's something you can both play with together

while Jana and I talk,' I said casually, wanting Laurie to feel she was unobserved.

As Jana, Ed and I discussed the unusually mild fall weather and the heavy traffic on the main highway into town, I watched Laurie from the corner of my eye. She was concentrating on building a tower, the tip of her tongue protruding slightly between her lips. Periodically she reached out to pick up a block from the pile in front of her to add to her tower. Barney was watching her intently.

'I play,' he said, reaching out a chubby hand to pick up a brick.

Laurie didn't reply, so intent was she on making sure her tower didn't fall over. Barney's bottom lip wobbled.

'I play,' he repeated and placed his brick heavily on the top of Laurie's tower, sending the whole lot crashing to the floor.

While Jana chatted to Ed about the family's holiday in Vermont the previous summer, I waited, tense, to see how Laurie would react. She got to her feet and took a step towards the little boy. I could sense Jana watching, even while she carried on talking.

'No, Barney!' Laurie was cross. That much was sure. And yet it was nothing out of the ordinary, just a normal level of crossness for a child of not yet five. She bent down and started picking up the bricks which were littered across the floor around Barney's sandalled feet.

'Sowwy.' He bent down to help her pick them up.

The three adults let out the breath we'd all been holding.

'She's amazingly good really,' Jana whispered as the two youngsters chattered together about how best to rebuild the tower. 'She's really patient with him on the whole. More patient even than his own sister. There was only that one incident . . .'

Ed Kowalsky, who'd seemed distracted – almost bored – up to this point, swung around in his seat as though someone had wound him up like a clockwork toy.

'Incident?'

Jana glanced over to the small children on the floor. She was more formally dressed today in a midi-length blue dress that swirled around her legs, revealing a tan leather beaded thong around one ankle, and flat sneaker-type shoes, also in faded blue. The sleeveless dress made her brown arms appear endless and I saw how Ed's eyes, magnified behind his glasses, were drawn to the long slope of her collarbone, smooth as a razor clam.

'Why don't we call Kristen in to take the children off for a soda,' he said. 'Kristen is one of my research students,' he explained to Jana. 'Kids just love her.'

He looked at me, and I realized that when he'd said, 'Why don't we', what he'd meant was why didn't I. As I went out into the corridor I reminded myself that he was the one who'd given me this opportunity, and it was fair enough for him to ask me to do the things he didn't want to do himself. But still it rankled. As did the way he was looking at Jana. Let's get this straight, there was nothing attractive to me about Ed Kowalsky. He was a married older man who just happened to be my departmental senior. But I'd got used to a certain level of . . . appraisal. It gave me a slight feeling of power. And it was galling to discover that power was all in my head.

Kristen was a plump girl with a wide, doughy face,

75

who always blinked before talking to you as if trying to expel an unwelcome image that had come unbidden into her head. After she'd led the children off towards the lifts on the way to what was cheeringly called the 'cafeteria' on floor one but was actually just three vending machines and a few padded chairs in faded pale blue and orange, Ed depressed the pause button on the cassette player and we leaned in towards Jana, partly to better hear what she was about to say and partly because she was just the kind of person you instinctively want to get closer to.

'There were two incidents, but they're nothing really,' she said now, pulling her long silky ponytail forwards over one shoulder so she could play with the ends. The sun was slanting through the slats of the blinds, striping the planes of her face with golden bands of light.

'Everything you tell us is useful, Jana,' said Ed, leaning so far in I thought he would end up with his head on her lap. 'Every little piece of information helps us build a picture of what's going on inside Laurie's head. And that's the only way we're going to be able to really help her.'

'The first incident happened a few days ago. Laurie was playing with Barney and, as I say, normally she's very good with him but on this day she was tired and a bit out of sorts and he was playing with something she wanted and she gave him a little slap. Not hard, but I guess I rebuked her quite sharply. Anyway, she ran upstairs and by the time I followed her up there, she'd locked herself in the bathroom. I tried to talk to her through the door but she just said she was bad and bad children needed to be locked up. Then it went quiet for a while and when she came out, it was just like none of it had ever happened.'

Ed and I exchanged glances. This was distressing to hear, but at the same time not unexpected.

'And the second incident?'

Ed Kowalsky leaned still further, looking as if he would like to take a giant straw and suck Jana up in one big gulp.

'It's probably nothing, really. It's just that I was reprimanding Lisa – that's my eldest – about something. I can't even remember what it was now. Laurie was in the room colouring or something, but I hadn't really been aware of her, you know. Then all of a sudden Lisa says, "Mommy, what's wrong with Laurie?" and I looked and she was just standing there with this really kind of weird expression.'

'Weird?' I queried, wanting to understand.

Jana shrugged her shoulders.

'No, not weird – she's only four years old. More like disturbing. It was a kinda set expression like someone much, much older. But it was her eyes that were the problem. It's like they were totally empty, like there was nothing there.'

'Did she say anything?' asked Ed.

'She was muttering. I think she was saying something like "bad Lisa". Or "Lisa's been bad". But it wasn't really what she was saying as much as that dead look on her face.'

'How long did it last?' I asked.

'Oh goodness. Really not long, *at all*. Minutes. Seconds even. Then she was completely fine again. And like I say, most of the time she's a little doll.'

'And still no curiosity about her parents? Her brother?' My voice stumbled over the last word as if it contained an untruth.

'Like I said before, she mentions them from time to time but mostly in terms of things. Like she'll see someone wearing red shoes and say "Mommy has red shoes", or like when I was reading the other night, she said, "Daddy has lots of books in his study." But she doesn't really ask about them in terms of where they are. Debra, the child welfare officer, has told her that sometimes parents aren't very nice to their children and when that happens they have to go away for a while – and she seems to accept that without question. It's kinda scary.' Jana paused and bit down softly on her bottom lip.

'Scary?' Ed repeated.

'Well, Lisa and Barney are my whole world. If I was separated from them it'd be like my life was finished. It's hard to believe that they could be separated from me and for them it would be like I was just this person who came into their mind when they saw a particular colour of shoe.'

After Jana had left with the two children, hyped-up and fractious after their soda, Ed Kowalsky and I played back the recording of the session and made notes in silence. Eventually Ed sat back in his chair and clicked the end of his pen thoughtfully a few times before speaking.

'I'm encouraged by how Laurie seems able to compart-mentalize her experiences,' he said. Click, click, click. 'That suggests she might be capable in future of separating off those parts of her psyche where the damage lies.'

78

I nodded, but more because I was programmed to nod when someone senior was talking than because I actually agreed with him.

'But don't you think, Profess— Ed . . . that there's also a danger that she might be suppressing her thoughts, rather than dissociating from them? And could that kind of extreme suppression lead to psychological problems further on down the track?'

He leaned back and crossed one leg on top of the other, ankle to knee, in an oddly suggestive way.

'I understand where you're coming from with that, but as you know, the optimal outcome for Laurie would be if she was able to separate off the things that have happened to her and keep them separate until it's as if they happened to someone else.'

'But those behavioural patterns Jana mentioned – the aberrant reaction to punishment situations?'

'I don't think I'd call those a pattern, Anne.' Click, click. 'Jana stressed they were unrepresentative incidents. It might be that something was said – just a word, or a look even – that triggered a learned response. But the probability is, those triggers will fade now that she's been removed from the source of them. I'm by no means complacent, but I am cautiously optimistic.'

I think it was then I felt the first prickling of unease. True, my name would be on this report alongside Ed's – but what if the conclusions were his alone?

13

Chloe

Chloe had never had someone dislike her before. At school she'd been one of those girls teachers appoint to show the new kids around. She captained the school netball team and when they won the county trophy she was careful to stress it was not her victory but totally down to the other players. Boys both liked and fancied her, even if secretly they sometimes wished she'd let rip a bit more. And girls were generally happy to be her friend.

As a result things had tended to fall into her lap. Three decent but not brilliant A levels from a leading North London state school ('I came through the state system,' she'd say modestly, choosing not to add that her parents paid over a million pounds for a house in the school's tiny catchment area) led to an English Literature degree from Bristol University – missing out on an upper second by only the narrowest of margins, she'd inform people, shrugging her narrow shoulders in a what-can-you-do gesture. She hadn't intended to go into recruitment but her mum knew someone who'd got her an internship and then Gill had offered her a junior role. Really she wanted to go into TV production but there was plenty of time. She was still very young, as she pointed out to her older colleagues with some regularity. The other reason she stayed in the department was Ewan.

Chloe had had boyfriends before. From year ten to year thirteen she'd gone out with Alex Macdonald, ending the relationship by phone once she was safely ensconced in Bristol and receiving the attentions of a boy who'd once modelled for a high-street chain. Then in her last two years at university she'd gone out with an American exchange student and had even talked about moving out to live with him after they graduated, but somehow that had just fizzled out once he went back to Illinois. Only when she met Ewan Johnson on her first day in the office did she properly fall in love.

And he'd seemed right up for it.

That first day he'd made it his personal mission to show her where everything was, how to put paper in the printer without it being chewed up with a horrible grinding noise. He'd taken her out for a sandwich and given her the lowdown on who was who in the office. He'd warned her that Amira had a thing about the smell of Pot Noodle in the microwave and Paula got upset if anyone used her special mug.

At twenty-eight he was four years older than her, but over the days and weeks following her arrival he'd deliberately allied himself to her as the younger element. They developed a signal that meant 'meet in the kitchen for coffee' and went out for a quick drink after work at least once a week. And though he hadn't made a pass at her – yet – he flirted relentlessly.

Yes, there were things she wasn't entirely comfortable with. She'd grown up in a house where it was considered vulgar to talk about money but Ewan openly speculated about how much other people in the office were on, and how much he intended to be making by the time he was thirty. He drank too much and could be patronizing, like when he referred to Paula as an 'old dear' although she was younger than Chloe's mum who would have been furious at that description. He was also cocky, insisting Charlie had the hots for him, although Chloe had never seen any indication of that. And he definitely had a chip on his shoulder about not going to university. 'Come out owing £50K just so you can move back home with Mummy and Daddy and send CVs to people like me begging for a job? No, thank you.'

But despite these niggles, she was smitten. When he turned his green eyes on her, she felt as if the rest of the world was just sliding away like one of those special effects where the outside edges blur into soft focus. He was good-looking, he made her laugh uncontrollably, and unlike most of her other friends, he wasn't living at home with his parents but in a flat share in Clacton, which seemed to her the height of glamour. All of which accounted for why, when Gill – to whom, anyway, she had difficulty saying no – called her into her office after a largely uneventful three-month internship and asked if she'd consider staying on as departmental assistant at a salary she later overheard her father describe as 'border-line exploitation', she'd jumped at the chance. And why Rachel Masters's unaccountable but evident dislike of her was so unsettling.

'She hates me,' she moaned to Ewan as they followed the others back to the office after that departmental lunch with Rachel, taking their time on account of

Ewan's leg feeling stiff – an old footballing injury, he'd once told her, which only added to his allure.

'No, she doesn't. She's just straight-talking, that's all. I like that approach. Makes a welcome change. Can't be doing with all this "Let's not say what we think in case someone's feelings get hurt" business.' Ewan put on a high-pitched voice that grated.

'You just fancy her, that's all.'

Chloe kept her muscles tensed into a tight smile so he wouldn't know how much it had cost her to say that. Her face ached from the effort of willing him to deny it.

'Course I do. Every bloke in the building does. Well, apart from Charlie, and he doesn't exactly count. She's gorgeous . . .'

Chloe made a noise she hoped sounded like a giggle, but inside, the arteries and veins that led to her heart were being tightened like guitar strings.

'. . . for an old bird.'

Ewan grinned, and it was like the sun coming out after a long grey winter. Everything inside had unfurled.

Thinking about that moment now, as she carefully felt-penned *Gill's leaving present* on a large padded envelope, Chloe once again had that dissolving feeling she'd experienced when she sat down at her desk on that first day in the office in front of an unfamiliar computer, squinting nervously at the yellow Post-it on which the guy from IT had written down her new ID and password. She had been trying to get up the nerve to turn the computer on when Ewan had looked across at her from the next desk and smiled, and something somewhere had gone *ping*.

83

It was only 8.50 a.m., still a full ten minutes before the official start of the day, and the office had that eerie living-museum quality you find in stately homes where the rooms are empty but the family is still in residence, subtle traces of them everywhere. Rachel Masters had already been installed in her office when Chloe had arrived five minutes earlier. Did that woman even have a life outside work?

A few members of the sales team whose desks were hidden behind a grey padded partition were already in, and Chloe decided to begin her collection there, slipping discreetly behind the screen with her envelope to a welcome of mock groans. By the time she emerged a few minutes later, her envelope clinking reassuringly, the office had filled up. Sarah was there, looking flustered as usual. Amira was clutching a large cardboard takeout cup – it always took her at least two strong filter coffees before she could function properly. Disappointment twanged at the sight of Ewan's still empty desk but then she heard a familiar roar of laughter and followed the sound to the boss's office where the object of her affection was standing in the open doorway, leaning casually against the frame.

'Wonder if he brought an apple in,' whispered Charlie as he dug around in his pocket for some change to chuck into the envelope.

'Apple?'

'You know, for the teacher.'

Charlie was looking at her as though she was being particularly dense. After a rocky start, Chloe had come to like Charlie, but she wished she didn't always feel so stupid around him.

Amira pulled a ten-pound note out of her wallet.

'Really hate to be tight, but can I ask for a fiver back?' She looked embarrassed and kept her voice low. 'It's just that we're so skint at the moment and Tom keeps making me account for every single bloody penny.'

'Sure. No prob.'

Chloe felt for Amira. She didn't know how much she was earning, but even though she knew it had to be way more than her, it was never going to be enough to pay mortgages and gas bills and Council Tax and God knows what else. Chloe's dad had once sat her down and gone through his bank statement to show her how much he paid out each month. 'You're an adult now, it's about time you realized just how much things cost,' he'd said, but her eyes had glazed over before they'd even gone through the first page of figures. Still, she knew it added up to many times more than the paltry sum that went into her bank account each month.

'Chloe!' That distinctive high-pitched voice cut like a knife through her thoughts. 'I'm curious. Care to tell me what you're doing?'

Rachel Masters was standing outside her office with her hands on her hips. Ewan was back at his seat and turned to see what was going on, along with everyone else. A horrible hush fell over the office.

'I'm just taking a collection for Gill.'

'What time is it?'

Chloe swallowed and glanced over to the clock on the far wall.

'Five past nine.'

'Actually it's seven minutes past nine, which means you've been doing that for seven minutes since the working day officially began. I take it that means you're

85

up to date on all your stuff, like that mailing list you're doing for me.'

Chloe stood frozen as if her legs had grown roots and dug down into the floor. Her face was on fire and she wasn't sure she trusted herself to speak.

'No, but . . .'

'Actually I asked Chloe to do the collection.'

Paula's voice sounded strange and unusually gravelly in the tense air. Chloe felt weak with gratitude as Rachel Masters's attention shifted suddenly to her deputy.

'And you specifically asked her to do it on company time?'

Paula's cheeks flushed a vivid fuchsia at odds with her burgundy-coloured top.

'No, of course not. I assumed she'd have the sense to do it at lunchtime.'

Chloe felt a stinging in the back of her eyes at Paula's uncharacteristic unkindness. Please God, don't let me be about to cry, she thought.

'Right, Chloe. I suggest you take your envelope and go back to your desk and get on with what you're actually being paid to do.'

Rachel turned on her heel and Chloe's feet finally recovered their function enough to allow her to slink back to her desk. She could feel eyes on her as she moved but refused to look at anyone for fear a sympathetic glance would unleash the tears she was only just managing to hold back.

Her computer pinged with an email. The name Ewan Johnson appeared in her inbox in bold.

Bit harsh that. U ok?

She bit her lip and typed back, No. *She is a total bitch. Am going to start looking for new job.*

Seconds later came the response. *Shes tough but thats what shes here for*

No *please don't do that.* No *I'll miss you if you go.*

Chloe minimised her inbox and called up the mailing list she was in the middle of putting together for Rachel Masters. She stared at the names until the letters became random black dots on the page.

Her eyes burned.

14

Paula

Paula had once tried to describe anxiety to Ian – when they were still married and he was still obliged to feign an interest.

'It's like my nerves are made up of tiny ants and most of the time they're all asleep but then they'll wake up and start crawling around and as they crawl they bump into each other and more wake up and they start crawling faster and faster and suddenly there are masses of them swarming around like crazy until it feels like my insides are on fire and I just want to rip open my ribcage and claw great big holes in myself.'

He hadn't asked again.

Normally she kept the worst of it at bay with pills she got from the doctor that sometimes made her feel like she was looking at the world from behind a thick pane of glass, and that reduced her to fits of mid-afternoon yawns. Recent hormonal fluctuations had reduced their effectiveness, however. Either that or her anxiety levels had outstripped the medication. Whatever the reason, she was once again waking in the night with her heart racing, her tormented brain forcing her through the litany of catastrophes awaiting her – bankruptcy, illness, death.

Six years ago, when Ian had left his job in IT to set up an eBay shop buying and selling vinyl, she'd generally been supportive. She knew he was miserable at work and she reasoned he'd either make a go of things with the new business or, more likely, grow tired of it when it proved harder than he'd imagined and get another full-time job. What she hadn't bargained on was his doing neither option. The vinyl business had been sluggish at best, even with him travelling the length and breadth of the country trawling through charity shops and car-boot sales, but when he tried, reluctantly, to find a new job, his fifty-something age counted against him. Gradually he stopped the excursions out, buying and selling exclusively online, with increasing apathy. In the two years since they'd split up, he spent most of his life holed up in the back bedroom in which he now both slept and worked, but his contributions to the household budget were minimal and unpredictable. They'd already remortgaged once to release equity, with the result that they now owed more than ever on their South London Victorian terrace – just at the time they'd envisaged being mortgage free. Such pension as he'd accrued, Ian had already spent establishing the business, so the future they'd once planned of long-haul travel, hikes along the Inca Trail and Nile cruises evaporated. Not that they'd be doing any of that now they weren't together any more. And anyway, with the kids still at home, the empty nest they'd pictured themselves coming home to after their long sojourns away was as much a figment of the imagination as the financial security she'd once taken for granted.

No wonder she tossed and turned wide-eyed in the

dead hours of the night while her ex-husband snored through the wall and her son and his friends dragged kitchen chairs outside and sat on the patio smoking spliffs and giggling and her body alternately heated itself to boiling point then cooled suddenly, turning the sweat on her skin to ice. No wonder she arrived at work in the mornings half crazed with tiredness and struggling to think of anything except the low-level nausea that had been an internal fixture ever since Rachel Masters came on the scene.

Today, though, that low-level nausea had switched up a gear. Several gears. She should never have got involved with organizing Gill's leaving do. Even though she'd worked so closely with Gill these last years that people assumed she'd sort it out, she still ought to have said no. Someone else would have done it. Someone with less to lose.

'I just hope everyone is being discreet about it,' she told Amira when she ran across her in the toilets. 'I deliberately kept it low-key.'

'I don't know why you're being so paranoid,' Amira replied. 'It's not in work time. It's not on work property. There's absolutely nothing anyone can object to.'

Paula found it odd that Amira, with whom she'd always got on so well, wasn't meeting her eyes. Was something going on? Maybe she was getting paranoid, after all. All day she carried around a heavy nugget of dread in her heart. Despite paying her lip-service at the start, Rachel had since made no secret of her scorn for the way Gill had run the department and her suspicion of anything connected with the Gill era. By organizing Gill's leaving do, even though it was just drinks at the pub a few doors down from the office, Paula couldn't help feeling she was allying herself too closely with her former boss.

'Can you get down there early to make sure everything is sorted and we've got an area cordoned off?' she asked Chloe at lunchtime when they bumped into each other in the kitchen.

'Not really. I've got mountains of work to do.'

Chloe had been noticeably off with her since the previous morning when Rachel had taken her to task in front of everyone for doing Gill's collection in work time and Paula hadn't backed her up. Afterwards she'd regretted not standing up for her younger colleague. Not that she felt guilty exactly, but she could see that Chloe had taken it as a public slap-down, which she'd never intended. It was just that Rachel Masters had put her on the spot, trying to make her appear unprofessional – just for collecting a bit of money for a woman who'd worked hard for the company for eight years.

'I'm not asking you to skip work, just to get off on the dot of 5.30 to put a few nibbles and crisps out on tables. Amira and Sarah are off getting the present now so I can't ask them to do it. And anyway, it is the kind of thing the departmental assistant traditionally does.'

Chloe flushed and bit down hard on her bottom lip.

'Fine. If I have to. I'd better get back to work now then so I don't get completely behind.'

She flounced off and Paula briefly closed her eyes, knowing she'd been tactless drawing attention to Chloe's junior status. It wasn't like her to keep blundering like this. She'd always been quietly attentive to other people's feelings, earning herself, she hoped, a reputation for quiet diplomacy. But now she felt that she was constantly upsetting people.

Settling back down at her desk, she glanced across to Rachel Masters's office. As usual, her new boss was intent on her computer, frowning at the screen. The dark-framed glasses gave her a permanently angry look.

Three-quarters of an hour later Paula's anxiety levels were once again rising. Amira and Sarah still weren't back from their shopping trip. Surely it couldn't take that long. She'd told them to get some nice-smelling stuff – scented candles and bath oils, or failing that a voucher. It was just a gesture. But they seemed to have turned it into an epic expedition.

She sent an email to Charlie.

Any idea what's happened to S&A?

His reply pinged back almost instantly.

No clue. Have they absconded with the money? You can get a long way on £72.38, an extra-strong mint and three weird foreign coins.

The clock on her computer showed 2.10. They'd been gone well over an hour. From the corner of her eye she saw Rachel Masters glance up before going back to her screen.

By 2.30, Paula felt clammy all over as if she'd been out running all lunchtime instead of sitting hunched over her desk. Finally, at 2.43, they returned. Amira was first, sliding into her desk which, luckily for her, was the door side of the office, followed by Sarah, trying to hide her coat from view so it didn't look as if she'd just arrived back. Rachel Masters's head remained bent and Paula started to unwind. She needed to get a grip! Trying to second-guess the boss's erratic moves would just mean she was anxious all the time. She called up her calendar. She had a list of calls she had to make before leaving work today. Better get started.

Sarah looked over and caught her eye. She shook her head and mouthed 'nightmare'. Paula raised her shoulders in a questioning gesture and Sarah reached inside her handbag and held up a small bag with a reassuringly expensive brand name emblazoned on the side.

Paula began working through her list, but she was only a third of the way down when Rachel Masters flung open the door of her office.

'Sarah? A moment, please.'

Immediately the tiny ants were on the move again inside her, swarming around until Paula's very veins itched. If Sarah and Amira were going to get into trouble for being late back from lunch, would they tell Rachel it had been Paula's suggestion that they go out shopping for Gill's present? Three minutes later, Sarah emerged from Rachel's office clutching a white envelope, her face pale in contrast with her red-rimmed eyes. She resolutely avoided looking at anyone as she sat back at her desk, but as she put her hand over her computer mouse, Paula could see it shaking. She glanced over at Amira, who was looking uncharacteristically grim-faced. She shrugged her shoulders almost imperceptibly when she caught Paula's eye.

But though Paula was braced for Rachel to come through her doorway and call for Amira, the summons never happened. Instead the afternoon ticked on in tense silence. A couple of times Paula tried to smile at Sarah, but the younger woman stared at her computer screen as if her eyes were magnetized to it. Finally, Paula snapped and emailed her.

Everything ok?

Twenty minutes later, the reply pinged back.

No. She has given me a formal disciplinary letter.

Paula stared at the words on her screen. In all the time she'd been working for the company there had only ever been a couple of disciplinary warnings and both for serious abuses. One a woman who'd taken so much stress leave half the office had never even met her, and the other a young man who'd started as a junior but clearly thought it beneath him and openly took time off to go for interviews and assessment days with other firms. Sarah had only been late a couple of times. And anyway, why hadn't Amira been called in too?

The tense, bad-tempered afternoon seemed never-ending.

Finally, at 5.30, Chloe discreetly gathered her things together and stood up to leave.

'You off, Chloe? Is that spreadsheet done?'

Paula hadn't even noticed Rachel getting up, so her high-pitched voice came as a shock.

'Not quite.' Chloe's cheeks were flushed. 'I'll come in early tomorrow and finish it off.'

'Only I need it tonight. I did tell you.'

Chloe stood by her desk, uncertain. Finally she sat back down and turned her computer on again without speaking.

By the time Paula arrived at the pub where Gill's leaving drinks were being held, she was twenty minutes late and her white shirt was sticking uncomfortably to the small of her back. The guest of honour was sitting alone at a table in the corner nursing a glass of white wine. To her surprise Paula found her eyes pricking with tears at the sight of her former boss. Suddenly those years with Gill seemed like a halcyon era.

'Sorry. We couldn't get away.'

Though it was only a week since Gill's sacking, already she seemed like a stranger, or someone visiting from abroad after a long absence.

'I was beginning to think you'd all forgotten about me already.'

Despite all the time they'd spent together over the last eight years, some of it in this very pub, Gill seemed ill at ease. Gone was the effortless camaraderie of the office, replaced by an awkwardness that increased as Paula put the bottle of house white she'd bought on the table and struggled to find something to talk about. The trouble was, she felt that bringing up anything to do with the office would be insensitive, given that Gill had so recently been sacked from there. And yet, what else did they have in common? Paula had met Gill's husband, Martin, a few times at various functions. He was short and bespectacled and worked in a conveyancing firm based in St Albans. They'd had a few conversations, mostly about the nightmarishness of the North Circular and how much more house you got for your money outside the M25. But she'd never seen Gill in her home setting, never really socialized with her outside the official work dos. She knew she sang in a local swing choir and that she and Martin made an annual trip to Spain to walk the Camino de Santiago. But about Gill's personal life – the things she loved, the things that made her cry, her disappointments, her regrets, her secret hopes – she knew very little.

'I thoroughly recommend being a lady of leisure,' Gill said now as they sat self-consciously at a table in the centre of their empty section. 'Getting up late, going out for brunch, watching *Homes Under the Hammer*. I absolutely love it.' Gill's smile never moved as she spoke, as if it had been glued into place, and Paula felt a shiver of unease.

'So you haven't been applying for jobs?'

'I've put out a few feelers – you know, just letting people know I'm available, but I'm not in a rush.'

'Of course not!' Paula's own voice was unnaturally bright. She was relieved when the door burst open and Chloe came in accompanied by Amira.

'Really sorry,' said Chloe, hugging Gill tightly. 'She wouldn't let me leave.'

Paula remembered then that Gill had given Chloe her first ever job. There was a particular kind of bond formed when that happened, although Paula had occasionally wondered if it was entirely healthy.

Gill visibly perked up, her smile losing the fixed quality it had earlier.

'What's she like then? Come on, I want to hear all the gossip.'

'Oh my God, she's a total bitch.' Paula had never seen Chloe so impassioned. She and Amira had poured themselves large glasses of wine from the bottle Paula had bought, and Chloe had already downed half of hers.

'She's not *that* bad.'

Paula looked at Amira sharply, not sure she could

have heard her right, but Amira had her head bent, her glossy black hair covering her face.

'She seems to be nicer to some people than others,' Paula told Gill. 'She favours a divide and rule style of management. For instance, Amira and Sarah were both late back from lunch but only Sarah got a bollocking. How come you escaped, Amira?'

Amira shrugged. Then asked: 'How do you know – that Sarah got a bollocking, I mean?'

'She emailed me about a disciplinary letter.'

The others gasped.

'I don't believe it,' said Gill. 'I haven't even been gone a week.' Her expression was one of concern, but there was an edge of excitement in her voice. 'Actually, it doesn't completely surprise me. I wasn't going to say anything, but . . .'

'What? *What?*' Chloe, who'd already downed her first glass of wine, was impatient.

'Well, a good friend of mine met someone who'd worked at Rachel's last company. He wasn't in her department but apparently it was not a happy ship.'

'But I thought she was the golden girl there,' said Amira. 'I thought she'd turned the place around?'

Gill made a dismissive gesture.

'Her results were good but she upset a lot of people and something happened that got her into trouble with her bosses but he didn't know exactly what.'

Paula got the distinct impression Gill was relishing dishing the dirt on her successor. It made Paula's muscles clench uncomfortably. Somewhere inside her, those armies of little ants were on the move again.

Charlie appeared by the table clutching a fresh bottle

of wine. Sarah was just behind him, her eyes puffy and red-rimmed.

'Come back, Gill. We need you,' he said, sinking to his knees in mock supplication.

'You OK?' Paula asked Sarah in a low voice as the others laughed.

She shook her head. 'Not really. I'm not going to stay long. I only really came to say hi to Gill. I need to get back to the boys.'

'I don't understand though. Why you and not Amira?'

'Wish I knew. Although Rachel had already had a go at me for being late, don't forget. And maybe she just doesn't like me.'

'I'm sure that's not—' Paula broke off to stare open-mouthed at the door.

'Oh my God!' came Chloe's high clear voice to her right.

'What?'

Sarah, who'd been facing Paula, now turned around to see what they were all looking at, just as Ewan approached the table, closely followed by Rachel Masters.

15

Ewan

'She asked me where I was off to. I couldn't lie, could I? And then she said it sounded like fun and stared at me. I felt sorry for her. It's not easy being new.'

Ewan was getting annoyed. Why were they all making such a big deal of it? So Rachel wasn't the most popular person in the office. She was having to make difficult decisions. That's why she'd been brought in. And at least she was being upfront about it, instead of saying one thing to their faces and something completely different behind their backs like everyone else seemed to do.

When Ewan first joined the company, he'd been excited about working in a department that was almost exclusively female. He liked women, plus he imagined he had a better chance of rising through the ranks more quickly in a female environment. He'd reckoned without the culture of passive-aggressiveness that ruled the office. While Gill and Paula appeared calm and mild-mannered and reasonable, he soon learned they were also totally intractable. When Ewan came up with suggestions for ways to improve some of the frankly archaic systems in place in the office, they'd thanked him and made encouraging noises and then never mentioned any of them again. And when he'd pressed them, they smiled and said how pleased they were he was coming up with ideas . . . and then added something that made it clear his idea was dead in the water. The office politics were a minefield – no one saying what they really meant, no one allowed to raise their voices. Having to preface every sentence with 'I understand where you're coming from' or 'I respect your opinion' and always you knew there was that great big BUT coming. At least Rachel just came out and said it.

'You didn't have to invite her. Didn't you think about what it would be like for Gill? The woman took her job. Her seat was still warm.'

Ewan had rarely known Sarah get angry. Her face was blotchy and her red hair around her face was stringy with sweat as if her skin was overheating.

'You can't blame Rachel for that,' he said. 'She didn't ask for Gill to be fired. She was offered a job and she took it. Same as any of us would have done.'

'Speak for yourself,' Sarah retorted.

They were at the bar buying more wine. After all the fuss she'd made about having to leave early, Sarah didn't seem in any hurry to go. Instead she'd spent the last half-hour talking to the sales team who were gathered around a different table.

'It'd look bad if I left,' she told him. 'Rachel will think it's because of her.'

This was just what Ewan hated about working in a female-heavy environment. Everyone second-guessing what other people might be thinking. Why couldn't Sarah just do what she wanted and then if there was a reaction she could deal with it, and if not, then no problem?

'Actually, Ewan,' Rachel was calling across from the table. His stomach liquefied when she said his name. 'Could you get me a vodka and tonic? I can't do pub wine, I'm afraid.'

'Jesus Christ,' Sarah muttered under her breath.

Rejoining the main group at the table, Ewan could sense the hostility coming from the others. He wasn't the world's most sensitive bloke, he knew that, but even he could feel the tension. Gill was wearing that fake smile he recognized from various meetings over the years where things weren't going to plan. Paula was perched awkwardly on her seat as if she was sitting on a pineapple or something. She looked hot and bothered. Probably she wasn't used to going out at night, he supposed. She was getting on a bit now. Fifties? Sixties even? Seeing her next to Rachel was like putting an aged, slightly manky pet cat next to a cheetah.

'Thanks for the drink,' Rachel said as he sat down. She'd tied her long black hair up, but silky tendrils escaped at the front and neck. He fought back an urge to blow on them, just to watch them flutter against her skin.

Instead he turned to Charlie, next to him. 'You looking at porn?' he said, to cover his sudden embarrassment. Charlie's head was bent over his phone, revealing the thinning patch at the back he was so sensitive about.

'Grindr,' came the reply. 'Although it might as well be porn. Look at this fox.'

He flashed Ewan an image of a paunchy, middle-aged man sitting back on a sofa with his legs splayed, wearing a pair of boxers and a big smile.

'Euw. That's disgusting.'

Charlie smiled.

'Actually there is someone who's pretty hot. What do you think?'

He called up a photograph of a man Ewan reckoned to be in his early thirties, with curling dark hair and chiselled cheekbones.

'Not my type, mate.'

'His name's Stefan. He lives in the next road. And he's at home now.'

'What – and you'd just go round there? Even though you've never met the guy before and he could be an axe murderer?'

'Which is exactly my type, as it happens.'

'Seriously, though, wouldn't you be worried? He could be anyone. Maybe that's not even his photo. Maybe he's some fat old geriatric bloke in a string vest.'

'Nothing wrong with a string vest.'

Ewan smiled, but he didn't feel nearly as comfortable with this conversation as he was trying to appear. Charlie was OK – although Ewan had never completely shaken off the conviction that the guy secretly fancied him – but this side of his life was just a bit, well . . . grubby. One time when Charlie got drunk at a Christmas party, he'd confided in Ewan that he was lonely. Ewan, who'd only been in the job then for a couple of months, had been mortified by the unwelcome confession. 'I'm sure you'll find someone,' he'd said lamely and immediately changed the subject. Charlie had never mentioned it again. It wasn't that Ewan had anything against Charlie, he just didn't feel comfortable discussing other people's private lives. He'd always been like that, always struggled with intimacy.

'Anyway, think I'll slip away in a bit. See what he's like. Gives me an excuse to get out of here. Can't handle this crazy party atmosphere.'

Ewan half expected Rachel to leave too. She must be able to tell that her presence was putting a damper on things. But she stayed in place at the table sipping her vodka and tonic through a straw and making small talk with Gill, quite as if she hadn't just swiped her job from under her, even if it hadn't been her fault.

Paula got up to make a speech. She looked nervous and Ewan wondered if she was having to revise what she'd been planning to say in view of Rachel being here. She was never particularly confident talking in front of a group of people. When he got to her position, no one would be able to shut him up. Even so, surely there must be something more to say about Gill after eight years than that she was 'firm but supportive'? What was she, a sofa?

Someone from the sales table shouted something, and there was a resounding roar of laughter. The sales team was almost entirely male. Sometimes Ewan wondered if he'd be happier on that side of the divide.

As soon as the speech was over and the present – a massage voucher and a scented candle – ceremoniously handed to Gill, and the card chuckled over, Ewan noticed Charlie making a quiet exit, mobile in hand. At least he was going to get some action tonight. It had been three weeks since Ewan had picked up that girl on his friend Jack's birthday night out. Yet for the first time the prospect of another emotion-free one-night stand seemed strangely unappealing.

'She's got a nerve.'

Chloe had come up behind where he was standing and was leaning heavily on his shoulder.

'I mean, she must know no one wants her here.'

Her voice was thick and he could feel her skin burning through her thin cotton top.

She was very drunk.

'Get us another drink.' Her breath was hot in his ear. 'The wine's all gone.'

'Sounds like you might have drunk it all. Ow.' He rubbed his arm where she'd punched it.

'Sorry. Let me stroke it better.'

As she ran her fingers up and down his arm, he realized two things: firstly, she was even drunker than he thought and, secondly, she was coming on to him.

'Steady on. You trying to give me a Chinese burn?'

'Sorry.' But still her hand lay on his arm, damp like a warm compress.

'Maybe we should go back to the others. We're being a bit anti-social staying here.'

Even from where they were standing, Ewan could sense the ill-feeling among the group at the table. He knew it was illogical to feel responsible for Rachel just because she'd invited herself along with him, yet he couldn't help it. Nor could he help being hyper-aware of her all the time – where she was, what she was doing, who she was talking to. Yet still Chloe's hand rested on his arm and now he could feel her pressing up against his back. Almost against his will he felt a heat stirring inside him.

'I'm too drunk to sit back down there. I know they're all silently disapproving. It's like being with my mother, times four. Come on, Ewan, let's get out of here, please?'

Ewan knew it was a bad idea. He liked Chloe. They had a laugh together and he enjoyed flirting with her, but sleeping with someone you worked with was a mug's game. But now the heat inside him was spreading and he found himself pushing back against Chloe in a way that was impossible to misinterpret.

'We shouldn't . . . we work together . . .' He tried to protest, then gave in, 'It could only be a one-off,' he warned her. 'Just a bit of fun.'

'Absolutely. Just fun. No strings.'

He didn't believe her. He'd seen the way she looked at him. But being around Rachel Masters for the last week had built up a level of frustrated energy inside him and suddenly the prospect of going home alone was too depressing to contemplate.

'OK, but we can't leave together. You go first and wait for me outside. I'll leave it five minutes and then join you.'

She squeezed his arm.

They rejoined the table and Chloe made a big deal of retrieving her stuff and saying goodbye to Gill.

'I still can't believe you've gone. You were the best boss ever,' she slurred, ignoring her new boss, sitting just a couple of feet away.

As soon as she'd left, Rachel turned to Ewan.

'I've been wanting to talk to you all evening, but you've been monopolized,' she said in a low voice. 'Come and sit down next to me and keep me company for a bit. We can get to know each other a little.'

He felt a rush of liquid joy flood through him.

'Sure. Love to. Only I can't stay that long. I need to be getting back.'

'Just five minutes.'

But five turned into ten, and still Rachel was talking to him, asking him about himself, laughing at his jokes, leaning in very close to catch what he said above the noise of the suddenly full pub. He felt his phone in his pocket vibrate with an incoming text. A minute or two later, it did so again. He slid it into his palm and glanced down under the table. Chloe. *Where r u?*

He wished he hadn't made the arrangement with her now, wished he could stay here with Rachel all night. But he couldn't text her back, not with Rachel sitting right here. And he couldn't leave the girl standing outside.

'I've got to go.' He wondered if his reluctance showed in his voice.

'Really? That's a shame.'

Was she flirting with him? The thought was a butterfly fluttering in his chest.

As he shrugged on his jacket and got ready to tear himself away, she put a restraining hand on his arm. He was surprised to feel her fingernails digging into his flesh.

'Tread very carefully, Ewan.' Though her voice was as high-pitched and girlish as ever, her eyes when they met his were suddenly hard and he felt a prickle of cold on the back of his neck.

'You could go far in the company. Don't blow it.'

Did she know that Chloe was waiting outside? Was that what the warning was about?

His thoughts, after he'd said his goodbyes and threaded his way through the post-work drinkers, were a heavy mix of apprehension, confusion and disappointment.

'Where have you been? I thought you were never coming.' Chloe peeled herself off the wall she'd been leaning against and looked up at him, pouting.

He felt a rush of irritation.

'Come on then, if you're coming.'

And when she took hold of his hand a few metres up the road, he imagined she was someone else.

16

Anne

From the outside, the house where Laurie grew up wasn't a million miles away from the house in which she now lived with Jana and her family. A different suburb, but the same wide tree-lined streets, the same sense of everything being exactly as it should be. The house itself was situated on the corner plot of a block, set back from the road with only the overgrown lawn and scraps of police crime tape, still fluttering uselessly from garage handles and porch posts, to show that anything untoward had ever happened here.

'The American dream, right?' said the heavyset man behind the wheel as the Pontiac in which we were travelling pulled up to the kerb.

Sergeant Dean Cavanagh had been sitting in the driver's seat when he picked us up from the medical school, and it wasn't until he was out of the car that his true size was revealed. The man was enormous. Next to him, Ed Kowalsky seemed insubstantial, as if the policeman could snap him in two like a twig if he so decided.

'You kinda expect a big spooky old place with turrets, doncha? Maybe a coupla bats flying around the top.'

Sergeant Cavanagh hoisted up his pants so the waist-band nestled just under the hang of his belly. I stared at the gun that revealed itself as his suit jacket swung open. Nowadays I wouldn't turn a hair. I've seen guns a lot closer up than that. But standing outside that house where so many unspeakable things had happened, I shivered at the sight of that moulded metal glinting in the sun and glanced quickly away towards the neighbouring house.

'You gotta ask yourself what exactly they were doin'' in there, right?' said Sergeant Cavanagh, misinterpreting my look. 'I mean, you're telling me all those years they never heard nothing? No shouting? No screaming? No little kids crying?'

'As I understand it, the neighbours never knew there was a second child in there.'

Ed seemed to be trying to make himself look taller, raising himself high and straight out of his brown suede desert boots. I wondered if it was a response to the gun, whether he felt threatened by it. Whatever the case, the policeman wasn't impressed.

'Ya see what ya wanna see, hear what ya wanna hear. Sometimes it's easier just not to know. Get my drift?'

There was still a car in the driveway, a Buick with a child's booster seat in the back. As we walked past, I saw Ed Kowalsky hesitate and knew he was thinking about the seats in his own car, and his own children, and for the first time I wondered what toll this case might be taking on him. I'd never thought before about his wife or the three small faces smiling gappily out from the framed photo on the desk back in his university office two doors down from the one I occupy today. For the first time I allowed for the possibility that he might exist outside of his relations with me, that he might have layers concealed underneath the surfaces he showed me. Already, even at that stage, I'd begun what has turned into a lifelong habit of trying to corral and order events into a set pattern in my head, rather than reacting to them as and when they arise, and this evidence that Professor Kowalsky might have a rich, hidden life did not sit well with the narrative I'd created. My husband Johnny always used to tell me to stop writing the end of the story before it had a chance to evolve naturally. When we divorced after just three years of marriage, he considered himself vindicated.

The porch area of the house was accessed via two steps from the front path. I was wearing shoes with a small heel that gave me an uneven, hesitant walk, and as I placed my right foot tentatively on the first step, that's when I first felt it – that sense of treading where her small foot had gone, looking at the same things she'd have seen . . . the white paint peeling on the post underneath my fingers, the small tear in the screen door up by the top left-hand corner. There was a neglected jasmine plant growing up the far side of the porch and I imagined how it would have smelled to her on summer days, the heady scent rising to meet her as she came home from kindergarten in the afternoons. How did she feel as she climbed these two steps towards her front door? I asked myself. Was she apprehensive? Did she wonder what kind of atmosphere would greet her today? Did she glance down towards the line of vented bricks at the base of the porch and feel a tug of . . . what? A sense that things were not right, that she was part of something that other people would find unacceptable. Did her heart start hammering in her narrow little chest? Did she clutch on to her school bag as if the connection to school and everything that was good and proper and normal might offer some protection against whatever was inside the house?

A child's scooter lay abandoned on its side at the far edge of the porch. Its central stem was pink and there was a sticker halfway up with a picture of a rainbow on it. Silver streamers that had seen better days hung from the handlebars.

'Prepare to enter the House of Horror,' said Sergeant Cavanagh, making quote marks in the air with fingers plump as chicken breasts. The wooden porch floor creaked where he trod. Withdrawing a key from the pocket of his pants, he inserted it into the front door.

'Never used to bother locking up crime scenes, but now everyone wants a souvenir, know what I mean? Everyone's gotta try to be part of the action.'

He turned the key and as he did so, I had a sudden strong memory of being a child myself, just a few years older than Laurie, unlocking the door of my house with hands that were stiff with anxiety, and pausing on the threshold to try to gauge by the weight of the air in the hallway which of my mother's various personas she would be wearing that day. As the sweating policeman nudged open the door, the dread that had been crawling slowly through my veins ever since we pulled up at the house came whooshing to the surface and I had to stop and take a deep breath in.

'You OK, Anne?'

Ed had a hold of my elbow and was looking at me with concern from behind his glasses.

111

'Sure. I'm fine.'

I broke away and carried on into the house.

There are some places that have their own kind of personal scent, just like people do, that gets into your nose and under your skin. Well, Laurie's family house was like that. Although there was nothing in the hallway, with its polished wood floor and pale paintwork and the wooden stairs that curved around the walls, to say that anything bad had ever happened here, there was just this smell – this sour, stagnant, sad smell – that stoppered up my nostrils until I could hardly breathe.

'You folks looking for anything in particular?'

Sergeant Cavanagh filled the hallway like a piece of outsized furniture. I wondered if he could smell it too, but he gave nothing away.

'I think we'll just have a general look around,' said Ed. His voice sounded small and tinny.

'Sure. Well, here's the living room.'

We followed him through a door to the left of the hallway and found ourselves in a wide room that might have been pleasant if it wasn't for the heavy drapes in the windows that, together with the screens, blocked out most of the daylight. There were two sofas, one a three-seater and one a two-seater, and a leather arm-chair with a footstool. All the seats faced towards a small TV in the corner. The sofas were a curious colour, almost two-tone, and it was only when I got nearer that I realized the original green upholstery had been covered in a sheer, dark-blue cover, almost like a fitted dust sheet. On the wall there was a framed family portrait, the type people have taken in a photographic studio and give prints of as presents to grandparents or have made into

Christmas cards. There were only three people in the portrait.

I'd caught sight of pictures of Noelle and Peter Egan on the news, but I'd tried to avoid looking too closely at any of the coverage for fear of influencing my dealings with Laurie, so this was the first time I was seeing them up close. If you've ever had someone pull back the collar of your shirt and drip ice water down your back for a joke, you'll have some idea how I felt looking at that picture. There was Laurie, a year or so younger than she was now. Still padded out with toddler fat with her hair pulled tight into two little braids that stuck almost straight out from the side of her head. To her left, her father gazed at the camera through close-set blue eyes. His mouth was stretched into a tight line as if the photographer had told him to smile but that was the most he could do, like a smile that had been ironed flat. I stared at the dip in his cheek where you could almost see a muscle moving, and at the long, hard line of his nose that ended nearly at a top lip so thin it was hardly there at all. I stared at his hand around his daughter's chubby shoulder, the large, meaty fingers resting on her perfect creamy skin. I thought of what those fingers had done, and something bitter rose into my mouth.

At first glance, Noelle Egan was more pleasant-looking than her husband, attractive even, with high plump cheeks and a smooth forehead framed by dark, natural-looking curls. But closer examination revealed her skin to be caked with thick paste-like make-up that gave her a waxy appearance, and there was a plasticky gloss to her hair. She was leaning her face in towards her daughter and her mouth was cracked open in a wide smile that ended by her daughter's ear as if she would gobble it up. But her eyes, with their coating of frosted blue and their thick black mascara'd lashes spiky as bee stings . . . I'm not someone who is inclined to be melodramatic. I wouldn't get far in my job if I was – but Noelle Egan's eyes were the deadest eyes I've ever seen.

'Ya can't imagine, can ya?'

Sergeant Cavanagh was standing so close to me I could feel the heat coming off his bulky body. I shook my head.

'They just seemed like everyone else. That's what the neighbours say and the teachers and the guys at the realtors where he headed up the billing department.'

Like they ought to have had crosses on their foreheads or horns or someone walking in front of them ringing a huge bell. But of course I didn't say any of that.

We wandered into the kitchen, a large but curiously sterile room. The family had clearly been disturbed mid-breakfast by the police arriving, but even so the dishes left out on the table were orderly, no smears of strawberry jelly across plates, no crumbs on the polished wood surface. A cupboard was open as if someone had been in the act of retrieving something. Inside, the cans and jars were neatly arranged in height order, their labels uniformly facing out. The only outward sign of family life was a notice pinned to the refrigerator door by four round black magnets. It was immaculately typed and laid out as a table. When I got closer I saw that down one side were the days of the week and across the bottom were the initials N, P and L. Across the top, the words

FEEDING SCHEDULE were typed in bold capitals and underlined.

'Doesn't look like the kind of household to have a pet,' I remarked.

Sergeant Cavanagh made a snorting sound through his flattened nose.

'There's no pet,' he said.

The dawning of truth was as sudden as it was sickening.

17

Amira

'So you'd like me to consider you for the job?'

Rachel had one eyebrow raised in a gesture that instantly infuriated Amira, but she took a deep breath and tried to keep her voice neutral.

'Yes, please.'

She still couldn't quite believe she was doing this. Right up until a few seconds before, she'd been telling herself she could still change her mind. She could pretend she'd had another reason for requesting a few minutes with the new boss – booking holiday leave, asking for clarification on the new catering contract. Even when she opened her mouth she'd been half expecting something else to come out of it. Instead she found herself saying that she was, after all, interested in the deputy position. She hadn't said the phrase 'Paula's job', but they both knew that's what they were talking about. Now everything inside her was screaming 'traitor'.

It was all Tom's fault.

When she'd come home on the day Rachel had sounded her out about being her deputy, she'd still been bristling with outrage, but instead of backing her up, Tom had been non-communicative and almost sullen.

All evening it had been as if a dark cloud was shadowing him around the flat, and finally when they were in bed, she'd snapped.

'What?' she'd asked.

'What do you mean, "what?"'

'What's up with you. You've had a face like a slapped arse all night. What have I done wrong now?'

'Nothing.'

'Bollocks.'

'OK. If you must know, it pisses me off that I've got to go into work every day doing a job I hate, just so we can pay the mortgage on this place – that you talked me into, don't forget – and even then it's not enough. Do you know, I lie awake some nights just eaten up with worry about how much money we owe and how we're ever going to keep up with all the bills and the Council Tax and the water – who knew you had to pay for water, for chrissakes – and everything else. And then you come home and say you've been offered a chance of a pay rise but your superior moral code won't allow you to consider it.'

It had all come out in a rush of words, as if they'd been building up inside him until they had to burst free. They'd had a big row then, which had ended with her telling him that if it wasn't for her he'd have wound up in ten or fifteen years just another middle-aged failed musician with nothing to show for himself.

The next day she'd felt awful and wished the words unsaid. Not that there wasn't some truth in them, but she knew she hadn't been kind, had said them just to hurt him. Worse than that, she knew he had a point. She had pushed to get the mortgage despite knowing they'd be financially overstretching themselves. Did she really have the right to turn down the chance of some extra cash just out of a sense of loyalty? Mightn't loyalty be a luxury she couldn't afford, especially in light of the store-card debts she'd run up that Tom had no idea even existed. In the end she'd apologized to him and promised to think about it.

'It's not as if Paula would ever know,' he'd told her. 'You could make it a condition of taking the post – that it has to look as if you were appointed after Paula left.'

'Was pushed, you mean.'

But now she'd actually told Rachel she was interested, Amira felt grubby, and she had the feeling that Rachel knew that and was enjoying it on some level.

'I'm happy to hear that, Amira. I'll keep you updated as things progress.'

Amira's stomach had lurched at that phrase, knowing that the thing that was progressing was Paula's dismissal from the company, whatever form that might take. It wasn't that she and Paula were best buddies. Though they got on well as colleagues, on a personal level they had very little in common. But they were part of a team. And team members didn't stab other team members in the back.

As she left Rachel's office, Amira took a detour around Paula's desk, pretending to check the printer, just so she wouldn't have to meet the older woman's eyes. Knowledge of Paula's impending fate was a hard, heavy stone in her gut. Her route back from the printer took her past Sarah's desk and she was both relieved and disappointed to see that she had her head bent over some paperwork. Sarah and Amira were friends. Proper friends. She felt bad not telling her about Rachel's offer. But as she passed, Sarah suddenly reached out and grabbed her arm.

'Was she having a go at you? About being late yesterday?'

For a second, Amira contemplated lying. She knew it wasn't fair that only Sarah had got into trouble for taking so long getting Gill's present. But she realized that if she pretended she'd also been reprimanded, Sarah would want to know the details and it would all get too complicated.

'No. Just going over the figures for March.'

Sarah's expression froze and her hand dropped to her desk as if burned.

Amira headed back to her seat, feeling even worse than she had a few minutes before. She texted Tom.

Told R I was interested in job. Feel like crap

She waited for him to reply but no message came.

18
Sarah

'Three dates. Is it too early to start redecorating his living room, do you think?'

'Maybe wait until you know his last name?'

'You're so old-fashioned.'

Sarah couldn't remember when she'd last seen Charlie this happy. It was as if someone had yanked the dial of the dimmer switch round, lighting him up from inside. Normal Charlie was an endearing if reserved mix of cynicism and kindness, warmth and resignation. Now he shone with an emotional energy so exposing you almost wanted to look away, as if you were seeing something you shouldn't.

She was nervous for him, slightly afraid of the new-found enthusiasm that bordered on mania. Though Charlie had more friends than anyone else she knew, it didn't stop him being lonely, and he'd told her so many times how much he envied her family life that she couldn't bear to tell him that it sometimes swamped her, that she felt she was drowning in other people's expectations of her, other people's demands.

'I assume he's removed himself from Grindr now he's met the love of his life?'

A shadow flitted across Charlie's face and Sarah caught her breath. He'd made himself too vulnerable. She could already tell. His soft brown eyes looked suddenly uncertain.

'It's maybe a bit early to be exclusive, don't you think?' he said.

'I'll take that as a no then.'

'I don't want to push it. I don't want to come over all jihadi on him: *You will deactivate your social media accounts and wear a veil at all times so other men cannot look upon you.* To be honest, Sarah, I don't think I'm successful enough for him. He was a bit underwhelmed when I told him what I did. He's after someone with a more impressive bank balance and job title.'

'And lunchbox.'

'Oi! Anyway, how are you? You're looking a bit stressed, sweetie, if you don't mind me saying. Is it the thought of that disciplinary letter?'

'Yes. It's really doing my head in. "Consider this a final warning." It's so apocalyptic. I feel like there's a great big sword hanging over my head wherever I go.'

While this was the truth, it wasn't the whole truth. But Sarah couldn't tell Charlie what else was bothering her because that would mean articulating it in words, and once she did that, she'd have to deal with it . . . and the thought of *that* made her entire nervous system vibrate like a dentist's drill. She was trying not to think about it, but the effort of not-thinking about it was making her jumpy and nervous. She envied Charlie his new-found passion and his lack of ties that meant he was answerable to no one but himself. If Charlie had been hit with a totally unfair and unwarranted disciplinary warning, he could choose to tell them where to stuff their job, but because she had Oliver and Sam and Joe to consider, she just had to suck it up.

Oliver had tried to be supportive about all the crap going on at work, but that deep vertical groove in his forehead that she'd only recently noticed had got even more pronounced, and she'd ended up reassuring him that it wasn't as bad as all that. She hated seeing him worried. He looked so old all of a sudden.

'She's a piece of work, isn't she, Rachel?' Charlie said. He was leaning against the work surface in the office kitchen while they waited for the kettle to boil. One of his legs was crossed in front of the other so he looked shorter than usual, and he was hardly the world's tallest man to start with. Sarah had an urge to step forward and give him a hug but she held back. He was a forty-two-year-old man. Dealing with toddlers was now so ingrained in her psyche that she waged constant battle with herself not to greet friends and colleagues by kissing the tops of their heads or wiping the noses of perfect strangers on the tube.

'I can't believe she stayed right up until the bitter end on Friday night,' he went on.

'I know. Paula says it got so embarrassing, even Gill made an excuse to leave.'

'Do you think there's actually something wrong with her?' he wondered. 'Like some sort of mental illness where you can't judge social situations properly?'

'Don't try to make excuses for her.'

'No, really. Maybe it's not her fault. Maybe she has Asperger's or something. Or maybe she really is possessed by the Devil like that email said.'

Charlie was talking about a disturbing message that both he and Paula had received from a weird email address made up of seemingly random letters and numbers. *Rachel Masters is an evil bitch. She destroys people.* They'd discussed showing the email to HR or Mark Hamilton or even Rachel herself – but in the end Paula had decided they should delete it. Malicious gossip, she'd called it. Sarah knew she was probably right, but when Charlie had forwarded the email to her, it had left her shaken.

'Anyway,' Charlie went on, 'no doubt we'll find out soon enough what she's really like. You've heard the latest plan, I take it?'

Sarah's already leaden heart grew still heavier inside her.

'Don't tell me.'

But Charlie was already visibly perking up at the prospect of sharing whatever it was that was coming and he paid her protests no heed when he shrilled: 'A team-bonding weekend!'

'Oh dear God, please tell me you're joking.'

'No. It's management's grand new idea.'

'I don't believe it. Surely Rachel won't agree to it?'

'Don't think she has much choice. We're all going – edict from above. Come on, Sarah, it'll be fun. Up at dawn to run five times around the grounds dressed as cartoon characters with our legs tied together, then back for room inspections and then all into the hall to reveal our innermost fears through the medium of interpretive dance. Can't wait.'

Back at her desk, Sarah tried to dispel the dread that had crept over her at Charlie's news by focusing on the day ahead. She had a whiteboard on her desk where she wrote down on a Friday afternoon all her appointments and important calls for the following week so that when she came in on Monday morning, she knew exactly what she had to do. She frowned at the cramped black writing. The anxiety over Gill's leaving do had meant she'd been in a rush when drawing up the lists at the end of the last week and some of the entries were barely legible. Luckily this afternoon's meeting with White & Co was clear – 3 p.m. – which was just as well because they'd changed the arrangements so many times she'd completely lost track of them. If they weren't her biggest client she'd have made a fuss, but as it was she'd bent over backwards and rearranged her schedule to accommodate them each time they rang to say they couldn't make it. Sarah was proud of the relationship she'd built up over the years with the biggest brewery in the country. The deputy director now asked for her by name. It would probably be her single biggest bargaining tool when it came to arguing her worth with Rachel Masters.

The brewery headquarters was in Milton Keynes so, as usual, the meeting was to be held in a private room in an upmarket gastropub in West London which was the flagship pub for the chain. Even allowing a full forty minutes for the journey, it still left her three hours to get on with the rest of today's to-do list. She'd refuse to think about the team-building weekend, or that other thing that was like a cheesewire around the chest every time it flitted into her mind. Sarah worked through lunch, which wasn't unusual these days. She'd already primed Paula that she would be out most of the afternoon, and she knew Paula had let Rachel know. After the débâcle of the shopping trip for Gill's present on Friday, no one was taking any chances when it came to being considered late.

At two, she discreetly unhooked her bag from the back of her chair and made her way into the toilets. The face that looked back at her from the mirror in the brightly lit room was the grey colour of old grout and she quickly extracted a small red make-up case from the depths of her bag and began applying foundation and then something from a small tube she'd ordered online on impulse after seeing it advertised in a Sunday supplement as a miracle product. It was supposed to give her cheeks a dewy sheen but Sarah couldn't help thinking it made her look as if she was permanently in a light sweat. Kevin Bromsgrove, the brewery's deputy director, was old school and set a lot of store in appearance, so she knew it was worth making the effort. By the time she swiped open the door of the main office, she was feeling almost human. She'd used the green eyeshadow that set off her red hair and for once she hadn't ended up looking like she had two three-day-old black eyes.

Seeing Rachel Masters standing by her desk with a face like thunder burst her buoyant mood like an overblown balloon.

'What the hell is going on?' Rachel's sculpted face was distorted by anger.

'I don't understand.'

'I've just had Kevin Bromsgrove on the phone. Apparently you were due in Notting Hill twenty minutes ago.'

'No, you're wrong. Our meeting was for three o'clock.

Look.' She pointed to her whiteboard, and was mortified to see how much her finger shook.

'You've obviously written it down wrong. What's the matter with you? This is one of our best clients.'

Sarah felt sick. She was cold all over.

'I wouldn't have made a mistake. I know I copied it exactly from my notebook. I was really careful because there had been so many changes. Look, I'll show you.'

She snatched up her weekly desk organizer and started leafing through it frantically.

'Here,' she said, landing on the page for the previous week. 'It clearly says . . . Oh.'

Kevin Bromsgrove, 2 p.m.

In her mind she saw herself writing it down and confirming it three times with Bromsgrove's secretary on the phone. Then later, standing at her whiteboard with the notebook open in front of her, copying down the time. Double checking. Triple checking. She didn't make mistakes like this.

'I'll go right now. I can be there in twenty-five minutes—'

'It's too late. He's gone.'

Rachel wasn't so much saying the words as spitting them out like apple pips.

Sarah felt like Joe or Sam when caught out in some naughtiness, all wobbly bottom lip and frozen-faced fear. When Rachel had stalked off back to her office, Sarah slumped into her desk and put her head in her shaking hands. No one approached her.

19

Anne

After the shock of the pristine kitchen with its chilling feeding rota stuck to the fridge – that 'L' written against Monday and Friday, evidence of Laurie's forced involvement – Ed Kowalsky and I stayed close by each other. I was glad he was there, as if his glasses and his corduroy pants and his rubber-soled suede shoes could somehow mitigate against the sheet of paper on the fridge and the sourness of the air and those regimented supplies in the cupboards and Noelle Egan's dead eyes.

'Shall we go upstairs?' asked Sergeant Cavanagh as if we were prospective buyers and he was showing us around.

By the time we'd reached the upstairs landing, he was already wheezing. He paused at the top, leaning heavily on the post.

'You guys help yourselves. I'll be right here. Kid's bedroom kinda creeps me out, to be honest.'

There was a tight feeling in my chest as I walked into the first room, so it was a relief to find it contained mostly office equipment. There was a large desk along one wall, its surface completely clear of clutter. A leather swivel chair was neatly tucked underneath. On the wall directly in front of the desk was a framed needlepoint sampler which read *The price of greatness is responsibility* with Winston Churchill's name in smaller letters underneath.

'Guess this guy Egan really rated himself.' Ed was trying to lighten the atmosphere but he sounded false and unconvincing.

'You're assuming this is his office? It could just as easily be hers.'

I was playing devil's advocate, of course. We both knew this was Peter Egan's lair. Though I'd tried to avoid the news, I'd have to have been living on another planet not to have heard about his obsession with tidiness, how the sheets had to be changed every day, how he was fascinated by war and collected medals from dead soldiers that he bought on eBay or at private auction and which the police had found in special leather-bound display cases. Though conspicuously empty, the sterile room felt oppressive with his presence. I thought back to those close-together eyes, that paper-cut smile . . . and shivered.

Next door was the master bedroom. The bed was narrow for a double and of course meticulously made up: the coverlet, with its fussy little green and yellow flowers, was perfectly smooth, the matching pillows neatly aligned. I wondered which side was which. I tried to imagine the couple in the photograph I'd seen downstairs lying next to each other knowing what they'd done, knowing what each was capable of. Did they ever talk about it, I wondered. Did they ever express remorse, regret, ever wonder how they'd ended up in this situation? Did they ever wake in the night with guilt gnawing away at their insides and turn to face each other and ask themselves who it was they'd married, who they'd become? Did they lose sleep, knowing what was down there in the basement?

I knew the answer.

'Check out the closet,' called Sergeant Cavanagh from the landing.

Ed cautiously opened up the double doors of the white wardrobe that took up half of the far wall. The two of us took a sharp intake of breath as the contents were revealed.

'Wow. These two really were something else,' said Ed.

The rail was hung with clothes. On the left-hand side were six or seven suits all in different shades of grey, the same number of white shirts. On the right were brightly coloured women's dresses and blouses. All the hangers were facing the same way. And each and every item of clothing was wrapped in an individual clear plastic cover.

'Like Howard fucking Hughes, huh? Am I right?' Sergeant Cavanagh was standing in the doorway watching. His bulk blocked up the only exit, making the already stuffy bedroom feel doubly claustrophobic. I could feel the sweat breaking out under my arms and when I moved, the thin material of my skirt clung unpleasantly to the back of my thighs. I glanced again at that immaculately smooth bed with its puffed-up pillows where once Noelle and Peter Egan would have laid their heads down and slept despite everything they'd done.

'Excuse me.' I pushed past Sergeant Cavanagh so abruptly he almost overbalanced.

129

'You sure you're OK, Anne?' Ed said in a concerned tone, following me out of the room.

I nodded, not trusting myself to speak.

The third doorway off the landing was closed.

'That's the kiddie's room,' said Sergeant Cavanagh. 'Don't worry, there's nothing real bad in there. It's just a feeling I got when I went in there. You got kids, Doc?'

To my great surprise I found he was looking at me. Instantly my face burned, and I knew I was blushing.

'Me? No. That is to say, not yet.'

When I look at that younger self across the divide of decades, I want to cry. Either that or scoop her up and run with her and hide her away where nothing can get to her, none of the things that will eventually turn her into me. Back then, I really thought it was all ahead of me. I always had career ambitions – Harvard, Yale, Stanford. I thought I'd take my pick. But more than work, I thought the rest of it was there for the taking too – husband, a fleet of dimpled children, to be plucked from a shelf whenever I felt like it. Where does it go, that assumption of options? Did my nerve fail because the options dried up, or was it the other way around? Was it when I realized Johnny wasn't, after all, going to rescue me from myself? When I knew there would be no more children after Shannon? I no longer know. All I do know is that when the overweight detective in the low-slung pants asked me if I had kids, I was embarrassed. I was working on the most important case of my life and I thought I'd be reduced if I exposed myself like that, my personal aspirations and assumptions, the soft under-belly of me.

'Well, see, I'm a father,' Sergeant Cavanagh went

on. 'I have a daughter the same age as this kid, and a son the same age as the brother. You know what I'm saying? I go in that bedroom and it gets me thinking about my own kids and all of a sudden my heart is thumping and my blood pressure is going through the roof and I'm full of rage and sadness and it's not good for me. I need to avoid that kinda stress. When you're a parent it's like you wear your heart on the outside of your body. Case like this comes along and you gotta protect yourself from it. You'll learn that soon enough, Doc.'

So he stayed on the landing, while we nudged our way into the room, and I could feel instantly what he meant about the sadness. It was in the neatly made bed and in the three dolls on the shelf next to it, each stored in its original packaging. It was in the framed photograph on the wall, a smaller version of the one in the living room downstairs. It was in the three pairs of tiny shoes neatly lined up under the bed.

I thought back to my own childhood bedroom. One time when I was eight my mother had sent me to stay with her parents overnight and by the time I came back she'd painted a giant rainbow across one wall. It wasn't perfect and some of the colours were fat while others were disproportionately narrow, but I loved it. My father had raised his eyebrows when he saw it and muttered something about resale value, but to me it was perfect. That was before my father died and before I realized that some of my mother's enthusiasm was vodka-sponsored, and way before all her enthusiasm drowned completely in a 42 per cent proof bottle.

When you're eight years old you think life will be full

of big acts of love, but looking back now I don't think anything really came close to that rainbow ever again. Not until Shannon came along anyway.

'There's so little personality in here,' said Ed Kowalsky, and once again I knew he was thinking about his own kids' bedrooms at home. Since we'd got to the house, he'd dropped his authoritative, teeth-flashing persona and in its place was a diffident man who seemed to have shrunk physically.

'What does it tell you, Anne, that this little girl was able to so subliminate all traces of herself?'

'That she has learned how to suppress her true nature?'

'Or maybe she has learned how to adapt?'

We stood for a moment looking around and I think we were both relieved when Sergeant Cavanagh asked if we'd seen enough.

'Right, folks,' he said, as we followed his lumbering frame back down the stairs. 'Are you ready for the *pièce de résistance*?'

He pronounced *pièce* as if it was an acronym: 'PS'.

At the back of the hallway, under the stairs, was a doorway. I'd noticed it on the way in, but had studiously avoided thinking about it. As Sergeant Cavanagh turned the handle, I fought back an overwhelming urge to yell, 'Stop!' Suddenly, it felt too much. I knew that by going through that doorway I'd be crossing a rubicon. Despite my training and my ambition and my curiosity, I wasn't ready. I didn't want to see what human beings are capable of doing to each other, or of enduring. But Sergeant Cavanagh was already squeezing himself through the narrow doorway.

'This woulda been kept locked at all times. See how heavy that door is? It's reinforced with steel on the inside.'

We were in a cramped store-room lined with shelves which housed all manner of household items – various tools, an iron, tins of used paint, a stack of lightbulbs in their boxes. Multi-packs of washing powder. As you'd expect, everything was neatly arranged with different shelves for different categories of stuff, all with their labels facing out. At the end of the room was what looked at first glance like a wall with yet more shelves. Only when Sergeant Cavanagh reached up under a shelf in the top left corner and slid open a bolt did I realize that the whole wall was actually another door. To the left of it was a plastic bottle on a small purpose-built shelf. As the burly cop reached down, with obvious effort, to slide open another bolt at the bottom of the door, I peered closely at the label on the bottle. Antiseptic handwash. Something way down in the pit of my stomach lurched to the side.

We all stepped back as the door swung open, revealing steps going downwards into what appeared to be a fathomless black hole. Even Sergeant Cavanagh was silenced by the wave of damp, stale air that rose to greet us and the overpowering smell of something decaying under rotten floorboards. The only light came from the three vented bricks I'd seen from the outside which were ahead and to the left, the air vents covered over with a thick sheet of clear safety glass.

'There's a switch around here somewhere,' said Cavanagh eventually, feeling around on the wall to the left of the staircase. There was a clicking noise and suddenly the whole scene was illuminated in a brutal white light. I instinctively closed my eyes, and when I opened them again the world tilted and it has never been straight since.

20

Chloe

It was Wednesday morning and Ewan had been ignoring her for the best part of two days now. Not quite ignoring her but doing that thing where you smile but let your eyes slide off a person as if they're made of soap and address your comments in a bright, shiny voice to a point by their shoulder.

Chloe was beside herself.

She'd always been secure in her own attractiveness to the type of man she wanted to be attractive to. After spending the night of Gill's leaving do squashed together with Ewan in his narrow, frankly rather rank-smelling bed, she'd noticed he seemed subdued the next morning, but put it down to a hangover. Her own head had felt like her skull was shrink-wrapping itself over her bruised brain.

So she tried not to read anything into the way Ewan hadn't bothered to get up, simply calling out, 'Bye, babe,' leaving her to let herself out, or the fact that he hadn't asked her what she was doing for the rest of the weekend. And when he didn't call or text that day, she reasoned he was still shaking off the night before. She was happy to snuggle with her mum on the sofa in her onesie, watching

135

non-stop telly and listening to her dad shouting at the football in the next room and remembering with a warm thrill in the bottom of her stomach the things they'd done on Ewan's unwashed sheets the night before.

But by Sunday afternoon she was getting irritable. Something small and rodenty was scrabbling at her insides as if it wanted to get out. She made excuses – a string of them that she threaded together like a daisy chain. He was so busy. He didn't want to look too eager. He was sitting staring at his phone waiting for her to ring.

At 8 p.m. she sent him a text. By that time she'd agonized over it for hours, rewriting it again and again on a Post-it pad. Even so, her finger hovered over the send button. She'd aimed for casual – joking about her monumental hangover and enquiring about the state of his head. Directly after sending it, she experienced a moment of paralysing regret. She should have held out longer; she'd played her hand too early. She thrust her phone under a cushion on the sofa and tried to concentrate on the television screen where an actor with nineteenth-century clothes and twenty-first-century stubble was smouldering on a hillside – which made her think of Ewan and the dangerous, alien feel of his biceps under her fingers. She snatched up her phone again to check she hadn't missed an incoming message beep.

Finally, twenty-five minutes and seventeen snatched glances later, she received a text.

Yeh was not feelin 2 clever yesterday but better today tnx. See you tomoz.

The rush of euphoria that greeted the arrival of the message fizzled into flatness. She'd been hoping, she now realized, that her message would kickstart an evening of intimate text exchanges, the kind where you wear a private half-smile as you compose your messages and a full-on one when you read the replies. But this wasn't the kind of text that encouraged a response. It was impersonal and throwaway.

It made her feel like *she'd* been thrown away.

All that night, she'd had a lump lodged in her throat and in her dreams she ran endlessly from unspecified dangers, her breath torn in ragged strips from her throat. She went to work the next morning with puffy eyes and a hardened heart. Then, miraculously, Ewan was attentive again. He'd brought her in a croissant in a brown paper bag and picked a crumb of it out of her hair with gentle fingers. When he went to the kitchen he came back with a cup of coffee for her, and even though he'd put sugar in it, forgetting she didn't take any, and even though there was a trickle of coffee sludge down the outside, she drank it just because of his fingers spooning in the sugar and his hands wrapped around the mug.

'You're looking altogether too well for someone in the state you were in on Friday night,' he said when he brought the coffee to her desk.

'That's due to my fast metabolism.'

She glanced up to see if he was smiling, and then had to look away in case she burst with pride when she saw that he was.

Only after he'd gone to sit down did she question fleetingly this seeming change of heart. It was almost extravagant in its total reversal of the weekend's silence, as if he was doing it to make a point. If they'd been somewhere other than at work she might even have suspected him of putting on a show to make someone jealous, but they were in the office and it was Monday morning and Ewan had looked at her with eyes that had flecks of amber in them which caught the sun as it slanted through the slatted blinds.

Happiness poured over her as she laboured through all the dreary Monday-morning tasks that Rachel had assigned her in a long, bullet-pointed list she'd printed out and left lying on Chloe's keyboard for her to find when she came in. She was conscious of Ewan mere yards away, but she concentrated on her screen, content just to know he was there. An email popped up.

Lunch?

She'd smiled to herself but didn't reply immediately, already secure enough in her beloved status to take him for granted. Her pampered past had bought her the sense of entitlement that allowed her to do that. They'd gone to the sandwich shop around the corner, Chloe trying not to check to see if Rachel was clocking them out as they left. She'd had a grilled panini and regretted it when she bit into it and melted mozzarella dribbled down her chin. They'd been for lunch here loads of times in the past but now she felt self-conscious, sure the other customers could feel the electricity in the air.

Then, without warning, Ewan had gone all quiet on her, eating his chicken wrap with a kind of taciturn intensity that made her talk far too much to compensate. On the way back to the office, she thought he might take her hand and made sure it was fully accessible, hanging down invitingly on the side nearest to him, but then he'd taken his phone out so both his hands were

138

occupied and she'd withdrawn hers, putting it up to scratch her nose as if there'd never been any other plan.

'Fancy a drink after work?' She'd been rehearsing the words in her head all the way back to the office, but even so, hearing them said out loud came as a shock.

'Sure.'

It wasn't the enthusiastic 'I thought you'd never ask' she'd been hoping for but it wasn't a 'no' either and she'd gone back to her desk feeling buoyant, though her heart sank at the prospect of an afternoon of invoicing, still the air around her desk had thrummed with possibility.

Halfway through that Monday afternoon, just at the point where Chloe was contemplating heading to the kitchen to make tea in the hope that Ewan would follow her, the door to Rachel's office had swung open.

'Ewan. A word.'

That day, Rachel was wearing a sky-blue silk blouse tucked into a slim charcoal skirt, with high-heeled dark grey suede shoes with straps that went around her narrow ankles. Chloe felt suddenly shabby in the khaki top and brown skinny trousers and brown suede boots she'd agonized over before leaving for work.

The slatted blinds in Rachel's glass office were closed so Chloe couldn't see what was going on inside. There was something quite chilling about those blank white windows like giant backs turned to her. She went to the kitchen anyway, hoping that by the time the kettle boiled, Ewan would be out and he'd sneak in to join her and fill her in on what Rachel Masters had wanted. Perhaps he'd do one of his impressions like he used to do of Gill. But when she slid back behind her desk a few minutes later, Rachel's door was still shut.

By the time Ewan had finally emerged, Chloe was on the phone and she missed seeing his expression. She tried to catch his eye as he sat down, but he was already concentrating on his computer screen. She saw a little muscle twitch in the side of his jaw and it reminded her of Friday night in his narrow bed and something turned to warm liquid inside her.

She tapped in an email.

Well?

From the corner of her eye she saw him click his mouse and then frown briefly at the screen before clicking it again. If he'd read her email, he didn't respond.

When 5.30 came around, Sarah was first to leave as usual, trying to gather her things as discreetly as possible. Did she really think she was fooling anyone by leaving her coat off until she got out of the office doors? Gradually the others also got up to go until only Chloe and Ewan remained. And Rachel Masters.

Finally Chloe cracked. She stood and picked up her jacket and phone, lingering as if her attention was caught by something on the screen, hoping Ewan would turn around. When he didn't, she took her things over to his desk.

'Guess you're too busy for a drink then?'

Before looking at Chloe he glanced over to Rachel's office where the blinds were still down.

'Sorry,' he shrugged, drumming his pen on the desk.

Still Chloe hesitated, knowing she should leave but unable to tear herself away.

'Is everything OK?'

140

Again that flick of a glance in Rachel Masters's direction.

'Look, she gave me a bollocking, all right? She didn't mention your name but she asked me if I wanted to get ahead in this business, because having a fling with a co-worker was a sure way of stopping my career in its tracks. And she's got a point, you know. It's a mug's game, isn't it, getting involved with someone you work with? Well, isn't it?'

His eyes had locked on to hers as if pleading with her to agree.

Chloe had smiled her default smile and nodded her head, up down up down up down, but really her mind had stopped working when he'd said that word. Fling. That's how he saw their night together. She'd been thinking of box-sets with a blanket over their laps and mini-breaks to Rome or Berlin and making love in front of an open fire or on a deserted beach with the sun reflecting gold in those amber flecks in his eyes . . . and he'd been thinking 'fling'.

Since then they'd hardly communicated at all, avoiding each other's eyes and making sure they didn't cross paths in the kitchen. And now it was Wednesday and her jaw ached from forcing a smile and there was an unfamiliar hard, metallic taste in her mouth, and when she looked at Rachel Masters's office she experienced a rush of something so shockingly intense, she didn't even dare try to analyse it but swallowed it with a gulp. She felt it burn as it went down.

21
Charlie

Charlie had come to believe himself an outsider to love. Not that he was incapable of it, or immune to it. Not at all. He was an incurable romantic, as many inveterate cynics often are. It wasn't that he didn't believe love was possible because he absolutely did, but rather that he didn't believe it was possible *for him*. So he was doomed to live in a permanent state of quiet unfulfilment. And then he met Stefan.

Stefan had smooth olive skin that shone where the light hit it. His face was all planes and hollows in soft woody shades like beech and walnut, and when he smiled it was like the sun coming out so you just wanted to make him smile again and keep on smiling and never stop. But only for you. And that was the problem with Stefan. It was never really only for Charlie.

Stefan was one of those people who knew everyone. He had over two thousand friends on Facebook. His phone was always buzzing with incoming texts, Instagram messages, tweets, voicemails that started 'Hey, babe . . .' He was eleven years younger than Charlie, and it showed in the way social media came as naturally to him as breathing. Ten days after their first meeting, his profile was still up on Grindr though he swore he wasn't active on there any more, but Charlie didn't believe him.

Charlie had never felt so happy, or at the same time so utterly afraid. It was as if someone had stripped the top layer of skin off him, leaving every nerve-ending exposed. Stefan cancelled dates at the last minute, but when they did meet, he made Charlie feel that he was the wittiest, sexiest man alive. At least some of the time. He told Charlie he wanted to show him off – and then once they were out, flirted outrageously with everyone he met – men *and* women.

Stefan called himself a freelance design consultant, but Charlie had little idea what he actually did. When Charlie got up to go to work on those rare mornings he was allowed to stay over, Stefan remained fast asleep; he seemed to spend his days flitting here and there, lunching or drinking with this person or that. He lived in a rented flat in a trendy central London neighbour-hood, but he expected Charlie to pay when they went out. He asked about Charlie's job but didn't bother to disguise how his eyes glazed over when Charlie replied. Charlie found himself talking up his position and his level of responsibility in the department, just so he could bear to look at the image of himself reflected back through Stefan's dismissive gaze. For the first time ever, he wished for a more impressive job title – and an accom-panying pay packet. Charlie was both miserable and ecstatic and it was driving him crazy.

And all the time, he was having to come into the office and deal with the shit that was going on. Chloe seemed constantly either on the verge of tears or else adopting this grating loud and gregarious 'let's go and get hammered' persona – clearly for Ewan's benefit. Like he even noticed she was there when Rachel was around. Amira was preoccupied, Paula on edge, and Sarah, who was his natural ally in the department, was almost like a ghost person. She slipped in and out as unobtrusively as she could and spent the day with her head bent over her desk. Since the disaster of her missed meeting with Kevin Bromsgrove the previous week, she'd stopped taking lunch breaks even. He was worried about her. She had a pinched, haunted look, but when he tried to catch her on her way to the kitchen or the loo, she made it clear she didn't want to talk. Her eyes would flit anxiously towards Rachel's office or the door. 'Got to be on best behaviour,' she'd whispered the day before when he finally cornered her by the kettle.

'She'll forget about that Bromsgrove business soon enough,' he'd said, trying to cheer her up. 'It'll be someone else's turn to be the new whipping boy.'

But Sarah hadn't been convinced. 'There's something else,' she'd said. 'And I'm dreading Rachel finding out.'

'What?' he asked. But Sarah had just shaken her head. 'You don't even want to know,' she sighed.

On the Tuesday afternoon, Mark Hamilton came down from his penthouse office to talk to them all about the forthcoming team-building weekend.

'It'll be great fun,' he said, his strangely colourless eyes with their sandy lashes flicking from one person to the next as if inviting agreement. 'It's being organized by a company who specialize in this kind of thing. It'll be a mix of cognitive exercises, boardroom games and Outward Bound stuff.'

At the phrase Outward Bound, Charlie felt as if

someone had snapped an elastic band against the inside wall of his stomach. There could be no two words more guaranteed to strike fear into the heart of a man who'd had a migraine all through school that only visited him on PE days, and who had never completely got over the pain of discovering as a teenager that his newly divorced father had failed to turn up to see him two Sundays in a row because he was standing on the touchline supporting his girlfriend's soccer-playing son. 'It must make a lovely change for you being around someone who understands the offside rule,' he'd said cuttingly. But his dad – who he now accepted had been loving in his own way – had just said, 'Ah well, that's the thing about families – you don't get to choose each other.'

Wasn't that the truth!

Stefan was into fitness. He wore a lime-green plastic band around his wrist that measured his steps. Sometimes if he felt he'd underperformed that day, he'd leap to his feet when they were on the sofa – or, once, in bed – and run around the room a few times, stopping to lunge forward on to one leg. The band told him how many calories he'd burned and how well he'd slept. Charlie had come to dread a low reading, since it could send Stefan's mood plummeting. He hated that band with a passion, feeling it to be a personal reproach, a kick in the teeth for everything he was.

Rachel had been listening to Mark's speech with her strange flat smile. After he finished and repaired back upstairs, she approached Charlie. His mouth became suddenly dry.

'Could you come with me for a moment, Charlie?'

Reluctantly he got to his feet. He could see Sarah

darting hollow-eyed glances at him from her desk and felt unaccountably guilty.

'Have you had a chance to think?'

'What about?'

Rachel frowned. She was leaning against her desk with her arms crossed across her chest, and her posture stiffened with disapproval.

'About the deputy position. I do hope you're taking it seriously, Charlie. I had a good feeling about you. I hope it wasn't misplaced.'

'No. Of course not.'

Charlie cursed himself for sounding so obsequious. What he should do was tell her to stuff her job. He was conscious of Paula sitting outside in the office, just feet away. She wasn't exactly the kind of deputy that set the world on fire. They all knew that. But that didn't mean to say Rachel could just get rid of her.

'You're not getting any younger, Charlie.'

That stung. Charlie wasn't vain though he had minded when his hair started to thin and spent a chunk of his monthly pay on a hormonal treatment that was supposed to stimulate new hair growth. But being with Stefan had made him sensitive to the lines around his eyes and the way the skin puckered around his belly button. It was as if Rachel Masters was tapping into the thing that lay at the very heart of his self-doubt.

'Is this enough for you? Really?' She gestured at the desks in the office outside and the bent heads, and Charlie mentally added in the strange new deadened atmosphere that had descended since she arrived.

'I'm talking about you giving yourself the chance to get ahead and start building a career, before it's too late. Do you want to still be out there in ten years' time, plodding along? "Good old Charlie," the bosses will say. "He's got no ambition but at least he's reliable."'

'But Paula . . .'

Rachel made a *pff* sound with her mouth, as if she was blowing a small fly off her lower lip.

'Paula is my concern. Obviously we'll make sure she's well provided for. All you have to think about is whether you've got the guts to lift yourself out of the rut you're in. I need somebody with a bit of get up and go as my right-hand person. If it's not you, I'll have to bring in someone new. And obviously there's no guarantee you're going to like them. What are you afraid of, Charlie? What's stopping you from stepping up?'

Normally Charlie hated that whole Californian thing about stepping up and making the grade and going the extra mile, but something in Rachel's little speech resonated. He saw himself through Stefan's eyes, a mid-ranking worker in a not particularly exciting sector, treading water until retirement. But if he was deputy, he could be running his own department within a year or two. Charlie had no illusions about the glamour, or lack of it, of the industry he'd somehow ended up in, but if he made manager it would in theory be easier to shift across into another managerial role in a different, perhaps more stimulating working environment.

'If I was interested what would I have to do?'

Afterwards, he felt grubby. Passing Paula's desk, he pretended not to see her thin, almost non-existent eyebrows raised in question. The spurt of adrenaline he'd felt in Rachel's office when he'd seen a more dynamic version of himself materializing in front of him had died away, leaving a sour aftertaste.

Clicking open his computer screen, he noticed he'd had two emails while he'd been in with Rachel. The first was a dull round-robin from Security about how they all needed to get updated passes. Yawn. The second looked like spam and he was just about to bin it when something about the address – a random selection of numbers and letters – struck a chord in his mind. He double-clicked.

Have you asked her yet? Have you asked Rachel what she did?

A chill ran through him as if he was swallowing ice. He called up the anonymous email he'd received before, the one calling Rachel a bitch who destroyed people. Same address. Someone really had a grievance against his new boss. He could understand how Rachel's abrasive management style might have ruffled a few feathers, but to go to the effort of creating a fake account just to send these creepy messages . . . Should he contact HR or even Rachel herself? He forwarded the email to Sarah with a line saying, *Look what I just got. Should I report it?*

Seconds later, he had a reply.

Shit. That's a bit OTT, isn't it? Not surprised R has enemies though. Bitter ex-employee perchance? I would bin it.

Charlie let out a deep breath. Sarah was right. It was sour grapes from someone Rachel had rubbed up the wrong way. Nothing to do with him. He deleted the message and got up to go to the kitchen.

'Fancy a cuppa?' he asked Sarah on the way.

'Oh God, yes, please.' She really didn't look well. Her complexion was pale and waxy.

As a special concession, he washed up the one decent mug left in the cupboard, the deep one with flowers on it. Most of the others were cheap promotional things with the company name emblazoned on the side, that chipped easily and stained brown at the base. He made Sarah's tea in the flowery one – remembering to take the teabag out in good time so it didn't go that orange colour she hated. In his own he put a spoonful of instant coffee and then two heaped spoonfuls of sugar from the packet that was out on the side. He knew he needed to cut down. It had never really bothered him until he started seeing Stefan, but now he felt a twinge of guilt every time he made a hot drink. A few years ago there were lots of them who had sugar in their tea or coffee, but now you felt a bit of a social pariah asking for it. It was like smoking, he supposed. It had just gone out of fashion.

When he gently placed the mug of tea on Sarah's desk, she gave him a look of pure gratitude and he could have sworn he saw her eyes film over with tears. He would have to persuade her to come out for a drink so he could find out what was wrong with her.

Back at his desk he took a swig of coffee. *Holy crap, that was bitter.* He wondered how long the coffee jar had been sitting there. Once, they'd checked the sell-by date on a container of hot-chocolate powder that had been at the back of one of the kitchen cupboards for ever, and found it was four years out of date. No one threw it away though.

He took another sip. Briefly he contemplated going back to the kitchen and making another cup, and hated the little voice inside his head that said, 'But what would Rachel think if you got up again?' He glanced at his phone and saw, with a rush of excitement, that Stefan had texted him. They'd had a tentative arrangement to go out tonight, but he'd learned quickly that all Stefan's arrangements were fluid, and Charlie had been gearing himself up to be disappointed. His joy at reading Stefan's confirmation of the date was slightly tempered by his insistence that they try some new hip Lebanese-Thai fusion place in Soho where you couldn't book. Stefan had dragged him to one of those places before and they'd ended up having to stand in line and wait for an hour glaring at other diners while music blared out so loudly they had to shout over the top, and all for the pleasure of sitting side by side at a bar facing forward, eating tiny portions of food in huge bowls, feeling the eyes of the people in the queue behind boring into their backs. But Stefan had wanted to try out this new place, and as usual Charlie gave in. What he really wanted was to go round to Stefan's house, order a takeaway and watch a box-set, and then rip each other's clothes off. Or, better still, rip each other's clothes off first. But at least Stefan wasn't cancelling him.

Occasionally, Charlie forced himself to look at the whole situation with Stefan objectively. If he was his own best friend, he'd have serious words with himself. He could see he was getting in too deep with Stefan far too quickly, being too needy. But the truth was, he was just so bloody lonely sometimes, and it felt good to be with someone. And Stefan already had this hold over him he couldn't even really explain. Just knowing he was going to see him this evening set his nerves buzzing in a most pleasurable way – even though he knew he'd hate the restaurant and resent paying the no doubt astronomical bill.

His desk phone rang and he checked the clock on his computer. 2.45. Margaret Hoffman. Right on time. Margaret was a client he'd been wooing for ages. It was almost impossible to get to speak to her. This phone meeting had been booked for days.

'Margaret? How nice to talk to you again.'

As they exchanged pleasantries, Charlie rifled through his in-tray before extracting the paperwork he'd already set aside for this much-anticipated call. Margaret Hoffman ran a string of highly successful shops selling fashion accessories and had just bought up a smaller jewellery chain which she needed to re-staff from top to bottom. If he landed the contract, Charlie would potentially be bringing in many thousands of pounds' worth of future commission. Tens of thousands. But he knew he wasn't the only recruitment agent she was talking to so he'd really done his homework, gathering in all the statistics and facts he could find about her company and the accessories market in general, creating an ideal personnel profile and setting out his ideas for a restructuring of staff hierarchy in each of the shops.

'So tell me, Charlie, how you envisage a possible long-term contract might work,' Margaret said in her peculiarly masculine voice. 'I haven't got long so you have twenty minutes to convince me to hire you rather than any of the other agencies.'

Charlie launched into his prepared pitch, but he hadn't been speaking long before he started to feel strange twinges in his lower abdomen. He tried to ignore them, but within minutes they'd worsened and now his stomach was cramping intermittently in painful spasms. Sweat broke out on his forehead, and his skin felt clammy under his shirt. He battled on with his pitch, but now, oh God, he needed the loo.

'Charlie, are you still there?'

A sudden sharp pain had caused him to stop mid-sentence and Margaret Hoffman didn't sound too impressed.

'Yes, sorry. Where was I?' His eyes scanned the printout in front of him, trying to regain his train of thought.

'You were telling me about your post-hiring assessment strategy?'

He started to explain his system for following up on appointments he'd made. Suddenly a horrible loud gurgling sound erupted from his insides. Sarah's head whipped around, her mouth open, her eyebrows raised in shock. Charlie's voice again dried up as his stomach spasmed with pain. Horror flooded through him as he realized what was about to happen.

'Sorry,' he gasped into the receiver, and then he dropped the phone and bolted for the door that led to the lobby where the toilets were.

When he emerged some twenty minutes later, his face pasty, but his gut slightly calmer, Amira was waiting outside.

'Sarah emailed me to tell me to come and find you. She was worried about you, but doesn't dare leave her desk. You look like shit – no offence. What happened to you?'

'I don't know. It just came out of nowhere. I've been trying to work it out while I've been in there glued to the toilet. Do you know, I think there was something in that coffee.'

'Don't be daft – how could there be? Anyway, we've all been drinking that coffee today and no one else has been affected.'

'Well, the sugar then. It tasted disgusting. Do you know, I think someone must have put something on it – some kind of laxative maybe.'

'Oh, come on. Why would anyone do that?'

Charlie put his hands on his belly, feeling the stirrings of something deep inside there.

'I don't know.' He shook his head. 'All I know is I was completely fine, and then I drank the coffee which tasted really odd, and then I was on the phone and all of a sudden . . . Oh God.'

He was remembering Margaret Hoffman and how he'd cut her off mid-conversation. What would happen now? He couldn't imagine her giving the contract to someone whose stomach erupted mid-sentence as if the creature in *Alien* was tearing out of it. And tonight – no way was he going to be able to make it out for dinner. And he didn't think Stefan was the type to volunteer to come round and hold his hair back while he hunched over a toilet bowl – or worse.

As if in sympathy with his thoughts, his stomach started to make a low groaning noise.

'I've got to—'

Amira pushed him back through the door of the toilet before he could finish what he was going to say. He made it into the cubicle just in time, which was probably the one good thing to happen to him that day.

22

Anne

As well as lecturing at the university and advising in legal cases, I also have private clients, some of whom I've been treating for years. Not so many new ones these days admittedly, but there was a period when I couldn't get enough. I was hungry to expand my knowledge and my reputation. During that time I dealt with some harrowing cases. There was a man who'd been sexually abused by a teacher from the age of six and suffered permanent and ongoing physiological damage, and a young woman who'd drowned her own baby in the bath because a voice told her that was the only way he'd be safe from her. There was a teenager who hadn't spoken in the three years since her father stabbed her mother in front of her, yet cut words and phrases into her skin.

Some cases made me question everything I thought I knew about human relationships; others made me go home at night and stare at my own reflection in the mirror, asking, 'Could you?' 'Would you?' Then I'd hug Shannon wordlessly till she got fed up and wriggled free. But nothing ever came as close to totally derailing me as that day in late summer when I stood at the top of a flight of basement stairs in an anonymous suburban house while a large cop in low-slung pants flicked on a light switch.

'Quite something, ain't it?' asked Sergeant Cavanagh, making his way down the steps so that Professor Ed Kowalsky and I could properly take in the scene in that basement.

'Jesus fucking Christ.' It was the first time I'd ever heard Ed swear.

'Yep,' said the cop.

The basement was a squarish room, probably around five metres by six. The floor was that grey concrete that starts to go greenish after a while. The walls were grey also. The smell was damp cut with decay and something darker and more rancid.

'These are getting on for half a metre thick,' said Cavanagh, patting the walls almost proudly. 'Two layers of bricks with a thick insulating membrane between them for soundproofing. Guy was a regular self-builder.'

But Ed and I weren't paying attention to the walls, or to the eight narrow steps that led down to where the outsized policeman was standing. Both of us were fixated on one thing.

The cage.

It took up over half of the floorspace in the basement and was just under adult height, with black bars up the sides and across the top. A wide wooden plank ran horizontally across the middle section of the top with a pulley and rope attached. At one end of the rope was a large hook. As I stared at it, something foul-tasting shot into my mouth and I tried not to gag. The only other things in the cage were a toddler-sized cot with the side down, a hard wooden chair and, at the far end, a large metal bin with a lid.

'Kid used to wear this harness kind of thing that wrapped around him and kept his arms by his sides with a ring on the back that the hook clipped into.'

Sergeant Cavanagh could almost have been a tour guide in a museum and I wondered why it was that Laurie's room had so affected him, while this horror show in the basement left him seemingly unmoved. Was it just because of his own children at home – so easily relatable to the little girl we'd met in the meeting room at the university medical facility – but a world away from the poor creature in the cage? Was it the depth of the boy's suffering that set him outside the cop's radius of empathy, like the blank-eyed refugees I see these days on the television news?

'They never let him out,' said Ed. He looked pale in the harsh overhead light and I remembered with a start that he was also dealing with the boy. David. Child D. We never spoke of this other assessment being run simultaneously. Ed felt it better that we kept the two completely separate until our reports were made, ostensibly so that Dan Oppenheimer and I couldn't be swayed by each other's opinions but also, I now believe, so that he would be the only one with full knowledge of the case, the only one qualified to write up the account. The result was that I'd forgotten how close he was to the things we were seeing now.

'Nope.' Cavenagh was matter-of-fact. 'This was it. The full extent of the kid's life. Going from the cot to the chair.'

'No toilet?'

'Diapers. Used to sling 'em into that bin every coupla days. Place absolutely stank when we found him. When you think of what it's like upstairs – everything all covered in plastic and lined up so neatly – and down here the place is crawling with flies and maggots. You know they used to scrape all their leftover food into a bucket and bring it down. He ate it with his hands.'

'The feeding rota on the fridge door,' I said, thinking out loud. 'So Laurie would have been down here pretty regularly.'

'Sure. Sure,' Sergeant Cavanagh agreed. 'Plus obviously you know they had her help out with the punishments.'

I'd seen the initial police reports and the accounts of the child welfare officers who'd interviewed Laurie after the gruesome discovery was made. The boy was found with marks all over his puny body. Some looked like they'd been made with a stick of some sort; others were burn marks – as from a heated hair device, the medical report had said. I thought now about Noelle Egan's dark glossy curls and shivered. And right at the top of one of his scrawny arms was a perfect bite mark scored purple into his flesh, and of such a size that it could only have been made, said the report, by a young child.

23
Sarah

'You don't have to go.'

Oliver had a hand on each of her shoulders to hold her in place and was gazing into her eyes. He looked worried.

'Don't kiss. Oh yuck, you're going to kiss. Disgusting.' Sam made vomiting noises behind Oliver's back.

'Mummy, stay,' said Joe, clinging to Sarah's leg.

'I do have to go, we've already discussed it.'

'No. It's not reasonable. It's the weekend, for God's sake. We hardly see each other as it is. And you look awful. When was the last time you had a proper night's sleep?'

'You're just fed up because you've got to look after the kids all weekend instead of going to poker at Jimmy's tonight.'

'That is so unfair.'

It was unfair, Sarah knew it. Oliver hadn't even mentioned the poker. But she was so tired. And he was an easy target.

'Look, there's nowhere in the world I want to go to less than this stupid weekend in Derbyshire. Last night all I could think about was how Rachel is going to manipulate the whole thing to suit her agenda. She'll do anything to humiliate me. But I can't give her an excuse to sack me.'

'You should take her to a bloody tribunal. That's what you should do. This is bullying.'

'Um, you said bloody. Mummy, Daddy said bloody.'

'Yes, I know he did, Sam, but sometimes people say bad things when they get upset.'

'*I'm* upset. I'm upset because you're going. Bloody. Bloody. Bloody.'

'Sam!'

'I'm allowed to say it because I'm upset.'

Still attached to her leg, Joe started crying.

'Look, it's only two days. I'll be back tomorrow. I've got to do it otherwise it's going to be even worse when I have to tell her about . . . that other thing.'

She dipped her head in Sam's direction and raised her eyebrows meaningfully.

Oliver sighed and dropped his hands from her shoulders.

'I suppose I could ask Mum to come over and help.'

'Are you serious? I'm away just one night and you can't cope without reinforcements? Anyway, the last time your mum came over while I was away she basically scalped Joe.'

'Oh come on, it was only a trim.'

'She knew I loved his hair long.'

'He told her he wanted it cut.'

'Only after she'd said it would make him look like a big boy, like Sam.'

They glared at each other. Oliver was the first to look away.

'Fine. I won't call her if it makes you happier. I'll look

after the boys and do the shopping because there's bugger all in the fridge, and clear out the stinking nappy bins and . . .'

'Bugger! He said bugger!'

'What you mean is you'll do exactly what I do ninety-nine per cent of the time.'

'That's not fair. I do more than my share.'

Sarah put up her hand wearily. 'There's no point having this argument. I'm too tired and I need to get going. Boys, you be good for Daddy.'

'That's right. Walk away. Just like you always do.'

'Mummy stay Joe,' said Joe, his chubby hands clamped around her knee, creasing up her dress.

'I'll be back before you know it,' she said, peeling his fingers off her and planting a kiss on the top of his head where his hair was still messy from sleep.

She went to kiss Sam but he darted away from her outstretched arms and climbed up on to the side and then the back of the sofa.

He folded his arms and glared at her.

'Bloody bugger,' he said.

She was meeting Charlie and Amira at St Pancras station to catch the train to the hotel in Derbyshire. Paula was driving and giving Chloe a lift. Ewan, he'd admitted the previous afternoon, was travelling up with Rachel.

'It makes sense,' he'd said defensively. 'She has a company car and she drives practically past my flat.'

'Since when was Clapton on the way from anywhere, let alone Islington?' Amira had asked him in the office, but he'd just smiled, looking pleased with himself.

By the time she arrived on the concourse, twenty

minutes late thanks to the argument with Oliver, Sarah was tired to the very bones of her, so that just lifting one foot in front of the other used up vast reserves of energy.

'You're late. We'd better put our skates on,' said Charlie. 'I don't think missing our train would be the best way to kick off all that lovely team bonding.'

'Team bonding my arse,' panted Amira. 'Team absconding, that's what I'll be doing first chance I get.'

It was a relief to find their reserved seats, just as the train was pulling out. Sinking down opposite Charlie, Sarah noticed for the first time how pale he was.

'You OK?' she asked.

'Of course,' he replied over-brightly, brushing a hand across his brow in a self-conscious gesture. Sarah gasped.

'Your arm! What happened?'

Instantly Charlie tugged down on his shirt sleeve which had risen up when he lifted his hand, trying to hide the jumbo-sized plaster on the side of his arm, just above the wrist, through which she could see a faint pink stain seeping.

'Oh, this – cut myself opening a can of tomatoes, can you believe? Got halfway round with the tin-opener and it got stuck so I was jerking at it and the bloody thing stabbed me. Hurt like a bugger as well.'

The story sounded as if it had been rehearsed, but Sarah knew better than to push Charlie. For all his gentleness, he was fiercely protective of his privacy.

'Only you could have a near-death experience over a tin of tomatoes,' said Amira.

During the course of the journey, the mood among the three of them picked up. Amira and Charlie bought canned gin and tonics and made Sarah howl with laughter by acting out some of the activities they imagined might be on the itinerary for the weekend.

'Someone I know had to rap all the things she thought were great about her company,' claimed Amira.

'We is the kings/Of spreadsheets and tings,' improvised Charlie.

'That's genius right there,' said Amira, approving. 'Make that man the boss immediately.'

'Well, I heard of one company that dropped the entire sales team in the middle of a wood in the middle of nowhere in the middle of the night and they had to find their way back to the hotel,' Charlie said. 'But because it was sales they were all über competitive and instead of working together they were trying to trick each other, and all of them ended up lost on their own and the police helicopter had to go and find them with heat-seeking equipment. Some of them had lost half their bodyweight and they'd actually started eating each other to survive.'

'I think you might be exaggerating just a wee bit there, Charlie,' said Sarah, but still something snagged at her chest at the thought of scrambling around the country-side in the dark. She couldn't remember a time Joe and Sam had both slept through the night and she'd been pinning her hopes on at least getting a proper night's sleep out of this hellish weekend away. The idea that they might be expected to stay up all night trekking through fields in the cold made her want to burst into tears.

'Do you think we're going to see a different side of Rachel?' she asked. 'I mean, maybe she feels that for whatever reason she has to put on this really hard act at work, play the big boss, and this is the point at which she unveils herself as a total pussycat.'

Amira snorted.

'Yeah, her interests are knitting little jumpers for penguins and meditating for world peace. Oh, and biting the heads off live babies.'

Sarah's stomach lurched and she fought back a wave of nausea.

They took a taxi to the hotel. Obviously they'd all Googled it before so Sarah had a rough idea what to expect, but it was like internet dating – hotels inevitably used misleading photographs of the sun dappling the honey-stoned entrance, or the chandelier over the beautiful sweeping staircase in the main hall, while neglecting to show the ugly modern extension on the side or the fact that it was actually situated in a layby off the A40.

In this case, the hotel itself was pretty close to how it had appeared online – a sprawling redbrick building set in parkland, accessed by a long driveway. As the taxi turned in through the iron gates and made its way towards the front entrance, Sarah felt a sense of foreboding. She tried not to look at the lawn to the side of the hotel where an awkward-looking group of people wearing matching yellow T-shirts bearing a company logo were doing some sort of line dancing at the behest of an energetic young woman in Lycra shorts, bellowing instructions into a megaphone.

'Oh God, please make her go away,' muttered Charlie under his breath.

Inside the lobby, a man wearing a dark suit and a

smile that seemed sprayed on allocated them their rooms.

'You have a nice day,' he called after them as they headed to the lifts.

'Hear that?' hissed Charlie. 'He's mocking us. He knows what's in store for us and he's mocking us.'

Inside her room, Sarah took one look around at the double bed with its dark wood headboard and crisp white pillows, and sheets tucked in smoothly beneath a claret-red bedspread, the dark-green walls with matching curtains and deep, plush patterned carpet, the russet velvet armchair by the window with the view out over the parkland at the back of the hotel, the ensuite with its fluffy white robe and towels and miniature toiletries . . . and she burst into tears. It was so peaceful. She could select a teabag from the basket on the tray over there on the desk and make a cup of tea using the kettle next to it, and drink the whole thing with one of those individually wrapped shortbread biscuits, without someone wanting something from her – a particular toy, a drink, to tell his brother off for bending his favourite Top Trumps card, a cuddle, a wee. She could lie down on that perfectly made bed that wasn't covered with children's books and changing mats, and climb inside sheets that weren't sandy with crumbs and close her eyes . . . and no one would prod her awake to tell her there was a child crying or insist it was getting-up time even though it was pitch black outside the window. She could run a bath in a tub that wasn't ringed with grime because neither she nor Oliver had the energy to do more than the most perfunctory wipe around the rim with a damp sponge, and lie back without spearing the back of her head on a plastic soldier, his plastic gun raised in front of his face. Instead she sank down on to the velvet armchair and sobbed, missing her babies with an intensity that made her heart hurt.

She called Oliver. His 'hello' was flustered and she could hear a high-pitched reedy cry in the background.

'Who's that crying? What's happened?'

'Nothing's happened. Everything's fine.'

'But I can hear someone crying.'

'It's nothing. Just a stupid argument.'

'It doesn't sound like nothing.'

'For fuck's sake, Sarah. They were perfectly OK until just a second ago. It'll be forgotten in a minute. I can manage, you know. The world doesn't fall apart just because you've gone away for a night.'

'Sorry. I know you can manage. I'm just jittery, that's all. I'm dreading what's going to happen next. We've all been summoned to the lobby in half an hour's time in exercise gear.'

'I did say—'

'And please don't say you told me not to come because I don't think I can bear it.'

'All right.' His voice was gentler now. Conciliatory. 'I know you're having a tough time. Just grit your teeth and keep remembering it's only one night. I'd kill for a night in a hotel. Uninterrupted sleep, big telly to watch whatever you want on. Room service. And isn't there a pool and a spa in the basement?'

'Yes, but we won't have time to do that.'

Even as she was saying it, Sarah was remembering with misgiving the email that had gone around the department from Rachel listing what they would need to bring with them for the weekend. The words 'swimming cossies' had been slipped in far enough down that Sarah had been able to gloss over it. There was no way she was getting into a swimming costume in front of her workmates.

After she'd put the phone down to Oliver, Sarah lifted her case on to her bed and stared at the contents. They'd been told to bring 'active wear', everything in her weeping at the phrase. She extracted the faded blue sweatpants she wore around the house. Oliver loathed them, but that didn't stop her slipping into them the minute she came home from work at night. They were so comfortable. But in the setting of this grown-up, almost luxurious hotel room, the sweatpants looked cheap and shabby. She'd brought one of Oliver's T-shirts to wear with them and, modelling the mismatched ensemble in front of the full-length mirror on the wardrobe, she knew it had been a mistake.

She bumped into Amira by the lifts. The younger woman was wearing a zip-up black top over black Lycra leggings. Her long dark hair was pulled back into a ponytail. She didn't exactly exude glamour but at least she didn't look like someone who last exercised when the Beatles topped the charts.

'I feel like I'm in some reality TV show,' said Amira. 'Like *The Apprentice*. I'm expecting Alan Sugar to pop up any moment and tell us we're all fired.'

'Do you know, I'd welcome being fired right at this moment. At least then I wouldn't have to go through with this.'

In the lobby, some members of Sales and Marketing appeared to be doing warm-up exercises in a joky way that definitely wasn't a joke. At first Sarah had been encouraged by the fact that other staff members were going on the dreaded weekend, thinking their presence might defuse the Rachel Effect – until she'd found out they were forming a separate team, to be 'hosted' by someone else.

'My God, this is like one of those Iron John male-bonding weekends, isn't it?' whispered Charlie, who was waiting on a sofa wearing a pair of long baggy shorts that were clearly from a different era in his life and an ironic 1D T-shirt. 'We're all going to have to go into the forest and daub ourselves with wode and hunt each other with spears.'

The lift doors pinged and Chloe and Paula stepped out, both walking in that stiff way of people trying desperately not to appear self-conscious.

'I look like such a dork,' said Chloe, gesturing down at her endless bare legs in their Lycra shorts. She took off the elastic band holding her hair back and shook it out before putting it back up again.

'Er, hello?' said Paula flatly, standing still to model her outfit, one foot extended in front, arms bent out to the sides. It had to be said, it was not the most flattering look. The trousers were an indeterminate brown colour and rolled up at the ankle and they were teamed with a maroon-coloured hoodie that, judging by the size of it, probably belonged to Ian or her son. What was his name – Cameron? Sarah still found it impossible to believe her own sons would one day become big man-boys, lurching out of bedrooms in their boxers at midday. She was shocked at how much older Paula was looking suddenly. Paula had always seemed older than her years, because

167

of the way she dressed and her air of quiet resignation, but now it was as if she'd aged ten years in the last weeks; her face was leached of colour, her eyes disappearing into swollen puffy cushions of skin.

The 'host' for the sales and marketing team had arrived – a stern-faced young woman in a purple tracksuit who wore a whistle around her neck – and instantly had them all running on the spot in the lobby. Sarah and the others looked on in silence.

'I can't even . . .' said Amira, before tailing off.

The door to the emergency stairs burst open and out came Rachel closely followed by Ewan. Sarah swallowed, her mouth suddenly dry.

'Hello, troops,' called Rachel, with that strange smile that wasn't really a smile. 'Hope you're all warmed up and ready to go.'

She was all in skin-tight Lycra, a silver and pale-blue vest and matching leggings. On her head was a pale-blue baseball cap, through the back of which her black hair was pulled in a sleek ponytail.

Ewan, walking a few steps behind in his Arsenal kit, was like an oversized puppy in her wake. Even through her own twisted-up nerves, Sarah felt a twinge of pity for Chloe. The first experience of rejection was never easy.

A large shape came bounding in through the main hotel doors like a force of energy.

'Howdy, folks.' The shape skidded to a halt.

Through her misery, Sarah registered that the man attached to the greeting was handsome. The kind of handsome you don't normally see outside a TV or cinema screen. He had floppy blond hair, close-set blue eyes and darkish, well-defined eyebrows that lifted when he smiled – as he was doing now. A way of appraising you that wasn't assessing so much as appreciating, as if you were both sharing a marvellous joke.

The effect on the rest of the group was instant. Amira, who'd been sprawling in a chair texting furiously, zipped her phone into her jacket pocket and sat up straight. Charlie peeled himself off the wall where he'd been leaning. Sarah was pretty sure he was holding in his stomach. Chloe reddened as the new arrival glanced her way and a pink flush bloomed like a sudden flower on her chest. Paula seemed to stand up straighter, hoiking up the elasticated waist of her trousers. Even Rachel wasn't immune.

'So you're the one in charge of whipping us all into shape,' she said, giving a smile in his direction that was quite different to the one she normally used. 'How frightened should we be on a scale of one to ten?'

'That'd be an eleven, ma'am.'

Rachel laughed, revealing a tiny dimple in her cheek Sarah didn't think she'd ever noticed before. Behind her, Ewan's face set hard. This would be interesting. Ewan was so used to thinking himself the alpha male of the group.

'I'm Will your personal trainer – or torturer if you prefer. Haha, just kidding. So, we're going to be doing an activity outside this afternoon where we take on the other team over there. Just look at them. It'll be a walk in the park.' He gestured towards the sales and marketing group who were executing a complicated stretching manoeuvre in pairs: this involved one person arching backwards with their arms behind them, while the other stood behind them and linked their own arms through their elbows before lifting. There was an awful lot of grunting.

'It hardly seems fair to pit them against us,' said the new, jolly Rachel. 'Like taking candy from a baby. Look at them, they're quaking in their boots.'

They weren't the only ones. Sarah was afraid, with the kind of low-level fear that winds itself around your internal organs like bindweed. She tried to get herself in check. She just needed to make it through the next twenty-four hours and then tomorrow she'd be home again. She should relax. But all the time she was conscious of the thing she wasn't saying like an abscess inside her waiting to burst.

Outside on the lawn an obstacle course had been laid out in two matching lines. The tightness in Sarah's chest intensified as her eyes took in the long tunnel made of netting and the hoops laid out in formation and what looked horribly like items of fancy dress.

The sales and marketing team were already running laps in preparation.

'I feel like I've died and woken up in student rag week hell,' said Charlie. 'Please tell me we're not going to have to put those hideous clothes on. Surely there's some clause in our contract that prohibits the public humiliation of employees by being forced to wear outfits from Stag 'n' Hen Warehouse? Those things don't look very hygienic.'

Will clapped his hands.

'Your attention, please, ladies and gents. Before the games commence, and just in case it wasn't exciting enough for you already, we have a special guest star joining us. It's your very own CEO, Mark Hamilton. Don't say we don't spoil you.'

A slight figure stepped out from behind an outbuilding, where presumably he'd been lurking all this time. Sarah couldn't remember ever seeing the company boss outside of the office, and had never spoken to him directly. He had thinning sandy hair the same colour as his eyelashes, and today he was wearing expensive-looking Italian shoes and grey trousers that certainly didn't look like 'active wear' – though as a concession to informality he'd teamed them with a navy-blue polo shirt that still bore the creases from the shop shelf. Beneath his golf-course tan he wore an expression that could either have been a painful smile or a look of grim resignation. Sarah thought about the disciplinary warning and the thing she hadn't yet told anyone. This was the man who'd be making the ultimate decision about what happened to her. And now she was expected to crawl on her stomach in front of him, wearing a nylon Afro wig.

Will whispered to the red-faced woman in charge of the sales and marketing team and then put his hand up, signalling for attention.

'Right, guys. First off we have the obstacle race, but we don't want you to just run through the course as you are, because that would be boring, right? So we're going to sex things up a little bit. What we want first is for you to get into pairs within your teams.'

Sarah felt a stab of remembered trauma, a legacy from schooldays when it was social suicide to be the one singleton who had to pair up with the teacher. She grabbed Charlie.

'Quick, for God's sake be my partner before I have to cosy up to Mark Hamilton.'

They looked around. Amira had paired up with Chloe, Rachel with Ewan, leaving poor Paula standing alone attempting a 'good sport' smile.

'Looks like it's you and me,' Mark Hamilton told her, trying his best to sound as if this was a delightful outcome.

'Right,' yelled the red-faced woman in an unmistakable Antipodean accent. 'I haven't introduced myself to everyone yet. My name is Yvette and I'm in charge of this bunch of reprobates.' Cue a dutiful cheer from sales and marketing. 'The aim of this exercise we're about to do is to engender a sense of cooperation. Working together.'

'Thanks so much for explaining what cooperation means,' whispered Charlie.

'So, one member of each team is going to complete the course while the other one shouts instructions from the side, but the complication is that the person doing the course is blindfolded.'

'Bloindfolded,' parroted Charlie in her ear.

'Well, baggsy you're the one being bloindfolded. There's no way I'm doing that.'

'Oh come on, Sarah. You know how crap I am at any kind of physical activity. Remember when we tried to do Ooops Upside Your Head at the Christmas party?'

'Yes, but that was after ten pints of wine. You're doing it, Charlie. I'm not even going to discuss it.'

Something in her voice, some edge of desperation perhaps, stopped him, mouth open ready to protest.

The race seemed never-ending. They had to take it in

turns to compete, a pair from each team racing against each other. By the time Sarah and Charlie were up, second from last, their team was trailing by one to two. Amira and Chloe had won their race – just – while Paula's reluctance to raise her voice to the company boss meant Mark Hamilton had spent a lot of time gazing blindly around, shouting, 'Where now?' into the ether.

'If that wig feels slippery to the touch, it's not going anywhere near my head,' Charlie warned Sarah. 'Just think of all those sweaty skulls that have already been in it.'

They were pitted against a duo of twenty-somethings from Sales and Marketing who delighted in playing to the crowd, making exaggerated limbering-up moves at the starting line and then the blindfolded one staggering about like Frankenstein's monster while his partner cracked an imaginary whip behind his back.

'Please God let this be over quickly,' said Charlie as Will tied the blindfold tightly over his eyes.

'You OK?' Will asked, catching sight of the plaster on Charlie's arm. 'That looks nasty.'

'I'm fine,' said Charlie. 'Extreme tin-opening injury.'

Ewan was jumping up and down on the balls of his feet.

'There's still time to catch up,' he said urgently. 'Just hold them off for this one and then Rachel and I will smash it in the next round.'

As soon as the whistle went, their opponents dropped the comedy act and revealed their competitive side.

'Forward, forward. Hit the floor! Wriggle, wriggle, faster. Come on!'

By the time they were at the second stage – the hoops

– Charlie was still attempting to find the entrance to the net tunnel.

'Left a bit. No, sorry, I meant right.'

'Oh, for fuck's sake!'

'Give me a break.'

Sarah heard the muttering but didn't dare turn round to see who was talking. The woman in the sales team put her foot out of the hoop formation and had to go back to the beginning.

'Go, Charlie! This is your chance! Take her!'

That was unmistakably Rachel's voice. High-pitched and reed-thin.

Finally Charlie was out of the netting and negotiating the hoops, at which he was surprisingly adept. Come to think of it, he had very small feet for a man, which probably helped.

By the time they'd been over the climbing thing, Charlie was neck and neck with his rival. Almost against her will, Sarah found herself getting drawn into the drama of the whole thing, her voice rising as she tried to navigate Charlie towards the fancy dress. 'Forward, forward. No – too far! Left a bit . . . a bit more. Right, pick up! PICK UP!'

Poor Charlie lumbered to a stop and swooped down on a pair of discarded sailor's trousers.

'On! On! On!' came the chant from behind Sarah.

Charlie dutifully flailed around to find the opening, only instead of stepping into them, he put them over his head, clearly imagining them to be some sort of sweater or jacket instead.

'Aargh. Ghmph,' he said from inside his polyester prison.

Sarah felt the adrenaline mixing with her heightened nerves and lack of sleep. She started laughing. He was so funny, staggering around with a pair of trousers on his head. Then she found she couldn't stop.

'Tell him what to do!' yelled Ewan.

But Sarah couldn't speak. Tears were running down her face as she convulsed with laughter. The giggling from behind her subsided as the sales' team candidate started pulling on her fancy dress costume at a rate of knots and now there came irritated entreaties to 'get a grip'. Still she couldn't stop laughing, or perhaps she was crying. Charlie was trying to get the trousers off but his head had become stuck in one of the legs. Her knees suddenly wobbly, Sarah sat down on the damp grass. She heard Rachel say, 'Bloody brilliant,' in a voice that dripped with disgust as the sales woman stormed across the finish line to resounding cheers from her team.

'Classic,' said Amira in Sarah's ear, but even she sounded like she was biting back disappointment.

'Never mind, guys. Good effort,' said Will brightly. 'Remember, we're all on the same side so let's pull together. It's all a bit of fun. Rachel and Ewan, you're up next.'

'Yes, but we can't win,' said Rachel, mock-pouting for Will's benefit.

'You're all winners to me,' he replied.

'Fuckwit,' said Charlie, flinging himself down next to Sarah. He looked puce-faced and flustered, his hair sticking to his forehead in damp curls. 'If I catch an STA from those trousers, I'm going to sue.'

'Everyone seems to be taking it very seriously,' whispered Sarah. Now she'd calmed down, the nauseous feeling was back, clogging up her throat like something she'd accidentally swallowed and couldn't cough back up. She thought about her boys and wondered what they were doing right this moment.

Ewan and Rachel predictably won their race, with Rachel doing the actions and Ewan bellowing commands from the sideline, his limbs in perpetual motion as if he could remotely propel her to victory. Chloe had turned her back on them to chat to Will. From the way her head was cocked to one side and the toe of one trainer was tracing a pattern in the grass, Sarah surmised there was some high-level flirting going on. Well, good luck to her. Rejection was a bitch. Sarah could still remember on her wedding day that sudden rush of relief that she never again had to go on a shitty date, never again had to feel the hot shame of having allowed herself to fall in love only to realize she'd read it all wrong. She thought about Oliver and the way he'd looked when he turned around and saw her coming down the aisle of the church, the gratitude in his face, and for a horrible moment she thought she might start crying again. Love was so tricky, with all its layers and pockets where things could get lost or tucked away so tightly you forgot they were even there.

'They may have won the battle, but we can still win the war,' said Will, when everyone was assembled again. 'Am I right?'

'Yesss!' yelled Chloe, her voice tailing off when she realized she was the only one.

'We were going to mix it up a bit here with an indoors activity, but the forecast is for rain later on, so we'll carry on out here while we're still all so pumped up.'

Sarah's spirits, which had momentarily lifted when he'd mentioned the word 'indoors', came slamming down again. As they followed Will around the side of the hotel and down a sloping lawn towards a field at the bottom hidden by a hedge of tall trees, Sarah watched his broad shoulders and his easy swagger and wondered if her boys would grow up like this, so completely at home in their own skin, so uncomplicatedly happy to be themselves. Or might she in fact prefer them to be challenging and spiky, all dark depths and deep hollows?

So engrossed was she in her ruminations that Sarah failed to give a thought to what the next activity might be until they were through the gap in the hedge. She stopped in her tracks.

'Now I know it might look daunting, but believe me, it's not once you get up there.'

Will was grinning as if his saying it should be enough to put their minds at rest. But nothing he could say would make it better. Sarah gazed at the structure: two towers at least ten metres tall and forty metres apart, connected by a wire with ropes to hold on to on either side.

'Don't look so horrified – it's Sarah, isn't it?' Will switched his smile in her direction as if he was adjusting the beam of an anglepoise lamp. 'It's really fine. And this one's not a competition. The other team are off doing their own thing. This is all about working together. So you'll all be wearing harnesses and be tied together with ropes so you'll have each other's backs. Literally. The idea is for the whole team to make it from one tower to the other. You'll be working together with the stronger

177

ones helping the weaker ones across, because if one goes, you all go . . . Only kidding. No one is going to go because you're all attached also to the top wire.'

Sarah glanced across at Charlie who was muttering something under his breath. It wasn't a prayer.

'I can't do this,' she hissed at him.

He shrugged and shook his head.

'No choice, babe,' Amira whispered. 'Anyway, I think it might actually be quite fun. There's no real danger.'

'No,' Sarah said, her voice wobbling. 'You don't understand . . .'

'Now, before we start, I just need to run through some health and safety stuff. Yawn, yawn, right?'

Mark Hamilton, who'd been staring nervously up at the climbing structure, gave a weak smile. 'Bane of my life,' he said.

'So,' Will continued, 'I just need to make sure none of you are epileptic, diabetic, pregnant, have a heart condition or breathing problems, blah, blah, blah.'

'Nope,' said Rachel. 'I checked all that in the personnel files to make sure we were all good to go.'

'Cool,' said Will. 'Well, if you'll just step this way, Katie here will give out the forms you have to sign for the insurance company to say I've told you the risks so if you all drop dead of heart attacks it's not my fault. Then we'll get you all rigged up.'

A young girl who'd just joined them raised a limp hand. She didn't look old enough to have left school, let alone work for the same corporate events company as Will. She didn't look old enough to be out of school, quite frankly. Maybe she was on work experience or something. Normally Sarah would have made a joke of it to Charlie but she couldn't bring herself to speak. Her heart was hammering against her ribs as she took the form from the girl's outstretched hand and waited for the one pen to make its way around. Her hand hovered over the paper.

'I can't,' she croaked.

'Course you can,' said Rachel. She had that smile on but behind it her voice was snappy, as if it was on a spring-hinge, the words rat-a-tatting out.

'There's always someone who's reluctant at first,' said Will. 'But you know I haven't had one single group where, when we finish, everyone doesn't say, "I'm so glad I did that."'

Sarah could feel one of her legs shaking as if it had gone into spasm.

'No, I can't.'

'Oh, come on.' Even Charlie was losing patience. 'The sooner we do it, the sooner we can get to the bar for a stiff drink. Look, Paula's signed it.'

Paula nodded. She looked pale, but determined. Sarah saw her glance over at Mark Hamilton and wondered if she was trying to impress him, and if so, was it because he was her boss, or whether in some weird, unfathomable way she might actually fancy him. But the distraction was fleeting. Her attention was once again drawn to the tower she'd be expected to climb, and that wire running from it to the next one. From this angle it looked finer than cotton thread.

'Stop overthinking it,' said Will gently. 'It's OK to be scared.'

'I'm not scared,' said Sarah, and to her horror she began once again to cry. 'I'm pregnant.'

24

Anne

The visit to the Egans' family home changed the dynamic between Ed Kowalsky and me. You might expect such a shared experience to bring us closer together, but in fact the opposite was true. It was as if we'd both participated in something shameful so that, once back in our own world, we couldn't quite meet each other's eyes. What we'd witnessed downstairs in that basement made us somehow complicit and we avoided talking about it as much as we could. For the first time since we'd started working together I began to wish Ed had picked someone else to help him with the assessment.

I knew this case was still my ticket to a different life. But in my weaker moments, lying awake trying to summon up sleep, when images of that pulley and hook would roll backwards and forwards across my mind, I'd find myself longing to go back in time to before we set foot in that house, before I even heard of Child L. Let someone else have the glory – and the nightmares.

We knew from the police and child welfare reports that Laurie had been actively involved in both the feeding of and the punishment of her brother, but we had no idea to what extent she'd been forced into these chores,

180

or whether indeed she just considered them to be a normal part of life.

Laurie's parents were being kept in separate jails on different sides of town. When Ed first told me Noelle Egan had agreed to see us, I felt utterly conflicted. Professional curiosity made me thankful for the opportunity to get up close to a woman who had dissociated herself so completely from one child while retaining a maternal connection to a second. But another part of me kept remembering that dank basement that smelled like something had died in it, and the hook on the end of the rope, and the hand sanitizer on the way out. The media called her a monster and while I didn't believe in monsters, I obviously had an issue with mothers.

'She'll only meet with us once. That's her condition for seeing us,' said Ed when he first told me the news, his eyes sliding off me as if I was coated in oil. 'Which is a pity because the rules only allow two visitors at a time. I had to make an executive decision whether to bring you or Dan Oppenheimer, but I decided that as Laurie is the one who has a chance of a new life, I would bring you with me today. It's a great opportunity for us to contextualize Laurie.'

Contextualize her. That's how he talked.

'Plus she also said she didn't want to discuss the boy.' He threw this in like an afterthought, rather than the deciding factor I guessed it to be.

The correctional facility where Noelle was being kept pending her trial was fifty kilometres out of town to the north. Once again we drove there in Ed's station wagon but this time he'd removed the child seats from the back. I wanted to ask him if it was to make sure he reacted to

Laurie's mother as a psychiatrist rather than a parent, but it seemed too personal.

The facility itself was small. There was too much interest in the case for the authorities to risk placing her in a larger jail where corruption was rife and staff morale rock bottom, and where gangs of inmates ran the show. Women who harm children don't fare well in jail. Women who harm their own children fare the worst.

After we'd gone through the two sets of gates, topped by whorls of barbed wire, we pulled up in front of a low-slung modern building.

'Looks like the kind of place you go to get your accounts audited,' I said.

We were thoroughly searched before we were allowed inside. Ed became agitated when the uniformed woman searching his briefcase pulled out his notebook and, holding it by the spine, shook it to see if anything was hidden within the pages.

'Be careful with that. There's important research in there.'

After crossing a small, empty yard, a guard unlocked a door which led to a cramped vestibule and a second locked door, which only opened once the one behind us had clanked shut.

Finally we were shown into a room containing a beige Formica table and four hard wooden chairs. The bars on the window blocked the sun so the room felt gloomy and noticeably cooler than the corridor we'd just exited. Ed and I arranged ourselves behind the table facing the door and sat side by side in silence. I'd been so taken up with the technicalities of getting into the prison that I hadn't given much thought to meeting Noelle herself, but now I found myself growing nervous.

Ed retrieved his notebook from his briefcase and dug around in the side pocket for a pen. He opened the book on a fresh page and wrote *Noelle Egan, interview* with today's date. Then he underlined it. Twice. We waited some more. By the time the door swung open, I had a dent in the pad of my right thumb where I'd been digging the nail of my index finger into the skin.

First through the door was a heavyset female guard wearing a uniform in different shades of brown polyester that made a loud rustling noise when she moved. Attached to her left wrist, so tight the skin was puckered around it, was a metal handcuff. And attached to that handcuff was Noelle Egan.

She bore no resemblance to the wedding photos the newspapers kept printing, nor to the framed family portrait I'd seen in her living room.

This Noelle had lank hair that hung from her head in solid clumps. Free from the heavy foundation she favoured in the photos, her skin was sallow, even yellowish in places, and lumpy with spots. Her eyebrows, which in the pictures were plucked into two perfect thin arches, had grown out and were sparse and unkempt, like randomly planted seedlings. The prissy blouse had been replaced by a regulation khaki prison uniform. Only the eyes, with that lifeless stare, were the same.

Ed stood up to shake hands before remembering her right hand was shackled. He froze, half standing, half sitting.

'Hi, Noelle. I'm Professor Ed Kowalsky and this is my assistant, Dr Anne Cater.'

I bristled at that word, assistant, though I had no illusions I was anything but the junior partner in this team.

'As I'm sure has been explained to you, the state has charged me with evaluating the um . . . *well-being* of your children so we can get a better understanding of the impact recent events have had on them, and work out the best long-term plan of action. As Dr Cater and I have been working with Laurie, we're going to focus on her and we're hoping you'll be able to . . .'

I stiffened in my chair. Please let him not be about to say 'contextualize' again.

'. . . fill in some of the background details so we can get a fuller picture.'

Noelle, who'd been uncuffed from her guard, sat down in one of the chairs opposite us and stared at him from her strange dead-fish eyes.

'There's no need to *evaluate* Laurie,' she said eventually. Her voice was as flat as her gaze. 'She's a perfectly normal little girl. She's never wanted for anything.'

Ed swallowed loudly enough for all of us to hear it.

'Yeah, well, that's why we're here. So that you can give us a bit more insight into her life at home and we can start to build up a picture that will help us work out how best to support her. I'm sure we all want what's best for her.'

The guard, who was standing against the wall behind Noelle, made a *pff* noise, blowing air out through her mouth as if to demonstrate what she thought about this statement. This was a woman who'd kept her son in a cage. Did we seriously believe she had her children's best interests at heart?

'You don't need to worry about Laurie, she's perfectly happy. She's always perfectly happy.'

I looked for any signs that she was aware how glib that sounded, any fidgeting of the fingers, or darting of the eyes in one direction or another. But there was nothing. Noelle Egan genuinely seemed to believe happiness was possible, even inevitable, despite what Laurie had experienced in the basement of her house every day of her life.

'Can you give us some kind of background, Noelle, to how this all started – the circumstances in which your son, David, was born?'

Noelle recoiled as if she'd been hit when Ed said the word 'David', and I wondered if this was his intention. For the three weeks after a pizza delivery boy who turned up at the Egan house by mistake heard a noise and pressed his eye up to the vent in the brick at ground level, the authorities had struggled to find a name for the child known to his family only as 'It' or 'Thing'. Noelle and Peter Egan refused to give up the name, perhaps because by naming him, they'd be humanizing him. And it seemed it had never occurred to Laurie that the Thing in the basement might have a name. Only when police investigators finally discovered Noelle's maiden name and traced her back to Missouri, where she'd first lived with Peter, did they find the birth records listing the boy as David Egan.

'I didn't have a very happy childhood.' I blinked at Noelle in surprise when she started speaking. I'd expected her to be unforthcoming, even though I knew she'd been told that helping us could improve her chances of avoiding a life sentence for child abuse and neglect, particularly if she could claim to have been unduly influenced or coerced by her husband.

'My parents were religious and very strict. I always knew my father had wanted a son, and he made it clear I was nothing but a disappointment to him right from the start. He avoided me wherever possible, and my mom, who was totally dominated by him, resented me for making him upset with her. So I got the message real early that I was a screw-up. It didn't help that something went wrong when she had me and she had to have a hysterectomy so they couldn't have any more children. By the time I was ten I was cutting myself with anything I could get my hands on. At twelve I was drinking hard liquor. By fifteen I was sleeping with guys twice my age. Sometimes two at a time. Until I met Peter, my life was one long spiral downwards.'

The words gushed out of her as if she'd been swilling them around her mouth just waiting for a chance to release them. She glanced up and caught my eye and I got the impression she was checking to see how they'd gone down. We'd already heard that Noelle's legal team was going to claim she was mentally unfit to stand trial, that her upbringing and early experiences had left her too damaged to be accountable. Maybe I should have felt sorry for her. There was no doubt life had dealt her a cruddy hand, but I couldn't get past the idea that she was practising for her eventual appearance in front of a jury. There was a throbbing in my temple when I thought of that cage in the basement and the possibility of Noelle avoiding jail, but I reminded myself she wasn't my concern. It wasn't her we were charged with assessing.

'Peter saved me from all that. I met him at a bar. I was

out of it. I'd taken something – pills or I don't know what. He sat next to me and started talking to me and I thought he was just one more guy hitting on me, but he wasn't. He was from Missouri. He worked for a huge firm of accountants there who had clients in lots of different states, so he was in town doing a huge audit.'

'We get it. He was a big shot. You fell for him.' I wanted to hear her say it. I wanted her to take responsibility for this at least, for allowing Peter Egan into her life.

'I was overwhelmed by him.' When Noelle turned her empty eyes to mine, I had to repress a shudder. It was like looking into a void.

'He was the first and only man to tell me I was beautiful – or he said I could be beautiful if I took more pride in myself. He bought me nice clothes, make-up, gave me money to get my hair done. No one had ever paid that kind of attention to me before. I was totally under his spell. He loved that I was so vulnerable. So alone.'

Now Noelle turned her flat gaze to Ed and it occurred to me that she wanted him to feel sorry for her, for what she'd been through. The woman had so little self-awareness, it was textbook narcissism. And of course as soon as that thought occurred to me I wondered if that was exactly what this was, an off-the-peg personality disorder she'd researched and adopted to help her case.

'And you were in love with him?' asked Ed.

'I was besotted with him. I thought he would save me from the hell my life had become. Isn't that a psychological condition? Don't you call that "rescue fantasy"?'

187

You had to hand it to her, she'd done her research.

'So you moved to Missouri with him. Got married. Tell me about Laurie's birth,' I asked, wanting to move the conversation on.

'Oh my. Never has there been a child more wanted or loved. I doted on her. We both did. Right from the first scan where I knew she was a girl I bought her clothes – the cutest, tiniest little pink dresses – and we both talked to her. Through my belly, ya know? Pete used to call us his two princesses – "how've my two princesses been today?" he'd ask when he came home. And for a few weeks after she was born, he was just euphoric. He couldn't do enough for me. Back then.'

She looked up. To make sure we'd registered that past tense.

'So what changed?' asked Ed, conscious of the time, the disapproving guard, the allotted visiting hour ticking away.

'He changed. Pete. He started getting jealous. I'd never made a secret of my past, but suddenly it was like he was obsessed by it. He kept thinking men were hitting on me, or I was hitting on them. Asking me, again and again. How many men did I sleep with? What did I do with them? You know, sex stuff. Now I know he was sick. All the time I knew him, he'd been on meds. I didn't know it then but it turns out it's seriously heavy shit. Then, around the time Laurie was born, he stopped taking them.'

'Allegedly,' I said, at the exact same moment that Ed said, 'That's all for his defence team to prove.'

Noelle's expression didn't change.

'How old was Laurie when you became pregnant again?'

'Around seven months. I was so happy when I got the positive test. I thought it would make Pete forget about all that other stuff, but instead it made him worse. He was convinced the baby wasn't his. Kept asking me again and again who I'd slept with, whose baby it was. He said the dates didn't match up. But they did!'

'So the baby *was* his?' I asked.

For the first time there was a flicker of something in Noelle's black eyes when she looked at me. The little hairs on the back of my neck stood up.

'Of course. But he wouldn't believe it. He kept on and on about the baby. He said everything about it was different to Laurie – from the shape of my bump to the way I was so sick every morning. When we had the first scan, he didn't say a word. On the way home he told me the baby was clearly deformed. He said it was obvious from the screen but the radiographer just didn't want to tell me. That's how he was for the whole pregnancy, telling me the baby wasn't his, that it was mutant, that it was bad.'

'Bad?' Ed asked.

'You know. Evil. And the thing was, I felt it too – that there was something wrong with the baby, some kind of bad energy. Do you know what I'm talking about?' She looked at both of us, as if waiting for us to agree with her.

'How was it when the baby was born?' I asked her. 'Did Peter come round?'

Noelle shook her head.

'Not at all. He wouldn't even stay with me in the hospital. Said he couldn't bear to see what was going to come out of me. I was so scared on my own in that hospital room. The labour was horrible. Thirty-six hours of agony. It was like my body was fighting against the baby, trying to stop it being born. When it came out, I couldn't look at it for fear that it would be some sort of monster.'

'He,' I said before I could stop myself. 'Your baby was a he, Noelle. And he was perfect, wasn't he, despite what Peter had said?'

'Some deformities aren't on the outside,' she said. 'The doctor gave the baby to me and tried to get me to put it on the breast but I didn't want it near me. I used a bottle, right from the start. Not like with Laurie. I breastfed her until she was three years old.'

Looking around as if she wanted a medal or something.

'How was Peter's relationship with the baby when you got home?'

'Relationship? I don't think you could call it that. Pete couldn't bear the noise it made. It was a real demanding baby. All the time screaming. Crying. No matter what I did. He made it sleep downstairs in the utility room so we couldn't hear it.'

'How about Laurie? How did she react to him?'

'She was only a baby herself. She just seemed to accept everything as it was. She didn't know any different.'

'You must have taken him for check-ups after you were discharged from hospital,' I said.

'Sure. One or two. But then Pete got offered another job. Out of state. With one of the client's companies, here in La Luz City. I didn't want to move. I had friends in Missouri – other moms, you know. But Pete, he didn't listen. He still thought I'd slept with half the state.

Wanted a new start, so we moved here, to the house on Franklin Street. Total clean break. I hoped at least the move might stop him acting so crazy, but it just made him worse.

'He said the baby would have to sleep in the basement. Said it would be too shameful for new neighbours to see it. Insisted they'd know it was deformed.'

'And you just let it happen, without raising any objections?' I tried to keep my voice level, but it rose up at the end.

'You've got to realize the kind of person Pete is. He's real clever, real powerful. He gets into your head, you know. He takes over your thoughts. Right from the beginning he was telling me there was something wrong with the baby. Then he started saying we needed to keep it away from Laurie, you know, so she wouldn't be affected by it. Polluted by it.'

'Surely one of the neighbours must have noticed you moving in with the baby?' Ed asked. 'I mean, you must have had baby stuff. A stroller, for example.'

Noelle stared at him dully. 'What did it need a stroller for? It never went out.'

'Well, a crib then?'

'We arrived in the evening, after dark. Pete made sure of that. So no one saw us going into the house. Like I said, Laurie was still pretty much a baby herself so if anyone saw us taking baby stuff into the house they'd assume it was for her. And if they heard it crying, they'd think that was her too. Anyway, Pete's very good with his hands and it wasn't long before he had that basement soundproofed, and he built that special room in there.'

'Room? You mean the cage?' I asked.

Noelle ignored me.

'It was quite comfortable down there. Kind of cosy, you know?'

'I still don't get why you didn't just leave it with the welfare services in Missouri?' asked Ed, not even realizing he'd fallen into Noelle's way of referring to her son. 'You clearly hadn't bonded with it. Why not get rid of the baby? Start again afresh.'

Noelle stared at him as if he'd said something outrageous.

'It was my baby. There was no question that it – he – wouldn't come with me. That's what being a mother is. You don't get to pick and choose. You deal with what you're given.'

She was something all right.

'And after you moved in, you never registered David with any health agency?'

'No authorities. Pete said it was better for us and for Laurie that no one knew about it, on account of it being so deformed.'

'Deformed?' asked Ed, scribbling furiously in his notebook.

'Deformed physically and mentally. It wasn't normal at all.'

'If a child doesn't get any mental or emotional stimulation and is kept physically bound, it won't develop normally. Surely you must see that?'

I'd spoken without thinking and Ed put his hand on my arm.

'Let's not forget, Anne, we're here to find out information to help us help Laurie, not to make judgements.'

192

I felt my cheeks flame.

'When did Peter start physically assaulting the boy?' Ed asked.

'Assault? That's not what it was. You have to understand this wasn't a normal child. You couldn't deal with it like you would a normal child. It didn't understand that sort of dialogue. It responded only to physical stimuli. Food . . . pain . . . it was that way from the time it first opened its eyes.'

'So Laurie grew up knowing only that there was this sub-human *thing* in the basement?'

'Pete thought it was important that she was exposed to it very early – so she wouldn't be fazed by it. So as soon as she could walk, he'd take her down there to feed it. And he taught her how to discipline it if it got out of hand. It's like those kids who grow up in houses where the parents speak different languages and turn out bilingual. If they're exposed to something at an early enough age, they absorb it naturally and it becomes just something normal. No big deal.'

'So he thought there was less chance of her talking to other people about it if it was just something run of the mill.'

Noelle nodded at Ed, as if she was pleased to be understood. Like we were agreeing with her or something.

'So from early on, she was feeding and disciplining her brother. Did she enjoy that?'

Noelle frowned.

'No. I wouldn't say she enjoyed it. It's like it was a household chore – you know, that she had to do, like scraping her plate into the trash or emptying out the kitty litter tray, if we had a cat. She put up with it.'

'But she must have asked you why he was down there?'

'Not really. She just accepted that it was bad. And that's why it was down there and she wasn't. She had a really good life, you know. We gave her everything, we took her everywhere. Pete doted on that girl. She knew we were good people, so she accepted what we told her without question, especially Pete. She'd have done anything he told her to.'

She paused. Then out of the blue: 'How is she? How's my baby?'

I started. It was the first time Noelle had shown any curiosity about her daughter. I stared at her, trying to work out if her concern was genuine or put on for our benefit, as if she had just remembered how a normal mother would act.

'She needs me, you know.' Noelle's hitherto emotionless voice now rose to a high, almost squeaky pitch. 'It's wrong to separate young children from their parents. You will tell them that, won't you? When you make your recommendations? You will explain that a child needs its mom?'

25
Paula

Sarah, pregnant *again*? Oh, she couldn't be, she just couldn't. Not when she'd only been back at work less than a year.

Paula vividly remembered what a nightmare it had been trying to cover for her while she'd been gone having Joe. The original replacement had left after only four months and then there'd been a succession of temporary placements each more useless than the last, meaning they'd all had to shoulder a lot more than their normal workload until finally Sarah returned, having taken her full year's maternity entitlement. And two years before that, she'd had another year off to have Sam. Paula didn't begrudge any woman having a family. But the thought of going through all that disruption again set her nerves crawling. And just when they were trying to prove that the department didn't need shaking up. Paula had always liked Sarah, always considered them to be friends – so why hadn't she come to her first instead of blurting it out so publicly?

'Rachel, I take it you didn't know about this?' As they gathered around the base of the climbing tower on the first day of the team-bonding weekend, Mark Hamilton turned to face his most recent employee.

Rachel shook her head. Her face was flushed red, and Paula could tell from the twitching muscle at the side of her mouth that she must be biting down on her back teeth. This bombshell was not going to make her look good in front of her boss. In spite of Paula's own frustration at the news, she couldn't help feeling a twinge of satisfaction when she observed Rachel's discomfort. It was the first time she'd seen her boss this nonplussed. It made her seem more human.

Sarah was still crying, slow tears that slid down her cheeks and left drip marks on her T-shirt. Charlie stiffly put his arm around her, but Paula could tell from his stunned expression that he too was learning this news for the first time, and that it wasn't exactly a welcome surprise.

'Well. Nothing like a bit of drama to blow off the cobwebs,' said Will, grinning round at everyone as if the force of his niceness might be enough to get them all back on an even keel. 'Sarah will just have to shout encouragement from ground level. Shall we start?'

But the atmosphere of that first race where they'd all been rooting for each other – well, until Sarah and Charlie had spoiled things – had completely evaporated. Paula felt its loss keenly. There had been a moment when she and Mark Hamilton had been the only ones left unpaired and he'd turned to her and given her a mock bow, and just for a minute the tension that was as much a part of her as the rheumatism in her left thumb, or the mole on her shoulder that she checked religiously in the mirror every night in case it had changed shape during the day, had lifted and she'd felt pounds – no, stones – lighter. Not that she thought Mark Hamilton fancied her or anything. The few times they'd met in the office, his eyes had slid right over the top of her, even while his smile was still aimed in her general direction. But still in that moment she'd felt acknowledged, and that was enough.

Now, though, the mood was sombre as they queued to be fitted into their harnesses. Paula, being the most reluctant, was at the back. She noticed that Rachel's face was stretched tight as if she was clenching every single muscle simultaneously.

'I'd love to take a year-long holiday every couple of years,' muttered Ewan, out of earshot of his bosses.

Paula rolled her eyes. Ewan would find out soon enough that babies were about as far away from a holiday as it was possible to get. But for now she was too ruffled herself by Sarah's news to set him straight.

'Well, I think it's really lovely,' said Chloe, whose arrival in the office had coincided with the end of Sarah's last maternity leave so she'd hardly been affected. 'Honestly, I don't think it's very feminist of you all to be so mean about it. It's a woman's right to have children and just because it's not very convenient for the rest of us doesn't mean we can all act so snotty about it.'

'You won't be saying that when you have to do loads of extra work to make up for us being a person down,' said Amira.

'Bet Rachel's gutted. Just let her try sacking Sarah now,' said Charlie.

'Do you think that's why she did it?' asked Ewan.

Charlie made a snorting noise. 'Pregnancy on demand? It doesn't quite work that way. Even Sarah isn't that fecund.'

By this time Chloe, Mark and Rachel had started climbing the tower. The others, having been clipped into their harnesses by Will's child-like assistant Katie, were lined up waiting for their turn.

'It's Paula, isn't it?' Will was standing so close she could virtually feel the warmth from his wide beam. 'If you're a bit nervous, it might be an idea to swap places with Ewan here so that he's behind you. That way, you'll feel a bit more supported.'

Ewan obligingly unclipped his safety harness and the belt tying him to the person in front and Will helped Paula to get her own harness on. Only now, standing at the foot of the tower that looked a lot taller from this angle than it had from afar, did she start thinking about what she was about to do. What was she thinking? She was far too old to be doing this. It was irresponsible. How would her family cope if anything happened to her? Ian wouldn't be able to afford the mortgage. The kids would lose their home.

She tugged on the thick cord that attached her to Ewan, now bringing up the rear. Her palms were slick with sweat and she wished she wasn't wearing Ian's bulky sweatshirt but couldn't take it off without having to undo the whole harness.

'Gosh, it's hot, isn't it?' she asked Charlie who was now in front of her.

He looked at her as if she'd just said something incomprehensible.

'Not so much,' he replied eventually.

'Just me then,' she said. And tried to smile.

Now she noticed that Charlie was also looking pale and apprehensive. Poor thing. He was also way out of his comfort zone. It must be hard being a non-alpha man in this sort of environment. At least everyone *expected* her to be rubbish at it.

As if on cue, Will shouted over: 'Right, next one up. Come on, you guys are doing seriously awesome. Give yourself a cheer.'

There was a resounding silence followed by a thin 'yay' from Sarah, standing next to Will, looking cold and miserable in her T-shirt. So it was just Paula then, feeling as if there was a microwave heating her up from the inside out.

Ahead of her, Charlie had started climbing. He took delicate but deliberate steps, setting his dinky feet on the rungs in a rhythm. Paula's heart pounded as she watched him, knowing she was next. Was it too late to pull out? She pictured herself unclipping the rope that connected her to the others and stepping out of the line. 'Sorry,' she'd joke. 'I wouldn't make it far on *I'm a Celebrity*, would I?' She looked across at Sarah who was going to be staying safely on the ground and felt a whoosh of envy.

'Right, Paula. Let's see what you're made of,' shouted Will. 'Let's see you shimmying up that tower.'

Paula put one foot on the first rung of the tower, cursing her imitation Converse shoes that her daughter Amy had giggled about for a good ten minutes when she'd spotted them that morning. Amy had even taken a selfie of herself wearing them to send around her friends, using that application that erased photos almost instantly so that no one could pass it on. Thinking about Amy and Cam and how they'd kill themselves laughing if they could see her now spurred Paula on to go up another two rungs. It wasn't so bad as long as you didn't look up or down.

Below, she heard Sarah shout: 'Brilliant, Paula. You're doing really well!'

As she neared the top, she could feel her legs starting to wobble. The rungs were slippery under her hands and she paused and hooked an elbow through so she could hug the ladder with one hand and wipe the palm of the other on her trousers.

Charlie's face appeared over the top looking slack with relief.

'Come on, Paula. If I can do it, anyone can. Just one little vault and you'll be here.'

By now everything was wobbling – arms, legs, even the soles of her feet as they balanced on the metal rungs – and the sweat was pouring down her back inside her sweatshirt. She was conscious of Ewan standing just beneath her. His fingers tapped impatiently on the metal of the rung just below her feet. Paula took a deep breath in, trying to still her rising panic. Just one more rung. She reached up with her right arm, then her right leg and then felt hands reaching out to clasp hers and . . . she was up.

For a moment, she thought she was going to collapse, but then Amira's arm was around her.

'You did it. Bloody well done.'

Mark Hamilton came towards her with his hand raised so at first she had the alarming impression he was about to hit her.

'High five, teammate,' he said. She wiped her palm surreptitiously on her trousers again before raising it to his.

'Way to go,' yelled Will from the bottom as Ewan, eschewing offers of help, swung himself into the tower. Paula saw him glance across at Rachel to see what sort of impression he'd made. Did he really think he had any chance with their boss? Why couldn't he see that she was just playing him along, keeping him in reserve like a little lap dog?

When Paula was younger, she'd had a friend a bit like Rachel. Claudia had arrived at the school mid-year and Paula had been put in charge of showing her around, after which Claudia had adopted her – at least until something better had come along. All these years on, Paula could still remember the euphoria of those days when Claudia would seek her out or laugh at something she said or, as occasionally happened, invite her back to her rambling Victorian house with her four wild brothers and her bohemian parents who let them drink a glass of wine with their dinner. And then the agony of those times when Claudia would cold-shoulder her in the lunch queue or swap in-jokes with the other girls about funny things that had happened at gatherings Paula hadn't been invited to.

Claudia had soon moved on. Found her natural milieu among the popular kids and by the end of the year Paula found it hard to believe they'd ever hung out together. But since Rachel arrived, Claudia had been popping into Paula's head a lot. Sometimes, during one of her nocturnal insomnia sessions where she'd lie awake listening to Ian's snoring through the wall and worrying about money and how her children were ever going to be able to afford to leave home and whether her life would always be this much of a struggle just to keep

201

going, things that Claudia had said to her would come zinging across the decades. The awful time Claudia had told a mutual friend that Paula didn't even know how to put a tampon in. But over the top of it all, that sense of terrible grief at being cast out without even a chance to prove herself, without even realizing it was happening until it was too late. No question, Ewan was heading for a fall if he kept on running around after Rachel.

'How are we feeling, guys? On top of the world?'

Will looked very small from the platform at the top of the tower. His voice sounded like it was coming from very far away.

'How about giving yourselves a group hug for getting this far. Come on, don't be shy. That's what you're here for.'

'If he has us singing "Kumbaya", I'm jumping,' said Amira.

Still they shuffled into a circle and put their arms stiffly around each other. Paula, who'd found herself suddenly next to Rachel, hoped the other woman couldn't sense her discomfort. Rachel's touch on her back was as light and fleeting as a falling leaf.

Then it was time to cross the wire to the other tower. Paula had deliberately not been allowing herself to think of this part, that endless thin line stretching into oblivion. The way it would wobble under your feet, the way you would look down and see nothing between you and the ground far below.

'It's really not bad,' said Katie, Will's waifish assistant who was buckling a safety cord to their harnesses to attach them to the top wire running parallel to the one they were supposed to walk on. 'That cord is amazingly solid.'

Chloe was first, followed by Rachel. 'Once more into the breach,' Rachel said gaily before stepping out on to the wire. She seemed to be making a concerted effort to put the business with Sarah behind her. Paula wondered whether it was for Mark Hamilton's benefit, then berated herself for being so cynical. She never used to be. Sometimes she wondered if the antidepressants she'd been taking since she and Ian split up were changing her personality. The small print on the leaflet that came with them had said that might be a side effect. Mood altering, it had said. Paula had found that strange, seeing as the whole point of antidepressants as far as she could see *was* to alter your mood – otherwise, really, what were they for?

When Rachel was partway across, the tightening of the cord between her and Mark indicated it was time for him to set off.

'Paula, just so you know, my will's in the top drawer of my desk,' he joked, turning towards her. She was touched when she noticed his hand was shaking and she again had that sense of connection with him that gave her a warm glow, even in the face of her own growing fear.

But by the time a wan-faced Charlie had started inching his way across to the other tower, Paula had forgotten about Mark Hamilton, forgotten about Rachel and about Will standing down below bellowing encouragement beside Sarah, her red hair vivid against the lush green lawn. All she could think of was that thin wire stretching out across the chasm of thin air.

'Off you go, Paula,' said Ewan. 'The quicker we get across, the quicker we can get down and start the party.'

He was trying to be relaxed and jolly, but Paula could see how his eyes kept darting over to the tiny figure in silver and pale-blue Lycra already over on the other tower. He was itching to have his turn in the limelight, to be impressive.

Paula grabbed tight hold of the hand ropes and put her right foot on the wire. It was a steel cord, made of thinner steel cords all wound around each other. It moved slightly under her foot but at least it didn't wobble. Her hands were slippery but she clung tight to the ropes on either side, keeping her eyes focused on the other tower where those already across were standing. She saw Mark Hamilton make a thumbs-up gesture.

She took another step forward and another, refusing to look down. Now she was a third of the way across, hands still gripping tight to the ropes. Ahead of her she saw Charlie reach the far tower – a fan of outstretched arms gathering him in. Paula's longing to get to the end was so great, she could almost experience what it was like to be him, feeling the grip of those hands pulling her to safety. She inched out further. And now the cord underneath her feet was beginning to sway. A splash of red moved in the very outer reaches of her vision – Sarah, changing position down below – making Paula mistime her step so that her foot came down on the outside of the cord. For a second panic stoppered up her throat, but then she slowly shifted her foot back into the right position. The breeze whistled in her ear as if it had been holding its breath.

'Wow, Paula, you're practically skipping across there. You sure you're not descended from mountain goats?'

Will's voice floated up to her but it was as if it was coming from another world.

Another two steps. And now she was in the very centre of the cord where the swaying was most pronounced and the breeze felt more like a gust that could sweep a person off her feet. Her legs were trembling and she'd lost the feeling in her fingers from gripping the ropes so tightly. And then it happened. A movement so quick it was almost like the wind whooshing, a blurred dark wriggling worm in the corner of her eye, there for a second and then gone.

'*Oh my God!*'

A woman's voice shouting out from the tower ahead. Chloe's? Amira's?

But what was it? What had happened? The cord was still solid under her feet, the ropes under her hands still taut. Then she glanced behind her. The safety cord that should have been attaching her to the top wire had come down and trailed uselessly from the harness on her back, its end dangling over the void beneath her feet.

Panic burst inside her like a firework.

There was nothing to stop her falling, nothing holding her in place besides the ropes connecting her to Charlie and Ewan and through them to the others.

'You're fine, Paula. Just wait there. I'm coming up.'

Will's voice, free of its joky sheen, was strangely thin.

Frozen to the spot, gripping the ropes on either side and gazing stiffly ahead, she dared not move her head but was aware of movement below her, the bright trail of Will's blond hair across the grass. The group of figures on the tower ahead of her changed formation, a space opening up in their midst. Time seemed to hang suspended, as she was, seconds refusing to pass, dragging themselves on for ever. She was aware of an ominous quivering of the cord under her feet and remembered Ewan, stranded there somewhere behind her.

'Should I go to her?' he shouted now. 'I could easily grab her and walk her over.'

'*No!*'

The vehemence of her own voice startled her, and for a moment she feared she'd unbalanced herself, her centre of gravity sloshing from side to side like a spirit level. She tightened her grip, trying to meld the individual filaments of rope into the skin of her palm. The thought of Ewan blundering behind her, heavy-footed, ripples spreading out along the cord and up through the rubber soles of her cheap shoes, drenched her in panic. He was impulsive enough to charge in and try to rescue her single-handed, using her nightmare to show off in front of Rachel.

Finally, Will was there on the platform of the far tower ahead of her, his once-easy smile now straining at the seams.

'Now here's what's going to happen, Paula. I'm going to come and get you.' He raised a hand to silence the anticipated protest. 'Don't worry. I'm so used to this wire, I can practically levitate across. You won't notice a thing. Then I'm going to take my safety cord off and clip it on to your harness, and then we're going to come back together.'

He stepped on to the wire.

'I'm going to fall,' she screamed.

'No, you're not.' His eyes didn't leave hers – deep set, blue. Somewhere in the tiny part of her brain that wasn't flooded with the battery acid of adrenaline, she registered the novelty of it. Ian's eyes were grey, actually pink-tinged now from his four-cans-of-beer-a-night habit. Once she'd thought him the most handsome man in the world, and the knowledge that most women wouldn't look at him twice only made him more special, as if he was a brilliant artist whose work only she appreciated.

'Oh,' she cried out as the ropes under her hands vibrated with the touch of Will's fingers.

'You're fine, Paula. You're doing brilliantly!' Sarah's voice wafted up from somewhere down below. Paula wondered whether she looked ridiculous, frozen here like one of those living statues that paint themselves silver or gold and stand stock-still in city centres. She gazed at Will, who seemed hardly to be moving. *Please hurry up*.

But now, at last, he was here, his arms, tanned and roped with sinew, outstretched towards her. And she was feeling her legs shaking and her nerve-ends fizzing until his hand was gripping on to the top of her arm and she felt the hard, solid proximity of him.

'You're OK now. I have you,' he murmured as he unhooked his own safety cord and then reached both arms behind her to clip it to Paula's harness.

Click. And just like that, she was reattached to reality, aware of the clamminess of her clothes under his hands, the way her thin hair was hanging in damp wisps around her face, the presence of her two immediate bosses a few metres away, their faces turned towards her, expressions unreadable from that distance. Following Will's instructions, they inched forwards in tandem towards the other tower, her feet treading obediently where his had just been, her hands gripping on to rope still warm from his touch.

And then she was at the other end, and he was scooping her up as if she weighed nothing and now her legs, on solid ground once more, were giving way under her and Charlie and Amira had their arms around her, stopping her from falling, and they were smiling as if it had all been a bit of a laugh.

'Blimey,' Amira said. 'I thought you were stuck there for life.'

'Hope that wasn't too traumatic for you, Paula,' said Rachel, coming over to hover nearby. 'Probably felt a lot more dangerous than it was.'

Paula couldn't believe she'd heard right. Was Rachel seriously dismissing what had just happened as nothing more than a slight mishap?

Back on the ground, Sarah came rushing over.

'You poor thing. Are you OK?'

Paula remembered suddenly about the pregnancy bombshell Sarah had dropped on them all just a short time before. Could there be a part of her that was enjoying the diversion Paula had created?

'I could have died,' she said, her voice wobbling. But even as she said it, she was looking up at the wire and noticing how much lower to the ground it looked from here than it had when she was up there. The distance between the towers, which, when she was stuck in the middle had seemed endless, was just a few metres. Nothing at all really. Yet the danger had felt so real.

Will had now made it down too and was talking to his assistant Katie in a low, urgent voice.

'Sorry about that, guys,' he said. 'We've never had a safety rope fail before. The clasp seems to have come undone but Katie has had a look at it and can't understand how it happened. It wasn't worn out at all. In fact, they're all pretty new. And we had another team on here earlier today using the same equipment and it was all fine.'

'Where is all the equipment kept?' Charlie asked. 'Could it have got mixed up with other older stock?'

Will shook his head.

'It's exactly the same equipment as we used earlier. It was all still set up from before. There's just no reason for it to have happened.'

'Maybe if you employed some more experienced staff?' said Mark Hamilton, sternly glancing meaningfully over at Will's baby-faced assistant.

'Katie's done this many, many times. It wasn't her—'

Bur Mark cut him off: 'As it happens, there was a happy ending, but it could have been a very different story.'

'Oh come on,' said Rachel, glancing over at Will, who was looking distinctly uncomfortable. 'It wasn't really that bad. Paula was never really in danger. It's hardly like we had her scaling the Shard or anything.'

Paula stole a glance at Mark, waiting for him to leap to her defence and was shocked to see him break into a smile, as if what had happened to her was some sort of in-joke.

'I tell you something,' said Will, who'd regained his air of relaxed bonhomie. 'In terms of team-bonding, that was truly excellent stuff. You all pulled together, rallied around Paula, supported her. Mark and I couldn't have planned it much better ourselves. In fact, how do you know we didn't plan it ourselves?'

He glanced around the group, eyebrows waggling. There were a few giggles.

A savage wave of heat swept over Paula, rising from her feet upwards until she felt as if her whole body was on fire.

Her skin burned with shame.

26

Amira

'Do you think someone did it deliberately?'

Amira would have laughed if Paula hadn't looked like she was blinking away tears. She'd been taken aback when the older woman had knocked on her hotel-room door just a few moments ago asking for a 'chat'. She and Paula had always got on well enough – at least until Rachel practically offered her Paula's job and it all became awkward – but they'd never been intimate. Now Paula was slumped like a bag of boiled rice in the armchair by the window, asking her if someone could have deliberately tampered with her safety cord.

'Blimey, not you as well.'

Paula blinked at her, not understanding.

'Charlie was convinced someone had poisoned him the other day,' Amira explained. 'Hey, have you two been at the skunk again?'

'Skunk?' Paula looked more confused than ever and Amira stifled an impatient sigh.

'Skunk. You know – weed. Gives you paranoid delusions.'

'Oh. Right. Yes. Funny.'

Amira felt a pang of guilt. Paula was entitled to feel

paranoid – her boss *was* trying to get rid of her. Maybe not by dropping her off a rope bridge but scheming behind her back to replace her was just as soul-destroying.

'You look nice,' Paula said now, as if to compound Amira's guilt. The automatic reply 'so do you' died on Amira's lips as she surveyed the outfit her companion had selected for the evening's dinner activities: the familiar voluminous beige tunic over baggy black trousers. Low-heeled black court shoes of a type that were last in style in the early eighties and a shapeless black cardigan completed the look.

'You're so lucky,' Paula continued. 'You can wear anything with your colouring. Which one of your parents do you take after?'

Amira shrugged, uncomfortable as always with this line of questioning.

'Neither really. My mum is Indian and my dad was Irish, so I ended up this mutant creature who doesn't look like anyone. What do you think of this dress? Be honest.'

She had got used to heading off enquiries into her complicated heritage, but immediately she regretted her choice of topic.

'It's gorgeous,' said Paula sincerely. 'Is it new?'

The guilt was instantaneous. Amira's fingers flew to the bold-flowered-print Ted Baker dress she'd agonized over a couple of days before. She hadn't meant to go shopping. She and Tom had banned themselves from buying any new things for the next, oh, fifty years or so. But as she'd been walking to the Tube after work she'd started thinking about Rachel and how she always looked so perfectly put together, and she'd allowed herself to think for the first time about the possibility of promotion. *If* she took the job – of course, she wasn't committed yet – she'd need to start looking smarter. And that had got her thinking about the weekend and how she had absolutely nothing decent to wear. What would be the harm in just going to have a look? She wouldn't buy anything. She'd only be thinking ahead to when she got the . . . well, when she'd need to dress better, and would have the salary to do it too. So she'd detoured via Oxford Street and gone into the department store, and there had been the dress and she'd tried it on and fallen in love. And even though they were on the very edge of their overdraft limit in their joint account, and her credit was maxed on the joint credit card plus the two store credit cards Tom didn't even know about, she'd still taken out yet another store card and bought the dress, her euphoria lasting as long as it took the sales assistant to wrap it up in tissue and deliver it into a thick paper bag. But back home she'd felt consumed by self-loathing. She'd shoved the bag into the back of the wardrobe, vowing to return it the next day. But somehow the dress had remained in the wardrobe. When she'd put it on earlier, she'd felt fantastic, but now Paula's well-meaning compliment reminded her of just how she'd be getting this promotion (if she took it) and then she had an image of Tom's face creased with worry, and she felt suddenly damp with shame.

Dinner was in the hotel dining room. On the way down, Amira and Paula agreed to make an effort not to be intimidated by the presence of their bosses and to just enjoy being in a nice hotel with everything paid for. But even before they'd sat down, their resolution floundered. Mark and Rachel sat on opposite sides of the table with a spare seat next to each of them. All the other chairs were occupied.

It wasn't much of a choice, but Amira would definitely prefer not to sit next to Rachel, not least because she'd have Sarah on her other side and she didn't trust herself to talk to her at the moment, particularly not when she'd had a few drinks (which she very much intended to do). Just what was Sarah playing at? She'd always sworn she was going to stop at two kids. Always joked that she and Oliver never had sex anyway, so it wasn't so much a choice as a fait accompli. If she'd changed her mind, the least she could have done was give one of them a heads-up. It was they who'd be picking up the slack for her. Again. No wonder there was a spare chair between Rachel and Sarah, who was looking very fed up. Just as long as she didn't have to sit . . .

Too late. Paula was already squeezing her way around to the far side of the table to take the empty chair next to Mark, who had the look of someone trying too hard to appear pleased. Resigned, Amira took the seat between Rachel and Sarah.

'Phew, thank God it's you,' whispered Rachel.

Amira was shocked. Though she knew what Rachel thought of Paula professionally, it still seemed horribly indiscreet of her to express favouritism so openly, even if no one else could hear. She glanced at the almost-empty bottle of wine in front of her boss and wondered how much of it she'd had. Those glacial eyes were sharp enough to cut yourself on. Once again, Amira was flushed with self-hatred – this time for allowing herself to be party to the kind of office politics for which she and Tom had always reserved their ultimate scorn, lying on the sofa watching the conniving and backstabbing in reality shows. She knew he'd be horrified about what had been going on in the office, which practically amounted to a witch-hunt of Paula and Sarah. But then almost immediately, she was switching the blame on to him. After all, it was partly his fault she had to compromise herself like this. If he'd just taken some financial responsibility earlier, they would not be so stressed about this mortgage and she wouldn't have to kowtow to a bullying boss.

The mortgage you pushed him into, said the voice in her head. She batted it away.

A loud whooping noise came up from the next table where the sales and marketing team were sitting, making Amira jump. They seemed to be playing a drinking game. The ginger-haired guy whose name she could never remember was draining a pint of something while the others looked on, chanting, 'Down in one, down in one.' When he smashed the glass down on the table, he had a foam moustache. Those around him clapped.

'Everyone's treating me like a leper,' whispered Sarah on her other side. 'It's not as if I planned to have another baby. It was a mistake.'

'Do you think maybe after two you ought to have learned how they're made?' Amira had meant it to be a joke, but it came out harsher than she'd intended.

'I know it sounds really lame but you don't understand how exhausted we are all the time, both of us. After seven thirty at night our brains just shut down. We're not thinking straight, certainly not thinking

215

about consequences. And I thought it was a safe time.'

Amira made a face. 'There *is* no safe time. Anyway, you're clearly not that exhausted if you're still having sex.'

'Once in a blue moon. Honestly. It's just so unlucky. I haven't even been able to bring myself to think about it. After I'd done the test, Oliver had his back to me, doing the washing-up. I tapped him on the shoulder and showed him the little stick thingy with the blue line and he just stared at it and then turned back round and carried on washing up. Didn't say a word.'

'You're happy now though, right?'

Sarah lifted her eyes to hers and Amira saw they were blurred by a sheen of tears.

'I just don't know how we'll cope with another one, Amira. We're so tired. Joe and Sam are so physically demanding. And I've only just really got back into work mode again. My career's hanging by a thread as it is.' She shot a meaningful glance in the direction of Rachel who had turned her back on them to talk to Ewan on her other side.

'You're not thinking of getting rid of it though, surely?'

Sarah looked stricken. 'No. I mean, I look at Joe and Sam and think, no way, but then I imagine what it'll be like to go back to the beginning again with the constant feeding and the not sleeping and that smell of shit and sour milk that gets into your hair and your skin and I just can't . . . Well, I just can't. That's why I didn't tell anyone. Couldn't face dealing with it.'

'Has *she*,' Amira jerked her head backwards towards Rachel, 'said anything to you?'

Sarah shook her head, and now there was a tear building in the corner of her eye, then spilling down her cheek.

'That's a conversation I'm dreading,' she whispered.

A screech of laughter cut across the table. Chloe was sitting next to Will and clearly finding whatever he had just said hysterically funny. Amira had been surprised to find Will here at dinner. She'd assumed his duties ended after the outdoor activities were over. On the itinerary they'd been given before they arrived, there had been an entry on the Saturday night reading 'after-dinner games'. She'd hoped it might be something like Scrabble or even pool, both of which she quite enjoyed, but Will's presence made her nervous in case it was something more elaborate. More scope for public humiliation.

'Amira,' shouted Chloe. She had those pink blotches that pale girls get after a few drinks. 'Tell Will that joke you told us last week. The one about the monkey on the bus.'

Amira groaned.

'That kind of is the punchline, Chloe,' she said.

Again the screech of laughter. 'Oh yeah! I'm such a div!'

The meal progressed without much incident, but Amira couldn't shake off that sense of feeling disappointed in herself. When Rachel started talking to her about her vision for the department, asking her advice on what she thought about offering a performance-based incentive – like a day at a spa – she couldn't help thinking about how it would look to the others, she and Rachel cosying up together making plans for the office. She knew that when the axe finally fell, Paula would remember this evening and wonder if they had been plotting her downfall. *'Did you know then,'* she could almost hear Paula's quiet voice in her ear, *'at that team-bonding dinner? Did you already know she was going to get rid of me?'* And what could she say to that?

'I'd like to propose a toast to the team,' said Mark Hamilton, once the plates were cleared away. 'And to say a big thank you to Rachel for helping to make this weekend happen. I think today has been a tremendous success in bringing everyone together, making us think about how we work with each other and the importance of cooperation within the department – as well as the benefits of a bit of healthy competition. Plus we had a lot of fun, which is always a bonus!'

'Well, apart from Paula getting marooned on the high wire,' said Charlie. He was smiling, but there was a hard undercurrent to his voice.

'Oh come on,' said Rachel. 'Paula's fine. I expect she's forgotten all about it. I really don't think we need to keep bringing it up.' Her voice was like flint hitting rock, fine splinters of words spraying into the air on impact.

'If I could just say something.' Will's interruption broke the tension. 'Though what happened to Paula was unfortunate and we'll certainly be having a thorough investigation into what went wrong with that safety cord, in many ways it was also an invaluable learning experience for you guys. The quality of a great team lies in how the stronger members bring along the weaker ones. Not that I'm saying you're weak.' He turned his smile on Paula, who had flushed so that her rounded face, damply glowing from all the rich food, took on the texture of lightly sweating red onion. 'It could have happened to anyone. But it was wicked how everyone rallied around. I think you should all give yourselves a round of applause.'

They all clapped politely, even though Paula looked as if each clap was causing her physical pain.

'And now,' Will went on, 'we're going to play a few after-dinner games. Nothing involving heights, don't worry,' he aimed that remark at Paula. 'Just a bit of fun to hopefully help us all get to know each other even better.'

Amira's stomach muscles clenched involuntarily at the last few words. She had a flashback to being the new girl at school and a well-meaning teacher sitting her at the front of the classroom with a tennis ball that she had to bounce to different children in turn asking them their name and then saying hello to Toby or Melanie or whoever when they bounced it back to her.

'So you might have played this one before,' Will continued. He was in his civvies tonight – plain black T-shirt, black jeans. Amira wondered what he made of them all. Was he really as enthusiastic as he appeared to be, or were they just another bunch of grey office types, interchangeable with the last lot he'd had in? Reason told her the latter, but still there was that foolish, hopeful voice that said maybe he'd found something unique about them, about her. Suddenly it seemed important that this man, this perfect stranger, didn't lump her in with all the other faceless workers who streamed in and out of this hotel. *I have a degree in Psychology with Criminology,* she wanted to tell him. *I once spent six months travelling around South America. I climbed a mountain without proper equipment and thought I was going to die, I surfed sand dunes and cycled down a road in Bolivia so dangerous the locals call it Death Road. I volunteer with the Samaritans and dance around my kitchen to the Black Eyed Peas on Saturday mornings. Don't judge me*, she wanted to say. *Don't judge me on my job and the person I have to be at work and the way I simper when my boss makes a joke.*

'This is a word association game. We take it in turns to decide on a category, say "colour", and then we go around the table saying which colour best sums up our neighbour and why. So I'd say, for example, "Rachel is red because she's powerful and sexy."' He broke off to wink at Rachel. 'Or you could choose sports, so I could say, I don't know, "Charlie is snooker because he's got a lot of balls."'

Everyone laughed obligingly, though Amira suspected Will had made that joke many times before. She was aware of a tightness around the table, as if people were holding themselves in, muscles tensed, nerves stretched out like the wire cord they'd been balancing on earlier that day. The air between them all vibrated as if someone was blowing one of those whistles so high-pitched that only dogs could hear it.

'This isn't going to end well,' sing-songed Charlie under his breath as he leaned across the table. Charlie was in a strange mood. He'd spent most of dinner looking down at his lap, texting – which was pretty rude, Amira thought. And even when he joined in with odds and ends of conversation, he seemed distracted, his eyes constantly drawn down to his phone. Though he was next to Sarah, he'd hardly said a word to her. He must feel shut out, Amira decided. Normally Charlie would have been the first person Sarah confided in.

'Right.' Will smiled. 'I'm going to sit this one out as I haven't had the chance to get to know you guys properly yet, but I want you to have fun. This is the chance for you to really think about each other's qualities. Be creative and generous and don't spend too long thinking about your answers. Spontaneity is key. Mark, as you're *The Man*, why don't you start. What category are you going to pick?'

Mark Hamilton looked startled under his tan. He was wearing a white shirt open at the collar and his Adam's apple moved up and down like an air bubble in a straw.

'Erm.' Mark's glance darted around wildly as if trying to locate inspiration in the space around him. His gaze fixed on the glass in front of him and his face dropped with relief.

'Got it. Drinks!'

'Great choice.' Will nodded. 'So let's start with Paula. What drink would you say Mark was?'

Paula blinked and pulled her face inwards so the entire thing rested on the cushion of flesh under her chin.

'Drink? Er . . .' She looked around the table for help.

'It doesn't have to be clever, Paula. Just say the first thing that comes to mind. As long as it's clean.' Will chuckled to himself. Paula, who was anyway looking flustered, now turned the deep pink of farmed salmon.

Then, 'Hot chocolate!' she practically yelled. 'Because he's warm . . . and tasty.'

A roar of laughter went up around the table, genuine this time. Paula's hand flew to her mouth as she realized what she'd said.

Will raised his own hand. 'It's fine, Paula. That's the

221

whole point of it – it's supposed to be fun. Right, Charlie. If Paula was a drink, what would she be?'

'G and T,' said Charlie, and for a horrible moment Amira thought he was going to say something about her being colourless, but instead, he said something clever about her either being neat, or a tonic.

Amira's mind was so busy whirring through the possibilities for Sarah that she didn't hear what Sarah said about Charlie; however, she was aware of a polite murmur. Sarah was a Bloody Mary, she said – red and with a hidden kick. Amira ignored Sarah's questioning sideways glance at that last description, concentrating on what Rachel was about to say about her. There was a sharp intake of breath when Rachel described Amira as Guinness – 'Smooth and you have to wait ages for her.' Amira realized that the others probably thought Rachel was having a go at her timekeeping, whereas she alone knew it was a comment on how long it had taken her to decide she was interested in Paula's job.

Ewan predictably described Rachel as champagne – sparkling and expensive and very classy. As Will was sitting on his other side, the game skipped a seat and moved on to the person in the next chair. Chloe.

'If Ewan was a drink . . .' she began, and Amira could see just how how drunk the younger woman was. 'If Ewan was a drink . . . he'd be whisky because he seems like a good idea when you're drunk but he makes you feel like shit in the morning. Haha!'

She spluttered with laughter, as if this had been a spur-of-the-moment witticism, but Amira knew Chloe's mind wasn't quick enough to come up with something like that unless she'd given it a lot of thought. Well, if she'd been aiming to humiliate Ewan in front of Rachel she'd probably succeeded, judging by the latter's set expression and Ewan's undisguised fury.

'Cool. Remember, guys, let's keep it light and fun,' said Will evenly.

Amira stared at Chloe, still finding it hard to believe she'd said what she'd said. It was so unlike her. Not just because it was clever, but also mean. Chloe could be sulky and stroppy, but this was the first time Amira had heard her say something so out and out bitchy. This thing with Ewan, whatever it was, must have hit her really hard. Amira felt a stab of anger towards him. Normally she liked Ewan. He fancied himself a bit of a jack-the-lad, and he'd never made a secret of his ambition. She was surprised he'd hung around as long as he had – she'd have expected him to be off climbing through the ranks by now.

Though they'd worked together for two years, Amira knew very little about him, except on a superficial level. But lots of people were like that. Private. As if giving things away about themselves might lend you some sort of power over them. She didn't mind that, but she did mind him being cavalier with Chloe's heart. Hearts were delicate. You couldn't take them out and pound them like fillet steak, then pop them back in and expect everything to be the same as it was.

After the drinks round came flowers and then pets. Everyone was trying to be funny as if their standing within the company could be gauged by levels of laughter. Amira was surprised to find her adrenaline levels building as her turn approached, frantically trying to think of witty things to say about Sarah.

'Faster,' Will said. 'These should be totally off the cuff.'

As they did a round of famous books, he speeded them up, clicking his fingers at each in turn so they blurted out the first things that came into their heads. On the next round, TV shows, Will changed the rules.

'I'm going to mix it up a bit, so as we go round the table I'll shout a name and you describe that person. *Go.*'

Amira's heart was pounding as Will yelled, 'Mark!' at her. 'The news,' she said impetuously. 'Because he's authoritative and . . .'

'Boring?' Mark interjected when she hesitated, raising a laugh.

The next round was capital cities. She felt her stress levels rising ever higher as her turn came closer. While Sarah next to her splutteringly described Rachel as Copenhagen because she was 'expensive, clean and organized', Amira was casting a frantic eye around the table, trying to come up with witty one-liners, but her mind was blank. The two cities that had lodged in her head – New York and Paris had both been used. Panic rose up inside her as Will nodded in her direction and said, 'Faster now,' and then, 'Paula.'

Amira's gaze swung across the table towards the departmental deputy who was looking hot and uncomfortable in her voluminous beige top. 'Montreal,' she blurted out. Will gestured to her to hurry, clicking his fingers in rapid succession – snap, snap, snap – and without pausing to think, she added: 'Because she's big and a bit dull.'

There are some silences that start out as one thing and

mutate gradually into quite another, as if the silence itself has caused a subtle shifting of tectonic plates beneath the earth. This was one such time, where what had begun as a pause, pregnant with soon-to-be-released laughter, changed to discomfort and finally, as the meaning of what had been said sunk in, to shock. Amira's hand flew to her mouth.

'Oh my God, Paula. I'm so sorry. I didn't mean . . . It was just the first thing . . .'

'It's fine,' said Paula, but her face had the set look of someone trying not to cry. Her surprisingly small fingers were gripping so tightly to the handle of her coffee cup that Amira could see the blue threads of her veins through the translucent skin of her plump wrists.

'I wasn't thinking.'

There was nothing Amira could say. No excuse. The words had come from a part of her she hadn't even known was there. She'd always been so careful of other people's feelings. Even when she was drunk she didn't let rip like some did. But now something was pricking like the rough ends of dried grass at the edges of her mind. Times as a child when she'd got into a temper and said or done things she afterwards couldn't remember, and would emerge from her bad mood as if from a dream to find her beloved father shaking his head with such sorrow in his moss-green eyes. 'Oh, Amira,' was all he'd needed to say in his lilting voice and she'd be instantly filled with shame – much as she was right now.

'I'm sorry,' she said again. But by now the others had moved on and someone else was talking and it seemed the moment had passed – until Rachel leaned in towards her, her perfume crawling into Amira's nostrils full-bodied and overpowering.

'Spot on,' she whispered, and giggled in a way Amira found more disturbing than her usual frostiness. It was as if she'd borrowed the giggle from someone else, or stolen it.

'Montreal was inspired!'

Rachel moved her hand and for a moment Amira thought she was raising it for a high five, but instead she touched her fingers to Amira's dress where the fabric stretched tight over her ribs.

'Nice frock,' she murmured and Amira went rigid as Rachel's knuckles brushed the underside of her breast, but were gone so quickly she thought afterwards she must have imagined it. She glanced up in time to see Paula turning her head and knew she'd been watching. She waited for Paula to look at her so she could mouth another apology, but the older woman kept her gaze averted.

I'm sorry, Amira repeated inside her own head.

27

Anne

My house is a new build so everything is perfectly squared off. No alcoves or fireplaces or hidden places where cobwebs can build. No high ceilings to which the heat gravitates, leaving sofas and chairs exposed and icy, no gappy floorboards through which the wind can whistle on winter evenings. Everything in my house is grey or white or oatmeal, everything has a place. The surfaces are clean and clear, not cluttered with every manner of ornament and relic of everyday life – postcards, ticket stubs, receipts, photographs, candle stubs, light bulbs, felt pens, their lids long lost. My house is nothing like my mother's.

Unlike her I live a life filled with purpose. I have a job that I take very seriously. I go out to dinner once a week with my daughter. I have friends. I even exercise. Every evening when I get back from work I put on jogging pants and do a three-mile circuit of the neighbourhood. Not exactly running but very brisk walking. I never cheat. I never allow myself a day off because it's raining, or because I have a sore throat or a pile of essays to mark. I pull on my trainers and plug in my headphones and do my three miles. And then I come home and shower and change and then, and only then, I allow myself a beer or a glass of wine. Just the one, mind. I am the kind of person who believes in delayed and earned gratification because if I allowed myself to waver, if I cut myself some slack, who knows where I might end up. I might turn into my mother. I might turn into Noelle Egan.

For days after we'd been to see her in jail, her dead, blank eyes haunted my dreams. How did a mother do what she had done?

'It could be acute Post Natal Depression Syndrome,' Ed had suggested as we drove away from the prison building. 'Left untreated, she would have had major problems bonding with the child, and might even have experienced strong hostility. The child is responsible for the death of the person she was before. The child has in a sense killed her. Or she could have experienced massive guilt feelings about her own inadequacy as a mother. She might have felt that sooner or later she would end up damaging the child, but by doing it first, she was somehow pre-empting her own worst self.'

I didn't believe that's what had happened to Noelle. Without Peter Egan's influence, she might not have been antagonistic towards her baby, but she'd still have been indifferent. Of that I was convinced. Peter hadn't had to change her mind, or even reinforce a course she'd already set upon. He'd just planted a seed in a void. My secret fear is that, deep inside, I'm just as emotionally lazy as Noelle Egan, just as open to corruption – wide and shallow as a Petri dish. Only my love for Shannon marks me out as different. That's why I structure my life around book deadlines and departmental meetings and lectures and my weekly writing group and my twice-a-week swim. The more strictly I timetable, the less space I leave for the bacteria to thrive.

By the time we met with Laurie for the fourth time, it was common knowledge that Noelle was going to enter a plea of diminished responsibility, claiming that her husband had a Svengali-like hold over her. She was hoping to get a lesser sentence by turning state witness against Peter. He had refused to comment at all. Those who'd dealt with him said he considered himself above the normal rule of law. Meanwhile witnesses were emerging from his past. An ex-girlfriend he'd left with a metal plate in her cheekbone, a half-sister who claimed he'd always been the black sheep. No criminal record, just a string of people who would be very happy never to see him again.

Whatever the outcome of the legal case, it seemed certain both parents would be behind bars for a very long time, if not the rest of their lives. Laurie was now officially a ward of the state. Our recommendation on her future was critical. Was she so damaged that she needed intensive ongoing treatment, or did her best hope for a normal life lie in adoption somewhere well away from all this, where she could start again, forge new memories, forget about monstrous goings-on in dark cellars? Forget she had a brother.

'I think maybe it's time to start probing,' Ed said when I arrived upstairs at the medical centre. 'If we decide adoption is the best course for Laurie, time is of the essence.'

'But obviously we need to be sure,' I said as he went

through his now familiar routine of checking the tape recorder was working and straightening the blinds. 'I mean, the last thing we want is to decide she's OK because that's what we want to believe, and then a year down the line or two years or even five years, something happens and it all comes back to the surface, but she hasn't got the support network around to help her deal with it.'

'I hear what you're saying, Anne.' Ed had now sat down in a chair next to me, and was stroking his chin. There was a patch of hair he'd missed while shaving and I found myself riveted to it. 'And absolutely we won't recommend on Laurie's case until we're satisfied about the appropriate course of action. But I have to say that so far I've been impressed at how resilient she seems. And seeing the house and talking to her mom actually made me believe there might be cause for some kind of cautious hope. She grew up believing she was loved – that counts for a lot.'

'And the fact that her little brother was kept chained up in the basement?'

'With luck that will just start to seem like one of those weird images that flash into your mind and which is just too bizarre to be a true memory so you put it down to a movie you've seen. She's only four years old. How much of what happened to you before you were four can you remember, Anne?'

I tried to think back. There was an image of being swung between two adult hands. *Higher. Higher.* Another of sitting on a chair gazing awestruck at my own bleeding knee while my mom knelt on the floor in front of me gently swabbing it with a tissue.

'Yes, but I think something that traumatic would stick with me.'

'But that's just it, Anne. It wasn't traumatic to Laurie. It was normal. She didn't know anything else.'

'And the bite mark? Her involvement in the punishment programme?'

Ed held up his hands.

'That's exactly what I think we need to explore in today's session. I'm hoping Jana will be able to guide us in terms of how far we can push her.'

In my imagination I have Ed turning pink when he said the name of Laurie's foster mother, but I think that might just be time's embellishment.

We'd arranged that Kristen, Ed Kowalsky's research student, should meet Laurie and Jana at the front door and take Laurie off straight away for another soda while Jana came up in the lift to find us and update us on what had been happening.

When the knock came, Ed practically flew from his seat, but if Jana was surprised by the door swinging open even before her knuckles had left the surface, she didn't show it. When she entered the room, she brought her peculiarly calm aura with her, along with her faded denim jacket and jeans and a light floral scent.

'I don't know if you guys knew that Laurie started at a preschool last week? Just a coupla days a week. I'm happy to say that's going really good. The teachers are really happy with the way she interacts with the other kids. There was just this one incident . . .'

I wondered if Jana could sense how Ed and I were leaning in towards her, not wanting to miss anything.

'Well. It was nothing really. The teacher said she

231

wouldn't even have mentioned it if I hadn't asked her to report back on every little thing. It was at recess and one of the boys pushed another boy off the swing set, and he hurt himself and was crying and Laurie picked up this plastic thing – I think it was a plastic rake or something, you know so they can pretend to do the gardening? – and she gave the little boy a bit of a whack before the teacher got there and stopped it all.'

'The aggressor, you mean? The boy who'd pushed the other one?' I wanted to get the facts completely straight.

'No, that was the odd thing. It was the one who'd been hurt. The teacher took her and the other boy aside and explained why it was wrong, and apparently she was very contrite and even gave the boy she'd hit a big hug. Like I say, it wasn't a big deal.'

Jana's hair was long and loose today and she shook it back in an unconscious gesture like you'd shake out a sheet before pegging it out to dry. A brown hair elastic was looped loosely around one narrow wrist and she slipped it off and tied her hair back in one fluid, practised movement. It made me aware of my own hair, coarse and yellow, tucked behind my ears, the ends of it brushing my shoulders. What is it about women that we allow ourselves to be so defined by the things we are not? By the qualities we lack?

'Do you remember, Jana,' Ed said, 'that we talked before about how Laurie was during these episodes which, as you rightly say, are hardly unusual in a child of her age? Do you remember you said she was almost dissociated from her normal self? Have you noticed any more of that behaviour?'

Jana cocked her head to one side in thought. The smooth slope of her cheekbone shimmered in a slanting shaft of late summer sun.

'She can sometimes seem like she's somewhere else, ya know, in a different world – but then kids are like that, aren't they? It's good for them to be able to escape into their own heads, don't you think?'

I frowned, wanting to pin her down.

'But there's a difference between daydreaming and entering a fugue state . . .'

'I don't think we need to bother Jana with the technical jargon, Anne,' Ed broke in. His voice carried an edge of something. Warning? 'After all, she's not here to diagnose Laurie but just to observe, right?'

'Sure. No, I totally get that. It's just I think we need to be absolutely sure what we're dealing with here, because if Laurie really is dissociating rather than just drifting off like any normal four-year-old might . . .'

'I do hope you're not expecting Jana to define normality, Anne?'

This time the warning was obvious.

'I mean,' he went on, 'the greatest philosophers in the world have struggled with that one, so I think maybe we'll just give Jana a break and allow her to do her job, which is to care for a very vulnerable little girl. I have to say, I think she's doing brilliantly well.'

Nowadays he probably wouldn't get away with it. A modern-day Jana, with her college diploma and her natural intelligence, might call him out on his patronizing tone. But those were different times. Men like Ed Kowalsky were still sure of their places in the world. They felt entitled to condescend with impunity, would certainly not have recognized it as that. Anyway, Ed was far from the worst in that regard.

'Like I say,' said Jana, her eyes flitting between me and Ed as if picking up on the tension, 'I haven't really seen enough evidence of it, and anyhow I'm not the right person to judge. All I can say is, Laurie seems to be super-adjusted, given the circumstances.'

'And your own kids get on with her?' Ed asked.

'Sure.' Jana nodded. 'Well, Lisa is kinda separate because she's older, and Barney has asked a coupla times when Laurie is going home, but that's probably because he just wants me back to himself.'

'Any questions about her parents? Her brother?' I wanted to reassert myself into the situation, to recover ground.

'Never about the brother. Occasionally she'll mention her parents in passing, but it's strange, it doesn't seem to upset her in any way. She might just be good at hiding things but I get the feeling they're already starting to fade from her mind.'

Ed picked up his notebook and scribbled furiously.

When Laurie came in, clutching Kristen's hand, she seemed in high spirits.

'There's a machine there and it has all this nice stuff in the window and you put in your money and it makes this really loud noise like this . . .' She stretched her mouth into a tall oval shape and made noises in the back of her throat. 'Then it gives it to you in this special place in the bottom. I wanted some candy but the lady,' she glanced up at Kristen, 'said I needed to ask you. Can I, Mommy?'

The word seemed to take us all by surprise. I glanced

over at Jana and she gave a faint 'what can you do' shrug.

'We'll see, Laurie. But listen, honey, what did I tell you about calling me Mommy? We talked about it, remember?'

Laurie smiled.

'Oh yes, I forgot. But can I have some candy? I've been really good.'

'We'll talk about it later, but first we're going to have a little chat to Professor Kowalsky and Dr Cater.'

Laurie bounced up and down on the chair Kristen had settled her into. She looked tiny. My heart contracted at the sight of her, taking me by surprise. Ed started by asking her questions about her new preschool. I was impressed by his gentleness. He was asking her about her favourite toys, and what she'd liked to play with in her other house.

'I had some dolls, but Mommy,' she glanced over at Jana, 'I mean the other mommy, wouldn't let me play with them all the time. Just sometimes when she let them out of their boxes.'

'We went to see your house,' I told her. 'You have a lovely room.'

She nodded solemnly, accepting it as perfectly normal that we should have been to visit the house where she used to live.

'I like my new room better. I have a box on wheels that comes out from under the bed with all my toys in it. I can push it in and out.'

'Was there anything about your old house you didn't like, Laurie?'

The room held its breath. Had Ed jumped in too soon?

Laurie shrugged.

'I didn't like the chair in the kitchen that was made of wood and gave me a splinter in my finger.'

'Anything else? How about the basement? Did you ever go there? Did you like that?'

Bounce, bounce, bounce. Was it my imagination or had the little girl's movements become more frenetic?

'I didn't really like the basement. I didn't like it.'

'It?' queried Ed. 'You mean the basement?'

'No. The Thing.'

'What thing, Laurie?'

'The Thing that lived in the basement.' Laurie was looking at Ed like it was too obvious to warrant spelling out.

'Can you explain what that was, Laurie?' I asked, trying to match my tone to Ed's effortlessly patient one.

She shrugged again.

'I dunno. Can't remember. It was a Thing that was sometimes bad and made Mommy and Daddy cross, and I didn't like going down there because it was kinda stinky.' She held her nose and giggled.

'Can you describe the Thing, Laurie?' I asked, trying to keep her on subject.

She wriggled on the chair.

'I can't remember. It was dark in there. I think it was a kind of, you know, an animal.'

'Like a pet?'

I fought a wave of irritation at Jana's leading question. Why couldn't she have let Laurie formulate her own conclusion instead of handing one to her on a plate?

'Yeah, I guess. Can we go get candy now?'

As Jana got up to go, she shot us a sympathetic smile, as if to say 'I don't envy you'.

'Laurie, say goodbye to Professor Kowalsky and Dr Cater,' she said to the little girl hanging off her arm.

'Goodbye,' Laurie sing-songed, turning to us and shooting us a radiant smile.

Long after they'd gone, the memory of that smile stayed with me. And superimposed over the top of it was the image of a perfect, small bite mark in a little boy's skin.

28
Ewan

He should just go to bed. That's what he should do. Ewan could feel the alcohol he'd drunk sloshing around in his system. Normally he stuck to beer, and tonight he'd been drinking wine in almost the same quantities until now he felt awash with it, his stomach bloated, his brain splashing about in an unpleasant sea of Sauvignon blanc and the rich peppercorn sauce in which his steak had been drenched. He should get in the hotel lift and go up to the fourth floor and find his room among all those identical doors and lie down on those crisply laundered sheets and sleep this off.

That's what he should do. But he wouldn't. And the reason he wouldn't was *her*.

Ewan hadn't admitted it even to himself, but he'd had high hopes of this weekend. Rachel had been giving out signals – very subtle ones – but he wasn't an idiot. He knew when women were responding and she had definitely responded. Nothing too obvious. She had her position in the department to think of. But she'd given him a lift here. You wouldn't do that unless you were just a tiny bit interested. He'd been nervous in case he underperformed in the physical tasks or went blank while they were doing word games or, God forbid, role play. But all of the activities had passed off pretty well.

Yet ever since they'd arrived here, she'd switched off. Suddenly it was as if he was nothing – some bit of lint she'd picked up on the sleeve of her jacket and thought she could just brush off.

The way she'd been flirting with that Will. To be taken in by that airhead in a tracksuit. She'd even been playing up to Mark Hamilton – and after telling him, Ewan, that he should keep away from Chloe as well! The hypocrisy of it took his breath away. He concentrated his thoughts on that to keep out the wave of hurt that ambushed him every time he let down his guard.

'I'll have another Scotch,' he told the barman, who was busy clearing away chairs and glasses.

Turning back, Ewan was discomfited to realize there weren't as many people left at the table as he'd thought. He could have sworn they'd all been there when he went to the bar, but now there was just Charlie and Amira and Chloe. The place was empty apart from them. His hopes had been raised when Rachel had accompanied them all as far as the bar after dinner, but when Will peeled off, saying he had to be up early the next morning, Rachel had suddenly decided she too needed to turn in. Watching her leave, a little unsteady on her feet, Ewan had felt himself burn with humiliation, feeling that he was being played with. Chloe seemed fed up too. Not surprising, given that the energy she'd been investing in Will all night had just come to nothing. Well, she could join the club. The Mugs Club. Maybe they should have badges made.

'You're not still texting, are you?' he snapped at

Charlie as he sat down. 'Can't you put that bloody phone down?'

'Or what? You going to send him to the naughty step?'

That was Chloe, sounding like someone pretending to be more fed up than she actually was. Ewan allowed himself a moment of triumph as it dawned that she hadn't after all defected from him to Will. She'd been putting on a show to make him jealous. He felt himself softening towards her. She was still such a kid really, hadn't learned how to be hard and two-faced like the rest of them.

He gulped down his Scotch, wondering why he was even drinking it. It wasn't as if he was enjoying it. And he already knew he was going to feel like shit in the morning.

'Bloody Sarah, hey,' said Amira, apropos of nothing. She was slumped in one of the velvet bucket chairs turning a black cardboard coaster over and over between her fingers. 'I mean, don't get me wrong, I'm happy for her and everything, but seriously, I'm sick of covering for her. She says it was all a mistake, but when you've already got two kids under four, I'd say you kind of know how mistakes happen.'

'Next you'll be saying kids are a lifestyle choice,' said Charlie. 'And then you might have to start wearing a tall pointy white hat and carrying a burning cross over your shoulder.'

'You can dig all you like, Charlie, but I'm just saying what everyone is thinking.'

'Are you sure you're not saying that because you'd secretly like a baby too?' Chloe blurted out.

240

Bloody hell, she wasn't very tactful, was she? Even Ewan wouldn't have come out and asked that. Some people just couldn't have kids. You had to be careful.

'Tom and I couldn't afford to have a baby even if we wanted one, so no, actually.'

They remained at the table in bad-tempered silence until Charlie received a text that made him glare at his phone and then snap the case shut and stand up so suddenly that the table shook.

'Right. Bedtime.'

Drunk as he was, something in the tone of Charlie's voice made Ewan sit up a bit straighter and scrutinize him through the alcohol fug in his brain. Charlie had always been so easy-going, one of those men who called himself a total wimp almost as a badge of pride. But now his features were set hard, those brown eyes so narrowed as to be almost hidden. Together with that mysterious wound on the side of his arm, it made Ewan feel uneasy. Why couldn't people just be who they appeared to be? Why did they have to keep chopping and changing? He thought he'd left all that behind him at home where his normally loving mother would change for a few days every month into someone who seemed to view everything he did as a personal affront. And now here was laid-back Charlie acting all moody and uptight and it just made him nervous.

Now Amira was on her feet too.

'Gotta get my beauty sleep in preparation for what-ever delights we have in store for us tomorrow.'

'Orienteering,' muttered Chloe.

'Oriental what?' asked Amira.

'You know, where we get dropped in the middle of a

wood with a map and have to find our way back. Will told me. We're in competition with Sales and Marketing again.'

Ewan was starting to feel very sluggish, as though the Scotch was mixing with the blood in his veins to form a thick paste that was clogging everything up, making it hard to think. Still, he registered that he didn't like it when Chloe said 'Will' like that. So casually. Like they had some kind of special relationship or something.

'Fantastic,' said Amira, gathering up her handbag from the side of her chair. 'Just when I thought this weekend couldn't get any better.'

After she'd gone there fell a silence as dense as the fog in his head. Chloe tossed back her hair and combed her fingers through it, looking off to the side. He was touched at how much effort she was making to appear unbothered. She was so young, he remembered again. He hadn't behaved well towards her.

'Sorry,' he blurted out, even before he knew he was going to say anything. 'I was a bastard to you.'

She flicked her hair back again, still gazing off to one side, and shrugged her shoulders.

'Yeah, you were a dick, but I'll live.'

'No, I mean it. I'm sorry. I really do like you, Chloe.'

He stuck his foot out under the table, meaning just to nudge her leg as a peace gesture, but instead he found himself rubbing the toe of his shoe up and down her shin. She looked down at the table, as if studying something written there but, despite her flaming cheeks, she didn't move her leg away.

How did it happen? How does it ever happen? One

242

moment he was running a toe down her leg and the next they were in the lift, kissing, her mouth tasting of the crème brûlée she'd had for dessert. And then he was sliding her hotel key card into the slot and they were falling inside the room and on the bed and it was hot and sweaty and fun and straightforward and he was drunk and horny and not thinking about anything except what they were doing. And everything was good until . . .

Afterwards he tried to make sense of it, to remember when it changed and what changed it, but all he could think of was that one moment they were rolling around on the bed play-wrestling in the way drunk young people do when they're enjoying themselves and their bodies and the anticipation of what's about to happen . . . and then Rachel had popped into his head. He couldn't remember if it was something Chloe said or just one of those random thoughts. He remembered how Rachel had seemed to lead him on, singling him out in the office, offering him a lift to the hotel. And then she'd ignored him all day. Humiliated him. Flirting with Will in front of him. Anger pulsed in his veins, hot and insistent. And after that it wasn't fun any more.

'What's wrong?' he heard Chloe say, but it was like she was in a different room. Somewhere far away from the fury that was smothering him, making it hard to breathe.

'Ewan?' said the faraway Chloe, but all he could see in front of his eyes was Rachel raising her face to Will's, her whole body leaning towards him. What a bitch she was. He wanted to do something to make her sorry for the way she'd treated him. He wanted to hurt her like she'd hurt him, so she knew how it felt. He wanted to—

'Ewan, you're hurting me!'

Now Chloe's voice wasn't far away. It was right here in the room. He looked down at his hands which were pressing down on hers, pinioning her arms above her head, and her blue eyes which were wide with alarm.

He sat up, head suddenly clear.

'Oh God! I'm sorry. I didn't mean to . . . Are you OK?'

She grabbed the sheet and held it up against her, her breath tearing from her chest in rasps. He reached out a hand to stroke her cheek, but she flinched from his touch.

'Get away from me!' Her voice was croaky, but there was no mistaking the fear embedded in it. 'You scared me.'

'I didn't mean to. I don't know what happened . . . God, I'm so sorry.'

Ewan was aware he wasn't making sense, but shock seemed to have robbed him of the ability to carry a sentence or a thought through to its end. All he knew was that for a few seconds, the woman on the bed beneath him, the woman he'd wanted to hurt, had not been Chloe.

'Get out of my room.'

'Please let me explain.'

But when he tried to find the words, he couldn't. He hadn't been himself, hadn't been in his body or in his head. And she too had been someone else, but how could he make her understand when nothing made sense?

'I'm sorry,' he said again eventually. 'I'm so sorry.'

He picked up his clothes from around the bed, and tried not to look at Chloe's tear-stained face. He'd never laid a finger on a woman in anger. Ever. And, despite the tough-guy persona he liked to adopt, his experience of physical violence in any capacity had been limited to a few playground scuffles at school and a Saturday-night shoving contest in a pub with some body-building type clearly wired on steroids whose girlfriend he'd smiled at.

He felt like crying himself. He felt sick. He felt guilty and ashamed and unable to meet her eyes.

'Sorry,' he said again. Then he turned the handle of the hotel-room door and stumbled out, blinking in the bright overhead lights of the corridor. He had on his suit trousers and his new floral shirt which was unbuttoned and, he noticed now, inside out. His shoes and socks were in his hand.

In the lift, his reflection in the mirror scared him. His face was white and clammy, sweat beads popping on his skin like mini blisters. His eyes seemed hooded, the pupils staring wildly out from the bottom of a long dark tunnel. He leaned back against the wall and put his head in his hands so he wouldn't have to look at himself.

When the lift pinged two floors up, Ewan remained in his slumped position. Everything about him felt too heavy, as if he himself was a dead weight he couldn't face carrying around any more. His leg, which hadn't given him any trouble on the high wire earlier in the day, was now aching in that dull but persistent way that usually presaged an uncomfortable night ahead. Eventually he peeled himself off the wall and limped out into the corridor.

'Hello, Ewan.'

After everything that had just happened, Rachel Masters standing in the deserted hotel corridor in the middle of the night felt unreal. In his blurred head, he wondered whether perhaps the whole night had been some sort of test, culminating in him standing here, half dressed in front of his boss.

'Been sleepwalking, have we? Or sleepstripping, maybe?'

'It's not what you think.' He had a flash of Chloe's terrified expression, and felt as if he was about to throw up. What *had* it been exactly?

'Please don't try to make excuses, Ewan. I made it perfectly clear where I stand on personal relationships between staff members. I'm going to have to think about this very carefully. Clearly you and Chloe can't work in the same department. One of you will have to go. Now I think you should get back to your room.'

Letting himself through the door, he lay down on his bed without taking off his clothes and focused on the ceiling, trying to work out what was real. The ceiling was blank, white, giving nothing away. He studied it until he located, in the far corner by the window, a hair-line crack. The tiny imperfection convinced him that this wasn't all in his head, a nightmare from which he would soon wake up, hungover, but not ashamed.

He knew there'd been a moment when he was in bed with Chloe where he'd genuinely lost control. And he knew that she knew it too. And tomorrow she would tell everyone what he'd done, what he was.

The room, like a womb with its burgundy curtains and walls, pressed in on his already thumping head until it felt as if his skull was caught in a vice. He fell asleep with his hands pressed together on his chest, as if he was praying.

29

Sarah

No signal.

Sarah knew she shouldn't be surprised. After all, they were in the middle of nowhere. Literally. But still the fact of being cut off from her children, from Oliver, made her feel nervous and panicked. Twenty years ago, before everyone had mobile phones, no one was able to stay in touch all the time. When you went out of the door, that was it until you stepped back in again. Unless you hovered by a landline all day. Under different circumstances maybe she'd see it as quite liberating, this being apart from her family, out of range of their demands, but she felt so low, so miserable and exhausted. And it didn't help that the wood they were passing through was so dank and gloomy.

'No point looking at your phone,' said Will cheerily. 'There's no signal out here, otherwise it would defeat the point of the exercise, wouldn't it? Can't have you all ringing your mates to navigate your way out or ordering yourselves a Domino's pizza when you feel peckish.'

As soon as he mentioned pizza, Sarah felt ravenous. She'd thrown up her breakfast shortly after eating it far too quickly on her own in the hotel restaurant and now she was hungry again in that early pregnancy way where your body feels like a black hole sucking food into it without enjoyment. They weren't going to be eating again until they'd found their way to base camp, aka the minibus in which Will had driven them halfway here and to which he would presently be returning. The idea was that he would then drive it to a new location marked with a cross on the Ordnance Survey map they'd been given. Then it would be up to them to navigate their way to it – once they'd worked out where they were. They'd already been walking at least forty minutes through these woods and, before that, across a few fields. They'd even crossed a couple of sizeable streams by stepping from one strategically placed rock to another. 'Watch out, the water is much faster-moving than it looks,' Will had warned them. Sarah hated it all. Despite a fear of confined spaces that extended way back into childhood, she'd never felt comfortable in the country-side either. The idea of being cut off from everything left her feeling exposed and vulnerable. She was someone who needed human contact to an almost embarrassing degree. Her unease wasn't helped by being grossly over-dressed. As it was November, she'd come prepared for Arctic conditions in a down jacket of Oliver's that was like wearing a maximum-tog duvet at all times. But the weather was damp and sluggish rather than cold and she was hot and clammy inside the coat.

'Kinda creepy here, isn't it?' Will said. 'Apparently, until recently the locals used to avoid coming here. There are lots of really wild stories about this place being haunted and stuff – which is a good thing because you won't want to hang around, which means you'll be first back to the van . . . and the champagne is all yours!'

The sales and marketing team were being taken to a different spot that was equidistant to theirs, from where they'd be making their way to the same end point. Whichever team arrived first would win a magnum of champagne. It was supposed to make each team work together so they came back bonded and thinking as one well-oiled machine. Sarah looked around at her markedly subdued co-workers. It was hard to think of a group of people who less resembled a well-oiled machine.

Ewan was striding ahead through the half-light of the wood, his hands thrust into his pockets, head down. He'd been plastered last night, so his head must be pounding – but he could at least make some effort to be sociable, she thought. And he wasn't the only one. Charlie, who'd been glued to his phone all the way in the minibus until the signal abruptly stopped, was now making very sparse conversation with Paula and Rachel. Amira was walking slightly apart from everyone, not surprising after what she'd said last night. Sarah had been so shocked. There had been a few seconds' gap between Amira speaking and her words actually sinking in, when time had stood still. Poor Paula, she'd looked so stunned. Sarah knew Amira was mortified; she had apologized time and again, but the damage was well and truly done by then. Even Chloe, who could usually be relied on for a bit of light chatter, was silent, bringing up the rear, looking as if she was being led out to the gallows. She wore her North Face jacket zipped right up so it covered the bottom part of her face. At least Mark Hamilton was tagging along with the other team this morning so they didn't have to be on best behaviour for him.

It seemed almost incredible to recall it now, but a few short weeks ago, work had been just another part of Sarah's life. Now it was as if the office was her *whole* life. It was the first thing she thought of when she woke up and the last thing on her mind before she went to sleep. The sick feeling never left her, that churning sense of imminent confrontation, of being always at fault and one step away from being caught out. It had got so that Oliver and Sam and Joe were like bit players in her life, secondary to her co-workers and, more particularly, Rachel. 'Get her out of here,' Oliver had taken to saying, tapping the side of her head when he saw her gazing anxiously at nothing, knowing she was consumed with thoughts of her new boss. Sarah had always struggled with authority and Rachel's abrasive managerial style left her nerves permanently shredded.

No one was talking to her and she couldn't entirely blame them. She knew everyone had had to shoulder more work when she'd been on maternity leave with Sam, despite the promise of extra cover. She remembered what it had been like when Paula had been off for six weeks when her mother died – how they'd all had to divvy up her workload between them. Even though there'd been quiet rumblings about how so and so had managed to do a specific task in half the time Paula normally took, or how someone else had restructured the way Paula normally did something to make it twice as efficient, still they'd all been overworked and couldn't wait for her to come back. So she could understand their ambivalence about her news, but people were allowed to have children, weren't they? Surely it was a funda-mental right?

Most hurtful of all was Charlie's reaction. He'd hardly said two words to her since that scene at the rope bridge. Every time she tried to catch his eye he'd pretended to be engrossed in something on his phone. She felt so wretchedly lonely, but when she'd phoned Oliver just to hear his voice, he'd been distracted and irritable. Joe had just spilled a jar of red lentils all over the kitchen floor. 'Why'd you put the lentils in such a low cupboard anyway?' Oliver asked her crossly, as if the kitchen design was entirely her doing. And though he apologized later on for being snappy, the moment had passed then where she could whisper, 'I'm having such a horrible time,' and be comforted.

Sarah was relieved to notice that the canopy of leaves and branches overhead seemed to be thinning out. Up ahead, the light was still grey but less oppressively so. Emerging from the final ring of trees, she found they were in a clearing. There was a carpet of dead brown leaves on the ground, made mulchy by the fine rain that was falling in a light mist. A stream ran diagonally across the clearing, flanked on either side by steep banks covered with weeds and shrubs, and flowing rapidly over flat, grey rocks. They all stopped walking while Will pointed to a particularly large rock in the middle of it.

'Around there is where the stream crosses over with a ley line, or so local legend has it. That point is called Devil's Cross. Apparently these woods used to be full of devil worshippers and that's where the locals used to drown women they accused of being witches.'

Swaddled inside her suffocating coat, Sarah nevertheless felt a chill pass through her.

'Cheery thought, isn't it?' Will grinned, noticing her

shudder. 'Anyway, this is where I say my goodbyes. But not before I've collected up all your phones so no one is tempted to download a Compass App. It has been known!' Will held open his backpack and they all dropped their phones inside. Sarah was amazed how naked she felt without it.

'Adios amigos,' called Will, already heading back the way they'd come. 'See you on the Other Side.'

Although Sarah had begun to find Will's relentless chirpiness grating, still a heavy weight settled inside her as she watched him walk away. She couldn't remember the last time she'd felt so alone, and now she was feeling dizzy too, the trees in her peripheral vision blurring and swaying.

Amira held the Ordnance Survey map.

'Anyone have a clue how to read one of these things? What do the dotted green lines mean? Charlie, I'm guessing you must have been a Cub Scout in a previous life. You seem like the type.'

Sarah knew that Charlie actually had been made to go to Scouts when he was younger, and had loathed every minute of it. It had been part of his father's strategic campaign to make a man of him. Charlie claimed he'd got only two badges the entire time he'd been there – drawing and cooking – but he was prone to exaggeration and not above milking his unhappy childhood for a few laughs. It wasn't that his parents hadn't loved him, he'd once explained; more that he'd felt a monumental disconnect from them. Still, it was something she'd told him off about on more than one occasion, this tendency to offer up his private sadnesses as a form of mass entertainment.

'I haven't the foggiest,' Charlie said, peering over Amira's shoulder. 'Are you even holding that the right way up?'

'I'm sure Chloe did Geography A level,' said Paula. 'Chloe, come and take a look.'

To Sarah's surprise, the younger woman didn't come bounding over as she'd normally have expected her to.

'I'd just be useless,' she said instead, speaking into her jacket in a low, muffled voice.

'Come on. Just take a look, see if any memories are jogged.'

Chloe shuffled reluctantly over, her face still half hidden in her jacket, hands shoved deeply into her pockets. Will had marked the new position of the van on the map with a biro cross, but they still had to work out exactly where they were now and then work out which direction to go – no mean feat without a compass.

'Well, clearly we're here,' said Rachel, stabbing at the map with one of her clear glossy nails, 'where that blue line crosses over the clearing. So all we have to do is get from here,' she jabbed the page again, 'to here.' Now she jabbed the biro cross Will had drawn. Her face had lost the fixed smile it had worn in front of Mark and Will and once again her mouth was set in the hard line familiar from the office. 'Except how do we know which direction to go in?'

By now Sarah was feeling faint, and sat down on a felled tree trunk with her head in her hands. She'd had 'funny spells' as she called them, throughout her two previous pregnancies, times when she felt dizzy and lightheaded, as though the world was receding in front

254

of her. Her stomach lurched and she retched, but without any food left to throw up, she managed to swallow it down.

'Hang on. Isn't this something?' Charlie was squinting at a point on the map very close to the clearing. Sarah knew he had been prescribed glasses by the optician but was too vain to wear them. 'These two faint crosses here?'

'Graveyard,' said Chloe. 'Little one from the looks of it.'

'That be where the witches be buried,' said Amira. No one laughed.

'According to the map, that graveyard is directly north-east of us, really close by, so all we need to do is find it, and then we'll be able to work out which direction is south-west, which is where the van is.'

With her head still in her hands, the others' voices were indistinct and Sarah had trouble following what they were saying. Someone was suggesting they go off in pairs to look for the graveyard, but Ewan and Chloe, who'd been put together, were insisting it made more sense for everyone to go off independently, so they'd cover more ground. The crosses appeared to be really near. They wouldn't have to go far.

'I'm afraid I think I'll have to stay here,' Sarah said, without looking up. 'I'm not feeling well.'

Instantly Amira and Charlie came to stand on either side of her, worried.

'I'll be fine. I just need to be still for a few minutes.'

Really, she wasn't fine at all. It wasn't just that she felt so awful, there was something about this place, something about the way the trees merged into blackness on all sides, and the fetid air that seemed to suck the air from her lungs.

A figure appeared in front of her. With her head bent, Sarah could just make out Rachel's skinny black jeans and black leather and Gore-Tex hiking boots.

'I'll stay with her,' said Rachel. 'The rest of you go off and look for the graveyard and report back.'

Dread fought with nausea inside Sarah as she hunched over on the tree trunk. But she was feeling too dazed to protest. She heard the others talking in low voices before disappearing off in different directions through the trees.

Then they were alone.

'I'm sorry,' Sarah whispered. She was too hot inside her jacket. She felt as if her veins and arteries and all the little capillaries were on fire and her head was filling up with smoke. 'I'm just being a wuss. It's always like this at the beginning of a pregnancy.'

'Stupid bitch.'

Sarah's head jerked up so that she was staring straight into Rachel's blue eyes. For a moment, shock burned a path through the wooziness in her brain so that she was able to take in clearly the edges of cheekbone, the upper lip twisted into a snarl. Then the dizziness returned and she once more dropped her face into her hands to steady herself. She was vaguely aware of Rachel wandering away towards the stream, but by now she was swaying and everything was spinning, and the heat from her coat was overwhelming and the ground, with its carpet of dead brown leaves, was rising up to meet her . . .

A voice brought her back to reality. Someone shouting 'found it' from somewhere far off. She opened her eyes and found she was slumped on the ground with her back against the tree trunk; everything felt heavy and unreal. She ran her tongue around her dry lips as she heaved herself to her feet and stood blinking in the grey drizzle.

Footsteps in the leaves announced someone's arrival.

'I found it,' repeated Ewan. 'The graveyard. It's just up there.' He pointed in the direction behind the tree trunk, and then picked up a stick and drew an arrow in the leaves and mud just to be sure. 'Horrible place, actually. Gave me the creeps.'

Almost immediately the others arrived, summoned by Ewan's earlier shouts.

'Well done,' Amira said, slapping Ewan on the shoulder. 'Let's get going. There's a bottle of fizz somewhere with our names on it. Where's Rachel?'

Rachel. Something inside Sarah contracted suddenly at the name. And now the fine hairs at the back of her neck were pricking, remembering her boss's face as she said that thing. *Stupid bitch.*

'I don't know where she is. I was—'

The scream cut Sarah off mid-sentence. Chloe.

'Oh my God! Quick! Help!'

She was standing at the top of the steep bank looking down at something in the stream below.

Sarah felt a knot of dread forming in the pit of her stomach.

By now the others had joined Chloe.

'Is she breathing?' asked Charlie.

Sarah made her way slowly towards the cluster of figures in nylon jackets and hoods until she could see what they were looking at.

Rachel lay at the foot of the bank, her legs and feet

submerged in the water, her head buttressed up against a protruding rock. Sarah clapped a hand to her mouth as she noticed the blood trickling from somewhere in Rachel's hairline.

'There's definitely a pulse, thank God,' Ewan called up. He'd been first to scramble down the bank and was now on his knees in the water, leaning over Rachel's motionless body.

As Ewan gently shook her arm, Rachel began to moan softly. If it wasn't for the blood, Sarah would have sworn she was acting the part of someone injured, so perfect was her dramatic timing.

By this time Amira and Charlie were also down on the bank, crouching next to Rachel.

Amira held her boss's hand in hers. 'Are you OK, Rachel? Can you hear me?'

Nothing. Just that soft, ominous moaning.

Ewan looked up so he was staring right at Sarah. 'What the fuck happened to her?'

Now everyone was looking at her, and Sarah felt herself flushing inside her too-hot coat.

'I don't know. I was kind of passed out over there.'

Ewan's heavy dark brows knitted together. 'You didn't look very passed out to me when I got here.'

'She's coming round!' shouted Amira, bending her head towards Rachel.

Rachel slowly sat up, blinking in the dull grey light. She put her hand to her head, looking shocked when her fingers came back covered in blood.

'What happened?' she asked. 'Where are we?'

Between Ewan and Amira, they set about getting Rachel back up the bank, with Charlie hovering ineffectually around them giving instructions. 'Left foot higher, Ewan. Watch that loose stone, Amira!'

Finally they were at the top, leading Rachel towards the tree trunk where she sank down until she was sitting, then slumped forwards. Her face, always pale, was alabaster white against her dark hair. She opened her mouth as if she was about to speak, then exhaled heavily. Some few seconds later, she tried again.

'Someone pushed me,' she said at last.

Chloe let out an audible gasp and Sarah felt herself growing cold.

'What do you mean?' Ewan demanded. 'Who pushed you?'

'I don't know,' snapped Rachel, sounding more like her usual self. 'I was right here, talking to Sarah, and then I walked over to the stream and was looking down, and all of a sudden someone shoved me from behind.'

And now everyone was turning to look at Sarah.

'I . . . I don't know what happened,' she stammered. 'I passed out for a bit.'

Rachel fixed her with the shards of her eyes.

'Passed out? I don't think so. We were talking.'

And now Sarah remembered something.

'Yes. We *were* talking. You called me a bitch.'

'What?' You had to give Rachel her due, she looked genuinely surprised. 'I didn't call you a bitch. I said I was going to look in the *ditch*.'

A wave of heat swept through Sarah and she fumbled to unzip the down jacket as if it was on fire.

'That's not true. You said . . .' But now doubt was creeping in. 'Well, whatever you said, I was sitting here on this trunk, feeling sick and faint and you walked away and the next thing I knew, Ewan was here.'

'No. You were standing up and wide awake when I arrived.'

She couldn't believe how confrontational Ewan was being.

'You woke me up!' She knew she was sounding defensive. 'When you shouted! I came to, and stood up – and Rachel was gone. I didn't see anyone else here. Are you sure you couldn't have slipped?'

She'd turned to face Rachel, but couldn't bring herself to look her straight in the eye, focusing instead on a point just underneath where the dim light was picking out leftover glints from last night's make-up.

'I didn't *slip*.' Rachel pronounced the word as if it was something distasteful. 'I was pushed.'

There was a silence while everyone tried to absorb what had happened. Paula, who'd been largely silent since returning from her solitary exploration, was the first to break it.

'I think we should talk about all this when we're safely back at the hotel. Rachel should probably get that head looked at.'

They set off in the opposite direction from the arrow Ewan had drawn in the dirt with a stick, heading, they hoped, in a south-westerly direction to where the van was. With Chloe dredging up her A-level Geography knowledge to read the Ordnance Survey map, they navigated their way through the seemingly never-ending wood, eventually coming out into a field from which they were able to pick up a public footpath that would lead them to the pick-up spot.

While Ewan and Amira followed behind Chloe and Paula, supporting Rachel who seemed to be recovering quickly from her ordeal, Sarah and Charlie fell back behind the others. Shock had jolted Charlie out of the strange mood he'd been in since her pregnancy announcement of the day before.

'What really happened?' he asked her, his voice low.

Sarah felt another stab of misplaced guilt.

'I told you. We spoke. She called me a bitch, out of the blue. Or at least I'm pretty sure she did. Then I passed out.'

'What, literally blacked out?'

'Yes. Well, no, not literally. It's more of a wooziness that comes over me. It's a pregnancy thing.'

She thought she could sense Charlie stiffening beside her at that word 'pregnancy'.

'So you didn't see or hear anything?'

'No, Charlie, I didn't. What is this? You don't believe me? You think I *pushed* her?'

'No, of course not. I mean, everyone knows you're pissed off about this disciplinary threat – not to mention hormonally unbalanced – but that doesn't make you a homicidal maniac, does it?'

Sarah glanced at Charlie and saw that the corners of his mouth were twitching. She relaxed slightly, hoping they were friends again.

'I bet she slipped down there, and was too humiliated to admit it,' she said. 'So she made the whole thing up.'

'Yeah, or maybe she planned the whole thing and bashed herself in the head with a rock to make it look good.'

They both giggled, and Sarah could have cried with

relief. It felt so good to be sharing confidences with Charlie again after feeling so cast out.

But as they emerged through another copse of trees and saw the minibus in the distance, with the sales and marketing team already gathered around it, swigging from plastic cups, the knot in her stomach returned. Surely no one would believe she'd actually done anything to Rachel? The rain was starting to come down in earnest now, soaking through her jacket and dripping off her eyelashes. Yet with every step they took towards the bus, her trepidation grew. Something bad had happened back there. But she had a terrible feeling that things were about to get a lot worse.

30
Anne

There was another photograph on the news last night. Taken with friends outside a café or bar, three faces smiling into the camera, arms around each other's shoulders. I knew instantly which one was you. I'd kept tabs over the years, through Barbara. When a case affects you that much, you don't let it go easily. Until that picture flashed up last night, though, I hadn't recognized anything of the child from all those years ago in the photos she'd sent me. But something about that picture, a familiar look in the eyes, brought it all back.

I wondered then about your life. Were you close to the two women either side of you? That would mean you were at least capable of forming friendships. Have you been happy? What had turned the person smiling at the camera into someone capable of doing what you did? Was this in some way my fault?

Before our fifth session with Laurie, Ed Kowalsky and I met up with officials from the Child Welfare Department. Hurrying up the steps to the brownstone building downtown where the Welfare Department was housed, past the flagpole where the Stars and Stripes hung, noticeably faded after a relentless summer, I felt nervous. Underqualified.

I'd arranged to meet Ed there, ostensibly because it was more convenient but really to avoid another tense journey in Ed's dog-hair-ridden station wagon. Ever since we had stood side by side in that dank basement, we'd been awkward around each other. Whereas a few weeks before, he would lean into me in that way he had, as if personal space was an outdated concept, now he seemed to shrink back.

I was late to the meeting. I'd spent too long preparing, trying to pre-empt the questions I'd be asked. Determined not to be found wanting. By the time I arrived at the meeting room, having had to retrace my steps to reception after failing to find it on the first attempt, I was out of breath and flustered. It was an unseasonably warm day and I regretted my choice of a long-sleeved shirt and thick cotton pants. From the heat coming off my skin, I could tell that my face would have gone the deep red I hated.

Walking into the room, I had the strangest feeling of intruding. Ed sat at a round table flanked by Debra, the thickset welfare officer who'd accompanied Laurie the first time we met her, and another woman with short cropped salt and pepper hair and tanned leathery skin, against which her teeth appeared unnaturally white when she smiled.

'Dr Cater?' she said. 'Please come in and take a seat.'

There was another person seated at the table, a slight man with thinning strawberry-blond hair and a short-sleeved white shirt. He had freckles on his face and arms and a strangely shaped nose, as if someone had pinched it until it stayed that way. Jana sat to his left, looking cool and smooth.

'You know Debra Albright, Laurie's personal case-worker, and Laurie's foster mother Jana Green, of course. This is George Sullivan, who runs our legal team, and I'm Nancy Meade, head of the Child Welfare Division. I'm afraid we couldn't wait to get started. We're all on a tight schedule.'

Her eyes darted towards the clock on the wall to make her point.

'So, we've just been discussing Laurie's case with Professor Kowalsky and agreeing that we're all pretty encouraged by the progress she's made since her parents were arrested. As you know, Laurie and her brother David have been made wards of state. David's case is, of course, very different, owing to the level of neglect he suffered in his early years. At four and a half, Laurie still has the potential to put this part of her life completely behind her. There is an enforced adoption order in place so regardless of her parents' wishes, we can push ahead with that if that's what we decide is most appropriate. We have reciprocal adoption arrangements with organi-zations in Canada, Australia, New Zealand, the UK – places where Laurie could be completely anonymous. Mrs Green here is of the opinion that would be the best thing for her in the circumstances, and Professor Kowalsky has just told us that, from your sessions so far, the two of you are inclined to agree, which makes me wonder if we should start the ball rolling. George, can you explain to us the legal steps in this process . . .'

'Wait a minute.'

The words were out before I'd even had a chance to

work out what would follow them. Five pairs of eyes turned towards me.

'It's just that Ed and I – that is, Professor Kowalsky and I – haven't really discussed this properly. The sessions are still very much ongoing and I think it's too early to completely rule out the possibility that Laurie will need extensive long-term therapy to fully process what has happened to her.'

Nancy Meade blinked in surprise, although her ultra-white smile remained in place.

'Well, obviously we would need to be completely sure, but I should remind you of the time constraints here. Of course the two of you,' she nodded her wiry head in the direction of first Ed and then me, 'know much more about the cut-off age for childhood amnesia, before the formation of long-term memories begins, but I would imagine we're pretty near. Plus I don't need to tell you that it's far easier to find adoptive parents for a four-year-old than an older child.'

'I think Dr Cater is just erring on the side of caution,' Ed broke in, and I could tell from the way he stressed the first syllable of my surname, that my intervention had embarrassed him.

'We know that the hippocampus and the prefrontal cortex – the two parts of the brain responsible for processing memory – become fully developed around the age Laurie is now, so we're well aware of the need for speed. We still have another couple of sessions scheduled and we will hold off from making any final decisions until we're completely satisfied that adoption is the way to go, but I can say that at this moment in time, that seems like a more likely outcome.'

He glared at me through his reading glasses as if daring me to contradict him. I pinched the skin of my left wrist between the fingers of my right hand and didn't look away.

Jana raised one of her long, slender fingers. 'Could I say something? I know I'm only a mom and you all are the experts.'

A collective murmur of dissent went around the table. Ed shook his head vigorously.

'I just wanted to give you my take for what it's worth as I probably see more of Laurie than anyone else. She's a dear little girl. That isn't to say there aren't aspects of her behaviour that concern me. She has occasional tantrums like all kids that age and she still over-reacts in situations when there's strong disciplining going on. And she has those kind of trances, you know, like we talked about before.' She was appealing to me and Ed.

'Barney – he's my younger one – gets a little spooked by her when that happens, and he has started asking, "When is Laurie going back to her people?" He's such a character. But given everything she's been through, I think she is doing really, really well. Like amazingly well. And I just think she deserves the very best chance of being able to lead a normal life. Anyway, like I say I'm no expert.'

She shrugged her shoulders. Today she was wearing a cheesecloth top with a slash neckline that showed off her long throat. The two men around the table lapped her up like a dish of milk.

'I like to think I've also built up a bit of a rapport with Laurie.' Debra, Laurie's case-worker whom we'd met during our first session with Child L, sounded usurped.

'After all, I was the first person she met here when the police first brought her from that house.'

Nancy's nostrils flared as if stifling a sigh, but her smile remained fixed.

'Of course, Debra, you've been a real constant in Laurie's life since she's been with us, and I know she's very attached to you, so we'd certainly value your input as well.'

Debra pressed her lips together and a flush of pleasure spread over her wide cheeks. Her tone, when she started speaking again, was softer.

'I guess all I'd say is that Laurie is real keen to please. You know, you just have to ask her to do something once and she's already jumped right up and done it. Do y'all know what I mean?'

'And you think that bodes well for her being able to make a fresh start?' Nancy was holding a pencil poised over a notebook but her arm was laid across the page, shielding it from my view.

Debra tilted her head and gazed thoughtfully into the middle distance before replying.

'Yeah, I do. I think it's got to be a good thing, doesn't it, for a child to want to make authority figures happy. It means she'll take her cue from the adults around her. And she's whip-smart. She'll learn real fast.'

I felt my pulse speeding up and my mouth went dry, but I couldn't help myself.

'With all due respect, I'm not sure I entirely agree. The desire to please isn't always a positive thing. Sometimes it can be a sign that a person is sublimating their own feelings in favour of other people's, and that's not always what we would consider healthy, particularly given Laurie's background. For me it's a concern that Laurie hasn't acted out more. This is a child who has been torn from her family, from her home, from everything she knows. I would have expected there to be more displays of anger, more challenges to authority. The fact that she is exhibiting this kind of docile behaviour that seems built around a need for adult approval makes me worry that she isn't processing what's happened to her but is just suppressing it because she's learned that her real feelings aren't valid, and, not only that, will probably get her into a whole heap of trouble. We shouldn't underestimate the effect of exposure to extreme punishment at such an early age.'

I was long-winded in those days. Verbose. We all were. All of us women academics. We didn't dare launch our opinions straight at people, didn't have the confidence in our own judgements, so instead we dressed them up with flounces and fancy bows and nestled them in tissue paper so it was impossible to tell what they were without rooting around and peeling back layers. We worked twice as hard as our male contemporaries, men like Dan Oppenheimer, but then we offered up our knowledge like a present to be cast aside or else opened at leisure, its contents accepted or rejected on the whim of the recipient. On this occasion, the latter held true.

'This is Dr Cater's first major case study, and I'm sure I'm not alone in commending her thoroughness and commitment,' said Ed, looking around the table with a smile. 'As I said earlier, we'll obviously be making sure that, whatever recommendation we arrive at, it's in the best interests not only of Laurie herself but also whoever she's going to come into close contact with in the coming years. So we won't be reaching any conclusions without plenty of thought and discussion, but at the same time we completely take on board the need for a speedy resolution so that Laurie can move on to the next stage in her life, whatever that might be.'

As we stood up to shake hands around the table, I glanced down at Nancy Meade's notepad. She'd written down each of our names – Ed, Jana, Debra, me and even George Sullivan the lawyer. Next to each name was a scribbled version of what they'd said. All except mine. Alongside *Dr Anne Cater* was a series of question marks.

31

Charlie

Charlie's life was spinning out of control, and he was twirling round and round, grabbing at air, trying to hold it down. That's how it felt. The weekend in Derbyshire had destabilized some elemental thing in the universe and now everything was out of kilter, everything was wrong.

To be completely accurate, the problems had started before the weekend. For days now, Stefan had been growing increasingly distant. When Charlie tried to phone him, he didn't pick up. He'd return the calls hours later and always when he was walking to the gym or running a bath or some other activity that necessitated a curtailed conversation that rarely dipped beneath the surface. The one night they'd spent together the previous week had been soul-destroying. They were supposed to be meeting straight from work but Stefan had cancelled at the last minute, saying he had a dinner meeting and would call him afterwards, but it had been after 11 p.m. when he'd finally got in touch. 'I imagine you're safely tucked up with your camomile tea,' he'd said, not altogether kindly. And Charlie, who'd been sitting on his sofa wearing the brand-new Calvin Klein trunks he'd bought for the occasion, had humiliated himself by pretending he'd only just got home himself and offering to jump in a cab to go round. Which he did, to find Stefan already in bed. 'I'm exhausted,' he said, coming to the door in a tatty old dressing gown Charlie had never seen before. He'd been asleep before Charlie had even had a chance to take his trousers off.

The sane, rational part of Charlie knew Stefan had already grown tired of him, was just using him for the occasional meal or when his ego needed boosting by Charlie's undisguisable adoration. Yet, still he couldn't let go. Meeting Stefan had been like pressing the 'enhance' option on his digital photos, so colours that had previously been drab and monochrome sprang suddenly, gloriously to life. He'd never known such agony, but equally he'd also never known such exquisite euphoria as when Stefan laughed at something he said, or surprised him with a hug from behind as he was brushing his teeth. Charlie stored up those moments, rare as they were, like an alcoholic hides bottles, bringing them out to savour when no one else was around.

But last Friday, the day before the Derbyshire weekend, he'd been supposed to meet up with Stefan for dinner. He'd spent hours online, trawling through restaurant recommendations before picking a place he thought Stefan would enjoy. It wasn't the sort of place Charlie would have chosen for himself – too cool for its own good, too expensive – but it was new, and had featured in the gossip section of the free commuter paper the previous month when a hugely popular blogger Charlie had never heard of launched her new book there.

All day he'd been warning himself not to get too

excited, reminding himself that Stefan would probably cancel at the last minute. He'd tried to manage his own expectations so that the blow, if it came, wouldn't be too traumatic. And yet when Stefan rang at 5.25, to say something had indeed come up – a potential client who needed schmoozing – Charlie's expectations hadn't been managed at all. While he'd held it together on the phone, afterwards, alone at his desk, he'd felt a ripping pain in his chest as if someone was cutting him open, followed by a rage more powerful than anything he remembered feeling before.

On his way to the Tube, he'd logged on to Facebook, clicking on to Stefan's home page. Stefan used social media in the same way most people used food or air – posting photos or updates was a normal physiological reflex to him, just like breathing. Sure enough, there was an automatic tracking update showing a little map of a small section of Soho marked with red lines and accompanied by an automated message: *Stefan Lovato is at Buns 'n' Roses with Jacob Collins.*

Charlie knew exactly who Jacob Collins was – had observed the moment he and Stefan first met at a private view in a gallery a couple of weeks before. Jacob: early thirties, bearded, long hair tied up on his head in a top-knot. Cool. Stupidly handsome. He was no potential client.

That little update on Stefan's page turned a dial inside Charlie's head. *Click.* And suddenly he wasn't the Charlie who put up with disappointment, whose job it was to make other people laugh, or comfort them when they were sad and then go home alone. His heart was a wild, unpredictable animal released from its cage. Instead of going home, he'd gone to Soho. He'd tracked down Buns 'n' Roses (which was every bit as hideous as its name suggested). He'd stood on the pavement opposite the restaurant looking in at the man he loved leaning over a small table so that his head touched his companion's ridiculous topknot – and something had gone off in his head like a mini explosion.

Rage mixed with heartbreak and frustration and self-disgust, forming a toxic liquid that travelled through his veins and arteries until it reached every part of him, and not one cell of his body felt known and familiar.

He'd taken a taxi round to Stefan's flat and broken in through a back window that he knew didn't lock properly. Half an hour later, when he finally let himself out, his anger was still churning and he'd been carried home on a tide of blind fury. So it was only when his alarm went off on Saturday morning to wake him up for Derbyshire, and he discovered streaks of blood across the sheets from the arm he'd cut breaking into Stefan's flat, that the reality of what he'd done hit home. He had a sudden image of how Stefan's bed had looked by the time he left, with the duvet ripped up, feathers strewn around the room like confetti, and he thought he was going to be sick.

On the journey to meet Amira and Sarah at St Pancras station, he'd rehearsed his story for how he cut his arm. Opening a can seemed like a lame excuse but it was the best he could come up with. His core muscles were clenched so tightly, he'd given himself a stomach ache, and a couple of times he thought he might actually throw up, imagining that at any moment, he might feel a hand on his shoulder and turn round to find the police standing there. But as the morning wore on with no irate messages from Stefan accusing him of trashing his flat, he began to relax. Maybe he hadn't made as much of a mess as he'd thought. Maybe Stefan would see it as fair retribution for what he'd done. It never occurred to him that Stefan might fail to link him to what had happened. In his mind it was too obvious. Too inevitable even. But by the time he'd had a couple of canned gin and tonics with Sarah and Amira, he'd calmed down and was even starting to enjoy the weekend in a 'so bad it's good' kind of way. Until the texts came. They'd started on Saturday afternoon and gone on all through that evening and Sunday. Stefan accusing, Charlie defensive, not admitting what he'd done, until it finally occurred to him that the reason Stefan had delayed contacting him was because he'd spent the night with Jacob. After that, the rage had returned until he'd had to turn off his phone just so he could breathe again. Then had come the business with Rachel falling in the stream, and the whole thing with Stefan had been pushed from his mind.

Now, though, walking back into the office on Monday morning, he was plunged into a kind of black gloom, torn between grief at the loss of Stefan, and fear about what he'd done to Stefan's flat. He kept imagining Jacob Collins with his stupid beard and stupid hair. Charlie knew Jacob ran a successful business selling artisan ice creams from pop-up vans around the capital. Money. With Stefan, it all came down to money in the end.

He made a decision. If Rachel came back in today, he'd march straight in there and demand to be put forward for the promotion. He knew it wasn't fair on Paula, but surely at some point he had to start looking out for himself. He couldn't carry on living his limbo of a life, aimless and lonely. Going nowhere. He may have failed in love but he could still achieve something at work, get out of the rut he was in. He had to try to rid himself of the feeling he'd had ever since he could remember that he was somehow unworthy of happiness.

'What's the atmosphere like in there?' he asked Amira when he popped into the kitchen straight from the lift, to find her filling up the kettle.

She shrugged. 'Like you'd expect.'

Black shadows ringed Amira's dark eyes, making them look as if someone had smudged them with a soft pencil.

'Maybe Rachel won't come in today – after what happened.'

She shrugged again. 'She's like one of those snakes who grow a new skin. She'll probably turn up right as rain.'

'What's up, Amira? You seem really down.'

A third shrug. Followed by a sigh. Then her shoulders sagged.

'I've fucked up, Charlie. Big time. Run up all these debts on store cards. Thought I'd be able to pay the interest when I got paid, but forgot about the bloody service charge on the flat. That came out automatically and now there's nothing left – no credit anywhere. And I got a bailiffs' notice in the post this morning.'

A tear formed in the acute angle at the corner of Amira's eye. Charlie followed its track down her cheek with dismay. Amira wasn't the crying sort. Sarah seemed to burst into tears with such frequency he sometimes found himself wondering if, behind the delicate membrane of her eyeball, there existed a reservoir of salty water, and one prick would send the whole lot crashing through. But Amira wasn't like that. It wasn't that she was hard, but she didn't wear herself as close to the surface as Sarah did. So the tear made Charlie uncomfortable.

'What does Tom say?'

Amira hung her head as the original tear was joined by another. And then another.

'I haven't told him,' she admitted eventually. 'He'd be so pissed off if he knew I was buying more stuff when we've just got this huge mortgage. But I thought I could pay it back without him knowing.'

Charlie felt suddenly exasperated. 'How on earth did you imagine you were going to pay it all back if you're so overdrawn?'

Amira looked up at him and an expression passed over her face that looked suspiciously like guilt.

'If I tell you something, will you promise not to say anything to anyone else?'

Charlie nodded, although part of him wanted to say no. There were already so many secrets in the office. He didn't know if he could face being burdened with another. But Amira clearly needed to talk to someone.

'Rachel called me into her office a while ago. It was completely out of the blue – I didn't do anything to encourage it.'

Amira was looking at him as if he'd accused her of something and he found himself nodding again, to reassure her, although he had no idea what he was reassuring her about.

'She asked if I'd be interested in a promotion,' Amira

continued. 'I said there was nowhere to be promoted to, no vacancy.'

Unease prickled on Charlie's skin, causing the hair on his arms to stand up.

'So then she said it was Paula's job and did I want it. Don't look at me like that, for fuck's sake! I said no, OK? I was really straight with her. I said it was underhand. But she kept bringing it up. Again and again. And, you know what? I'd be fucking good at it. And it would be a lot more money, and you know Paula really has been doing it too long. She's so slow, she's practically Jurassic.'

'So you changed your mind about taking it?'

'Yeah.' She nodded, looking utterly miserable. 'Don't get me wrong, I feel totally crap about it. But I need the money, and the department needs shaking up. Everyone knows Paula's just treading water until she can retire. So anyway I just figured that soon I'd be earning more money and the bills would all get paid. Why are you smiling? What's so funny?'

Charlie felt the laughter tearing painfully from him. Rachel was playing them both. What a bitch. What a total bitch.

'Guess what?' he asked Amira, still smiling although he actually felt like he might throw up. 'She offered me that job too.'

Amira stared at him, tears brimming unshed in her eyes, so that her irises looked like brown marbles bobbing under water.

'And you said yes?'

'Course not. I did exactly the same as you. I said no a couple of times. But then I started to think about it and how I might as well take advantage of it because she's going to get rid of Paula no matter what. Let's face it, she's just dead wood, isn't she?'

There was a noise behind him, like a sucking in of breath. Facing him, Amira's face changed, her mouth opening in horror. Dread rooted him to the spot, not wanting to see what she was seeing. But slowly his head turned, as if pulled by an external force outside his control.

Paula stood in the doorway, her round moon face frozen. Then abruptly it collapsed, the features folding in on themselves.

'I thought you were my friends,' she said in a voice so laced with hurt it seemed to be drawn out from somewhere deep inside her ribcage.

'We are,' Charlie began. 'It's just—'

But it was too late. Paula was gone.

'Oh fuck!' Amira said. But Charlie was too ashamed to look at her.

32

Paula

The anxiety, which before had been like an army of tiny ants swarming through her veins, had now turned into an endless oozing panic that pulsed and surged and tsunami'd inside her, sweeping in its wake all that had once been calm and ordered and stable.

Paula left work straight after the scene with Amira and Charlie, and for the first time in her entire working life she didn't give a reason, nor did she tell anyone she was going. It should have been liberating, but instead her head was churning with the words she'd overheard in the kitchen: 'dead wood', 'slow', 'Jurassic'.

All through her worst times with Ian, when she'd come home to a wall of resentment and all those little digs and put-downs that only someone who's been close enough to know your secret weaknesses and soft points can come up with, the image of herself at work, reliable and responsible, had kept her self-confidence from shattering like the fragile stem of a wine glass. When Cam was playing up and Amy dropped out of sixth form, and she and Ian couldn't talk about any of it without each blaming the other, work was her refuge – the still point of her turning world. The rest of her life might be crumbling, but there in the office, she was a professional, someone others counted on to hold things together, someone they looked up to.

Except it was all a lie.

Throughout that whole day, the thoughts she normally managed to keep at bay came flooding out, unchecked, thoughts she'd believed she'd left behind in childhood. She was useless. Bad. No one in their right mind would trust her, or like her, much less love her. Why had she ever believed she was good at anything?

If Rachel got rid of her, she'd have three months' money and that would be it. Rachel would call it a 'restructuring'. Paula already knew that much. Her exact job title would be scrapped, but whoever replaced her – Charlie or Amira, those snakes in the grass – would get a different title that would say much the same thing. Three months' money. That's all there would be to show for her decade of loyalty, all those mornings she'd got in early and the evenings she'd worked on long after the others had left. She'd never been ambitious, just imagined living out her working life in the office, the stabilizing centre while everyone else came and went around her.

Now who would employ her? She was fifty-five, and she both looked and felt it. Not one of those 'stay in shape, fifty-is-the-new-thirty' types. Everyone wanted the new thing, the latest model. Who would take on a dinosaur who'd been chucked out by her old department like so much rubbish?

'Are you even listening?' Amy demanded at dinner after recounting a long story about a customer at the pub where she worked who'd insisted that two separate bottles of wine were corked, only to be met with blank silence from her mother.

'Sorry,' Paula said. 'I'm not feeling myself.'

But if not herself, who even was she?

She didn't tell Ian about what she'd overheard in the office kitchen. They'd got well beyond the stage where they could give any comfort to each other. Instead, she went to bed early, shutting herself away with only her own destructive thoughts for company. Round and round they went like a washing-machine cycle of self-doubt.

Throughout that long, sleepless night, the pounding in her ears never left her – the noise of all her old insecurities whooshing around in her brain.

33

Anne

It had to happen sooner or later and now it has. Some UK journalist or other. They have no rules over there. There's nowhere their gutter press won't go. They uncovered the details of the adoption all those years ago. Traced it back to La Luz City and found a story bigger than they could have ever believed.

The first I heard of it was when the new departmental secretary knocked on the door of my office this morning.

'Sorry to disturb you, Professor Cater, but there's a journalist on the phone. He's asking lots of questions about a Professor Korsky who used to work here.'

'Do you mean Kowalsky?'

'Yes, that's the one. He's very insistent. Says it's in connection with some big case in England.'

'I'll talk to him. Put him through.'

As I listened to the secretary's heels clicking on the floor down the corridor, past the framed faculty photographs, I took a deep breath in and then held it, counting in my head, trying to control my thoughts. When the phone started ringing, I expelled the breath in a long, steady exhalation.

'Professor Cater? This is Derek Walsh from the *Sun* newspaper in London.'

'Hello, Mr Walsh. What can I do for you?' I aimed for warm but professional. If you smile while you're talking on the phone the listener can hear it in your voice.

He explained about the terrible thing that had happened in London and I pretended it was news to me.

'We tend to be very insular over here, Mr Walsh.'

He said that didn't surprise him, having spent a year in Massachusetts as part of his college degree. He sounded touchingly proud of that fact.

'The thing is,' he said, and there was no disguising the excitement in his voice, 'we did some digging and found out about the adoption and then we did some more digging and found there were rather sensational circumstances, and your Professor Kowalsky was the shrink who oversaw the adoption process. Looks like he rubberstamped the whole thing, said there was no lasting damage. So in effect he might be held partly accountable for what happened. Him and his assistant, I forget the name now. Hold on.'

The line clicked a few times as if someone was setting down a handset on a hard surface. I closed my eyes and breathed in slowly. Then came the sound of papers rustling and then the handset clicked back into life.

'Ah right. Here it is – knew I had it. Yes, Professor Kowalsky's sidekick was . . .' a sound like a biro tapping against a page, time slowing to a standstill . . . 'a Dr Oppenheimer. Ring any bells?'

Relief made my muscles weak. I had been given a reprieve.

At the time it was all taking place though, all those years ago, it hadn't been relief but pure fury that had flowed through my veins when my nemesis, Dan Oppenheimer, first encroached on what had been, up to then, my assessment, my territory.

I hadn't slept well in the days following the meeting at the Child Welfare Department. I was young and inexperienced when it came to judging personal inter-actions. (I still struggle. In fact, a shrink I was seeing a few years ago asked me if I'd ever considered whether I might be on the autistic spectrum. 'Most of us are,' he said glibly.) I could tell that something had been damaged between me and Ed Kowalsky, but not what or how deep the damage went.

We were due to meet with Laurie again. This time we were visiting the preschool she'd been attending two days a week. The idea was we'd chat to staff about her progress and observe her interacting with the other kids and then take her out for ice cream with Jana. We'd agreed it would be low-key and informal, so I was taken aback to arrive at the tiny school office to find that Ed had brought someone else with him. Daniel Oppenheimer. The two of them filled the cramped room.

'Ah, Anne. You know Dan, I take it?' said Ed casually.

I nodded, unable to look at my classroom rival – which was a tricky feat considering Oppenheimer's freakish height.

'He's going to be joining our sessions from now on. I felt we'd now reached a point in the proceedings with Laurie where a fresh pair of eyes would be a boon, and of course Dan knows the case inside out from his involve-ment with David's assessment.'

'But what about cross-overs? I thought you decided the two cases needed to be kept completely separate, to avoid the possibility of us influencing one another?'

Ed was nodding before I'd even finished, as if he'd anticipated the question.

'Quite so. Quite so. But now that the preliminaries are over and we've had time to, ah, get the measure of each child's needs, I think that danger is past. I'll level with you, Anne. I believe we've reached a critical stage with Laurie. Her age now makes it imperative that we reach a decision on her future quickly, and I think Dan is ideally placed to help us arrive at that decision.'

My heart was pounding so hard I thought it must be obvious, even through the sweater I'd put on against the sudden chill. After a mild September which had failed to distinguish itself fully from the sweltering months which preceded it, fall had finally arrived over the last couple of days, bringing cool winds which I welcomed wholeheartedly.

'Right. Of course. The more the merrier.'

My own jolly voice grated in my ears, but what else could I have done? It was obvious that, when faced with the choice between potential competition and potential dissent, Ed had chosen the former. Dan Oppenheimer would aim to build his career out of this case in a way I'd never dare to. I'd always suspected this was probably the real reason Ed had only allowed him to see half the picture. But now I'd proved less biddable than he'd imagined, he was going into damage limitation. If there were three of us, the majority view would hold. Oppenheimer would back up Kowalsky if it was strategically advantageous for him to do so. I was effectively being sidelined.

The women who ran the preschool buzzed around Dan and Ed. They kept calling Dan 'Professor', although he did try to correct them. To me they addressed all the practical questions – would we be wanting coffee, lemonade? – and the more domestic details about Laurie's life. So in the middle of an anecdote about how Laurie had helped another, younger child, the woman relating it turned to me to mouth 'to the toilet' before turning back to the others to continue her story.

And all the time, as I sat awkwardly on the tiny chair that was the only choice after the men had been offered the two spare full-size ones, anxiety was churning my insides. Should I have kept my opinions to myself? Followed Ed Kowalsky's lead? Stayed quiet for the sake of my career? I thought about Harvard and Yale and Cornell, the office I'd envisaged for myself in a redbrick building with ivy growing up the walls and a view out over the treetops as they turned from green to orange before shedding completely. Now, from my vantage point across the years, I call out to my younger self wedged into that little chair with her ungainly knees up under her chin. 'Toe the line,' I say to her. 'Nod when he speaks and agree when it's your turn. There'll be time enough to find your voice when you're out of there.' But, miserable and agitated, my younger self doesn't hear.

'Would you say that on the whole Laurie knows the difference between right and wrong?'

Dan's first question of the process caught all of us by surprise.

The Head of the preschool, a small blonde woman in a knee-length dress with a bow at the collar and flat white shoes with just the tiniest splatter of red paint on the sole to give away her vocation, bit down on her bottom lip in concentration before replying.

'Obviously she's very young still and there's a debate about how much of a moral framework any child of four really has, but on the whole I would say she has a fairly good idea of what behaviour is and isn't acceptable. I believe someone must have taught her the basics of right and wrong, although coming from that home it's impossible to imagine they knew the difference.'

If she was hoping to invite some broader confidences relating to Laurie's past life, she was to be disappointed.

'And there haven't been any incidents to give you cause for concern?' asked Ed, smartly closing the door on conjecture and bringing the conversation back to the here and the now.

The Head frowned.

'There have been minor issues, just as you'd expect with any child of that age. She reacts badly to being told off – sometimes running away to hide, other times getting angry or upset.'

'And if other children are being told off?' I asked her.

The Head swung round to face me with a look of surprise, as if she'd only now noticed I was there.

'She doesn't always respond well in those situations either,' she said at last. 'We have had occasions where we have had to gently remind her that *we* are in charge and the disciplining of other students isn't her responsibility.'

'Tell them about the Wendy house,' said a young woman with long brown braids, who'd been standing by the doorway clearly waiting for a chance to get involved.

'I'm not sure it's what you're looking for,' said the Head after another pause. 'But the other day – when we had that sudden scorcher, do you remember – anyway, the kids were all outside in the playground and, well, there's been some trouble between two of the little girls. You know how small children can be,' she said directly to me, before continuing.

'I'm afraid one of the two has been bullying the other a bit. We've been trying to deal with it, but such behaviour isn't uncommon. Laurie hasn't initiated any of the trouble but she's clearly been agitated by it, sometimes reporting back to us about what's been going on, other times joining in with some not-very-pleasant behaviour, like refusing to let the girl play a game the rest of them are playing or repeating some of the meaner things being said. All perfectly normal.

'On this particular occasion all the children were playing outside as I said. We were having a little staff conference over here on the porch about the afternoon's activities. We had a good view of the playground and we gradually realized there was something going on down at the far end, near the Wendy house – a disturbance. I went over there as quickly as I could and all the children were standing around outside. Some of them were laughing in a kind of nervous way but a couple of the girls were crying. The girl who'd been doing the bullying was outside the door, and as soon as she saw me she said, "It wasn't me." Just like that. So I knew something had happened.

'When I got closer, there was just Laurie in the Wendy house and the other little girl, Sandy, who she'd tied up with a skipping rope.'

'Well, that doesn't sound too bad,' said Ed. 'I mean, not ideal certainly but not entirely aberrant either.'

'Sandy was naked,' said the braided young woman in the doorway, seizing her opportunity to take centre stage. 'Well, near enough. Laurie had taken off her clothes before she tied her up.'

'Not *all* her clothes,' said the Head reprovingly. 'But yes, it was . . . unfortunate. The child told her parents and we had to call all the girls and parents together for a meeting.'

'When was this?' I asked, wondering why Jana hadn't mentioned anything the last time we'd met.

'Just a couple of days ago,' said the Head. 'To be honest, it probably sounds more serious than it actually was. Aside from the skipping rope and the clothes, Laurie hadn't done anything to hurt her. And as I said, she wasn't the instigator of the bullying campaign. In fact, the little girl's parents were far more concerned about the girl who'd started the whole thing.'

'Did you notice anything about Laurie's state of mind when you found her in the Wendy house?' I asked. From the corner of my eye, I saw Ed Kowalsky stiffen and straighten, as if he'd thought the questioning was over.

'Well, she certainly wasn't angry or agitated, if that's what you were hoping to hear,' said the Head tartly. She glanced over towards Ed and Dan, and I wondered if she'd picked up on the tension between us.

'In fact, she was unusually calm, almost like she was in a trance.'

Wandering outside to the playground, we spotted Laurie straight away. She was playing with another little girl in the sandbox at the far end. We watched them for a few moments. They were deeply involved in their game which involved digging tunnels with their hands through a mountain of sand.

'She looks very settled,' said Dan. 'Can you point out the child she had the altercation with?'

'Well, I wouldn't call it that,' said the Head, her lips pulled together like a drawstring purse. 'But that's her – the one she's playing with now.'

I glanced over at Ed just in time to catch on his face a fleeting flash of satisfaction. The Wendy house incident must have momentarily rocked his confidence, but here she was, calm and sociable and conciliatory.

Later, after Jana arrived to collect Laurie, we took them both to a nearby diner. If the little girl thought it was odd to be seated in a booth surrounded by strange adults, she didn't show it. As I watched her, I felt a chill creeping up through me. There was something so preternaturally contained about her. Shouldn't a four-and-a-half-year-old be asking questions, like who Dan was? There was no squirming, no fidgeting, no 'can we go now'? Just this blank conformity. Where was she hiding it – all the anger, the grief, the confusion about what was happening to her and where her old life had gone?

'Do you like school?' Dan asked Laurie. He was sitting opposite her and his height made his head curl down across the table towards hers. He looked uncomfortable, as if he wasn't used to talking to small children.

Once, in our first year of studying together, Dan made a clumsy pass at me. I'd been so surprised I hadn't properly recognized it as a pass until I'd got home. We'd bumped into each other in the library and gone for a coffee and he'd pressed his leg up against mine under the table while staring at me purposefully. For a few moments I'd let it stay there while the heat travelled through my body until I felt I would ignite. Then I moved my leg away and suggested we get the bill. That was two years before, when I had very definite ideas about romance. Back then, I was looking for the big love story, the charismatic stranger. I didn't learn until it was way too late, until long after my failed marriage to Johnny, that love doesn't ride into town and sweep you off your feet, but sometimes looks at you in a certain way and you realize it was there all the time, right under your nose. Anyway, I digress. The point was, whatever my definition of love, Dan Oppenheimer wasn't it.

At the time of the Kowalsky assessments, he was dating an attractive undergraduate from Stanford who came to stay every other weekend. The rumour was that Dan himself had his sights set on a teaching post at Stanford. This case might get him there.

'School's OK, thanks,' said Laurie, without looking up from her ice cream, which came in one of those tall glasses which meant she had to dig around with a long spoon to dislodge the chocolate from the bottom.

'And how about the other children?' Ed was sitting at the end of the booth. 'Have you made friends there?'

'Yeah.' She scraped her spoon down the side of the glass.

Ed tried again.

'I heard you had a little falling-out with Sandy.'

Laurie shrugged.

'Want to tell us about that, Laurie?'

In contrast to Ed's practised manner, Dan's question sounded clumsy. Laurie looked up. Blinked. Then went back to her ice cream.

'It's all OK now. I said sorry and she said that's OK so that means we are friends again. We don't have to talk about it any more.'

'That's what they're told at school,' explained Jana, reaching a slender arm around Laurie's shoulder and giving it a squeeze. 'They're told that once a situation has been dealt with and everyone has said sorry and apologies have been accepted, they need to move on and put it behind them.'

''S not important anyway,' said Laurie. ''S all finished with.' She carried on fishing around with her spoon in the bottom of her glass, even though there was no ice cream left.

'Laurie?' I asked her diagonally across the table. 'When you and Sandy were having your . . . falling-out in the Wendy house, can you describe how you were feeling? Were you very cross with Sandy?'

Laurie shook her head emphatically. Next to her, Jana bit down on her lip as if stifling a protest. My lips were suddenly dry and I took a quick sip of my Coke before pressing on.

'But you must have been a little bit cross with her or you wouldn't have tied her up.'

293

Again the shake of the head.

'I wasn't cross with Sandy. I like Sandy. She's my friend.'

'Then why did you tie her up?'

I could feel Ed's eyes boring into me through the lenses of his glasses, but I kept my own gaze fixed on Laurie.

She shrugged once more.

'I dunno. I think the other Laurie must have done it.'

Well. That made us all sit up. Dan leaned back in the booth as if to better assess the situation, while Ed's response was to start combing his fingers through his hair in that nervous fluttering way he had.

'Honey.' Jana was looking down right into Laurie's eyes. 'What do you mean by the "other Laurie"?'

'I dunno.'

'Can you see her, this other Laurie?' Ed's voice was now slow and controlled.

Dan broke in, his voice too quick, too loud. Too eager. 'Or can you hear her? Is she talking to you inside your head?'

Laurie stared at him blankly.

'No. I can't hear her in my head. That would be funny.' She giggled. 'Just sometimes she does things when I'm not looking.'

Ed caught my eye and I gave the faintest shake of my head. Laurie's bombshell had caught us all by surprise.

'Can you explain, sweetie,' asked Jana, 'what you mean when you say "when I'm not looking"?'

Laurie was already appearing bored with the conversation. Her ice cream finished, she was bouncing up and down impatiently in her seat.

'Just sometimes it's like I go like this.' Laurie closed her eyes. 'And then like this.' She snapped them open again. 'And something happened and it wasn't me.'

'You mean something bad has happened?'

'Not really bad.' Laurie frowned. 'Just a little bit bad. But it wasn't me.'

After Jana had taken Laurie home, the three of us stayed behind in the diner. Dan was the first to speak.

'Wow,' he said, a smile stretching out his long, thin face. 'That was interesting. What do you think? Dissociation? Fugue? Psychosis?'

He sounded thrilled with the choices on offer, as if they were dishes on a menu, not acute psychiatric disorders he was wishing upon a four-year-old girl.

'I'm not convinced we can read that much into this,' said Ed eventually, stirring sugar into his second coffee. 'Many young kids invent alter egos who act in ways they know they're not really supposed to. My own kids have done it. Jon – he's eight now, but when he was younger, he used to talk about himself in the third person a lot like he was a completely separate entity, especially when he was in a morally ambiguous situation. So if he was watching a movie with a bad guy, he'd say "Jon is going to beat that bad guy up." It was dissociating, but not necessarily in an unhealthy way.'

'But surely,' I said, 'given the context, given her background . . .'

'I know we did a lot of work at the beginning of this process to contextualise Laurie,' Ed responded. 'But we have to be very careful, Anne, that we don't allow the context to dictate our responses to her. We need to react first and foremost to what she presents to us, rather than our interpretation of how what she presents fits in with what we know about her context. That could be dangerously loaded.'

'I couldn't agree more,' said Dan. 'I mean, the incident in the Wendy house and this talk about "the other Laurie" – they're actually only one part of the picture.'

Ed nodded.

'As someone who's coming fresh to this case, Dan,' he said, 'what's your impression of Laurie? Putting those two factors aside for a minute.'

'To be honest with you, sir . . . '

'Enough of the formalities, Dan.'

'Sure. Sorry. To be honest with you, Ed, I'm kinda amazed how *even* she is. You know, balanced. She seems very close with her foster mom and she has friends at school so she's obviously capable of forming emotional bonds with other people, which is really fundamental. And she seemed genuinely sorry about the Wendy house thing, which means she's capable of remorse. So I'd say those were pretty major tick points for me. In fact, I'd say I was pretty encouraged by what I've seen today.'

'With all respect, Ed,' I said. 'I don't know how we can set those two factors aside. I mean, they're directly relevant to what we've been asked to assess, wouldn't you say?'

Ed Kowalsky stared down into his coffee dregs as if trying to read his future there.

'Of course they're relevant, Anne,' he said eventually. 'But I worry you might be seizing on them to back up a narrative for Laurie you've already created in your head from things you've seen on the news. We have to be totally objective. That's our job.'

On the way back that night to my little room in the student house I shared with three other girls, I stopped by the liquor store and stood looking in the window for a very long time.

34

Chloe

'Chloe, where are those reports? I asked you to have them on my desk at ten thirty.'

'Sorry, Rachel. They're taking a bit longer than I'd thought.'

'Try to keep to deadlines, please. I shouldn't have to remind you.'

Chloe's cheeks stung as if she'd been slapped. She focused her eyes on the plaster on Rachel's forehead, half hidden by her hair, and tried not to cry.

'Sorry,' she mumbled to Rachel's retreating back as the latter swivelled on her heel and returned to her office.

Chloe had never felt so wretched. She longed to talk to someone about what was going on, but her dad had had to fly off to the USA on business, and her mum had gone with him. They were so inseparable still. Chloe usually loved how close they were, but this thing with Ewan had her doubting everything she'd ever thought about relationships. She'd always just assumed things would happen for her the same way they had for her parents, but now she questioned if that was true. Maybe the men she loved would all turn on her, as Ewan had done. She'd tried to imagine her own mother being treated like that – rejected and then physically intimidated – thinking perhaps if she convinced herself it was a rite of passage it wouldn't hurt so much, but she couldn't. It must be something uniquely to do with her.

She glanced towards Paula, hoping for a reassuring look. She'd realized that Paula wouldn't stick her neck out to defend her from Rachel's barbs, but she could usually be counted on for a sympathetic eyebrow-raise. However, Paula was hunched over her desk, head down, as she had been ever since arriving that morning. Chloe had tried asking her where she'd got to yesterday afternoon, when she just disappeared without telling anyone, but Paula had given her a really strange look, as if she had no idea who she even was, and it had freaked Chloe out so much, she'd just said, 'Oh well, never mind, you're here now,' or something equally silly, and retreated to her desk. Across the office, Sarah got up and scuttled off towards the double exit doors. Acting on a rash impulse, Chloe followed her. Rachel couldn't stop her going to the loo, could she?

In the toilets, she glanced in the mirror, remembering her shock when she'd caught sight of her reflection in the hotel bathroom after Ewan had left, the ghostly pallor of her face. Her stomach spasmed as it always did when she thought back to Saturday night, the way his eyes had glazed over. She'd wondered if she should have reported him to someone. But then what exactly would she have said? That he'd been a little too rough? She'd been scared of him – she could remember that. And yet there was a small part of her, a part she was deeply ashamed of, that felt a kind of thrill that he'd felt strongly enough about her, passionately enough, to get carried away like that. And besides, as time passed, she started to wonder whether it had really been as bad as she remembered, or whether she had over-felt it, the way she did sometimes. Her mum was always telling her not to let her feelings carry her away, to be more self-censoring. Could she have exaggerated what happened? Ewan had tried to talk to her several times yesterday and this morning, but she'd ignored him. Still, it made her feel better in a way, that it was *him* pestering *her* for a change.

She heard retching sounds coming from behind the closed door of one of the cubicles.

'Sarah? You OK?'

A noise. Something between a moan and a sigh.

'Sarah?'

The door opened, and Sarah emerged, wiping her mouth on a length of toilet paper. Sarah had always been on the curvy side, and her body was still round but her face looked gaunt, as if someone had ironed the plumpness out of it so that her skin clung, grey and uncushioned, to her cheekbones.

'You all right?'

Sarah shook her head. 'Not really,' she said in a small voice.

'What happened in there this morning?'

When Chloe had arrived at 9 a.m., the blinds were down in Rachel's office and Amira told her that Sarah and Mark Hamilton were esconced in there with Rachel and James Ellis, the head of HR.

'She wasn't still going on about you pushing her down that river bank, was she?' Chloe asked Sarah now, who flinched as if she'd been hit.

300

'No. God, no. She couldn't. I'd have grounds to sue her, wouldn't I, for defamation of character or something. No, that meeting this morning was her saying I'm a slacker, always late, always behind, and trying to make out I'd deliberately got pregnant because she'd threatened me with disciplinary action.'

'She didn't say that!'

'Not in so many words, but the implication was clear. Luckily James from HR has some basic conception of how biology works and pointed out that it wasn't likely I'd be able to conjure up a pregnancy just like that. And he also made it very clear that it would be extremely hard for her to get rid of me because the rules protecting pregnant women are so strict.'

'So she backed down?'

'No. She said she couldn't work with me because I was so bad at my job. And I said she was discriminating against me for having small children as well as for getting pregnant.'

'Good for you.'

'Yes, except I was practically in tears by then, and she said that she couldn't deal with staff who were so overemotional they couldn't take criticism. So Mark Hamilton suggested I could be moved into a different department. As if I was some sort of item of unwanted furniture. Honestly, Chloe, it was so humiliating!'

Her voice had risen until she was practically screeching and her fingers clasped around Chloe's narrow wrist in an uncomfortable echo of the way Ewan's hand had gripped hers on Saturday night. Sarah was so quiet normally.

'Any idea what's up with Paula?' Chloe asked, changing the subject.

301

The disappearance of the deputy manager the morning of the previous day had left her deeply perplexed, but when she'd tried to discuss it with Charlie and Amira they'd frowned at her as if she was being out of order in even bringing it up. Charlie reckoned Paula probably felt ill, while Amira just said, 'None of our business, is it?' Neither of them seemed bothered by how out of character it was. Even when Rachel came in at lunchtime, showing off that plaster on her forehead, and made a great big fuss about Paula not being there, and got Chloe to leave hundreds of messages on her answerphone asking where she was, Charlie and Amira hardly looked up from their desks. They'd said they were really busy, but later on she'd seen them huddled together by the lifts looking as if they were arguing about something, so clearly they weren't as busy as all that.

'No idea,' Sarah said, dropping her fingers from Chloe's arm. 'Maybe she's having some sort of post-traumatic meltdown after the rope-bridge incident. I'm surprised we're not all falling apart right, left and centre. The atmosphere in this place is so toxic.'

'Are you OK, though?' Chloe asked. 'With the baby and everything?'

To her consternation, Sarah put her hand to her mouth, as if she'd said something shocking.

'God, I'm sorry. There's nothing wrong, is there?' Chloe asked, alarmed. 'Have I put my foot in it?'

Sarah's voice, when she finally spoke, was choked.

'No, don't worry. It's just that you're the first person who's asked me anything about it. Anything nice, I mean. D'you know, in some ways I wish Rachel *had* sacked me. It's so horrible, knowing everyone resents me. Even Charlie.'

That reminded Chloe of the argument she'd witnessed between Charlie and Amira, but just as she was about to ask Sarah if she knew what was going on with those two, the door to the toilets was flung open and Rachel came stalking in on those vertiginous heels. Click clack, click clack.

Chloe's throat turned instantly dry.

'Chloe, I assume you've finished those reports?'

'I was just . . . going to the toilet,' Chloe muttered, before slinking back, humiliated, to her seat.

After she'd finished the dreaded reports, which she knew Rachel would anyway find fault with and get her to change, Chloe logged on to her emails. Her inbox was reading 73 new messages. Chloe's heart sank. She'd never been particularly ambitious, always imagining that life would come and find her rather than the other way around. But still, the idea that she'd gone through all those years of education – those private tutors who'd shown up at the door on a Wednesday afternoon with cycle helmets swinging from their hands and hi-vis reflector strips around their ankles, the 9 a.m. university lectures she'd dragged herself up for, the heart-stopping moment where she held the results envelope in her hand – all in order to sit at a desk in a demoralized office on a Tuesday morning dealing with seventy-three emails about health and safety initiatives, the new canteen policy, plus numerous queries from the Accountancy, IT and HR departments filled her with sudden panic. She glanced over at Paula and shuddered: a fleeting glimpse of an unwelcome future.

Chloe tried to push aside these morbid thoughts. She was normally such a positive person, regularly posting gratitude lists on social media, but the oppressive atmosphere in the office ('toxic', Sarah had called it) was seeping into her. She didn't look at Ewan, sitting two desks away, yet she was acutely conscious of his every movement, the rise and fall of his chest as he breathed, the flick-flick-flick of his pen against his desk as he held his phone to his ear, waiting for someone to pick up.

She forced herself to focus on her screen and began scrolling through the endless emails until her eye snagged on a familiar name. Gill Marsh. *Greetings Fledgling!* read the email. It was the nickname Gill had affectionately given her right from when she first took her on as a green intern not long out of university, but it no longer invoked that warmth of feeling. Instead she felt a prickling of unease. *Just checking in for news of the weekend. Any gossip I should know about?* Chloe glanced around the the office, feeling as if everyone must be looking at her, knowing what she was doing, what she'd done. Even when she'd reassured herself that the others were all occupied with their own stuff, she couldn't shake off the idea of being judged. *It's not my fault*, she wanted to say to them. *I'm only twenty-four.*

She wouldn't answer the email, she decided. She'd done enough. Gone above and beyond what Gill could expect, really. The trouble was, she'd been so grateful to Gill – for giving her a full-time job, for taking her under her wing and being so nice to her, even at the start when she got everything wrong. Gill was the kind of patient, understanding boss everyone should have at the beginning of their career. She'd stood up for Chloe on the rare occasions when one of the others had got irritated with her for making a mistake, and she'd taken time out from her own busy schedule to mentor her, explaining how to prioritize her time and how to cope with criticism without taking it too personally. They'd been sort of friends, despite the age gap. Chloe had been outraged on Gill's behalf when Gill had been so suddenly and summarily dismissed, as well as being upset for herself. She knew she'd miss her terribly. So when Gill had started pumping her for gossip barely hours after being escorted from the building, Chloe hadn't minded in the least. As far as she was concerned, Gill had been treated appallingly and was still the rightful boss. Hadn't all the big clients they were working with been secured by Gill? Weren't all the systems they used ones that Gill had come up with? So when Gill had suggested that some gentle, behind-the-scenes 'disruption' might ensure that Rachel didn't get past her probation period, Chloe hadn't needed too much persuading. It was second nature for her to do Gill's bidding without questioning it.

Changing the time on Sarah's whiteboard so she'd messed up that meeting had been easy enough to do, but Chloe had felt a real pang of guilt when she'd seen how upset Sarah was, and how much flak she'd got from Rachel. Crushing up the laxatives to sprinkle in with the sugar had been Gill's idea. 'Just a tiny bit,' she'd said when they'd met for an after-work drink and she'd handed Chloe the blister pack of pills. 'Don't worry, it won't do any damage, just the odd dash to the loo to shake things up a bit.' Obviously Chloe hadn't done a good enough job of mixing the pills in because poor

Charlie seemed to have borne the whole brunt of it, but Gill had been right. There was no long-term damage and he'd been right as rain after a few hours.

Gill had left the team-bonding weekend up to Chloe. *I bet Mark Hamilton will go along*, Gill had emailed Chloe. '*Any excuse to get away from his wife. So it's a great chance to do some low-level sabotage and make it really obvious Rachel isn't in control. Just keep your eyes open for mischief-making opportunities.*'

The safety-cord thing had been a momentary mad impulse, and of course it had proved to be a terrible mistake. When she'd realized how easy it would be to loosen the strap on the clasp that linked to the harness, she hadn't thought for a minute that she might put anyone in danger. She'd been so angry with Ewan at that stage, she'd decided to give him a scare, ruffle him up a bit – maybe even humiliate him a little (that word again). When she'd got to the top of the first tower and everyone was in that euphoric giggling mood and helping each other up, she'd noticed the line of safety cords hanging from the top wire, waiting to be attached, and she hadn't even stopped to think. She knew Ewan was second from the end because she'd seen him lining up before they started climbing, and she counted and recounted to make sure she got the right cord. How could she have guessed he'd switch with Paula at the last minute? Chloe hadn't known what the expression 'having your heart in your mouth' was about until she'd stood on the far tower watching poor old Paula wobbling around in the middle of that rope bridge, scared out of her wits.

While she was waiting for Paula to be rescued, her stomach folding in on itself like cake batter, Chloe had made a mental vow to stop doing Gill's dirty work. But then had come that moment during the orienteering when she'd entered the clearing and seen Sarah asleep and Rachel with her back to her, standing at the top of the bank by the stream, and she hadn't been able to resist. One little shove. Not even a shove really, more of a tap, and down she'd gone. Chloe hadn't wanted to hurt her, hadn't even known there were rocks down there. All she'd been thinking of was how mortified Rachel would be, to be found sprawled in the mud in front of her staff.

And Ewan especially.

Then that had gone wrong too, when Rachel hurt her head. There'd been a sickening moment when Chloe actually thought she might be dead.

Well, no more. Chloe understood why her former boss felt aggrieved, and she'd have loved to see Gill triumphantly reinstated after the department fell apart under Rachel's leadership, but she'd done her bit, and now two people had very nearly come to harm because of her, and she felt grubby and guilty and didn't want any further part of it.

In truth, Chloe was beginning to feel a bit freaked out by how Gill had acted since her sacking. On the surface of things, she always pretended things were great, as if she'd been deluged with offers and was just taking her time deciding which one to pick. But Chloe knew from things she'd let slip that prospective employers weren't exactly beating a path to her door. And while no one could blame Gill for being resentful of Rachel, there was something about her obsession with her successor that was kind of creepy.

If only she could talk to Ewan about it. All of it.

Hurriedly she tapped out an email: *Cheeky pint in the Blue Posts after work?* But then an image came into her head of his face looming up over her in that hotel room in Derbyshire, and she quickly pressed delete, feeling lonelier than ever.

With a leaden feeling like there was a large lump lodged inside her gut, Chloe went back to dealing with the mass of unanswered emails in her inbox, but her focus was once again interrupted when the door to the main office swung open and Mark Hamilton walked through. His appearances on this floor were rare enough for this to pique Chloe's curiosity, especially when he paused by Amira's desk. To Chloe's astonishment, Amira nodded at him before pushing back her chair and following him across the office to Rachel's door, where Mark rapped once before barging in, Amira on his heels. From inside came the sound of raised voices. Chloe locked eyes with Sarah, who shrugged almost imperceptibly in an *I don't know anything either* way.

The mystery intensified a few minutes later when the door was once again flung open and Rachel appeared, looking unusually agitated.

'Charlie. A moment.'

Charlie? What now?

At his desk, Charlie exhaled, a lengthy sigh that whooshed across the office. Then, slowly, he got to his feet and he too disappeared into Rachel's office. Chloe tried to catch Sarah's gaze again, but Sarah had turned away when Charlie walked past. Chloe felt for her. Losing an ally was gut-wrenching. Still the voices in the office went on. And now the door was opening yet again to reveal a very pale Rachel.

'Paula. Can you join us, please?'

Chloe's head swung around towards Paula's desk, expecting her to be springing to her feet as she normally would. But the deputy manager remained still, gazing ahead at her screen with that strange look she'd worn all day. Something was very wrong.

'Paula, did you hear me? I'm asking you to step into my office.'

Still Paula didn't respond, just stared at her screen as if she was playing a videogame and they – Rachel, Chloe, Amira, even Mark Hamilton – were just characters in it, not real people at all.

'Paula?'

For the first time, Chloe detected a waver in Rachel's voice and was astonished to feel a pang of sympathy for her. There was something so weird about Paula's refusal to engage. So unsettling.

For a few seconds, Rachel stood in the doorway of her office as if uncertain what to do next. Paula didn't alter her expression at all, didn't give anything away.

The silence stretched out across the office like an elastic band until it was tight enough to snap.

35
Sarah

'You'll just have to tell them he's ill. They'll understand.'

'Are you insane? There was a meeting yesterday basically trying to work out how to get rid of me. If I get the sack there'll be no maternity pay, no nothing. And no one will give me a job while I'm pregnant. So unless you've suddenly had a pay rise that can support us all, *you're* going to have to take the day off.'

'But I've got a ton of stuff to do today . . . Oh, bloody hell. All right then, but I'm telling you, Sarah, you'd better not come home in the same state you did yesterday.'

Oliver glared at her as if she'd chosen to be bullied at work and have her job threatened. Then he relented.

'Come here.' He opened his arms and she gratefully fell against his chest, wishing she could climb inside his ribcage and be someone else for a while. She was so tired of being herself.

'Mummy, you stay here.' Sam had got out of bed and was clasping on to her from behind, his hot cheek resting against her back.

'Go back to bed, sweetie. Daddy's going to stay with you today.'

'Don't want Daddy. Want you.'

Sam burst into snotty tears, which she could feel soaking through the back of the only clean shirt she'd been able to find that morning. She tried to explain to him about needing to go to work, but his sobs just became louder, which set Joe off, so that when she finally left the house, the sound of her sons' cries followed her halfway down the street.

Outside the office building, she hesitated, reluctant to go in through the heavy main door. Already her heart was beating too fast and there was a nasty taste in the back of her mouth. Fear. The receptionist gazed at her blankly as she made her way to the lifts. Her feet felt like they were weighted down with breezeblocks. Everything inside her was screaming at her to turn around and go back to her family.

She'd half expected to find the office empty. Paula had been in such a strange state yesterday, Sarah actually thought she might be in the early stages of a breakdown. And just what was going on with Charlie and Amira? Or Ewan and Chloe, for that matter? But when she arrived on the fifth floor everyone was present and correct. Maybe they too feared the consequences of being away from work even more than they feared being there.

Sarah sat down heavily in her seat and tried not to catch anyone else's eye. The tension in the office was palpable. She could feel it in her nostrils, and pressing on her eyeballs. She'd just started calculating how many weeks she'd have left before her maternity leave would start when Chloe leaned across towards her desk.

'How are you feeling?' she whispered.

311

Despite herself, Sarah felt touched. Chloe was so clearly canvassing for new buddies since whatever had happened between her and Ewan. Sarah could probably guess what it was, but things were bad enough without inventing scenarios that might not even be true.

'I'm fine. Well, apart from feeling completely shit.'

'Ha. Yes.' Chloe had the air of someone skimming over the niceties in order to get on to more interesting matters. Sure enough: 'Guess who's in there?'

The girl jerked her head towards the glass walls of Rachel's office, where the slatted blinds were once again pulled firmly shut, blocking any view inside.

Sarah shrugged.

'Mark and Rachel,' Chloe informed her. 'He looked very grim when he came in. Do you reckon he might be about to give her the sack?'

A flare of something in her heart that she tried to dampen down.

'I don't expect so, Chloe. He might be giving her some advice though. She needs it.'

Chloe looked disappointed.

'I wish he would. She's ruined this department. It used to be such a fun place to work, didn't it?'

Sarah thought about it. Had it been fun working here under Gill? It had certainly been more harmonious, less stressful. But fun?

Rachel's door opened and Mark Hamilton emerged, followed by Rachel herself.

Mark's face had lost the expression of studied bonhomie it had worn throughout the team-bonding weekend. Back in a jacket and tie, after the weekend's ill-suited leisurewear, he exuded an authority he'd lacked in Derbyshire. Next to him, Rachel seemed diminished.

'Can everyone gather around, please. Quick as you can.'

Even his voice had grown in stature since the weekend, reverberating off the grey laminate desks and the computer screens whose customized screensavers provided the one hint of personality in the otherwise anonymous office environment. A close-up of Ryan Gosling (Amira), a beach in Thailand, all white sand and palm trees and colourful wooden boats (Chloe), two chubby toddlers, their mouths smeared with chocolate, beaming proudly as if their gluttony was an achievement to bask in (Sarah herself).

Sarah pushed herself reluctantly to a standing position. Though her bump was still hardly noticeable, blending in effortlessly with the extra cushion of flesh she had acquired since her last pregnancy, she felt leaden with tiredness as if the baby was draining the energy out of her. She longed to be at home, lying on the sofa watching cartoons with Sam, both of them wrapped in the soft woollen blanket they kept folded over the sofa arm.

But curiosity over what Mark had to say propelled her from her desk. She wondered if Chloe could be right. Was Rachel about to be publicly sacked? After all, the last time Mark had summoned them together like this out of the blue was to tell them that Gill was leaving and Rachel was taking over. She caught Charlie's eye and he stretched the corners of his mouth down in a 'don't know, but it's unlikely to be good news' face. At least he was acknowledging her again.

'Right,' said Mark when they were all gathered around. He was half sitting on the edge of Paula's desk so that one black leather, slightly pointed shoe was firmly planted on the floor, while the other dangled inches from the ground. He raised a hand to rub his nose, revealing an inch of tanned wrist, scattered with freckles and fine golden hairs against which gleamed a silver watch so chunky it might have been intended for a larger man.

'I'm not going to beat about the bush. I think we're all aware the atmosphere in this office isn't all it should be. The weekend away was supposed to get you working together properly as a team, but instead it just seems to have highlighted the divisions between you. Now I understand many of you were loyal to Gill and may have found the transition period difficult, but you are professionals and your loyalty must first and foremost be to the company that pays your salary. Rachel was brought in for a specific reason – to raise this department's productivity levels and boost profits, bringing it in line with the rest of the company. Do you think this is a charity?'

When he threw out the surprise question, Mark was looking directly at Chloe, who started as if she'd been slapped, her mouth falling open in a perfect 'o' of alarm, closing again only when his stern gaze abruptly altered direction, panning around the assembled company who shifted uncomfortably, gazing down at their shoes or at a point just above Mark's head, anything rather than meet his eyes and be obliged to answer his challenge. Sarah felt herself shrivel as his eyes passed over her.

'Rachel and I have had a long chat and we both agree that it is untenable for her to implement the changes she was brought in to effect unless she has a supportive team behind her giving her one hundred per cent loyalty and dedication. I don't intend to single individuals out here and now, but there are some members of staff who have been at best obstructive, at worse destructive – and let me be very clear, such behaviour will not be tolerated. Rachel is a highly skilled executive with an exemplary track record who has been brought in to do a job and we are very lucky to have her. Anyone who has an issue with that might be advised to start looking for employment elsewhere.'

Again he allowed his eyes to sweep across the gathered staff members and again Sarah felt herself shrinking under his gaze. Was she the one he was accusing of being obstructive, or destructive?

Finally, when Mark seemed satisfied that he'd made his point, he continued: 'Now, I came down here yesterday determined to make sweeping changes, but Rachel has persuaded me to give this department one more chance to get its house in order. She believes, and I support her in this, that what's needed is a clearing-of-the air session, somewhere neutral, away from the office. To that end, she has generously offered to host a meeting tomorrow morning at her own home, which is not far from here. I wouldn't normally allow an entire department to be absent for a few hours during the working week, but I think these are exceptional circumstances.

'After the débâcle of the weekend, I very strongly suggest you all take the rest of the day and this evening to think about areas where things have been going wrong and ways in which you can make improvements. I don't want this to turn into an excuse to vent grievances. I want to hear positive suggestions for how to best introduce changes so that this department starts pulling together and brings its performance up in line with the rest of the company. But there will be no more chances. If you cannot reconcile your differences, there will need to be significant restructuring.'

Mark glared around one more time and then strode from the office with the gait of someone much more powerfully built. Sarah found it hard to reconcile the man who'd gamely launched himself across the rope bridge and offered himself up for comparisons to a flower and a pet animal to this tough-talking executive. She turned to see Rachel's reaction to the managing director's speech, but caught a glimpse only of her retreating back before she closed the door of her office behind her. Now she sought out Charlie, but Charlie was staring down at his arm, scratching at the deep cut that had been concealed by a plaster all through the weekend and was now scabbed over with beads of dark dried blood. As she watched him, Sarah shivered, not because of the fresh blood that appeared where he scratched the old away, but because of the look on Charlie's face, the way his features appeared wiped of all the things that made them his, as if he'd been put back to factory settings, as he gazed fixedly down and scratched and scratched until the new blood was smeared in crimson streaks against the pale skin of his arm.

36

Anne

I'm watching him on the news. He hasn't changed much. Still the same confidence. More. Because now it's confidence born of authority rather than confidence born of youth. He looks very much at home on camera, which isn't surprising really. He's been a regular expert on documentaries and news shows for years. Decades. He knows how to talk in soundbites. And he knows how to say 'we got it wrong' so it doesn't sound like an admission of guilt but an honest summation of a difficult situation. Maybe we didn't draw the right conclusion but our methods and motives were beyond reproach.

'No one could have known,' he says now. 'We gathered all the evidence and, based on intensive assessment, made a professional judgement call in the child's best interests – which was all anyone could have done in the circumstances.' He looks straight at the camera as he speaks. His meaning is clear: you win some, you lose some. What can you do?

'So you wouldn't say your judgement was flawed, Professor?' asks the interviewer.

Dan Oppenheimer shakes his head with a kind of half

smile on his face as if to say, 'I know you're required to play devil's advocate, but sheesh . . .'

'You have to remember these were very different times. Our understanding of child psychology and the effects of early trauma on the psyche has changed beyond all recognition since then. And obviously we were up against huge time restraints. We wanted to give that child the very best chance at leading a good, normal life – which incidentally I think we did, up to now – and in order to do that, we had to make decisions very quickly.'

'Would it be fair to say you built your career on that case?' the interviewer breaks in. 'The book you wrote at Stanford – *The Boy Who Lived Downstairs (and the Girl Who Kept Him There)* – was what first propelled you into academic stardom. Isn't it still the best-selling publication by an academic press ever?'

'In the States.' Dan shrugs modestly. 'But you know I should point out I've published plenty of other material subsequent to that, moved into other fields.'

The interviewer isn't to be fobbed off.

'But this was the book that cemented your reputation. And now it turns out you and . . .' He glances down at the notes on the table in front of him. '. . . Professor Kowalsky made a wrong call when you decided to fast-track an adoption overseas. And as a result of that, you put people in danger and ultimately contributed to the terrible events in England we've seen unfolding on our newscreens.'

'As you know,' Dan says, all trace of levity gone from his expression, 'Professor Kowalsky was the lead psychiatrist on this case, and there was also another junior academic who was involved in the assessment process.'

Alone in my living room, still wearing my sweatpants with my greying hair pulled back off my face by a thick black band, every one of my muscles tenses. Is this it, finally? The point where I'm unmasked? My own involvement finally recognized? I find myself both dreading and longing for it.

'I don't believe it would serve any purpose to name her now. She was a young woman not long qualified and I know she found the case ... emotionally challenging.'

I breathe in sharply.

'Obviously as Professor Kowalsky has since passed away, you're the only one who can tell us what went on back then. Maybe you can give the folks back home an idea of what the child was like, Professor Oppenheimer. I mean, you green-lighted the adoption.'

'Well, Brad, you have to understand we're talking about a very young child here, so the personality is far from fully formed, but I will tell you this seemed like a smart child, very quick to learn and capable of showing empathy and remorse and forming relationships with others. Despite the terrible things that had happened in the family home, there was no hostility that we could determine and surprisingly little aggression.

'Ultimately, as you know, it was Professor Kowalsky's call. He was the senior psychiatrist. I was really just starting out, and though I have to say there were a few red flags for me, I very much bowed to the professor's superior judgement.'

I am grasping the remote control very tightly. For the

first time it occurs to me that there is to be no restitution, no righting of wrongs. Ed Kowalsky is dead – felled by a catastrophic brain haemorrhage as he was queuing at the juice bar after coming a respectable sixth place in the veterans' cycling race. The irony was lost on no one. To everyone's surprise, he hadn't, in the end, capitalized on the sensational House of Horror case beyond using it to consolidate his role at the college here. His children had been his excuse. They were settled here. But really I think he just lacked the ambition. He liked being a big fish in a small pond. He liked the way the Chancellor and Vice Chancellor took him for dinner at their golf club and described him as one of the 'jewels in the university's crown'. And I don't think he ever quite recovered from Dan Oppenheimer's meteoric success. Ed published his own papers on the case, of course. All of them well received. But none of them ever made him a star outside the narrow walls of academia. I used to think I was the only one left scarred by the Child L case, but after Ed's death I was able to see it wasn't so.

Up until he died, which incidentally allowed me to step up to the position I have now, I admit I fantasized about him being held to account. Well, him and Oppenheimer. And now that day is finally here, and only Oppenheimer is left, I realize it's not going to happen. Nothing can now discredit Professor Dan Oppenheimer, because all those years of success and fame in themselves create their own credibility, regardless of what went before.

37

Rachel

Rachel felt nervous, as if she was a home-owner preparing for a potential buyer, not a boss getting ready to host her own team. She ran a critical eye over her kitchen, taking in the wall of gleaming white units, its satin sheen unbroken by handles just as she'd envisioned when she first sat down with the kitchen designer. 'No, it has to be clean,' she'd insisted when he'd suggested breaking up the vast expanse of white with the odd splash of block colour or a textured finish, or even a mellower shade, ivory. He'd been disappointed when she'd stuck to her guns, but then he hadn't come as far as she had come, hadn't cooked in a kitchen so tiny it was as if the walls, with their imitation-wood units, doors hanging off hinges, were pressing in on you as you stood on a chair to stir baked beans on the hob. Hadn't made a vow that if you ever avoided the crappy jobs your mother had no choice but to take, the parental absence that ground your brother's ambition and self-respect to a dirty-grey powder to be snorted off cracked toilet cisterns, that meant your baby sister was permanently in your care, even though she was only two years younger than you . . . If you escaped all that, you'd live somewhere clean and light-filled that was all your own.

Rachel loved her home. When she and Ronan had first come to look around, it had been divided up badly into studio flats and he'd been put off by the layout and the sour smell of other people's belongings, spilling out from the flimsy furniture. He thought it was too poky. His colleagues at the investment bank lived in penthouse apartments with river views or mansion blocks in Kensington or Notting Hill, so he'd had something more impressive in mind. But as soon as they'd pulled up in front of the house on the end of a row of white Georgian terraces in Islington, and she'd seen the perfect symmetry of its three tall windows on each level, and the wide steps leading up to a graceful doorway, she knew she wanted it.

'We'll pull down all these internal walls and restore the rooms to their original size,' she'd said, knocking on plaster, looking for the answering hollow echo of a stud wall.

'But then it won't be big enough,' he pointed out. 'We're looking for a family house, that was our criteria.'

It was a pointed reminder of the children they'd agreed they wanted, but that she kept putting off. There was always just one more career milestone she needed to reach before she was ready to take a break. Ronan knew better than to suggest she didn't need to work. While he didn't know exactly what she'd come from – no one did, she made sure of that – he knew enough to realize that when you've had to work that hard for everything you have, you don't give it up without a struggle. When work has saved you, you owe it.

'Space isn't an issue,' said the estate agent, clearly sensing a sale. 'Half the houses in this street have extended down into the basements and added another one or even two storeys. You excavate from the back and put in as many windows as you like so it doesn't feel dark. Most of them have a kitchen down there, and sometimes a gym or cinema room or even a swimming pool underneath that.'

Which is exactly what they'd done, and when it was finished even Ronan had had to admit she'd been right. The two airy upper floors with their floor-to-ceiling windows were complemented by a basement kitchen into which light flooded from a wall of windows giving out on to the newly dug back garden, and then underneath that, a gym area and sauna and wet room. As that level had no natural light, Rachel had decided to go for a cave-type atmosphere down there with natural black slate floors and walls made from rough dark stones. An inbuilt feature on one of the walls created a waterfall effect, with clear water running down the stone as if over subterranean rock. Low-energy bulbs hidden in the stone provided the only source of light in the room, adding to the intentionally claustrophobic ambience. Rachel had been against the gym to start with, fearing it would be out of keeping with the Georgian elegance of the rest of the house, but now she spent hours down there, pounding the treadmill in the semi-darkness, enjoying the feeling of being cut off from everyone and everything, buried in the bowels of her own beautiful home. Afterwards she'd strip off her clothes, toss water on the coals and fling herself down on the wooden bench in the sauna, sweating out the dirt and the impurities until she emerged twenty minutes later rejuvenated and reborn.

No matter how stressful her day had been, Rachel would feel the tension lifting when she walked through her front door into the wide hallway with its broad limed floorboards and staircase that curved delicately up towards the first floor. So it had seemed natural to her to offer to hold this emergency staff meeting at her home. In her experience, very little in the way of air-clearing could productively be accomplished at work, where office politics and hierarchies wormed their way into every conversation. She hadn't wanted to go on the team-bonding weekend, but she'd hoped it would at least sort out the issues within the department, shaking out the wheat from the chaff so those remaining would come back streamlined and re-energized. But it hadn't worked out like that. There had been something unsettling afoot over that weekend, right from the beginning. Rachel had tried to chivvy everyone along, wanting to impress Mark as much as anything else, but the atmosphere had become increasingly unpleasant.

Rachel wasn't the fanciful type. When you came from the background she did, you learned very early on that only the real and the tangible have value: nothing else is to be trusted. So she knew she hadn't invented that feeling of something pushing against the small of her back as she stood on the bank of the stream. But could she be totally certain it was a hand and not someone brushing past, oblivious, or a strong gust of wind, or a trick her mind played on her as she passed out? Uncertainty was a condition Rachel found impossible to live with.

The poisonous office politics were getting to her. Rachel had always had to fight for everything and to her it was natural to view work as a competition. People didn't produce their best unless they had something to lose. So she had always encouraged healthy rivalry between her staff members. But now Amira and Charlie had discovered she had been pitting them against each other, and were both openly hostile to her, while doe-eyed Sarah, without doubt the weakest link in the office, was now pregnant and therefore unsackable. Mark was pretending to be supportive, but had pointedly reminded her she was still on her probation period. It would be career disaster for her to be 'let go' so soon into a new job, particularly in view of what had happened in her last post.

Rachel pressed on the top edge of one of the sleek kitchen cupboards, causing it to slide soundlessly open. She reached in and withdrew two large Moroccan-style bowls, one orange, the other cobalt blue, which she proceeded to fill with crisps and nuts. She'd toyed with getting food delivered from the caterers she had sometimes used when she and Ronan were entertaining, but she didn't want to appear to be showing off. It was important to strike the right note. Taste wasn't hard, you copied it from other people, from magazines, until it became your own, or as near to it as made no difference. But this question of nuance, of judging social situations, of knowing when not to go charging in guns blazing, that was more complicated. And negotiation went against Rachel's nature, as did holding back, knowing when to play your hand and when to hide it modestly away.

She was still learning. And she still got it wrong a lot

of the time. To Rachel, the endless compromises and little niceties that went into fostering 'harmonious office relationships' (how she hated HR jargon) were tortuous. The world wasn't like that. The world was dog eat dog, from the little kids in India scavenging on the rubbish heaps to survive, to the heads of state meeting at this very moment to discuss the worsening refugee crisis. So why should they have to pretend that working life was some tea party where they all 'validated each other's opinions' and gave each other only 'constructive feed-back'? She came across so many Paulas and Sarahs, plodders and wimps, trailing their personal lives into the office like snails. They wouldn't last a day in Ronan's office, where the air was so thick with testosterone it left a residue on your fingers, in the back of your throat, and you had to grow a hard enough skin for fear to run right off it.

Of course, the downside of that was that Ronan had found it increasingly difficult to detach from the person he was at the office, bringing more and more of his brash office persona home with him at night. Rachel didn't know if she would ever forget the way he'd said, 'Don't take it so personally,' when she'd discovered the secret email account he'd been using to send texts and dick-pics to the twenty-two-year-old intern he'd been sleeping with for the last eight months. He'd left Rachel the week before she took up the new position at Mark Hamilton Recruitment.

The sound of the buzzer made her start. A glance at the video-com revealed Paula standing outside the solid black gate they'd had installed between the edge of the front garden and the pavement. *Fuck*. Rachel hadn't been sure Paula would even come. Rachel was sorry that the quiet, doughy deputy had found out the way she had that she was surplus to requirements, but in a sense it was a relief. Far better to get things out in the open than all this whispering behind closed doors. More troublesome was the bad feeling it had engendered with Amira and Charlie. Those were the two staff members she least wanted to lose.

'Come on through,' she called into the intercom, and pressed the green key to open the gate. Before Paula passed out of sight, she scoured her face for hints as to her state of mind. Rachel didn't scare easily, but something about the supernaturally calm way Paula had reacted to the whole business of finding out that two of her colleagues were being considered for her job had creeped her out. The woman hadn't once come to her to ask questions or demand explanations, but instead had stayed at her desk, placidly working through her usual caseload while it was Amira and Charlie who'd raged behind her door, insisting she call Mark Hamilton down to hear their complaints.

'Neither of you said "no",' Rachel had told them in the end. 'It's not the fact that I was offering you Paula's job while she was still in it that offended you, it's the fact you've now discovered you were not the only ones in the running. This is about your hurt pride and nothing more.'

That had shut them up.

But Paula's strange closed-up silence, the way she'd ignored Rachel in the office as if she wasn't even there . . . that was something else and it made her feel uneasy. As she ran up the flight of stairs leading from the basement kitchen to the front door, Rachel found herself hoping that one of the others would hurry up and arrive soon so she'd spend as little time alone with Paula as possible.

She was relieved to open the door and see Ewan slipping through the still-open gate behind Paula's shoulder. She continued to count on him as an ally despite the atmosphere at the weekend. She'd been wrong to flirt with Will so blatantly. Ewan had felt humiliated, she knew that. Toyed with. But surely she was entitled to a little harmless flirtation after being so humiliatingly dumped by Ronan? She would just have to work on Ewan to win him back. Though he didn't yet have the intelligence or maturity for a promotion, his ambition made him a valuable asset to her department.

As long as she played him properly.

But first there was the issue of Paula, standing here on her doorstep, gazing at her with unnervingly empty eyes.

'Hello,' said her deputy in her usual flat voice, giving nothing away. 'I wasn't sure this was it.'

Usually guests were more effusive on their first visit to the house. Ewan was more enthusiastic.

'Oh wow. This is incredible,' he said, entering the hallway and eyeing the two tall arched windows over the stairwell, which perfectly framed the two mature sycamores in the back garden, their branches silhouetted against the pale, washed-out blue of the early-winter sky. Rachel was relieved to see that all hint of the week-end's sulkiness seemed to have dissipated. Ewan gazed around him – taking in the sculpture of a woman's back carved out of white marble on the windowsill, and the original Peter Blake print opposite the front door – with a guilelessness that touched her. He was still such a boy, really.

'Oi. Hands off. I'll be checking your pockets when you leave.'

It was supposed to be a joke, but she realized instantly from the way his face darkened that she had wounded him. But just as she prepared to apologize, the buzzer sounded again and the others arrived, all in one clump as if they'd arranged to meet up beforehand. The idea that they might not have wanted to risk being the first and having to be alone with her was surprisingly hurtful. Rachel knew leadership was never going to be conducive to popularity, but still she was not a monster. She had little time for most of them, but Amira and Charlie she had thought, in other circumstances, might have been friends.

She ushered her team – a misnomer if ever there was one – down to the kitchen. She'd wondered about taking them up to the living room but decided against it. Though like the rest of the house it was decorated in clean whites, the perfect symmetry of the windows and the grand height of the room lent it a formality she worried would be counter-productive. The basement kitchen, running the full width of the house, with its wall of concertina glass doors that gave on to the newly dug-out patio with the Italian flagstones they'd had to have craned over the house, was less intimidating.

Rachel knew she'd gone too far.

When Mark Hamilton had first approached her about Gill Marsh's job, he'd made it clear he was looking for a radical overhaul of the department. He wanted someone

to come in and 'play hardball', he'd said. She remembered that because of the way he'd over-emphasized
those two words as if he'd been rehearsing them. She'd
been flattered to be headhunted, plus she hadn't been
altogether reluctant to leave her last position after the
unpleasant business with her second-in-command.
Although that hadn't been her fault. The woman had a
history of mental illness she'd kept hidden from the
company. It had been upsetting though. Watching
someone have a nervous breakdown right in front of
your eyes. And afterwards the woman's husband had
made things very uncomfortable, sending emails to staff
members directly accusing her of all sorts of ridiculous
and libellous things. The emails had been anonymous,
so there could be no legal repercussions, but everyone
had known it was him. Rachel wondered what he was
doing now with all his rage and vitriol. Perhaps he'd
started emailing the staff in her current job. She wouldn't
be surprised.

So she'd done what she was brought in to do. Easier
to go in strong and make the painful decisions before
you had a chance to get too close to anyone, then ease
back later. But maybe Ronan walking out had affected
her more than she'd thought. She certainly wouldn't win
any prizes for diplomacy. She had gone too far and this
was the result – this hastily scrambled summit meeting
to smooth out the ruffled feathers. Mark Hamilton had
been furious to be called in to mediate between Amira
and Charlie and herself. 'I don't care how you do it, just
sort it out,' he'd told her. Rachel had been shaken.
She wasn't used to being on the wrong side of
management.

The kitchen table was a 1960s vintage piece. White and circular with a chrome central column underneath, which flared out at the bottom. Around it sat six retro 1960s chairs, S-shaped, in chrome with different colour seat cushions – red, turquoise, yellow, orange, green, bubblegum pink – the only splashes of colour in the otherwise uniformly white space. They'd been Ronan's sole contribution to the décor. He'd bid for them on eBay, paying an over-inflated price to a dealer in Camden, who'd delivered them the next day. She supposed he'd be taking them to wherever it was he was living now. The thought of him sitting on those chairs in some other house, maybe even with the twenty-two-year-old intern, gave Rachel a shooting pain in her chest.

When she'd settled her staff in around the table, dragging a bar stool for herself over from the island in the centre of the kitchen – realizing too late that the extra height was not helpful to her objective of breaking down the barriers that had built up between her and her team – Rachel launched into her carefully prepared speech.

'I realize we've got off on the wrong foot,' she began. 'I always did have two left feet, so it's not surprising I failed to find the right one.'

Silence.

Rachel ploughed on. She'd been brought in to make some tough decisions, she said. Nevertheless she should have handled things better. She understood that Paula must be feeling upset and sidelined, but she assured her that her position with the company had never been in question. Rachel had never intended for her to leave, merely to move sideways to a position more suited to her skillset. And Amira and Charlie had never been in competition with each other; she was only weighing up different people's strengths to make sure she had the best person for the job.

Her own voice sounded fake in her ears. But still she ploughed on. She knew just what she needed to say. Just what they needed to hear.

She'd done all this before.

38
Charlie

Was this how it felt to have a nervous breakdown? It was as if Charlie's normal self had vacated his body and was observing from a distance as this other alien self twisted his limbs and guts into knots of hatred. Rachel's house with its classy address and expensive understated décor was the sort of place that would have impressed Stefan. Sitting in that fabulous kitchen with its clean, modern lines, listening to Rachel wittering on about 'unique strengths' and 'skillsets', Charlie felt as if the house was mocking him, as if *she* was mocking him, holding out this bricks-and-mortar embodiment of everything he was never going to be, everything he was never going to get.

Individuals like Rachel destroyed people, just like that first anonymous email had said. They got you to act like them even though it half killed you to do it, by dangling a prize in front of your eyes. And then, when you'd lowered yourself so you were sliming down on the floor alongside them, they snatched the prize away. And there you were. Nowhere. No one.

Charlie picked absently at the scab on his arm where he'd cut himself breaking into Stefan's flat. He remembered some of the words Stefan had thrown at him over the phone when Charlie had called him to try to explain: loser, stalker, maniac, freak. Charlie had always been hard on himself, his own worst critic. Nevertheless he'd felt a level of pride in his own integrity and loyalty. Those had always seemed to him to be non-negotiable. And yet for Stefan, he'd offered them up. No, not offered them up – but allowed them to be taken.

And what had he got in return?

He looked around the table at the people he'd once considered friends and saw only a bunch of strangers who'd all in different ways betrayed their best selves, leaving behind these empty husks.

There was a knife lying on the table in front of him that Rachel had used to cut the supermarket quiche she was warming up in the oven. Heavy, sharp, expensive. While Rachel was talking at them, Charlie picked it up and ran it gently against the soft pad of his thumb, enjoying how solid it felt, the heft of it in his hands.

If he looked closely into the blade he could see that other Charlie's eyes glinting back at him.

39

Rachel

It was rubbish. They all knew it and she knew it. Nevertheless, as she talked about creating the tightest possible team, about how thrilled she'd been to recognize the potential of the staff she'd inherited, Rachel glanced around, trying to gauge how what she was saying was going down. The biggest imperative now was to calm everyone down and get them working properly again, and then gradually she could once again try to shave off the weaker members. She couldn't get rid of Sarah, but she could start taking away her responsibilities. Then, by the time her leave started, she'd find she was doing a different job, and in the staff reshuffle Rachel was planning, Sarah would be given a different job title too – more junior to the one she had now – with a salary drop to match. Chances were she'd decide it wasn't worth coming back – not with the costs of childcare.

Chloe would doubtless apply for Sarah's old job, which would probably need to be retitled in order to get around HR regulations. It was a natural progression for the girl, and with any luck when she didn't get it, she'd start applying elsewhere. Instead, Rachel had decided to give Sarah's position to Paula. It would be an ignominious step down, and maybe that would help her decide that voluntary redundancy wasn't so bad, after all. But all that was in the future. Now Rachel had to start building some bridges. If only there wasn't such a sense of resistance. Hostility hung over the table like a bad smell.

'Forgive us if we're not exactly jumping for joy to hear all this,' said Amira. 'I think we all feel . . .' Then she tailed off, and Rachel had a sudden moment of clarity, realizing that Amira was regretting her presumption that she could speak for the others. They were not a united group, linked in opposition to her. They were not a group at all. The insight comforted her.

'Well, *I* feel,' Amira corrected herself, 'that since the moment you arrived, Rachel, you've tried to set us against each other so that you could implement whatever changes you wanted without fear of opposition. You've deliberately and systematically cultivated favourites and pets among the staff.' She didn't look at Ewan. She didn't have to. 'And done everything you could to undermine the ones who, for whatever reason, don't fit into your vision of what this department should be. I'd go so far as to say your tactics have amounted to bullying.'

Amira glanced around as if looking for support. Relieved to see that no one responded, Rachel was quick to seize the advantage.

'Bullying is a very strong accusation, Amira. I could almost say slanderous as it's a disciplinary, even a criminal offence. Do any of you others agree with her? Now's the time to get it off your chests, while we're clearing the air.'

She scanned slowly around the table, forcing herself to make eye contact with each person in turn. One by one they dropped their gaze, or found something interesting through the window, or over near the door. All except Ewan, who hadn't even raised his head, and Charlie, who was fidgeting with the kitchen knife.

For Rachel the silence was like someone opening a valve in her chest and releasing the pressure. She'd won. She would keep her team together. There would be no revolt. Mark Hamilton would not let her go at the end of her probation period. The relief was overwhelming. And was closely followed by a feeling of near-tenderness towards the people sat around her table.

'This is exactly why we're here,' she said, her voice soft. 'To air these festering grievances and then put them to bed. Thank you, Amira, for being so direct. In a moment we'll go round and see what everyone else has to say, but first of all let's eat!'

She flung open the fridge door, taking out clingfilm-covered dishes into which she'd already decanted the ready-prepared food she'd bought from M&S early that morning. 'And why don't we have a couple of bottles of wine as well. I know it's officially a work day, but it's more important that we talk it all through. And what better way to do it than with wine.'

Ronan had called it the Precipice, that critical moment in a deal where he'd delivered his spiel and was teetering on the edge, waiting to see if the client would bite or back down. That moment just then had been her Precipice. And now it was over, she knew she could afford to be kinder. But first, wine.

'Ewan, why don't you come and help me pick out a

couple of bottles of wine from the cellar downstairs?'

The 'wine cellar' was actually just a storeroom off the gym containing a drinks fridge and a few racks of red wine, but Ronan had always called it that, and the name had stuck. Singling Ewan out might make up for her earlier gaffe about checking his pockets, which she had instantly regretted. Plus it wouldn't hurt him to get a look at the gym and the sauna. Ewan was impressed by material things. He wanted her, but more than that he wanted what she had. She recognized that want.

Around the table, the atmosphere was still tight. People sat stiffly as if moving might cause them pain.

Ewan kept his eyes downcast.

'No, you're all right,' he muttered, not moving.

'Come on, Ewan. There's something down there I think you'd enjoy.'

She held her breath. The moment stretched out. Finally Ewan lumbered to his feet. *And – breathe.*

'It's down here,' she called, leading the way through the door separating the kitchen from the narrow staircase that led down to the basement. Only as the latch closed behind them, plunging them into darkness, did she remember the light switch on the kitchen wall outside the door. Damn. But it was just a few steps and then they'd be in the gym where the lighting was low, but better than nothing.

She heard Ewan's footsteps heavy behind her, and the harsh rasps of his breath.

338

40

Anne

'Can I just check my emails on your laptop, Mom? My piece of shit phone is acting up again.'

'Sure.'

By the time I remember what I have open on the screen it is too late.

'What are all these news reports up here? A London case? Hey, is that why you were so keen on watching the BBC news? What's going on? Mom?'

Shannon has always been able to do this, throw out a volley of questions without even stopping to draw breath. When she was a child it used to exhaust me, never knowing which question to answer first.

'Oh, it's just something I'm keeping an eye on for a course I'm running.'

Even to my ears it sounds fake. Shannon knows I haven't added any extra content to my courses for years. That's part of the reason I've stayed all this time. Coasting along without effort left more time for the things that really matter, more time for Shannon.

But now Shannon is frowning at something on the screen, and I can feel cold bumps popping up on my arms and legs.

'This guy – the one in the photos. He looks kinda familiar. Is that why you're so interested in this case? Because we know him?'

I open my mouth to say no. But find I can't get the word out.

Shannon looks up and sees something written on my face that shouldn't be there.

'Come on,' she says, squinting at me across the room. My house has one integral living space and I am sitting on the couch facing the TV, while she is perched on a stool at the breakfast bar in the kitchen, my laptop open in front of her. We have adopted these same positions so many times over the years, it's like we have worn a groove in time. I imagine us suspended here for ever, like tiny figures in a doll's house.

'Like I'm gonna buy that! We both know your courses haven't changed since the Dark Ages. I bet you still get your students to write in a quill and ink. Why the interest in this case? Where do we know this guy from?'

For the first time in years, I have a sharp yearning for a neat vodka I could neck down in one to give me strength. Shannon is still gazing at me, waiting for answers.

'Mom? Who is he?'

'Shannon . . . Baby . . . He's your brother.'

41

Ewan

They'd stood there in the wide, white hallway with the light flooding in through the huge arched windows over the stairs so all her lovely things – the paintings, the ornaments, even that funny naked back on the window-sill – seemed perfectly displayed like in a gallery. Rachel was dressed casually in tight dark jeans and a filmy white top with her black hair pulled back into a loose ponytail, smiling at him as if she was genuinely pleased he was there. He'd felt himself begin to unfurl for the first time in days; the fear that had coiled itself up inside him like a rope since Saturday night finally loosening. For a moment, he'd had an image of himself living in this house, or a house like this one, next to this woman, or a woman just like her. Nobody telling him what he could or couldn't do. Nobody belittling him or limiting him or joining forces so it felt like it was him against the rest of them. And then she'd said that thing about checking his pockets when he left and everything had gone red.

All through the time they'd spent downstairs in that big show-off kitchen, while Rachel had talked and talked until the words formed one big blur of noise in his head, he'd felt as if there was something pressing down on his chest. When he'd first started going to the gym, and bench-pressing weights, Ewan had had an irrational fear that the bar was going to fall on him, crushing him. He'd lie there on his back imagining the pain of all that pressure on his ribs, how they'd crack, how the lungs underneath would deflate like balloons with all the air squeezed out of them. Sitting on a lime-green-cushioned chair at Rachel's circular white table, he felt just as he'd imagined he would, all that time ago in the gym.

And then she'd asked him to go down to the cellar. He'd stayed in his chair, unable to move. So she'd asked again, and everyone was staring, and the silence was so big and solid you could have cut it with the knife Charlie wouldn't stop playing with. He'd found himself getting to his feet, the pain still tight across his chest, the red in front of his eyes even when they were closed, as if his lids themselves were painted that way.

42

Charlie

The sound of the door closing behind Rachel and Ewan was like something breaking inside Charlie's head. He still felt split into two people, but now the old Charlie was fading, dissolving, leaving only this new twisted thing, full of rage and something else, sharp, like needles in his skull, that he finally identified as fear.

He was scared of them, these people he'd worked with, day in, day out for years. He was scared of what they were all capable of, scared of what *he* was capable of.

He struggled to bring himself back into focus. The others were discussing Ewan and Rachel.

'He must think his luck's in – an invitation to get down and dirty with the boss,' Amira said.

'I don't think so.'

That was Paula. Even through the confusion in his head Charlie registered surprise that she'd volunteered an opinion. She'd been so quiet for the last two days, ever since she'd overheard him and Amira scrabbling for her job like a couple of dogs.

'We arrived practically at the same time earlier on,' Paula continued. 'He was admiring the house until she said something really bitchy about him stealing the family silver. Then he clammed right up. I don't think he'll forgive that very easily.'

Paula's voice was flat and deadened, as if she was speaking through a layer of thick foam.

Charlie tried to summon the old sense of shame that had been with him ever since he'd decided to apply for Paula's job, but he couldn't. It was as if the anger and hatred and fear had pushed all other emotions out. Everything was foggy, untethered. The voices around him arrived through a mist as if disembodied.

Only the knife was real. Solid. Hidden by the table, he ran the tip of the blade across his thigh, over the thick material of his suit trousers. Then he rested his injured arm on his lap and gently traced the contours of his cut with the knife's metal edge. As if in a trance, he pressed down on the top of it, observing as spots of fresh blood emerged like rubies on the surface of the old.

Chloe's voice drifted past his ears. 'He's a big boy. Old enough to sort out his own shit.'

She sounded sad and so much older than her years, and Charlie wondered briefly if maybe she was experiencing the same thing as him – that feeling of being replaced by an alien Chloe.

But the thought was driven out almost as soon as it arrived, and Charlie was lost once again in the crimson brilliance of his own arm.

He pressed harder, enjoying the savage spurt of pain. He deserved it. They all deserved it. Rachel might have been pulling the strings but they'd all been complicit, all instrumental in making themselves victims or bullies at her whim. They made him sick. All of them. Himself most of all.

His head was throbbing, the blood pounding in his temple. He put his hand up to his forehead and a spray of blood arced across the table.

Someone screamed.

43

Anne

My daughter has always known she was adopted. We've never had secrets on that score. Her almond-shaped eyes are the colour of sea-glass, while mine are blue. I've always had a boyish figure, straight up and down with a slight stoop as if to apologize for the space I take up, while Shannon is unashamedly curvy, with the kind of figure that fits with the retro-style fashion she favours – tight sweaters and pencil skirts that hug her hips and swish when she walks, and long, honey-toned hair that falls in waves around her shoulders. She is beautiful. Of course she isn't biologically mine.

And yet she is mine in every other sense. The light of my life. The reward for every good thing I ever did in my life, or even thought about doing. The only reason I haven't drunk myself to death, or ended up like my own mother, alienated from friends and family, playing online poker with strangers just for the interaction.

Shannon Laurie Cater. Child L.

It was not easy.

When it became obvious that Ed Kowalsky and I had very different views on whether or not Laurie was capable of being assimilated into a new family, a new life, a new country even, capable of putting everything that had gone before out of her mind, he brought in Dan Oppenheimer to support him. At that time, Early Years psychiatry was still an under-researched area. I believe that in some more progressive academic institutions, there had already started to be a recognition of just how crucial experiences during the first two years of life, even before a child is capable of speech, are to their development in later life. But in our little backwater, that wasn't the case. So Professor Kowalsky and Dan definitely held the prevailing view. This was before the definitive studies showing that in cases of severe abuse, memory recollection was delayed, starting at the age of six or even seven, but there was enough anecdotal evidence to convince them time was on their side.

But something about Laurie, about the way she looked at me with those clear green eyes, her stubborn determination to try to make good of the shitty hand she'd been dealt, made me stick to my guns. Like Ed and Dan, I could see she had the potential to be happy, well-adjusted even, but unlike them I believed – no, I *knew* – that in order to achieve that bright future she would have to work through the darkness of her past. The lapses in her behaviour were too striking to ignore. Rather than going to a new environment and suppressing her past, folding it up into a tiny pocket inside her where it wouldn't show but would always be there, she needed intensive ongoing therapy. She needed to talk about what had happened to her, to take it out of whatever box she'd put it in and shake it like a dusty tablecloth and expose it to the air so it lost its power.

I knew this in my gut. So I stood my ground against

Kowalsky and Oppenheimer, and when they threatened to overrule me, I brought in my own experts, mostly from the very same elite universities Oppenheimer would later go on to work for. I called these experts in the evenings, leaving long messages on their answer-machines. There were a couple of 'no's' but mostly they were keen to get involved, to bring their new theories to bear on this high-profile case. There was growing evidence to show that intensive early therapy in the first three years of life when the brain was still developing was much more effective in cases of serious trauma than waiting to treat problems that emerged in adulthood. I worked through the night in the university library so I could provide study after study to support my conviction that Laurie needed to stay where her past was acknowledged and dealt with, so that eventually she could be done with it and move on.

I was not popular. But I did my homework, and impressed the right people, and in the end an extraordinary meeting of all the relevant authorities ruled that Laurie should remain under our supervision and the adoption order was rescinded.

Her brother was a different matter. David. Child D. Aka The Thing.

A year and a half younger, he had been treated by a range of medical experts. In addition to Oppenheimer and Kowalsky, he'd received intensive therapy to deal with the physical effects of being kept incarcerated and intermittently restrained at such an early and vital stage in his development. He had to learn to walk properly, using muscles that had atrophied through lack of use. Vocally his development was also severely retarded.

He'd been denied even the most basic social interaction. He'd never had the chance to absorb language or to develop his own speech. A small but dedicated team from the university's Department of Cognitive and Linguistic Sciences had worked tirelessly with him over a period of months to overcome the delays to his communication skills.

But while physically he responded to treatment better than anyone dared hope, it was his emotional development that was deemed most critical, and in this respect, too, his progress far exceeded all expectations. Dan Oppenheimer and Ed Kowalsky were the ones who had ultimately rubber-stamped the adoption order, some months after the battle for Laurie's future had been concluded. Their earlier pessimism had been misplaced, they decided. He would recover. He would forget.

'Did you meet him? My brother?'

Since I asked her to come sit with me on the couch, so we could talk properly, Shannon has listened to me in virtual silence. That's always been her way. Though naturally voluble and inclined to speak without thinking first, when the stakes are highest, she waits and considers before deciding on a reaction or an emotion, as if she is selecting clothes from an open closet. She has always known her early years were traumatic. She knows she was made a ward of state after her parents failed to take care of her. She knows she had a brother who was adopted overseas. She knows she had years of therapy when she was very young, and that's how we met. She knows both her parents were incarcerated for what they did to their children.

The facts I haven't shared with her are these: her

parents were sentenced to life imprisonment for their maltreatment of their son. Her father has been on the psych ward of a medical centre for federal prisoners in Missouri for over two decades since he started believing he was God. Her mother – dead-eyed Noelle Egan – was released from prison five years ago. Her willingness to testify against her husband and her insistence that she'd been in thrall to him, incapable of independent action, worked in her favour. She was also, by all accounts, an exemplary prisoner. When I learned she was free and had been sniffing around after her daughter, I went back through the files making sure there was no trail leading to Shannon. Noelle has always believed both her children were adopted overseas. That way, I was able to keep my daughter safe.

Shannon's brother was indeed adopted abroad, but rather than being lost in the system as I've always allowed her to believe, I've been keeping tabs on him through Barbara Campbell, the original social worker who handled the adoption.

I've been amazed at Shannon's capacity for self-invention over the years. Or is it merely self-preservation? Whatever it is, I've always told myself I was following her cue, keeping from her only what she didn't choose to know. For two years before I formerly adopted her, we worked hard on exploring her feelings about her parents and about what had happened in that house. But after the age of six or seven, after the final papers had been signed and she was finally mine, she was ready to move on. By that time I was married to Johnny whom she still calls Dad, even though she doesn't see him so much since he remarried and moved away. I would have told her the truth then, or at least I like to think I would, but she never asked me. And gradually the details of what happened before seemed to fade from her mind. And now here she is, fixing me with her inquisitive eyes and asking me, finally, about her brother. And I owe her the truth.

'I met him once,' I tell her. 'Well, not really "met". I saw him through a pane of glass.'

'What did he look like?'

'Like you, baby. A lot like you.'

I've already explained the basics of his early life, trying to keep to the facts and avoid commentary or emotion.

And now she asks me the question I've been dreading since I formally signed the adoption papers all those years ago. All the while she is speaking, I am urging her, silently, to stop, change direction. But still she continues.

'What was I doing while he was down there in that cage?'

I know what she wants to hear. I know she wants me to tell her she didn't know he was there. It's not impossible. I've heard of an Austrian man who kept his daughter imprisoned in the basement of his family home for twenty-four years, even having seven children with her – and all without his wife and other children suspecting a thing. It's so tempting to lie to her. Or if not lie, to omit the truth. But I don't. I tell her what happened and what she did. I tell her it was not her fault, and I know she understands that, but she still cries – not heaving sobs but fat tears that build in her eyes until they spill over like a slow-leaking faucet.

'He must have felt so alone.'

I reach out and take her hand and squeeze it so I don't give in to the temptation to tell her platitudes like 'He was too young to fully comprehend what was happening', or, 'He didn't know anything else'.

I am waiting for her to turn on me, demanding to know why I never told her this before, how I could have kept it from her. But she doesn't. Instead she asks me about David. She wants to know why he was adopted and not her, and I try to explain about Kowalsky and Oppenheimer and about how it was back then, that they thought the younger you were, the greater your capacity to forget.

'Was he happy?' she wants to know then. 'Did his new family love him enough to make him forget what went before?'

In this at least I can tell her what she wants to hear. Child D's parents were good people. Barbara made sure of that. Though they never knew the particulars, they were told the little boy had had a traumatic start in life, the subject of abuse and neglect, and they'd done their very best to make up to him for it.

'He's had a good life,' I tell her, still holding her hand. 'He's been loved.'

'Then why this?' she says, waving a hand towards the laptop, still open on the news report that bears a photograph of a man with features that mirror her own.

I shrug.

'It could be anything. Maybe there was something personal between him and the victim and something just snapped or, I don't know, he'd been smoking crack or something. My fear was always that if he suppressed memories without dealing with them properly, something could trigger if not the memories themselves, then at least the feelings he had from back then. Fear, anger, confusion.'

'But who was she? The victim, I mean.'

'She was his new boss, apparently. Barbara describes her as a bully. Says she managed people by pitting them against each other, praising some and punishing others so in the end there was no trust left and everyone suspected everyone else of conspiring against them. That might trigger someone like David.'

'What is the British press saying? Surely the courts will be lenient, because of his history?'

'The press can't report details now until the trial starts. That's the system they have over there.'

'So we don't know if he was provoked. It could have been self-defence. She sounds like a prize bitch. Maybe she was goading him. She could have been, right?'

My daughter is already jumping in to defend the brother she has only just discovered, and my heart aches remembering how she was at school, in the post-therapy years, when confronted with an underdog, with someone being bullied, how upset it made her, how strident on their behalf. Over-compensating? Maybe. And perhaps she'd have done the same even without the therapy. Perhaps left to her own devices she'd have rebelled against the patterns of behaviour learned in infancy anyway and grown from bully to defender of the weak. It's always the way with children. They drag behind them the different versions of themselves so you're never really sure which one is real, but you love them all just the same. I want to take her in my arms and make it go away. I want to take the burden of everything I've just told her about herself away, so she can't lie awake in the dead early hours and wonder just who and what she is. I want to let her think that her little brother is still the victim, more sinned against than sinning. But she deserves the truth.

'Sweetie, it was bad. What he did to her. It was real bad.'

44

Ewan

When he'd walked through the doorway off the kitchen and seen the narrow stairs plunging into the darkness below, with another door at the end, there had been a thudding in his head, as if someone was inside his skull, hammering to get out.

'This way,' she'd said.

And then the kitchen door had slammed itself shut behind them, blocking out the light, and now it was pitch black and the thudding in his head was so loud as they felt their way down the steps that his whole body was vibrating with it, as if he himself was the thing hammering to get out. His chest felt like it was about to explode, and his breath tore from him, ragged and far too loud. The air down here was different than it had been in the kitchen. Several degrees colder, damp.

'The door handle should be somewhere around here.' Rachel's voice ahead of him sounded as if it were coming from a long way away.

And now, along with the pain and the lack of breath, there was another sensation building, building, building inside him. Terror. *Don't open the door. Please don't open the door.* He didn't know what he was afraid of and the words stayed trapped inside him along with the fear.

'Aha, here we are. I think you'll love the basement.'

The door creaked open.

'The light switch should be somewhere around here, don't worry.'

Click. The gloom ahead was lit up by a dim, yellowish light, reflecting off some sort of wet, rocky surface. Another memory flashed into his head. *Dark. So dark. Water running down rough walls. A smell of damp stone. Cold bones*. He didn't know where the memory had come from. Only that it made him feel weak, like he was disappearing.

'What do you think? Not bad, hey?' Rachel was gesturing around the dimly lit room, which turned out to be some kind of gym. A rowing machine crouched in one corner black and low, next to a treadmill, its inbuilt screen now blank. There was a shoulder press and a spin cycle and a machine for working abs. In a normal situation he would have enjoyed checking them all out, but this wasn't normal. He wasn't normal. Another flash of memory. *Water. Damp. A hollowness in his tummy. Pain. Pain. Pain.*

Rachel was bending over a black crate by the wall. When she straightened, she was carrying something in her hands.

'What do you say?' she asked. 'Skipping contest?'

She held out the thing in her hands. She was carrying a rope.

'Don't,' he said. Or perhaps he just thought about saying it, because she didn't stop coming towards him, the rope wrapped around her hands. And he remembered something, or thought he did. Cords cutting into soft skin. A bare mattress. Longing to wrap his arms around himself, just so he could feel some human warmth.

And still she came.

She wanted to hurt him. Then she'd get the others to hurt him. That's why she'd brought him down here alone. To this dark place that smelled of cold, and where the *plop plop plop* of water on stone was like a physical pain in his heart.

The anger came out of nowhere, arriving with such force that it was as if it had been gathering inside him for his whole life, just waiting to be unleashed.

Too late, Rachel realized that something had changed. He saw her expression go from challenging to uncertain and then to something else. Scared. She turned towards the door, but he grabbed her arm.

'Leave me al—' Her command was cut short by his right hand clamped over her mouth from behind.

Power surged through him, mixing with the fear and the anger and those weird memories he couldn't place. He reached his left hand around to her neck and jerked her head back so her throat was stretched out. Then he ran his thumb up her windpipe, increasing the pressure each time. She hurt people, this woman. She'd hurt him before and she would do it again if he gave her the chance. More memories: *blows raining down on a body too small to resist. Not bothering to cry because what was the point?*

Now Rachel was struggling, writhing around under his grip, trying to prise his hands away with her fingers. With each of her movements, more of his old self was dislodged, crumbling away like broken cement, leaving behind only the fury, the red-hot core of him. He grabbed one of her fingers in his. The snap of bone breaking was the sound of his molten rage crackling.

45

Anne

'How bad?'

Shannon jumps to her feet, goes back to the laptop and begins scrolling through the news reports I have up on-screen. The British sub-judice laws mean the respected papers haven't yet reported on the crime in detail, but no such scruples operate on the internet. The first time I'd read what Child D was supposed to have done, I had to run to the bathroom to vomit. Some of the more salacious descriptions are up on my screen and I look away so I don't have to watch what reading them does to her face.

'Oh my God!' She has a hand clasped to her mouth and her eyes over the top are round like marbles.

'Baby,' I say. 'It might not be as bad as it seems. She could have been dead before he even . . .'

But it is no good.

'He cooked her?'

'Shannon, honey, don't believe everything you read there. It's rumour. Unsubstantiated.'

'Oh my God.' She is reading from the screen. '*He tied her up, laid her on the top bench of the sauna and turned the heat up to maximum as if he was roasting a chicken.*'

She stays in her seat as if the sheer force of her horror is keeping her there.

'Why didn't the others come down? They were having a fucking meeting a floor up. Why did nobody come stop it?'

'He'd locked the door,' I say. 'David – or Ewan as he's now called – had locked the door. At first the others thought there was something . . . well, sexual going on, so no one did anything. And then there was some sort of distraction. One of the others had a kind of mini-breakdown – cut his own arm in a desperate cry for help. By the time they realized something was seriously wrong downstairs and called the police, it was too late.'

Shannon is still scouring the news report, and I wish she'd stop. There are horrible things written there. Details about blackened features and melted skin left behind on the sauna floor.

I stand up and head towards my daughter. Reaching over her shoulder, I gently close the lid of the laptop and then, finally, I put my arms around her. At first she resists and is stiff, and for a moment the old fear returns, that I won't be able to get through to her, that she'll never truly allow me to love her. But then a little noise escapes her, like the sound a baby makes before it starts to cry, and she turns to face me, her whole body sagging as if she can't bear her own weight any more, and she collapses into me and I bury my face in her coconut-smelling hair, and we stay that way for a very long time.

46

Anne

The first surprise is how modern it is. I had been expecting dark Victorian brick, the colour of dried blood. But instead it is modern, bland even. Beige. Like the low-slung buildings on the industrial estates we passed on the train coming up here. Later we will discover there is another, older wing, a former hospital, vast and forbidding, but as we walk up the path, past neatly manicured lawns and in through the double doors, we might just as easily be going to get mortgage advice from some faceless finance company or do a wholesale deal for staple guns and other office supplies. Only the imposing metal gates we drove through in our taxi from the station, manned by an unsmiling guard and flanked by impossibly high fences topped with coils of razor wire, give away the true nature of the place.

'Put your belongings in here, please.'

Even after two days in the UK, I can't get used to the accent. Shannon and I have finally stopped digging each other in the ribs every time someone opens their mouth, but still those blunt vowels come as a shock. The woman behind the table has a different way of talking from the people we met in London, even though we're only two hundred miles north-west of the capital. In the States that's practically like visiting the next town, but here distance seems to matter more.

Shannon and I dutifully place our bags and coats in the plastic trays as if we're going through airport security, except that this time they are stored in lockers instead of given back to us. Suddenly relieved of my outerwear, I feel bizarrely like I'm going to a party or a social function and have checked my coat in at the door. But then we are searched and patted and questioned, and then questioned again for over half an hour, and we fill in form after form and it no longer feels like a party but the worst journey ever, assailed by bureaucracy every step of the way, and a building sense of menace with every fresh signature.

Finally we are escorted down newly painted corridors with soft magnolia walls and pale-green doors. We could be in any respectable but anonymous motel. Except that from far away I can hear the desolate sound of a man crying. Shannon takes my hand. Presses it tightly, as if it is me who needs bolstering. I am shocked by the miracle of her. This strong, courageous woman. My daughter.

We are ushered into a visiting room. It has a low coffee table, four comfortable chairs and opaque blinds at the window that shut off the outside world.

'Ewan will be along shortly,' says our escort, a short, bearded man with thin greying hair greased back from his face, and eyes so close together they seem almost to be touching. He makes it sound as if we have just popped in for a cup of tea.

'Oh God, I'm so nervous,' says Shannon when the man has left us alone. 'What if he hates me? He has every right to. I'm part of the reason he's ended up here.'

'Shannon, you were four years old,' I remind her.

We've had this conversation so many times I dream about it in my sleep. Since making her momentous discovery five months ago, Shannon has read everything she can get her hands on about her family background, trying to understand. To my amazement and vast relief she has never blamed me for not telling her the full truth. She now admits that she always knew there was something very dark crouching in her past but she preferred not to confront it. She says she used to resent the way I encouraged her to talk about everything, the constant question, 'How did that make you feel?' Yet now she realizes why I did it. She remembers how, as a child, she used to have what she calls 'blanks'. When something was too confusing or scary to cope with, she'd just check out of her own head and allow her body to go on to autopilot. By forcing her to relive those moments, analysing what was happening at the time, and why she was reacting the way she was, she gradually learned to anticipate the triggers and deal with them in a way that, she's convinced, her little brother couldn't.

'He was frightened of everything when he first arrived,' Sheila, Ewan's adoptive mother, told us when we visited them yesterday morning at their neat, ordinary house on the outskirts of Coventry.

'At first we worried that we'd taken on too much with him. I mean, we knew he'd had a difficult past. We knew there'd been abuse and neglect. We were prepared for that, or at least we thought we were. But we didn't expect him to be scared of us. That came as a shock.'

'So how long did it take him to settle in?' Shannon asked and I knew she was itching to get to the bit where David was finally allowed to be happy.

'It was a few weeks, I think, wasn't it, love?' Sheila turned to her husband, Neil, a heavyset man with a drinker's deep-purple cheeks, who studied his hands the whole time we were visiting, as if he might find written there the answers he needed to know.

'That's right, a few weeks,' he agreed, without looking up. 'He was such a sad little scrap at first. Didn't say anything, just followed you around the room with those big eyes. And then one day Sheila had been out some-where, I forget where, the shops or something, and she came into the kitchen and he said "Mummy". And he smiled. And that was that, really.'

'I'll never forget it,' said Sheila, and her pale-blue eyes, which had been shot through with pink when we arrived, as if she'd just been crying, now filled once again with tears.

'People are saying he's a monster, but he isn't. What he did . . . what they say he did . . . Ewan just wouldn't. Not to a woman. He was so protective of me, wasn't he, love?'

Neil didn't reply, just nodded and breathed a deep sigh.

Sheila was perched on a leather footstool as there wasn't enough space in the cramped living room for anything more than the three-seater sofa where Shannon and I sat and the armchair in which Neil was slumped. You'd think I'd be the one who'd know how to deal with tears, right? I'm the professional, after all. But it was Shannon who got up and knelt down on the dusty pink carpet next to the grief-stricken woman and put an arm around her heaving shoulders and said the things a woman in Sheila's position wanted to hear. 'You did a good job', 'He wasn't himself', 'It's clear how much you loved him'.

And it was. It really was. The photographs around the living room and in the narrow hallway were all of Ewan Johnson at various stages of growing up. As an angelic, if nervous-looking young boy on his first day of school in a uniform that was several sizes too big. Slightly older, tousle-haired and grinning straight into the camera to reveal a black hole where his four front teeth should have been. A handsome teenager, sitting in a kayak, wearing a life-vest over a tanned bare chest, gazing out at the photographer through Shannon's clear green eyes. The obligatory school prom photograph, sandwiched between Neil and Sheila, over whom he towered, with an arm around each of them, wearing a smart new suit, all of them looking proud and happy.

Photographs do lie. We all edit our own pasts, picking out what conforms best to the picture of our lives we most want to paint. But there was love there, in that modest house. We truly felt it. It was what we needed – what Shannon needed – to know.

Later, Neil admitted that Ewan had been no angel. He'd got into a few fights at school, though never too serious. Sometimes he hadn't even been able to give a reason beyond that an 'angry mist' had taken him over. He'd suffered off and on from stiffness in one of his legs, clearly the legacy of his incarceration in the cellar, although Neil and Sheila had been told only that it was the result of an early injury. Boys who'd made fun of his occasional limp had more often than not ended up regretting it. Ewan hadn't always been kind either to the besotted girls who called round all through his teens. 'Tell her I'm not here,' he'd hiss, running upstairs to hide in his room.

There'd been a period between the ages of fifteen and seventeen, Neil said, when the two of them had locked horns, Ewan pushing, always pushing, against his father's authority. 'I was stuck in the middle of them,' Sheila said. 'But that's normal, isn't it? All young lads go through a phase of trying to prove themselves to their fathers.' He'd got drunk one time and had to have his stomach pumped. Another time Sheila had found a little bag of white pills hidden in his bedroom. Once, Neil recalled, his friends had brought him home from a party raving like a lunatic. They said he'd been smoking skunk and it had done something to his brain. He was convinced people were trying to kill him, even his own parents. Sheila had wanted to take him to the hospital, but Neil had persuaded her to wait for a few hours and luckily it had passed. Their son had never touched the stuff again.

As he hit his early twenties he'd calmed down, become less confrontational, more considerate. And he'd seemed to be doing so well at work.

Until Rachel Masters arrived.

Neil's voice dried up as he said the name of the woman Ewan had killed, and Sheila began crying again.

'He wasn't in his right mind,' she said. 'He would never . . .'

We sat for a while, not speaking, the silence punctuated only by Sheila's sobs, tiny hiccuping sounds that seemed to catch in the back of her throat.

I could feel Shannon building up to say something. When you've lived with someone a long time you get a sense for things like that. Even before she spoke, I knew what she was going to say. It was what we'd travelled all this way to find out.

'Did he ever ask you about his early family life? Did he try to find out where he came from?'

Did he know about me, is what she was really asking. *Did he know what I did*?

Sheila shook her head.

'He knew he was adopted, of course. And he knew his biological family had been very . . .' she glanced at Shannon warily '. . . dysfunctional, and that's why he was sent so far away to be adopted. Barbara, our social worker, never told us his biological family's surname. She said it was better that we didn't know. She didn't say why but we guessed it was because they had been in the news. So we couldn't look them up. Ewan asked about them a few times over the years, but not often. He knew it upset me.'

Without warning, she put her hand out to touch Shannon's face, running her trembling fingers softly down my daughter's cheek.

'I'm sorry, love, it's just that you're so much like him. So, so lovely.'

And now in this anonymous high-security psychiatric hospital, Shannon is about to find out for herself how much alike she and her brother are, and I know she's finding the prospect terrifying.

'OK?' I ask now, leaning across from my chair in the visiting room to put a hand on her knee.

She nods.

'Will he even know who I am though, Mom? He'll be on heavy-duty medication, right?'

I have used my professional privilege to find out all I can about Ewan Johnson's treatment. Through contacts in the UK I learned that he had been remanded from court to this place, displaying signs of acute psychosis. From what I can gather, strong medication and daily therapy have got the psychosis under control, but now it is the possibility of self-harm that medical personnel are more concerned with. We met briefly with Ewan's lawyer late yesterday afternoon, a tired-looking woman who played with her wedding ring as she spoke to us in the foyer of her offices, as if it were a good luck charm with which she could ward off the more distressing aspects of her job. She couldn't or wouldn't tell us much, citing client confidentiality, but she did confirm they're working on a defence of diminished responsibility when his case does finally come to trial. She seemed interested in Shannon, appraising her with her purple-shadowed eyes and asking if she'd be prepared to come to give evidence in Ewan's support if they decided to play the dys-functional birth family card. I knew what she was thinking. My daughter would look good up there on the stand.

'Yes, he's on pretty serious meds,' I confirm now. 'But he should still be compos mentis. Just a bit slower than usual, is all.'

We are both silent, thinking about the baby who wasn't loved enough to be called by his name, the little boy Kowalsky and Oppenheimer decided was balanced enough that a new start could paper over the cracks his mistreatment had left in his psyche.

'Oh my God, someone's coming.'

Shannon is half standing, unsure what to do with herself. I hear her swallow loudly. My own mouth is dry as dust, remembering the solemn-faced child I glimpsed through a panel of glass all those years ago.

The door opens and a prison guard steps inside wearing a dark-blue uniform and a stern expression. He glances at me, then at Shannon. And then at Shannon again.

'I'll be outside,' he tells her. It's as if I don't exist.

Then he turns to go and someone else is coming through the door. Someone tall who looks at me through Shannon's eyes as if he recognizes me. As the door softly closes behind him, he shifts his attention to Shannon and they stare at each other for a long time. I notice that Ewan Johnson has lost the chest-out stance of the photographs in Sheila and Neil's home. His shoulders are still broad but he is thinner than he appeared on the news bulletins, his sweatshirt hanging off him as if off a clothes hanger. I have never seen anyone look so lost.

I think about what he endured in that basement. I think about the cage. I think about how he was three years old before he heard a kind word or felt a gentle human touch. And I think about the little girl who grew up aware she was doing something wrong, something bad, but not knowing exactly what or how to stop it. I think about my own mother and how she chose the liquor over me, and just how many ways it's possible to fuck up a child so badly that ten, twenty, forty years later they're still trying to make sense of it.

And now Shannon is properly on her feet and taking two steps across the floor and she's opening up her arms, and her brother is falling into them like the baby he was never allowed to be.

And for this moment, just for this moment, love is all. Love is everything.

I close my eyes.

Epilogue

Julia Tomlinson-Harris had that fluttery feeling she got whenever she was nervous or excited or, as now, a mixture of both. Though there were several files open on the desk in front of her, her mind wasn't on the reports she was supposed to be reading; instead, her gaze flicked repeatedly to the glass window between her new office and the desks on the main floor where sat the staff members she'd inherited.

She'd met them when she first came in that morning, but only briefly. Mark Hamilton had brought her into the main office and gathered the staff together to introduce her and make a quick speech.

The words 'unfortunate', 'regrettable' and 'tragic' had featured strongly in the first part of the speech, to be quickly replaced by 'overcome', 'pull together' and once even, if she remembered rightly, 'transcend'. They were entering an exciting period, Mark informed them. 'The future starts now.' Then she'd shaken hands with each of the staff members and they'd told her their names, which she knew anyway from the personnel records she'd studied in depth. And since then she'd been in here, pretending to work, but really trying to get a handle on who they all were and to gauge the general mood.

That grim-faced man over there must be Charlie. Not terribly friendly, was he? Looked like he had the world on his shoulders. But then hadn't he had some sort of breakdown on the very same day of what Mark kept referring to as 'the unfortunate tragedy'? Slashed his own arm? Not deeply, thank the Lord, but enough to have everyone flapping about for a while. That was one of the reasons they hadn't noticed the other two had been gone so long apparently.

'Aren't you a bit freaked out, going into that office? After everything that happened?' her old assistant Naomi had asked Julia after she first announced her new job.

'It didn't happen in the office itself,' Julia had reminded her. 'And obviously Ewan Johnson isn't there any more.'

'Yes, but it's kind of like stepping into a dead woman's shoes, isn't it? Kind of creepy.' And she'd done a theatrical little shudder so that her narrow brown shoulders moved up and down like piano keys under her strappy top.

Julia actually hadn't felt at all freaked out when Mark Hamilton had first approached her about taking over Rachel Masters's job. In fact, she'd been flattered. With all the media reports both at the time of the *incident* and then again at the trial, this was by far the most high-profile recruitment department in the country – and she was the one tasked with getting it back into shape.

'They need a safe pair of hands,' she'd said when she handed in her notice at her old company. 'Someone to steer them back to health.'

Mark himself had been running things since Rachel

had been gone, in conjunction with Paula Hibbs. It hadn't escaped Julia's notice that Paula had failed to meet her eyes when she shook hands this morning. She looked so hot and flustered. What on earth was she thinking of, wearing all those layers on a day like today? The woman hadn't exactly been welcoming. She couldn't possibly have imagined she might be offered the job herself, could she?

But while Julia hadn't been freaked out before starting the job, she had to admit she'd had a few *moments* since arriving this morning. In her experience, when you took over someone's position there was nearly always a lingering sense of the previous incumbent. Even if there was no nameplate still on the door or mini-pack of tissues in the top drawer, there was usually a faint imprint of someone else's presence – the particular height of the office chair, the list of extension numbers stuck to the telephone written in a sloping hand, not her own, and in blue ink rather than her own preferred black.

Even though six months had passed since the terrible thing that happened to Rachel Masters, Julia fancied she got a whiff, just every now and then, of a musky, smoky perfume of the kind she'd never use. There was also a coat hanger on a hook on the back of the door that Julia kept being drawn to, imagining one of Rachel's neat fitted jackets hanging there, or a soft cashmere coat. She'd never actually met her predecessor, but obviously she'd read so much about her she almost felt like she had.

The knock on the door gave Julia a start.

'Sorry to bother you.'

The woman who walked in was early thirties, long

dark hair, big-boned. Julia's eyes flicked to the notebook where she'd scribbled down the names of her new team. Amira. It must be.

Julia beamed at her and got a weak smile in return. Not so much a smile, in fact, as a muscle twitch at the side of her mouth. The assessment reviews in her personnel file had described her as 'bright' and 'out-going'. But Amira's face was blank and smooth as if something elemental had rubbed it free of expression.

'I just wanted to remind you I've got the afternoon off. We're moving.'

'That's exciting. Where to?'

'Back in with my mum.'

'Oh. Maybe not so exciting then.'

Julia was encouraging confidences, but Amira clearly didn't want to elaborate. Still Julia persevered.

'While you're in here, perhaps you can help me sort out who everyone is. That pregnant lady over there is Sarah, right?'

Amira's eyes followed the direction of Julia's nod to a woman standing by the printer absently rubbing her very obvious bump. Julia had already decided that when Sarah went off on maternity leave, she'd bring Naomi in to cover for her. Reinforcements, that's what she needed. A friendly face out there on the main floor would make all the difference.

But Amira was frowning.

'No. *That's* Sarah.' She gestured to a desk at the side where a heavily pregnant pink-faced, red-haired woman was shifting around in her chair as if trying to get comfortable. Now the penny dropped. Julia turned back to the figure by the printer.

'Ah, so that must be . . .'

'Yes, Chloe.'

Julia felt a secret thrill of excitement. So this was the girl at the centre of all the media speculation. Chloe was sticking to her story that the father of her unborn baby was a foreign student with whom she'd had a one-night stand, but that hadn't stopped the rumours. Only last week, Julia had seen a photo of her in a magazine with the headline: LOVE CHILD FOR SAUNA KILLER?

She looked so young standing there on her own. So vulnerable. Julia felt the first stirrings of protectiveness towards her new, beleaguered team. She was known in the industry as someone who was fiercely loyal to her staff. No doubt that was part of the reason Mark Hamilton had brought her in.

After Amira had gone, Julia was thoughtful. She had expected that her new staff might be nervous, maybe even a bit hostile. But this polite guardedness was something she hadn't anticipated. Still, she'd win them over gradually. She just needed to get to know them a bit, to find out what made them tick. Maybe she'd move her desk out on to the main floor. Or take them all out to the pub or out for a meal. Alcohol was the quickest way of breaking down barriers, she'd found.

She logged on to her computer, following the instructions the gangly young man from IT had scrawled on a Post-it and stuck to her monitor. Then she put the company postcode into a local search engine and looked up neighbouring restaurants. She picked up her phone and dialled.

'Table for six, please.'

* * *

Four thousand, one hundred and twenty-seven miles away, Noelle Egan gazed at a magazine feature with her dull, dead eyes. She'd been out of jail for nearly six years now, having got time off her life sentence for cooperating with the state in the case against her ex-husband. Naturally, she'd gone looking for her daughter straight away but Laurie had disappeared – adopted overseas, apparently – absorbed so completely into the system it was like she had never existed at all.

But her son was different. Him, she couldn't avoid. The news stations, running endless discussions about whether he was really a monster or just a victim of his early upbringing, statements from police who'd worked on the case when she and Pete were first arrested. An interview with one of the psychiatrists who'd assessed him, a ridiculously tall pompous man who liked the sound of his own voice. She'd seen her son on the news and felt nothing. Not even the old revulsion. Just nothing.

But this snippet in the magazine changed everything. She studied the photograph again. The girl looked so young still. Pretty. Long hair. Tall. Nice clothes. But it wasn't her Noelle was interested in. Her eyes were drawn to the bump under her expensive-looking coat. Her grandchild. A girl. She was certain of it. A little girl to replace Laurie.

Noelle cut out the photograph neatly with a pair of nail scissors. After laying the scissors back down on the table, she changed her mind and picked them up again. *Snip.* She'd cut off the young woman's head. That was better. Noelle taped the picture of the headless female carefully to the fridge and gazed at it, lost in contemplation. Contrary to what the world believed, she'd been a good mom. She'd been a great mom. But twenty-five years ago, her children had been stolen from her. And now, finally, she had the chance to reclaim what was hers. Children didn't belong to the state. They were private property. They belonged to their parents.

Or their grandparents.

She sat down at her computer and logged into Facebook. After peering at the caption on the photograph on the fridge she typed the name Chloe Somerfield into the search box, absorbing the few biographical details on display. Not many, as the privacy settings were on high, but enough to get started. She noted the date of birth. Still so young. She could have other babies after this one was gone. Opening up Google, she typed: *Applying for a new passport.* Next she called up a map of the world and stared at it impassively for a long while. She hadn't realized just how far away London was. That huge expanse of ocean. She'd never even been abroad before. For a split second her resolve wavered. Then she glanced at the photograph on the fridge and the doubts vanished.

Her grandchild would be needing her.

After all, blood was thicker than water.

THE END

Acknowledgements

I'd like to thank the amazing Emma Herdman for the time and energy she put into helping me with this book. Her future authors don't know how lucky they are. Also at Curtis Brown, thanks go as always to Felicity Blunt, my fearless agent, and to Vivienne Schuster, Alice Lutyens, Sophie Harris, Katie McGowan and Luke Speed.

The Transworld team, as ever, have worked tirelessly to effect the usual sow's ear to silk purse transformation. Heartfelt thanks go to my brilliant editor, Jane Lawson, my publicist, Sarah Harwood, and everyone else who contributed to the book including Katrina Whone, Alice Murphy-Pyle, Kate Samano, Larry Finlay and Bill Scott-Kerr. Also to receptionists extraordinaire, Jeanette Slinger at Penguin Random House and Jean Kriek at Transworld.

The book blogging community has been a massive support to me over the last few years. First and foremost, thanks go to the wonderful Anne Cater, who lends her name to one of the main characters in this book (although the similarities stop there) and who has been a valued friend and cheerleader. I'd also like to thank

Cleo Bannister, Liz Barnsley, Pam McIlroy, Victoria Goldman, and of course the famously indefatigable Tracy Fenton who established The Book Club on Facebook.

Though it's been a while since I last went out to work, writing this book inevitably stirred up memories of various offices I worked in during my career as a journalist, and I'd like to pay tribute to the friends and colleagues who shared those endless mid-afternoon tea-rounds. Sharon Bexley, Jacky Hyams, Rupert Mellor, Bridget Freer, Sue Cocker, Sue Ricketts, Sue Garland, Graham Kerr, Philippa Gibson, Belinda Robey, Liz Garment, Suzy Barber, Maria Trkulja, Jonathan Bowman. I'm raising a plastic cup of lukewarm white wine to you all now around an imaginary desk.

The science of early years memory is ever evolving and could fill several volumes. In my efforts to distil various theories into a concise enough form to fit this narrative, I have almost certainly taken heinous liberties with the facts and I apologize in advance. Huge thanks to Dr Jez Phillips, deputy head of Psychology at the University of Chester, for his patient help in explaining some of the current research in this area. Any mistakes are definitely my own

In the absence of a real office environment, I rely heavily on my virtual workmates when writing a book, and I'd like to thank everyone at Crime Scene and Killer Women and The Prime Writers. Also Amanda Jennings, Louise Millar, Louise Douglas, Cally Taylor, Emma Kavanagh, Clare Mackintosh, Marnie Riches, Mark Edwards, Susi Holliday.

I also would not function without my friends, so

thanks once again to Rikki Finegold, Mel Amos, Juliet Brown, Roma Cartwright, Fiona Godfrey, Mark Hindley, Mike Wilkins, Sally Thompson, Steve Griffiths, Ed Needham, Jo Lockwood, Dill Hammond, Mark Heholt, Jos Joures, Renata Barcelos, Helen Bates.

To my family – Sara, Simon, Colin, Emma, Paul, Ed, Alfie, Margaret, Gaynor, and particularly to Otis, Jake, Billie and Michael, and even to Doris – once again all my love and thanks.

Dying for Christmas
Tammy Cohen

Sometimes, evil comes gift-wrapped . . .

I am missing. Held captive by a blue-eyed stranger. To mark the twelve days of Christmas, he gives me a gift every day, each more horrible than the last. The twelfth day is getting closer. After that, there'll be no more Christmas cheer for me. No mince pies, no carols. No way out . . .

But I have a secret. No one has guessed it. Will you?

The Broken

Tammy Cohen

Best friends tell you everything; about their kitchen renovation; about their little girl's new school. They tell you how they are leaving their partner for someone younger.

Best friends don't tell lies. They don't call lawyers. They don't make you choose sides.

Best friends don't keep secrets about their past.

Best friends don't always stay best friends.

'Get your hands on this thriller'
CLOSER

'I couldn't put this book down'
LISA JEWELL

'Gripping'
PRIMA

First One Missing

Tammy Cohen

A serial killer is at large after another child's body is found on Hampstead Heath.

Police race to catch him before he strikes again.

Families of the victims gather to offer each other comfort.

But someone is keeping a dangerous secret.

WELCOME TO THE CLUB NO ONE WANTS TO JOIN.

'Compulsive and gut-wrenching'
LISA JEWELL

'Everyone read it!'
EMMA KAVANAGH

'Head and shoulders above the rest'
DAILY MAIL

'A nail-biting thriller with a stunning twist'
MARK EDWARDS